PENGUIN BOOKS

THE RAFFLES AFFAIR

Born in New Zealand, Vicki always dreamed about travelling the world and writing about her adventures. At the age of nineteen, she set off on a solo expedition to Africa. Falling in love with the continent and the freedom of travel, she felt a yearning to go further and explore even more far-flung corners of the planet.

Vicki's advertising career helped power her wanderlust even further, taking her from New Zealand, to the concrete jungles of London, Dubai and Singapore. Travel writing soon followed as she chronicled her adventures of more than fifty countries that she had by now visited—from ancient souks in Yemen, to the glaciers of Greenland.

The idea of taking on the formidable task of writing a novel was conceived aboard a glorious dahabiya on the river Nile in Egypt, where the Victoria West series was born.

It was at this point that Vicki decided to bring back the fun and glamour of the old Golden Age detective novel in a new crime series that would put a modern twist on the classic murder mystery—each book set in one of Vicki's favourite destinations so readers could escape to exotic places and enjoy new cultures . . . all while figuring out whodunnit!

vickivirtue.com
/vickivirtueauthor
@VickiVirtueAuthor
@VickiVAuthor

ABOUT THE RAFFLES WRITER'S RESIDENCY

As for back as 1887, men of letters such as Rudyard Kipling and Joseph Conrad have inaugurated Raffles' legendary literary tradition which continues today. Raffles Hotel Singapore has long played muse to renowned writers whose creativity was sparked by our majestic setting, intriguing guests and timeless destination. As we write the next chapter of our rich literary heritage, the Raffles Writer's Residency programme was launched with Pico Iyer as the first Writer-in-Residence with his insightful compact volume, "This Could Be Home—Raffles Hotel and the City of Tomorrow".

The programme continues with Vicki Virtue as our second Writer-in-Residence, supporting and inspiring the art of the written word and the storytellers of today - aiming to create and nurture a pipeline of creative writing talents as well as to engage writers with a record of creative excellence, inspiring and stimulating them to create new literary works.

THE RAFFLES AFFAIR

A Victoria West Mystery

VICKI VIRTUE

PENGUIN BOOKS

An imprint of Penguin Random House

PENGUIN BOOKS

USA | Canada | UK | Ireland | Australia
New Zealand | India | South Africa | China | Southeast Asia

Penguin Books is part of the Penguin Random House group of companies
whose addresses can be found at global.penguinrandomhouse.com

Published by Penguin Random House SEA Pte Ltd
9, Changi South Street 3, Level 08-01,
Singapore 486361

First published in Penguin Books by Penguin Random House SEA 2021

RAFFLES
SINGAPORE

This book is published as part of Raffles Hotel Singapore's Writer's
Residency programme.

ISBN 9789814954402

Typeset in Adobe Garamond Pro by Manipal Technologies Limited, Manipal

www.penguin.sg

For Roy

One

A silver Daimler glided round gently onto Beach Road.

Victoria West laid her iPad to one side and glanced out of its window, her gaze settling on the grand, white façade of Raffles Hotel. She leaned back and sighed. She seemed to have been travelling for days. It was nice to finally arrive. Although part of her wished she had just landed in London and not Singapore, she was beginning to miss home.

Still, she did love Raffles with its colonial architecture and huge, white, airy verandahs; it always felt so tranquil and timeless. Aside from her last visit, which hadn't been particularly tranquil—the dead Chinese spy in the laundry basket had taken care of that. Fortunately, this time she was only here for her friend, Peyton Latchmore's wedding.

She scooped her long, brown hair up in her fingers and let her head fall against the backrest of the seat. The cold leather sent goose bumps tingling down the back of her bare neck. She closed her eyes. It had been a long day; the flight from Ethiopia had taken over seventeen hours and she had scarcely managed to get any sleep, the night before. No wonder she was feeling as if she were ninety-seven, not thirty-seven.

The Daimler crunched on to the gravel driveway and rolled to a stop.

Before the chauffeur had time to cut the soft purr of the engine, a small, balding man with a lively face dashed out from the doorway, dressed impeccably in a dark grey suit, a starched white cotton shirt and a pair of fastidiously polished, black, leather shoes.

He darted across the strip of red carpet at the entranceway, hastily stashing his mobile phone into a pocket, and descended the three small steps on to the driveway. With a tremendous flourish, he flung open the passenger door, offering his hand and an effusion of compliments. Victoria smiled. Mario Fabrizio had lost none of his exuberance since she had last seen him.

She placed her hand into his and stepped from the Daimler, pausing for a moment to savour the intense Singaporean heat, as it hit her skin. She towered, almost comically, above the pint-sized general manager. Fortunately, the largesse of his personality made up for his diminutive stature. With a series of commanding gesticulations, he issued instructions to the doorman, resplendent in his distinctive white Gieves & Hawkes uniform, for the collection of Victoria's luggage. She loved the tradition of the doormen at Raffles. Their grand, military-style uniforms with white turbans, black sashes and gold braiding, took her back to the Golden Age of Travel, when everything was slower and more glamorous.

The doorman hauled her old rucksack out of the Daimler's boot, then gingerly lifted the Hermès suitcase by its calfskin handles. 'It looks like you have been away travelling again, Miss West,' he said.

Victoria's green eyes sparkled with fondness. 'I have, indeed, Narajan, you're getting to know me too well.'

A broad smile broke out behind Narajan's greying beard as he slung the rucksack over his shoulder and wheeled her suitcase, with great care, into the cool, pillared lobby. With a low bow and an outstretched arm, Mario gestured for Victoria to follow.

'We are delighted to have you back with us again,' he said, falling into step beside her, 'We all hoped you wouldn't give up on Raffles after your last visit. Such a fiasco! How it would have ended without you, I cannot imagine. You saved us, Miss West. And at Raffles, we never forget a friend—especially one so charming and beautiful.'

Victoria attempted to parry his compliments in good humour, but he would hear none of it. That she had resolved 'that small business with the Chinese', little more than a year ago, without the slightest blemish on Raffles' (or rather, Mario Fabrizio's) reputation, was a matter for which – he fervently insisted – he would remain indebted to her until he drew his last breath.

'This time, your stay with us will be more comfortable,' he declared.

He reached into the breast pocket of his jacket and with a majestic sweep of his arm, withdrew a tan leather keycard to one of the Presidential Suites. He then offered his arm to Victoria—seemingly incognizant of the extraordinary difference in their heights—and proceeded to escort her towards the staircase.

But they had scarcely advanced ten paces, when a woman—her naturally pale face flushed and excited—rushed towards them. 'Victoria! You got here! I was so worried you were going to get held up.' She threw her arms around Victoria and hugged her tightly.

Victoria smiled at the enthusiastic welcome. She had never seen Peyton in such high spirits. Despite being American, she had always behaved as reservedly as an Englishwoman, probably because she spent so much of her childhood living abroad. 'Getting married clearly suits you,' she said.

Peyton laughed. 'It definitely does. I mean, I know it took me a while to find the right guy, but I got there in the end.'

'It sounds like he was worth waiting for.' Victoria ran her gaze over Peyton's blonde hair. 'You've cut it.'

Peyton nodded, fingering the blunt ends. 'I had it trimmed this morning, although I'm worried they've cut it a bit short.'

'No, I like it; it sits on your shoulders perfectly.' Victoria took a step back from Peyton and looked her over from head to toe. 'You look fantastic. This new Englishman of yours is clearly doing you a world of good.'

Peyton gave a small, contented sigh. 'He is so wonderful—and so totally different from American men. Why didn't you tell me Englishmen were such gentlemen? I would have started dating them years ago!'

Victoria laughed. 'Most of them aren't, I'm afraid. But I'm glad James is. And I'm pleased he makes you so happy; you deserve it.' She turned to Mario, waiting in polite silence behind them, 'Would you mind if I take the key from you and show myself up to the room? Peyton and I haven't seen each other in such a long time, we have a bit of catching up to do.'

Mario leaned forward, giving a small inclination of his head. 'But, of course.' He presented the room key to Victoria with both hands. 'Your suite is on level two, at the far end, overlooking the Palm Courtyard. I shall have your luggage sent up. And of course—' he held his hands out in a wide gesture towards Peyton. 'If either of you need anything, please don't hesitate to ask.'

With another low bow, Mario stepped backwards and spinning on his heel, disappeared towards the concierge desk, where Victoria's luggage was waiting.

Victoria linked her arm through Peyton's and slowly led her across the white marbled floor of the lobby, towards the Grand Staircase. 'So tell me, what's been happening—aside from meeting a gorgeous Englishman and getting married of course? Last time we spoke you were in the middle of negotiating the sale of your company; has that all gone through now?'

'Yes, thank God. Everything's finally been settled. Honestly, it has been a crazy year. But James has been such an angel; I don't know what I would have done without him. He's organized the whole wedding.'

'It sounds to me like you've found the perfect man.'

'I have. I didn't think men like him existed and I can't wait for you to meet him. Will you be able to join us for dinner or are you totally exhausted?'

'I'm sure I'll be able to make it to dinner, I just need to have a shower first.' Victoria ran her fingers through the knots in her long hair. 'I've got half the Omo Valley in here.'

'Is that where you've been, Ethiopia?'

'Yes, I had a few days to spare before coming here, so I went down to the Omo Valley to do some photography. And you know what the drive from Jinka back to Addis is like.' Victoria gave an exhausted sigh. 'It's been a long two days.'

'You are incredible. You come straight out of the bush, drive for ten hours over pot-holed roads; sit on a plane for another twenty and still manage to look like a supermodel. If it were me, I'd look like one of the Hamer tribesmen with my hair all matted and the rest of me covered in a layer of dirt.'

Victoria laughed and lifted her arm. 'This *is* a layer of dirt; it's not a suntan.'

Peyton smiled and shook her head. It astounded her that Victoria had no awareness of how stunning she was. She had always envied her tall, dark elegance. When they were younger, she had even tried dyeing her hair dark brown and cutting heavy bangs just like Victoria's—but it looked terrible on her. Even now, they were both in their late thirties and Peyton still couldn't stop admiring Victoria. She kept glancing across at her as they ascended the polished wooden staircase, trying to work out how she managed to appear so graceful in a pair of cargo pants and a white singlet. Her deportment had a lot to do with it. But she figured it had also partly to do with her accent. Peyton loved the way the English spoke—it sounded so much more refined than her American twang.

'Have you been working in Africa?' she asked.

Victoria nodded. 'Yes, I've been there for the last few months.'

'I thought you were going to take a break when you left MI6.'

'I was, but this job was too interesting to turn down. Speaking of which, have you said anything to any of the guests about what I do for a living?'

'I've told everybody that you're a travel photographer, like you asked me to. I've told Granny and Grandpa to say the same thing.' Peyton's gaze dropped to the pale pink tote bag Victoria had slung over one shoulder. 'Although I'm not sure exactly how you're planning to explain being able to afford Chanel on a travel photographer's salary.'

Victoria smiled. 'Every woman should have her secrets. Besides, I *am* a travel photographer in my spare time. I've just spent the last three days with the Karo people taking some shots for a friend's magazine.' She took her iPhone from her bag. 'It's a quarter to six now. What time is dinner?'

'Oh gosh, sorry, you're going to need to get into that shower. Drinks are from six thirty in The Writer's Bar and then dinner is booked in La Dame de Pic for seven thirty.'

'Will everyone be there?'

'Yes, but it's not a big wedding. We didn't want the media finding out about it and turning it into a circus, so we kept it small. That's why we asked you all to keep it quiet. So there are only fourteen people coming—plus James and me, of course.'

'The happy bride and groom.'

Peyton gave a self-conscious laugh. 'It sounds so weird when you say that. I mean I know the wedding is the day after tomorrow, but it still feels so unreal. I guess I wasn't one of those kids who grew up dreaming of her wedding day, so I can't quite get my head around the thought of being somebody's wife.'

Victoria smiled. 'It's not too late to pull out.'

'God! Could you imagine it? James' Aunt Patricia is already complaining about the long flight we made her take from the UK to get here. She'd murder me if I called it off.' They reached the door of Victoria's suite and Peyton glanced at her watch. 'I'd better get going. I'm the guest of honour, I can't be late.' She gave Victoria another hug. 'Thank you so much for coming, it means a lot to me. I'll see you down in the bar, soon.'

Two

Victoria stood beneath the shower, relishing the jets of hot water streaming down her head. Her suite, when she arrived, had been chilled to what felt like freezing point by the air conditioning. Slowly, the heat penetrated through her long, thick hair. She closed her eyes and lifted her head, letting the water cascade over her upturned face. It was her first shower in forty-eight hours and for a few brief minutes, she thought of nothing but the pleasure of the warmth tingling on her bare skin and the sweet fragrance of the lime and bergamot shampoo.

She lathered her hair three times to get it clean and scrubbed her body twice, first with shower gel and then with the chamomile exfoliant that she had found amongst the array of aromatherapy products on the bathroom shelf. As the orange swirl of Omo Valley dust began to slowly disappear down the plughole, so too, did the fatigue of her long flight from Ethiopia, along with the months of difficult work that had preceded it.

She knew leaving MI6 had been the right decision. Now that she was working for herself, directly with governments that *she* chose to work with, and on projects that she felt passionate about, it was much more satisfying. Not that the work had become any easier; in fact, if anything, it was more difficult now that she didn't have the British government to protect her. But at least she was in charge of her own destiny. She no longer had to execute orders from above, that often made no sense to her and sometimes, exacerbated the problems they were designed to fix.

She gave her hair one final rinse; then pushed her thick fringe aside to check the time on the iPhone that she had left outside the shower.

Six-fifteen. She groaned. She really had to get out and start getting dressed. Not that she was in any hurry to get down to drinks—she knew that would involve the usual round of small talk that she found so tedious—but she was famished and she didn't want to miss dinner.

She was also curious. In the twenty-five years that she had known Peyton, she had never seen her so besotted. Ever since her parents had died, Victoria had watched Peyton erect barriers to protect herself from getting hurt again. She sometimes wondered if Peyton deliberately chose men who were not right for her, just so they wouldn't get too close. As a consequence, her relationships never lasted long—until now.

Victoria was intrigued to meet the man who had caused such a profound change in her. She just hoped he was a better choice than the men Peyton usually dated.

Three

Peyton applied a final touch of lipstick and stepped back from the mirror. She smoothed down the red Giambattista Valli dress James had bought her as an engagement present. It was so much shorter than anything else she owned, she felt a little self-conscious wearing it. But James liked it and tonight, that was all that mattered to her. And he did have incredibly good taste. She ran her hands over the embroidered flowers on the bodice and stood for a moment looking at her reflection. She was so lucky. A little spark of happiness ignited deep inside her.

Really, she had everything. She was young and healthy. She had plenty of money, now that she had sold her company—more than she would ever be able to spend. She had a small, close-knit group of friends. She had grandparents who adored her. And now there was James, whom she loved more than anything and who, in two days' time, would be her husband.

She turned from the mirror and took in all the gorgeous opulence of the bedroom. The plush carpet, the gold, lacquered panels, the wooden ceiling fans, the four-poster bed and the long, silk drapes hanging over the French windows. It was all so perfect.

And yet, she crossed to the writing desk and looked down at the black leather notecase. Slowly, she traced her finger over the Raffles Hotel logo on the front. It was this exact notecase that she had taken down to the lobby during their visit, two months earlier, when the solemniser had come to the hotel to sign their marriage consent form. On an impulse, she picked it up and held it tightly against her chest.

Why couldn't she shake the feeling that something was going to go wrong? She threw the notecase down.

'Don't be such an idiot,' she told herself. 'You always worry about things that never happen.'

She grabbed her clutch bag from the bed and hurried along the airy hallway of her suite into its living room. The sun had already dipped low behind Singapore's skyscrapers and the room was shrouded in a soft, dusky, late afternoon light. It looked so beautiful. To think it had been only ten years since she and Curtis Butland had sat in her New Jersey apartment, dreaming of the company they wanted to build. Now here she was, having sold it, standing in the Presidential Suite at Raffles Hotel. Her entire New Jersey apartment would have fitted in its dining room.

She glanced towards the French doors. They had been left wide open and the tropical heat filled the empty room. Peyton felt the humidity wrap around her bare shoulders like a damp cloth.

Outside, she could see James sitting with his back to her. Only his tousled brown hair was visible above the high, wooden back of the rattan armchair. Peyton smiled as she stepped out onto the balcony. She loved every bit of him, even his scruffy brown hair. 'Aren't you hot sitting out here?'

James threw the magazine he was reading, down on to the coffee table and turned to look at her. He let out a long, low whistle. 'Wow. You look stunning.'

Peyton couldn't help smiling; she found his lilting British accent so sexy. And she loved the masculine way he creased his forehead when he spoke. It made her feel as if she were back in high school and had scored the captain of the football team. James was still a boy, in many ways: impulsive and uncomplicated. She liked those qualities in him. He didn't overthink things like she did.

James held out his hand and drew her towards him. He pulled her down on to his knee and she caught sight of the *Time* magazine he had discarded, with *her* on the cover. 'It's here! Why didn't you come and tell me?'

James laughed and picked up the magazine to hand to her. 'I didn't want you taking any longer to get ready.' He slipped his arm round her waist. 'Not that I'm complaining, it was worth every minute of the wait.'

Peyton ran her eye over the headline, 'Busting the boy's club in Silicon Valley. 38-year-old social media entrepreneur and now billionaire, Peyton Latchmore.' She threw the magazine back down on to the coffee table and groaned. 'What is it with the media? Why is it such a big deal that I'm a woman?'

James lifted her hand to his lips and kissed it. 'Because you're smart *and* blonde and gorgeous.'

Peyton looked into his soft, grey eyes. She had never had a man say such appreciative things to her before. All the other men she had dated scarcely seemed to notice what she looked like. She squeezed him tightly. 'I love you so much, James Winstanley. I don't want anything to ever change. I always want us to be as happy as we are now.'

James took a loose strand of her straight, blonde hair and tucked it gently behind her ear. '*Nothing* is going to change, so stop worrying. Except we do need to get downstairs for drinks; if we're late, mum will kill us.' He stood up and held out his arm. 'May I escort the most beautiful woman in Singapore down to the dining room?'

Peyton linked her arm with his and laughed. She imitated his proper English accent, 'That would be marvellous, thank you.'

Four

La Dame de Pic was even more exquisite than Peyton had remembered it. Gold chandeliers hung like strings of tambourines from the ceiling, the white plaster work above embellished with a bas-relief of delicate white peonies. Small, golden flecks of light from the wall lamps glittered gaily in the high-arched mirrors, which sat grandly against the wall in finely curved frames. Vases of bulbous, pink hydrangeas shimmered on a surface of mirrored, black glass in the centre of the room. The tables were laid with immaculately pressed, white linen napkins, and the crystal glassware and sculptured Laguiole knives seemed to sparkle at her, like precious jewels on a crown. She ran her hand across the back of one of the pink, leather dining chairs and smiled. Everything was so feminine and beautiful. And the long-stemmed, pink roses, sitting atop each table in perfect, white, bulb-shaped vases, were the same colour as the flowers that had been in their room at the George V in Paris, when James had proposed to her. Bathed in the light from the chandeliers, they were as divine as her mood. She could still feel the little sparkle of joy smouldering deep inside her. Filled with an overwhelming sense of tenderness, she took James' hand and pressed it.

He pulled her in close, and slipping his arm round her waist, nodded towards the far end of the dining room. 'It looks like Mum has taken charge. I hope you don't mind.'

Peyton followed his gaze. At the far end of the restaurant, Beverley Marsters was emerging from the wine alcove with Raffles' sommelier. She was dressed in the elegant, grey silk trouser suit she and Peyton had bought together, the previous day. It was so much smarter than the cream dress Beverley had brought with her from London. The slim cut of the short jacket suited her tall, solid figure; and the pearls she wore at her neck, along with the pink lipstick, softened her strong, almost masculine features. Seeing her dressed up, Peyton was pleased she had talked Beverley into getting her hair re-styled that morning. The feathering around the edges of the short cut made her face look less harsh. The gold streaks worked too; they lifted the brown colour, giving it some life.

'I don't mind at all,' Peyton said. 'I'm pleased she's taking such an interest.'

Peyton liked Beverley. It had taken a while to get to know her, but they had grown close during the two years that she had been with James. It was almost twenty-two years to the day, since she had lost her own parents to a car crash in Kenya and she missed them terribly—especially now when she was about to get married. So it was a nice feeling to have Beverley in her life, especially as Beverley had made the effort to get to know her and understand her, in ways few other people did.

James was nothing like his mother; from what she could see, he took after his father, Roger. The two of them had never met as Roger didn't want anything to do with his illegitimate son, but Peyton had found photos of him online—taken when he was younger—and James looked exactly like him. They were both tall and handsome with broad shoulders and had the same warm, mischievous eyes and cheeky grins.

Beverley strode across the dining room towards them, her gaze fixed on her son. Peyton was used to playing second fiddle when it came to Beverley's affection for James. No one could usurp his place as his mother's number one priority.

Beverley placed her strong hands firmly on James' shoulders and embraced him. 'I've suggested they serve Louis Roederer Cristal Rosé Brut 2007 when everyone arrives.'

James kissed her affectionately on the cheek. 'Your taste is impeccable as always, Mother.'

Beverley smiled, but the warmth in her expression quickly disappeared as something behind James caught her attention. Peyton turned to see what it was.

John Marsters rushed into the dining room, his wild, curly hair even more unkempt than usual and his shirt, straining across his large belly, half untucked. His tie was pulled askew and his hurried footsteps clattered noisily on the wooden floorboards as he approached.

It amazed Peyton that Beverley had ever married him. When they first met, she had imagined Beverley's husband to be a suave, corporate type of Englishman; somebody like James' father. She had never envisaged him to be a blunderer like John, and still couldn't quite work out what she saw in him—or why John put up with being constantly berated. But for some reason, he always did what he was told and Beverley seemed to like that.

John stopped to catch his breath.

Peyton stared at him. 'Is everything okay?'

He gave a quick nod. 'Yes, yes everything's fine.' He turned to Beverley. 'I just need to have a quick word with you, Bev.'

Beverley glared impatiently at her husband. 'The guests are about to arrive, John, can't it wait?'

John cast a quick glance at James. 'No, no, it can't.'

Beverley gave an irritable sigh. 'Fine, let's go outside.' She turned to James. 'I'll be back in a minute.'

Peyton watched her stride towards the French doors with John at her side, attempting to tuck his renegade shirt back into his ill-fitting trousers. She took hold of James' hand. 'I hope there's nothing wrong.'

'I'm sure everything's fine, you know what John is like—a born worrier.' James pulled Peyton towards him and kissed her red lips. 'A bit like you, my darling.'

Peyton returned his bright smile. But as they moved towards the Writers Bar to greet the first of their guests, she couldn't help casting a quick glance at John and Beverley. She was curious to know what they were talking about.

Five

More concerned about John's flustered appearance than he wished to let on, James left Peyton at the bar and went back into the dining room. He pushed open the French doors and stepped outside on to the polished, marble walkway. His gaze darted along to the far end, where John and Beverley were standing, framed between the two columns of a high, white archway. The deep lines in his mother's face seemed softer in the golden hue of the verandah lights, hanging like teardrops from the lofty, panelled ceiling above her.

James moved quickly along to his mother's side. 'Is there something wrong?'

Beverley raised her chin and smiled at her son. 'Nothing that needs to be dealt with tonight, darling.'

James glanced across at John. 'Then what was so urgent? What couldn't wait?'

'It's just George. But we'll talk about it later, darling.' Beverley placed a hand on James' arm and nodded towards the walkway behind him. 'Your brother is on his way over here.'

James felt his anger rising. Why couldn't his uncle just keep his mouth shut until after the wedding? He knew they shouldn't have got George involved; he was always causing trouble. Yet, John had insisted. Now, George was in a financial bind and of course, was trying to blame it on them. It was the last thing he needed right now.

James wanted to tell John that George was his brother-in-law and he needed to sort it out. But he couldn't say anything, now that his brother was approaching; that would only exacerbate the problem.

He watched with growing irritation as Tim Marsters' tall, lanky frame strolled nonchalantly along the walkway towards them. His irritation turned to anger as his gaze fell on Tim's blue-checked shorts and flip flops. 'What the hell is he doing, coming to dinner dressed like that?'

John took a white handkerchief from his pocket and dabbed at the beads of perspiration gathering on his forehead. 'He's been out shopping. I imagine he hasn't had a chance to get changed yet.'

'Then he needs to get a move on. I don't want him messing everything up tonight, like he usually does. Everyone is starting to arrive.'

'I'll tell him to hurry along,' John said. 'He probably doesn't realize what the time is.'

'He's not a child; he's twenty-two years old. And he does own a watch.' James' jaw tightened as he watched his brother's slow progress. 'Tim, would you get a move on, you're late. Drinks started at six thirty.'

Tim glanced down at the gold Rolex on his wrist. 'Five minutes ago—what's the big deal?'

'You're not dressed and the guests are starting to arrive.'

'So? It's only going to take me five minutes to get changed.'

'Nothing ever takes you five minutes. That's why you're always late.'

'I'll go in what I'm wearing, if you're so worried.'

'Don't be ridiculous, Tim,' Beverley interjected. 'Go upstairs and put your suit on. You're family, you should be making a good impression.'

Tim crossed his arms with a sullen shrug. 'Maybe I should just stay up there and keep out of everyone's way. I can't make a bad impression then, can I?'

Beverley sighed in exasperation. 'Your brother has booked dinner for sixteen people. We are not going to make changes at such a late stage in the day. Now, would you go upstairs and get changed, quickly?'

Tim mimicked his mother's voice. '*Your brother has booked dinner for sixteen people.* And we can't possibly let James down, can we?'

'For goodness' sake, Tim!' Beverley snapped. 'I'm not going to say it again. Would you get upstairs and put your suit on? I don't want you turning up when drinks have finished.'

'All right, I'll go. Jeez, why is everyone so stressed?'

'Because we're trying to organize a wedding,' James said, irritably. 'Not that you'd have any concept of that; you couldn't organize your way out of a paper bag.'

'I wouldn't *want* to organize anything as disgusting as this. I'd rather spend my money helping people who are dying from starvation, than worrying about whether to serve wedding guests caviar or lobster. You could feed a whole village in Africa for the cost of one dinner here.'

'*You* didn't have to come,' James said. 'It would have saved us some money if you hadn't.'

'I'll pay you back if you want.'

James laughed. 'With what—the money we give you so you can sit around doing nothing?'

'I'm not sitting around doing nothing. I'm studying, which is more than you ever did. All you want to do is make as much money as you can, so you can spend it on crap like this, to make yourself feel important.'

Beverley took a step towards her son. 'Tim, that is quite enough. Now, for the last time, will you go upstairs and get changed?'

Tim's thin lips curled into an insolent smile. 'I thought talking about money was what you all liked doing.'

James grabbed hold of his brother by the arm. 'Stop being such a jerk. Go upstairs and get changed, like Mum told you to.' He gave Tim a shove towards the courtyard. 'Go!'

Tim wrenched his arm free. 'Don't touch me!'

'Then stop acting like a child and get changed.' James gave him another push.

Anger flared in Tim's eyes. He spun round and slammed both hands hard into James' chest. 'I said stop it.'

James fell back, hitting the side of his head against a concrete pillar. 'You prick! Why don't you go get a life?' He lunged forward at his brother, his body coiled ready to deliver a punch.

Tim stumbled backwards as James lashed out, crashing noisily against the grey, filigree gate. Pinned into a corner, he thrust his left hand into the pocket of his shorts and pulled out a knife. Its silver blade gleamed in the verandah light. With his back pressed against the wall, Tim held the knife out in front of him, pointing it at James. 'Keep away from me!'

James froze, his clenched fists suspended in midair. 'Jesus Christ!'

'Tim!' Beverley almost screamed the word.

John rushed forward. 'What on earth are you doing, Tim?'

Tim's fingers tightened around the blue stones embedded into the knife's wooden handle. 'I told him to leave me alone.'

'Put the knife down, son,' John laid a hand on Tim's arm. 'This is no way to resolve an argument. Someone could get hurt.'

'It's all right,' James said. A mocking smile crept on to his lips as his gaze fell on the Chinese characters engraved into the knife's short blade. 'It's just a souvenir. He's not going to do any harm with it.'

'It doesn't matter,' Beverley said. 'You don't threaten somebody with a knife. I don't know what's got into you, Tim.'

Tim lowered the knife and slowly his white knuckles turned blotchy pink as the blood surged back into them. 'I told him to leave me alone,' he said, sulkily. 'He thinks he can push everyone around. Well, I've had enough of it.'

James gave a sarcastic snort. 'And what are you going to do? Stab me with your souvenir?'

'It's not a souvenir, it's a proper Yingjisha knife from China.'

'That's what they told you in Chinatown, is it?'

Tim turned the knife over in his hand. 'It's sharp enough to kill somebody with.'

Beverley drew in a sharp breath. 'Tim, would you put that knife away. Take it upstairs and leave it there. I don't want to see it again. I don't know what possessed you to buy such a thing. Now go up to your room and get changed.' She glanced down at her watch. 'We should all be inside. Peyton will be wondering what has become of us.'

Six

Zara Avery-Smythe placed the hair straighteners down on the dressing table. She stared at her long hair in the mirror, pulling the front strands with her fingers. It had looked perfect at the hairdressers but now, in the humidity, the ends were frizzing and curling. The highlights they'd put through to lighten the red didn't help; the softer colour showed up every wisp. Maybe if she curled the ends, it would look better.

She glanced across at the clock on the bedside table. Twenty to seven. There was no time; she was already late. And where was Tim, he was supposed to have been back half an hour ago. She picked up her phone and tried his number again. Still no answer. She checked her face in the mirror. Her makeup was perfect; she didn't want it to get shiny before she got downstairs. She ran her fingers along under her eyeliner to check for smudges. Maybe she should go down. Tim could meet her there.

She took her strappy, black stilettos from the wardrobe and went over to the padded bench at the end of the bed. Slipping the sandals on, she admired the pedicure she'd had done in the spa that afternoon. The coral polish looked perfect with her spray tan. She was so pleased she had made time to get that done before she left London.

She stepped back to check the effect of the shoes with the purple chiffon dress. They looked perfect. She felt so sexy in them. And the short skirt definitely wouldn't have worked with winter-white legs.

She gave her hair a final ruffle with her fingers and pulled it around in front of her shoulders. Turning towards the dressing table to pick up her handbag, she heard the sound of the front door lock releasing.

19

It swung open and Tim strode into the small entrance lobby, slamming the door closed behind him. He walked into the bedroom and tossed the key down on to the dressing table.

Zara glared at him, waiting for him to say something. 'Where have you been? I've been trying to call you. We're supposed to be down for drinks.'

Tim took his wallet and phone from the pocket of his shorts and threw them across on to the bed. He took the knife out of the other pocket and turned the jewel encrusted handle over in the palm of his hand.

Zara's eyes bulged. 'What's that?'

'It's a Yingjisha knife from China. They're famous.' Tim ran his fingers over the blue stones. 'They're known for their intricate workmanship and razor sharp blades.' He held the knife out towards Zara. 'Feel it.'

She shrank back. 'I don't want to touch it. Where did you get it from?'

'In town.' Tim's thumb caressed the Chinese characters engraved into the thick, silver blade. A half-smile played on his lips. 'James thinks it's a souvenir, but it's not. It's a proper knife.' He swiped the blade across the tip of his forefinger. Tiny droplets of dark blood bubbled to the surface.

Zara let out a small gasp. 'Tim, be careful! You've cut yourself.'

Tim sucked the blood from his finger and laughed. 'Don't you like the sight of blood?'

'No, I don't. Put it away. What did you buy it for?'

Tim tossed the knife down on to the bed beside his wallet. 'Why do you buy handbags?'

'It's hardly the same thing. Anyway, come on, we need to go down to drinks. We're late.'

'I'm not going.'

Zara stared at him. 'What are you talking about, we can't not go? Everyone is expecting us.'

'So?'

'So, it would be rude. It's your brother's function; we have to be there.' Zara flung her handbag down on to the dressing table. The gold clasp hit the wood with a dull thud. 'Why do you always have to be so difficult? It's embarrassing.'

A taunting smile spread across Tim's lips. 'And you wouldn't want to be embarrassed in front of James would you? Given how much effort you make to impress him.'

Zara's face flushed crimson. She turned her back on Tim and busied herself with tidying up the dressing table. 'I don't try to impress him; I just try to be polite. Unlike you.'

Tim strode across to the large mahogany wardrobe. 'Then why have you gone bright red?'

Seven

Lou Farmer stopped on the threshold of the Writers Bar. She brushed down the skirt of her black cocktail dress and shifted her beaded purse from one hand to the other. She looked about, poised to move, it seemed, the minute she found what she was looking for. Her dark hair, cut to the nape of her neck in a simple bob, swung heavily from side to side with each movement of her head.

Seeing her alone, Peyton rushed over. She took her by both hands and kissed her on the cheek. 'Lou, it is so wonderful to have you here. And thank you so much for everything you've done to help James organize all of this. I know he and Beverley have been working you into the ground lately, and then on top of all that, helping them organize all of this—I really do appreciate it.'

Lou stiffened a little under Peyton's embrace, with typically English reserve. But her face, which bore no trace of make-up except on her lips, warmed into a smile. 'It has been my pleasure. It'll be worth all the effort when you walk down the aisle.'

'I can't believe I'll be doing that, the day after tomorrow.'

'I'm sure it's going to be a wonderful ceremony.' Lou looked about the room, something else clearly on her mind. 'Are Beverley and James not here yet?'

'Yes they are. Beverley went outside with John for a private word. I'm not sure what it was about. And James is somewhere. He went to use the restroom.' Peyton took Lou by the arm. 'Come, I'll introduce you to my grandparents. They arrived this afternoon.'

'Oh, I'd love to meet them—' Lou hesitated, her gaze flitting across the bar and outside into the Palm Courtyard. 'But I should go and find Beverley first. I've got an urgent email I need to show her.'

'I hope they're not making you work while you're on vacation.'

'Oh no, not at all. I just like to stay on top of things. With all of us here for the wedding, there's no one in the office.'

Peyton smiled. 'They are so lucky to have you working for them, Lou. I don't know how any of them could cope without you.'

'Oh, I enjoy it. And they've been so good to me over the years.'

'And you've been loyal to Beverley, in return. Forty years is a long time to work for somebody. And I know you do a lot more than just the secretarial work they pay you for.'

Lou's cheeks flushed. 'Well, most of the time, it doesn't feel like work; we have a lot of fun together as well.'

'I know, and I think it's great you're all so close. But make sure you take some time out while you're here, to relax and enjoy this weather. It'll be freezing when you get back home.'

'Oh, don't worry, I'm having a wonderful time. Beverley and I did some shopping at Orchard Road this morning and then we spent a couple of hours relaxing by the pool, this afternoon.'

'Good, I'm pleased to hear it. James wanted us all to get away from the office, that's why we're having the wedding here. Although, would you believe it, he's arranged a meeting for himself, for tomorrow morning. I swear, he'll be working at our wedding breakfast. And he was the one telling me we needed to take a break.'

Lou smiled, but her attention shifted from Peyton to the doorway at the far end of the Writers Bar. 'Ah, there's Beverley now. I'll just pop over and have a quick word with her. Excuse me.'

Peyton watched Lou rush away, feeling mildly irritated by her subservience to Beverley. She behaved like a puppy around her— devoted, no matter how badly she got treated. And Beverley did take her for granted. They all did. Peyton knew Lou adored the family, but she wished that sometimes Lou would stand up for herself a bit more and not let them trample all over her.

Eight

Peyton glanced down at her watch. A quarter after seven. She did a quick headcount around the bar. Perhaps, they ought to delay dinner until eight; there were still a few guests yet to arrive. She ran through the menu in her head: brown crab, berlingots with cheese fondue, wild turbot, Wagyu beef and poulard. That should all be fine. Everything would be cooked to order when they sat down. But then if they were going to stay in the bar for an extra half hour, maybe she should order some more canapés.

She was thinking about which canapés to order, when she felt the touch of a cold hand on her bare shoulder. She spun round and her face lit up into a broad smile. 'Curtis! You made it! I got your message saying your flight had been delayed. I didn't think you'd get here in time.'

Curtis Butland ran his fingers through his floppy, sun-bleached hair. 'Me neither. We were three hours late leaving LA.'

'Oh God, you poor thing, you must be exhausted.'

'I'm not too bad, I got some sleep on the plane.'

'Lucky you; I still can't sleep on planes.' Peyton rested her gaze on his familiar face. 'It's so good to see you, Curtis. It feels like it's been ages since we caught up.'

Curtis shrugged. 'I guess that's what happens when you fall in love.'

Peyton felt a sudden pang of guilt. In the ten years she and Curtis had been business partners, they had seen each other almost every day and hung out together on weekends. But when she met James and then they sold the business, all that changed. And she knew it wasn't just because they weren't working so closely together anymore. The problem was that he and James didn't get along. So maintaining a friendship beyond work had become awkward. But Curtis had been such a good friend to her over the years—she didn't want to lose him altogether. She hoped that after she and James were married, it would become easier.

'I'm sure things will settle down after the wedding,' Peyton said. 'It's been a crazy year. I've hardly had time to see anyone.'

Curtis gave another small shrug. 'Yeah, I guess. It has been pretty busy.'

Peyton smiled. She took hold of Curtis by the arm. 'Come on, let me take you over and introduce you to a couple of friends of ours.' She pointed towards a smartly dressed couple in their early forties, standing with James. 'The guy with the shaved head is my attorney, Nick de Brouwer, and that's his wife, Kate, in the blue dress.'

'I thought Doug was your attorney.'

'He is. But because I've been spending so much time in the UK with James lately, I thought I should get an English attorney as well. James introduced me to Nick; they've worked together for years. Nick has been great with helping me set up everything. Actually, you should talk to him; he's an expert in setting up offshore tax structures. He's done everything for me.'

She led Curtis across to the other side of the bar. James didn't see them approaching, so she crept up behind him and slipped her arms round his waist. 'I hope we're not interrupting anything. I just thought I'd bring Curtis over to introduce him to Nick and Kate.'

'You're not interrupting anything important,' Kate said. 'Just these two talking about football.'

James stared at her in mock horror. 'Not important? It's the FA Cup we're talking about!' He leaned forward and held his hand out towards Curtis. 'It's good to see you again. Please ignore my friend over here; she's a little lacking in cultural sensitivity.'

Kate rolled her eyes. 'Cultural sensitivity?' She extended her hand. 'It's lovely to meet you, Curtis, we've heard a lot about you from

Peyton. And I believe congratulations are in order for the sale of your company. I imagine it feels rather good being all cashed up at last.'

Curtis' blue eyes brightened with a smile. 'Yeah, it feels pretty good. I bagged enough to go surfing for the next few years. So that's cool.'

'Ah, you're a surfer?' Nick took Curtis' hand in a firm handshake. 'I must say that's something I've always wanted to try. It's a bit cold in the UK, unfortunately. You're based in California, aren't you?'

'Yeah, Santa Cruz. We get some pretty good waves there.'

'And a good climate, too. At least, it's a lot better than the miserable weather we get in the UK.'

Peyton laughed. 'That wouldn't be too hard; it's always grey and drizzly.' She snuggled up to James. 'But then maybe that's why the people are so lovely.'

James pulled her in close and planted a kiss on her cheek. Peyton nestled into his arms. But as she did so, her eye caught Kate's and she felt suddenly self-conscious in her happiness. Kate was watching her, but there was nothing of the warm friendship they shared, in her expression. It seemed hard, perhaps even a little jealous. Peyton wondered if she and Nick had been arguing again. It had been happening a lot, lately. Still, Peyton didn't want Kate to begrudge her and James their happiness, especially two days before their wedding, so she disengaged herself from James and took a small step towards Kate. 'I love that blue dress on you; you look amazing in it.'

Kate groaned and tugged at the skirt of the dress. 'Ugh! I feel so frumpy and fat in it. I should have gone out and bought something new.'

Peyton looked at Kate's long, dark, wavy hair and curvaceous figure. 'Frumpy? You look incredible.' She put her hands on the strapless bodice of her own dress and laughed. 'At least you fill yours out. I keep thinking I'm going to lose mine.'

Nick glanced down at the shortness of her hemline. 'You've got the legs for it though. It looks terrific on you.'

Peyton fingered the folds on the full, red skirt. 'Oh, thank you, Nick. It was an engagement present from James. I wouldn't normally wear anything so short but—' she gave James a coy smile. 'He talked me into it.'

'Of course I did. It looks fantastic on you. As does the blue dress on you, Kate. You look stunning.' James gave Nick a playful pat on the stomach. 'It beats me how a skinny, bald git like you managed to get yourself such a gorgeous wife. But I suppose you must have some attractions.'

'It's my wit and personality.'

Kate rolled her eyes. 'Making bad jokes does not make you witty, Nick.'

Nick gave an exaggerated look of astonishment to Curtis. 'It must be my culinary skills, then.'

Kate groaned. 'Ignore him, Curtis, he can't even boil an egg.'

'Ah, but I do a mean takeaway curry.'

'Which you always get me to pick up on the way home from work.'

'Okay, you two are making me hungry.' James looked down at his watch and then at Peyton. 'We should probably start getting everyone to dinner.'

'I thought maybe we should push it back until eight,' Peyton said. 'Patricia and George aren't here yet. Neither is Victoria—'

'Ah Victoria, the elusive best friend. You think she's actually going to turn up, this time?' James gave Nick a nudge with his elbow. 'They tell me she's a travel photographer, which is why she's never around, but personally, I think she's just a figment of their imagination.'

Peyton laughed. 'You know she's real. We're just never in the same country at the same time; that's why you haven't met her.'

'I've met her,' Curtis interposed. 'She's definitely real.'

'And I've shown you a photo of her,' Peyton added.

'Ah yes, that's right, you did show me a photo. And I seem to remember she was rather beautiful.' James narrowed his eyes. 'Maybe you're trying to keep her away from me. Perhaps, you're worried she might lure me away with her mysterious beauty?'

Peyton met his gaze with quiet amusement. 'Victoria is the one woman in the entire world that would *not* do that. So don't get your hopes up.'

James turned to Nick with raised eyebrows. 'That sounds like a challenge.'

'One that you would both fail at, miserably.' Peyton glanced over his shoulder with a teasing smile. 'But you're welcome to give it a try. Here she is, now.'

It seemed as if the entire bar turned to look as Victoria arrived. Peyton couldn't remember seeing her friend look more beautiful. She wore an emerald green dress that wrapped around her tall, slim figure like a long roll of exquisitely sculpted cling film. The sheer folds of the fabric enveloped her long legs to just below the knee, leaving her slender calves bare. The thin straps of the green stilettos exaggerated her height, giving the impression of a long wisp of grass shifting gracefully in the breeze.

Hugging the waist of her dress, like large handprints, were two boldly embroidered leaves and on one of the thin shoulder straps was a tiny, gold insect encrusted with jewels. Otherwise, Victoria wore no adornments. Her dark hair tumbled loosely over her bare, suntanned shoulders and her makeup blended so naturally with her creamy olive skin, it was barely noticeable. Only the smudged, black kohl pencil was visible; making her translucent green eyes appear to smoulder as she scanned the room from beneath her thick, heavy fringe.

Nick watched her in silence with his mouth wide open. 'Wow, she's stunning. How do you know her?'

Peyton laughed. 'We were at school together in Ethiopia. Her father was there with the British embassy, while my dad was working for the UN.'

Nick's eyes gaped. 'She's English?'

'Half,' Peyton said. 'Her mother is Danish.'

James slapped a hand on Nick's back. 'Now don't go getting any ideas you old sod; you're a married man.'

Kate gave a short, scoffing laugh. 'Somehow, I don't think she'd be interested in Nick.'

Nine

The maître d'hôtel approached with a smoky pink, suede-bound menu clasped in his hand. He stopped a polite distance from the group and inclined his head. 'Mr Winstanley, Miss Latchmore, would it be possible for me to borrow you for one moment in the dining room, to run through the dinner service.'

'Of course.' James extended his arm towards the entrance to La Dame de Pic. 'We're at your disposal.'

The maître d'hôtel turned to Nick, Kate and Curtis. He gave a small bow of his head. 'My apologies for interrupting.' With an outstretched hand, he gestured for Peyton and James to precede him. 'Please.'

Kate turned and watched the maître d'hôtel follow her friends out through the doorway behind them. When they were out of sight, she turned back to Nick and Curtis, but fixed her attention firmly on the glass of champagne in her hand.

Curtis watched her for a moment. He shifted his weight from one foot to the other, pushing his outgrown fringe away from his eyes. 'I might go and grab a beer.' He pointed his thumb in the direction of the bar. 'Can I get you guys something?'

Nick shook his head. 'No, we're fine, thanks, Curtis. The waiters are circulating with champagne.'

'No worries. I'll catch you guys again soon, then.'

Kate's gaze followed Curtis as he sauntered towards the bar. Then she turned sharply back to look at her husband. Something resembling childish hatred flashed in her eyes. 'I'm surprised you're not going over to talk to Victoria, given how amazing you think she is.' She took a sip of her champagne. 'You know, if she is your ideal woman, you really should rethink who you're married to.'

Nick stared at his wife, his arms spread in supplication. 'I just said she was attractive. I didn't say I wanted to marry her.'

Kate glared at him. 'You said she was stunning. So why don't you go over and try your luck with her? See how far you get.'

'For Christ's sake, it was a passing comment. There's no need to turn it around and make a big deal out of it. And keep your voice down, she's heading this way.'

Kate glanced across at Victoria as she moved further into the bar. Their eyes met and Victoria acknowledged her with a smile. Kate gave her the briefest of nods and turned back to Nick. The last thing she wanted was Victoria coming over to join them—she felt so dowdy in comparison. If she had realized everyone was going to be so dressed up, she would have gone out and bought something new to wear. Not that she'd had any spare time before they left London; she was too busy working and stressing out about Nick.

'I'm making a big deal out of it,' she hissed at him. 'Because you seem to be incapable of taking anything seriously.'

Nick drained the remaining champagne in his flute. 'I'm not the one talking about changing spouses.'

'That's not what I meant and you know it. I was talking about your business and its lack of liquidity.'

'I've told you; there is nothing for you to worry about. Everything is going to be finalized in the next week or so.'

'You've been saying that for six months.'

Nick sighed. 'Okay, it's taking a bit longer than I thought. It's complicated. Start-ups are not that predictable. Things don't always work according to the timelines you want them to.'

'I run a hedge fund company, Nick. I know how things work; I deal with this sort of stuff every day. And I'm telling you this is not normal.'

'This is not a normal company I've invested in. Look, I can't share the details because I've signed an NDA. But it is going to pay back massively, I promise you.'

Kate studied her husband closely. 'You haven't put any of your clients' money into this have you?'

'For God's sake, can we stop talking about this? I know how to run my business.'

'If you did, you wouldn't be in this position. You haven't had any cash for over a year now. I'm footing all of our bills. Our business invests in new projects every day, but I still manage to earn an income. I'm warning you, Nick, if you've got yourself in over your head, I'm not bailing you out again. This time, you're on your own.'

Nick ran his hand over the top of his shaved head. 'I'm not asking you to bail me out. There's nothing to bail me out of. Like I said, everything is going to be sorted in the next few days. There is *nothing* for you to worry about.'

Kate's lips tightened into a dry smile, 'If only that were true.'

Ten

Victoria looked across the bar to the French doors and out into the Palm Courtyard beyond. The sun had just set and the courtyard was carpeted in the soft blueness of fading daylight. A string of verandah lights fringed the courtyard, casting a rich, warm, orange glow over the white colonnades of the grand colonial architecture. It was usually her favourite time of day at Raffles, when the tourists had left and everything had quietened down. But she felt suddenly weary and wished the evening were already over so she could crawl into the soft bed that awaited her, upstairs.

She gave her head a small shake to drive away the thought and brought her attention back to the guests mingling in the bar. She didn't recognize most of the faces there and in her current state of tiredness, didn't feel especially inclined to getting to know any of them, either. So she was delighted when she caught sight of Bill and Eleanor Springfield. She always enjoyed the company of Peyton's grandparents; they had invariably been on some new adventure together and unlike most couples who had been married for sixty years, they still liked each other. They were sitting side by side on a grey button leather sofa, holding hands.

Eleanor was as immaculately groomed and made up as ever, and looked beautiful in a long, black, velvet evening gown with an embroidered, red shawl draped around her shoulders. Her lipstick was a perfect match for the shades of deep crimson in the shawl and there wasn't a strand of lightly coiffured hair out of place. It was styled, as it had always been, ever since Victoria had known her—in short curls that swept softly away from her face. Her nails were painted in the same bright colour as her lips and a large diamond ring sparkled on her wedding finger.

Bill Springfield looked dapper beside his wife, in a dark grey suit with a red tie that matched Eleanor's shawl. He had a warm, cheerful face and eyes that glittered mischievously through the thick, tortoise-shell rim of his glasses. He rose to his feet as Victoria approached and she was astonished to see how agile and strong he still was, at ninety-one. He took hold of her in a firm bear hug. 'How's my favourite English gal?' He held her at arm's length. 'You know you had better watch yourself, young lady, you're getting to be almost as attractive as my wife.'

Eleanor's eyes sparkled with good humour. 'Don't believe a word he says to you Victoria; you are far more beautiful.'

Eleanor pushed her petite frame up out of the sofa with the help of an elegantly carved walking stick. Victoria bent down to kiss her. 'If I look half as good as you, Eleanor, when I get to your age, I'd be very happy. I don't know how you two do it, you still look like a couple of spring chickens.'

Bill gave a loud, infectious laugh. 'That's because of the chicken feed we live on. You should see the organic diet this one serves me.'

'Well, whatever diet Eleanor has you on, it's working. You both look fantastic.'

Bill drew his bushy eyebrows together. 'Do you know how much it costs to buy an organic onion?'

Victoria threw Eleanor an arch smile. 'Think of it as an investment, Bill.'

Bill's eyes widened. 'An investment in what; the livelihoods of onion farmers?'

'An investment in your future. Isn't that what you bankers always talk about?'

Bill gave another boisterous roar of laughter. 'Yes, I suppose I did talk about that, once, and some fool probably believed me. But Wall Street is a long time past. Nowadays, I'm just a poor house husband, counting out our nickels and dimes to make ends meet.'

Eleanor smiled at her husband. 'He's talking nonsense. He still does a wonderful job of looking after our finances. I don't have to worry about a thing.'

'You're still working, though, I see,' Victoria said. 'I picked up your latest book while I was in transit in Dubai.'

Bill smiled proudly at his wife. 'Ten weeks on the *New York Times* bestseller list. Not bad for an old hen.'

Eleanor batted the compliment away with a wave of her hand. 'I do hope you didn't waste time reading it, Victoria. Given your adventurous life, it's a silly bit of nonsense that would bore you senseless.'

'Of course I read it; I've read all your books. And I thoroughly enjoy them; they're fun! You make the business of spying sound a lot more glamorous than it really is. I suppose you've already started working on the next one?'

'I just signed off the proofs before we came out. As for another one? Well, that will depend on whether I can come up with a new idea. I think I might be starting to run out of those.'

Bill dismissed his wife's modesty with an exaggerated swat of his hand. 'She's been saying that for forty years and she always comes up with something. As soon as we set foot back in our apartment in New York, she'll be at her computer, dashing out the next one; mark my words.'

Victoria smiled at the affection Bill had for his wife. 'Do you still write every day?'

Eleanor nodded. 'Yes, but I just write in the mornings now. I only have to produce one book a year for my publishers, so it's not too arduous. Although at my age, it is quite enough.'

'You work more than just the mornings, my dear. She's up at five thirty every day and sitting at her computer by seven. Then she doesn't stop writing until one, and after that, we read what she's written. So her working day doesn't stop until mid-afternoon.' Bill paused and took hold of Eleanor's hand. 'Although things haven't been quite the same for the past few months.'

Victoria frowned, concerned by the sudden seriousness in Bill's tone. 'Why, is there something wrong?'

'Not with us,' Bill said. 'It's Peyton we've been worried about. This whole business with her and—'

Eleanor squeezed Bill's hand. 'Perhaps, we should talk to Victoria about this a little later.' With a forced smile on her lips, she nodded across to the other side of the bar, 'James and Peyton are on their way over and we should leave the young ones to catch up on their own.' She threw a conspiratorial smile at Victoria. 'I know Peyton is very keen for you to meet James.'

Eleven

Victoria watched the bride and groom-to-be strolling towards her, each holding a full glass of champagne. James was certainly very handsome. He had one arm draped over her shoulders and Peyton was laughing happily at something he had said.

She looked radiant. The red dress suited her blonde hair and alabaster skin—although it was much more risqué than anything Victoria had seen her wear in the past. Peyton had always dressed well; she loved designer clothes, but she would never have worn anything that finished mid-thigh. It looked stunning though; her legs were slim and toned enough for her to get away with it.

James was quite different from what Victoria had expected. In the past, Peyton had always gone for men with unconventional looks. They were usually creative, artists of some sort, and generally had a quirky rather than handsome appearance, whereas James' urbane good looks gave the impression of a dashing man-about-town. His dark brown hair was loosely ruffled, just enough to look masculine but not so much that he looked unkempt. His face was long with a chiselled jawline and he had light grey eyes that were framed by thin laugh lines, which added a hint of ruggedness to his otherwise rakishly handsome features.

He was tall and looked suave in a superbly tailored black suit with a crisp white shirt, unbuttoned at the top. He had an olive complexion, but his skin was pale for want of sunlight. He wore no jewelry, except for a gold A. Lange & Söhne watch that Victoria glimpsed under his cuff, as he thrust his hand forward to take hold of hers in a brief but firm grip. 'It's a pleasure to finally meet you. I was beginning to think you didn't exist.'

'James!' Peyton gave his arm a playful smack. 'Ignore him, Victoria. He's just having you on.'

Victoria inclined her head towards James with reserved friendliness. The ease of his self-assured manner intrigued her, as did his accent. She couldn't quite place it. Possibly Midlands, but it was very subtle. A touch of wariness crept into Victoria's smile. 'I'm sorry to have been so elusive.'

James thrust one hand into the pocket of his trousers and returned her smile with a ready familiarity. 'Peyton tells me you live in north London. We must be almost neighbours. I've just bought a place in Highgate.'

'Almost,' Victoria said. 'I have a flat in Primrose Hill. Although I spend very little time there now, I tend to go to my house in the South of France, when I have time off.'

James ran his fingers through his thick mop of hair. 'It doesn't sound like that happens very often. I gather from Peyton that you're a travel photographer.'

'Yes, I am. In fact, I've just come from an assignment photographing the Karo people in southern Ethiopia.'

James raised his eyebrows. 'That sounds very intrepid.' He ran his eye over Victoria's green dress. 'Beautiful *and* adventurous—a dangerous combination.'

'What about you, James?' Victoria said. 'What do you do?'

'Nothing as exciting as you, I'm afraid. I run a financial investment firm in the City with my mother and stepfather. So my travel doesn't get much more intrepid than the jungles of New York or Hong Kong.' He put his arm round Peyton and pulled her to his side with an affectionate squeeze. 'Although, my fiancée has talked me into going to Botswana for our honeymoon; so perhaps I'll develop a taste for more adventurous travel destinations, like the two of you.'

Victoria smiled. 'I'm sure you won't be able to help yourself, once you've been to Africa. It gets in your blood. Although they do luxury very well in Botswana, you won't have to be too intrepid.'

'So Peyton tells me.' James' gaze fell on Victoria's empty hands. 'But please excuse me, how rude I'm being. Here I am, chatting on about work and our honeymoon and you haven't even got a drink. Let me get you something; I know you've just got off a long flight. Perhaps a glass of champagne, or would you prefer something stronger?'

'A glass of champagne sounds perfect, thank you, James.'

'Consider it done.' He turned and raising his hand, caught the eye of a waiter. He lifted his glass of champagne into the air and gestured with his free hand that they required another. The waiter gave a quick bow of comprehension and made his way swiftly over to the bar. James lowered his arm and was just turning back to the group when John Marsters rushed into the bar, clutching his mobile phone. James' elbow almost collided with his head.

John raised both hands in apology. 'Oh, I'm sorry—' His eyes darted around the bar. 'I was looking for your mother, have you seen her?'

'Not for a little while, but she's here somewhere.'

'Yes, she was, a minute ago, but I seem to have lost her—' John stopped. His words hung in the air as his gaze fell on Victoria. 'Oh, please, forgive me, I didn't mean to interrupt.'

James gave an effusive smile. 'You're not interrupting. Let me introduce you to Peyton's good friend, Victoria West; she's just arrived from Ethiopia. This is my stepfather, John Marsters. Oh, and that,' he gestured to the waiter that appeared at Victoria's side, 'is your champagne.'

Victoria took the glass from the waiter's silver tray and ran a curious eye over John Marsters. He looked more like a mad professor than a City financier, with his disheveled hair and an overgrown moustache, that dwarfed his top lip like a clump of crabgrass. He wasn't a particularly attractive man. His skin was sallow with large, open pores and small pockmarks from which thin streams of sweat trickled, pooling in small droplets on his jaw line.

John took a white handkerchief from the pocket of his trousers and wiped his palms before extending a hand towards Victoria. 'My apologies, my hands are a little sweaty.'

Victoria returned his clammy handshake with a smile. 'It's an occupational hazard of holidaying in the tropics, I'm afraid.'

John scrunched the handkerchief up in his stubby fingers and dabbed at the perspiration on his face and neck. 'I've just been outside. It doesn't ever seem to cool down here, does it?'

He pulled at the collar of his shirt and shifted his neck from side to side, his sagging jowls undulating with the motion. 'Actually, James, I wonder if I might borrow you for a minute?' He glanced apologetically at Victoria; then at Peyton. 'It would be good to have a quick chat about that small issue at the office that we didn't get a chance to discuss earlier.'

James slapped an arm across John's shoulders. 'Sure, let's go into the dining room.' He winked at Peyton. 'It'll give the girls a chance to talk about me, while I'm not here.'

Twelve

Victoria watched the two men disappear through the hammered iron doors. They were certainly a disparate pair—she couldn't imagine how they managed to run a business together. Nor could she envision what sort of clients they attracted. She conjectured they would be an eclectic bunch.

She was absently contemplating how she would feel about letting them manage her money, when a young man seated at the bar caught her attention. He was sitting alone, dressed in a dinner suit and reclining against the grey, suede backrest of the barstool. One arm was resting on the bar counter, his fingers tapping in time with the jazz music, and the other on the arm of the stool with his hand clasped around a glass of beer. His blond hair was parted on one side and combed neatly back, away from his face.

'Is that Curtis over there?' Victoria asked.

Peyton followed her gaze across to the bar. 'Yes, it is. He looks different in a suit, doesn't he?'

'He certainly does. I've only ever seen him in jeans and a t-shirt.'

'Which is what he would be wearing tonight, if Isabelle hadn't made him a dinner suit and told him he had to wear it.'

Victoria smiled. 'And Isabelle can be very convincing.'

'Especially where her clothes are concerned.' Peyton lowered her voice. 'She's furious with me for not wearing something of hers tonight. I tried to explain to her that I wanted to wear this because James had given it to me as an engagement present. But you know what Isabelle is like. And it's not that I don't love her clothes, I do. That's why I wanted her to make my wedding dress. But she's not the only designer in the world. I can't wear *everything* of hers.'

Victoria laughed. 'She'll no doubt be furious with me as well, then. She offered me front row seats to her show at Paris Fashion Week. She wanted me to choose something to wear for this weekend. I would have loved to go, but I was in Africa and couldn't leave.' Victoria glanced across to where Curtis was seated at the bar. 'Anyway, at least Curtis let her dress him. Maybe she'll be happy with that and let us off the hook.'

'Luckily, Curtis is so laidback, he doesn't care what he wears. But I don't think that'll be enough to get her off our backs. Especially yours. Isabelle hasn't forgiven you yet for missing her seventieth, last year.'

Victoria raised an eyebrow. 'Really, has she not?'

Peyton's red mouth arched into a mischievous smile. 'No, she hasn't. And you know how Isabelle likes to hold a grudge. Anyway, let's go over and say hi to Curtis.' She tucked her arm through Victoria's. 'I must confess, I'm feeling a bit guilty about not having spent much time with him, lately. I've just been so busy; everything seems to have happened at once. Finalizing everything with the business and then getting organized for the wedding. I feel as if I've scarcely had time to stop and take a breath.'

'I'm sure Curtis understands.'

'I don't know. He doesn't get along with James that well. I think he resents me for spending so much time with him.'

'I'm sure he does. Curtis is in love with you; we all know that. But he's thirty-four-years-old, he'll get over it. And if he doesn't,' Victoria gave a small shrug, '*C'est la vie.* There's nothing you can do about it.'

'I wish I was as pragmatic as you. I've lost so many nights' sleep over it.' Peyton paused for a moment, then her face brightened, 'Anyway, you didn't tell me what you thought of him.'

'Of James?' Victoria hesitated. She knew from past experience she had to be careful about what she said. If she made any negative comments, Peyton would obsess over them. 'He seems very charming. And I don't think I've ever seen you looking so happy.'

'I never have been. It's funny; before I met James, I thought I *was* happy. I guess I didn't know what I was missing.'

Victoria's gaze rested on Peyton's blushing face. 'I'm so pleased for you. And happy that you've finally found someone you like—after all those false starts.'

Peyton rolled her eyes. 'Oh God, let's not even go there. I don't know what I was thinking. I'm just so pleased that none of those relationships ever worked out.'

'Sometimes, things don't work out for good reasons.'

'I know. It's just a shame we don't know what they are, at the time.'

'If we did, we'd never learn any lessons. Now come on.' Victoria took a firm hold of Peyton. 'Let's go and assuage your guilt with Curtis, while he's still sitting by himself. Then I can keep him company while you go and mingle.'

Peyton gave Victoria a grateful smile. 'You're such a good friend.'

The two friends made their way across to the bar. Curtis was staring absently into his glass of beer and it wasn't until they were standing in front of him, that he looked up. His pale blue eyes sparkled with delight at the sight of Victoria and he jumped off the barstool.

'Victoria, how's it going?' He leaned forward to give her a kiss. 'It's so good to see you. Peyton said you would be here.'

'It's good to see you as well, Curtis.' Victoria ran her eye over his new suit. 'You're looking great. It must be that smart tuxedo Isabelle made for you.'

Curtis laughed, running his hands over the black lapels. 'It's starting to grow on me. It's not as uncomfortable as I thought it was going to be.' He nodded at Victoria's green dress. 'Is that one of hers as well?'

Victoria grimaced. 'No, which means I'm going to be in the dog house when she spots me.'

Curtis nodded over Victoria's shoulder and smiled. 'I think she already has. She's making a beeline in this direction.'

Thirteen

Isabelle Sauveterre was striding across the bar towards them, her thin, birdlike frame bedecked in a bright orange and white silk dress, with dramatic puff sleeves and a thick waistband of faux hibiscus flowers. Her long, peroxide blonde hair was piled high on top of her head like a French wedding cake. Between two immaculately manicured fingers, she held a Gauloises Blondes cigarette. She fixed her attention on Curtis as she drew closer. Raising her hand with the cigarette, she spoke in a deep, raspy voice, her commanding tone accentuated by her thick French accent, 'Curtis, my love, will you get me a lighter?'

Curtis looked down at the Gauloises. 'You know smoking isn't good for your health, Isabelle.'

'I am seventy-one years old. I have got to die of something.'

Curtis laughed. 'I'll go and get you one then.'

Isabelle watched him for a moment, as if she were an art curator admiring a newly acquired masterpiece. Then she abruptly turned and fixed her attention on Victoria. For a moment she just looked at her and said nothing. But her pursed lips didn't need words to convey the disapproval that lay behind them. Isabelle drew herself up to her full five foot and three inches—and although Victoria was still a good nine inches taller—managed to look down her nose at the green dress. 'Dolce and Gabbana? I suppose you could have done worse.'

Victoria smiled. 'Thank you, Isabelle, I'll take that as a compliment. And we were just admiring the dinner suit you made for Curtis. I've never seen him looking so good.'

43

Isabelle shrugged away the flattery. But behind the gruff exterior, it was clear that she had swelled with pride. She stood for a moment, appreciating her handiwork. 'He is an easy man to dress. He is very handsome.' She cast a sideways glance at Peyton. 'He would make a good husband. It is a shame you are not marrying him.'

Peyton stared at her godmother. Isabelle's lack of subtlety was hardly a surprise. But did she honestly expect her to change fiancés, two days before her wedding? It wasn't as if Isabelle hadn't already made her antipathy towards James clear. Although, why she thought she was in any position to comment, Peyton had no idea. Isabelle's only experience with husbands was with those of other people's. 'I'm sure he would, Isabelle, for the right woman.'

Isabelle raised her chin in the way she always did when she was about to disagree with you. 'But you are not the right woman?'

Peyton shook her head. Sometimes her godmother was beyond reason. 'Isabelle, I am in love with James.'

'Ah, how little we understand love when we are young.'

'I'm hardly young, I'm thirty-eight-years-old. Surely that's old enough to know if I'm in love with somebody.'

'I thought that once, too, when I was your age.'

Peyton opened her mouth to respond but was stopped by the reappearance of Curtis. He held out a small silver tray to Isabelle with a box of Raffles Hotel matches on it. 'They didn't have any lighters. I hope these are okay.'

Isabelle took hold of the box between two long, orange fingernails. Then, with the haughty confidence of a woman who wasn't accustomed to having her opinions opposed, she threw a disdainful glance at Peyton. 'There is no need for you to make the same mistakes.'

She turned on her heels and with a flurry of orange silk, strode off towards the lobby. Curtis watched her retreating back. 'What mistakes is she talking about?'

'She doesn't think I should be marrying James. She doesn't think he's good enough for me.' Peyton shook her head with a desultory smile. 'But then Isabelle is hardly an expert on relationships.'

Curtis raised his eyebrows. 'I don't know about that. She's got enough experience.'

A burst of laughter escaped from Peyton. 'You are absolutely right, Curtis, she does. Although, I'm not sure quantity should surpass quality, when it comes to offering advice.'

'I don't know, relationships are no different to wine.' Victoria held up her glass of champagne. 'The more you sample, the better you are at choosing a good one.'

Fourteen

Victoria took a long sip of the Louis Roederer; then placed her flute down on the bar and helped herself to the porcelain tray of hors d'oeuvres. She took a breadstick, embedded with large crystals of rock salt and scooped up a thick dollop of the deliciously pungent black olive tapenade it was sitting in. She ate in silence, enjoying her first morsel of food since the bland lunch of buttered cod they had served on the plane.

Peyton picked up a tiny satay stick and dipped it in the bowl of peanut sauce. She carefully manoeuvred it to her mouth, so as not to spill anything on her red dress.

Curtis followed suit and helped himself to a handful of spicy nuts. His gaze drifted absently about the bar as he popped them, one by one, into his mouth. He stopped for a moment with his fingers poised in mid-air and watched a young man standing inside the doorway. 'Is that guy one of your guests? He looks a bit lost.'

Peyton looked to where Curtis was gesturing with his beer glass. 'Oh, yes, that's Tim, James' brother.'

'Brother?' Victoria raised her eyebrows. 'They don't look much alike.'

'They're half-brothers,' Peyton said. 'John isn't James' father. Not that Tim looks anything like John either, or Beverley, for that matter. I think his red hair must be a throwback.'

Curtis scooped up another handful of nuts from the bowl and threw them into his mouth. 'He looks like a bit of a dweeb.'

Peyton stifled a laugh. 'Shush, keep your voice down.'

Victoria tried not to smile. But as she considered Tim Marsters' long, thin, pale face and lanky body, she had to admit Curtis was right. Tim did look like the nerd at school that everyone picked on. She was thinking about how a new haircut and more modern wardrobe would make all the difference, when a young woman walked in from the lobby and hovered beside him. She took no notice of Tim, as she cast her gaze about the room. Her eyes were huge and round, giving her an almost doll-like appearance and her lips were set slightly apart, revealing a perfect set of white teeth that seemed too large for her mouth.

'Who's that?' Victoria asked.

'That's Tim's girlfriend,' Peyton said. 'Zara Avery-Smythe.'

Curtis took a swig of beer. 'She looks like a horse.'

Peyton laughed. 'She is a bit of a thoroughbred. Her father is a Lord or Baron or something; whatever they have in England. She and Tim are studying history and politics together at Oxford.'

Curtis rolled his eyes. 'Great, just what the world needs—more rich kids with useless degrees, thinking they can solve all of the world's problems.'

Peyton gave him a playful slap on the arm. 'Curtis Butland, you are such a cynic.'

Victoria laughed. 'Well, they might as well have a go. Everyone else has tried—' she was about to add 'and failed', when a frantic knocking on one of the French doors stopped her. They all turned towards the noise.

'Oh God!' Peyton groaned. 'It's Patricia.'

Victoria followed her gaze outside, where a rotund woman in a vivid pink, floral dress was standing with her face pressed up against one of the glass panels on the door. Her greying hair was set into a helmet of hair-roller curls. It didn't seem to move, as she jabbed her forefinger at the handle on the inside and mouthed something unintelligible.

'Is that James' aunt?' Victoria asked. 'The one you don't like?'

Peyton nodded and turned back to Victoria. 'I think I'll let James deal with her. It's his family.'

As if on cue, James appeared and dashed across the bar towards the French doors, holding a full glass of champagne and a cheese and pistachio cookie in one hand and pressed an iPhone against his ear with the other. He tucked the phone under his chin and began to fiddle with the latch. After a couple of minutes, it released and the door swung open. He slipped out into the courtyard, still talking on his phone, and Patricia Helstone ploughed past him into the bar; her head thrust forward, protruding from her thick neck like a turtle's. She was a stout woman with a firm, resolute frown that the thin strip of pink on her lips only served to enhance. She reminded Victoria of a small, angry troll.

Trailing a few paces behind, a tall, slim man meekly followed, closing the door quietly behind him. Victoria took in the finely chequered weave of his grey suit. It reminded her of the suits her grandfather used to wear when she was a child. The man scratched his head. His crown was completely bald, below which there was a thick band of fluffy white hair. He had a large number of freckles on his face, giving his complexion a faint yellow tinge.

'That's Patricia's husband, George,' Peyton whispered.

Patricia stopped stock-still in the middle of the bar. She pulled a white tissue from the sleeve of her dress and dabbed the beads of sweat on her neck. 'I don't know what made you think we could get in through the courtyard, George. I told you the entrance was through the main lobby. We saw it when we came out from lunch. I pointed it out to you.' She fanned her face with the tissue. 'It was ridiculous standing out there in this heat.'

Peyton gave Victoria an almost imperceptible smile and took a step towards Patricia. 'Come and sit down, Patricia. You'll cool down quickly, now that you're inside with the air conditioning.'

Victoria watched Patricia bustle after Peyton and plonk her ample figure down heavily, into one of the armchairs. 'I said to George that we should go through the main lobby. I knew that was the right way. I don't know why he doesn't listen to me.' She shifted her large hips to better fit between the two delicately curved arms of her chair and pulled at the front of her blouse. 'This heat is dreadful. Look how my ankles have swollen up. I don't know how you can put up with it, George.'

George dropped silently into the seat beside her. He had a forbearing smile plastered on his face, although to all appearances, he hadn't listened to a word his wife had said.

Patricia displayed her swollen, stockinged feet to her husband. They resembled small sausages bulging out over the tops of her cream court shoes.

George frowned as he looked at them. 'Maybe we should get you to a doctor?'

Patricia flopped her forearms down on to the arms of her chair and directed a heavy, irritable sigh at her husband. 'I don't need a doctor, George. I just need to take a minute to cool down.'

Peyton smiled at her. 'Let me go over to the bar and get you a glass of champagne. I'm sure that will make you feel better.'

Patricia mumbled something by way of an acknowledgement as she leaned forward, took a white linen napkin from the small table in front of her and patted the perspiration gathering on her upper lip.

George Helstone watched his wife for a moment, then let his gaze wander around the bar. First, to the antique writing desk by the entrance; then, to the silver champagne bucket, filled with ice, that a waiter placed beside him, atop a tall, elegant, silver stand. Victoria wondered what was going through his mind as he took in all the elegance of the bar.

He then turned his attention to the waiters, immaculately groomed in grey waistcoats and white cotton shirts, as they circulated with silver platters of fois gras and small squares of focaccia bread topped with proscuitto and truffle caviar. He gave a small grunt. 'I'd like to know who's paying for all this.'

Patricia looked at him sharply. 'Oh for goodness' sake, George, that's got nothing to do with us.'

George sat up in his chair a little straighter and stared at his wife, 'It's got everything to do with us.'

Fifteen

Victoria moved from the bar to one of the armchairs by the French doors in the lobby, taking a small crostini smothered in pâté de fois gras, from the tray of a passing waiter. Peyton was starting to usher the guests into the dining room, but Victoria wanted to enjoy a moment of peace on her own, before moving through. The fading light of dusk had almost disappeared and the sky had turned ink blue. The only light in the courtyard now was from the soft glow of the lanterns. It was such a peaceful time of day; she wanted to savour it for a moment longer.

Beside her, Tim and Zara were seated in one of the booths. He was hunched over, picking his fingernails with the short blade of what looked like an ornamental knife. Victoria could just make out a row of blue stones embedded into the carved handle. His face was set with an earnest frown of concentration.

Zara was engrossed in her phone beside him. Her cherubic features looked almost childlike in the glow from the screen; and yet, she, too, wore the same solemn expression.

She clicked her phone off and looked up at Tim. Her body stiffened as her gaze fell on the knife in his hand. 'Why have you brought that down?'

Tim shrugged. 'Why not?'

'Because it's creepy. Who goes to dinner with a knife?'

'Some people do.'

'Yes, people who live in Brixton!'

Tim mocked Zara's posh English accent. 'Oh and we wouldn't want to mix with someone who lives in Brixton, would we? James would never go there.'

Victoria tried to suppress a smile; they clearly didn't realize she was sitting right opposite, watching them, and could hear every word they were saying. Or maybe they did and they didn't care. There were plenty of couples who were quite happy bickering in front of others.

'You are so obnoxious.' Zara stood up and grabbed her small clutch bag off the table. 'I'm going to dinner.'

Tim rose to join her, stuffing the knife into his jacket pocket.

Zara took a couple of steps towards the dining room; but then looked down at her right foot and stopped. 'Just a minute, my shoe has come undone.'

She placed her bag back down on the small table and bent over to re-tie the satin ribbon around her ankle. Tim looked on impatiently. 'Shall I go on in?'

'If you want, but make sure we sit next to Eleanor Springfield.'

'Why?'

'I want to talk to her. I've read all her books. She's an amazing writer.'

Tim gave a contemptuous grunt. 'Zara, American crime fiction is hardly literature.'

Zara's face flushed as red as her hair. 'I never said it was.' She gave the ribbon a final tug to tighten it and stood up. 'Christ, Tim, what's got into you? You've been in a foul mood ever since we got here.'

'I'm not in a foul mood. I just don't see the point of all this.' Tim waved his hand round at the lobby. 'This obscene display of wealth.'

Zara glared at him. 'Raffles is not obscene, Tim, it's tasteful. I would have thought you could tell the difference.'

Tim brandished his champagne flute. 'Spending two thousand dollars on a bottle of champagne, when there are people in the world without clean drinking water is obscene. In fact, it's worse than that, it's criminal.'

'Are we all supposed to drink dirty water in sympathy?'

'I didn't say that. All I'm saying is, the money that's being wasted on this could have been spent on giving somebody a better life. I thought you, of all people, would understand that.'

'I understand, Tim. But linking the two things together is ridiculous. There's no reason we can't enjoy ourselves *and* help other people.'

Tim gave a sharp laugh. 'How is any of this helping other people? It makes me sick watching the staff fawn all over James and Peyton as if they were royalty. Just because they've made a lot of money doesn't make them better than anyone else.'

Zara held up her hand. 'Okay, Tim, that's enough; I don't need a lecture. Just drop it, will you? For once, I'd like to just relax and enjoy myself without you going on about your brother and his money.' She snatched her small, black clutch bag from the table and marched into the dining room.

Tim curled his lips back into a scornful smile, 'And to hell with everyone else.'

Sixteen

Victoria leaned back in her chair and watched Tim and Zara disappear into the dining room. She couldn't help wondering how much either of them knew about the lives of people with no access to clean drinking water—she suspected, very little, and her thoughts drifted to the child she had taken to hospital in Southern Ethiopia, only three days earlier. The boy's mother had pleaded with her for some medication. But it was clear that he needed a lot more than the Panadol Victoria had in her rucksack, so she had offered to pay for him to go to a hospital. The gratitude in his father's eyes was heartbreaking. For the duration of their two-hour journey, he cradled his son in his arms, trying to protect him from every bump on the track. From time to time, he gave the boy a sip from the plastic bottle he had brought along for the journey, filled with murky, yellow, river water. That was the reality for thousands of people living in the Omo Valley. Their only source of drinking water was the polluted, crocodile-infested river. Victoria was ruminating how long it would be before the child suffered another bout of illness, when the French doors behind her slammed closed and James stepped back into the lobby.

He didn't appear to notice her sitting in the armchair as he rushed past, downing the dregs of his champagne. He thumped the empty glass down on to a table and made his way across to where Peyton was standing outside La Dame de Pic, talking with Nick and Kate. As James slapped a hand on Nick's shoulder, there was a little less warmth in his cavalier smile and a hardness in his grey eyes. 'Sorry, Kate, I just need to borrow Nick for a minute, if that's okay. Something's come up that we need to talk about.'

Kate gave an indifferent shrug, and James, with his arm still round Nick's shoulders, began to draw him away. But Peyton's voice stopped them. 'James, can't it wait? They're about to start serving dinner. We should all go into the dining room.'

James' lips tightened into a rigid smile. He called back over his shoulder. 'You two go on. We'll be there in a minute.'

Peyton rolled her eyes at Kate. 'Men! I swear the two of them will be doing a deal during our wedding vows.'

Kate cast a frosty glance across at her husband. 'Or Nick will be getting James to help him fix one that's gone wrong,' she muttered.

Seventeen

Victoria made her way to the restaurant and took her seat between Tim and Isabelle. Magnificent, long chandeliers hung low in the centre of the room, bathing the wedding guests in a soft, golden light. Waiters circulated, pouring champagne into crystal flutes. The fine bubbles sparkled like tiny, honey-coloured diamonds.

Victoria leaned back in her chair and took it all in. She always enjoyed her evenings in La Dame de Pic, and it felt even more special having the whole place to themselves. The refined grandeur seemed to make time stand still, as if nothing mattered except that precise moment, when every taste and smell should be savoured.

Yet, running her eye around the table, Victoria couldn't help feeling that on this particular evening, she had just taken her seat at The Last Supper. Da Vinci would have found rich material amongst the gloomy faces, seething with anger at their petty feuds.

Sitting on her left, Tim and Zara were pointedly ignoring each other. John and Nick were huddled on the other side of them, earnestly discussing something on John's iPhone. Beverley had taken pride of place at the head of the table, but in between giving orders to the staff, she glowered disapprovingly at her husband, while Kate sat on the other side of her, throwing venomous glances across at Nick. George was beside Kate, patiently listening to Patricia complaining that there was nothing on the menu to suit her. James leaned in to offer a helping hand, but he soon gave up and turned to Lou, sitting on the other side of him. She was trying to make conversation with Curtis, but he looked bored. Bill was the only one who seemed happy. Seated at the opposite end of the table to Beverley, he had Eleanor on one side of him and Peyton on the other. Peyton looked anxious and Isabelle, who was sitting between her and Victoria, had an expression of ennui plastered on her face.

Victoria took the printed menu from her dinner plate and began to work her way down the degustation selection, consoling herself that even if the company wasn't much, the food, at least, would be agreeable.

The maître d'hôtel glided towards her, with a large bottle of Evian and Badoit balanced aloft in each hand. 'Sparkling water for you, Miss West?'

'Yes, thank you Thomas—that would be lovely.'

'And for you, sir?' The maître d'hôtel whirled around to face Tim Marsters. 'Would you prefer still or sparkling water with your dinner?'

Tim's thin lips twisted into a smirk. 'I'll have tap water, thank you.'

The maître d'hôtel bowed. 'Of course, sir. If that is your preference, I shall arrange for a carafe to be brought to the table.'

'Yes, that *is* my preference.' Tim looked pointedly across the table at his brother. 'I don't see why you would pay for bottled water, when water from the tap is perfectly drinkable.'

James met his brother's gaze with an expression of weary disdain. 'Given you're not paying for it, it hardly matters, does it?'

Tim straightened his gangling body and pressed the heels of his hands hard against the edge of the table. 'If you stopped to think about it for a minute, you'd realize it does matter. There are people in Singapore living on five dollars a day. And you're spending what, twenty on a bottle of water? They could live for four days on that.'

James lowered his gaze to the glass of Louis Roederer Cristal sitting in front of Tim. 'Then maybe you should stop drinking the champagne as well,' he taunted. 'They could live for eighteen months on that.'

Contempt blazed in Tim's eyes. 'Maybe I will.' He shoved his chair back and stood up. 'I don't want your stupid champagne, anyway.' With the back of his hand, he swatted the crystal flute, sending it clattering into the porcelain vase.

The single pink rose swayed precariously on its pedestal. Victoria reached out and grabbed hold of it, to stop it from falling.

Patricia shrieked as the river of Tim's champagne flowed into the bodice of her dress. She snatched up her napkin and began to dab at the patch of wet, pink flowers. 'Oh Tim, look what you have done. I'm covered in it.' She turned to her husband. 'Give me that napkin, George, this one is soaked through.'

James reached over in front of Patricia, using George's napkin to dab the leather top of the table. He glowered across at his brother. 'You idiot.'

Tim stood in frozen silence, staring at his aunt. 'I'm sorry, Aunt Patricia, I didn't mean to knock it over.'

Zara seized Tim by the arm and pulled him back down into his chair. Her pale cheeks burned fire engine red. 'Just sit down and stop making a scene.'

Ever the efficient secretary, Lou jumped up and rushed around behind Patricia, wielding her own napkin. She tucked her dark bob firmly behind one ear and threw a kindly glance across at Tim. 'Accidents happen; they can't be helped. And I'm sure it won't leave a lasting stain, Patricia; it's just white wine.'

Lou crouched down and began mopping up the few drops that had dripped on to the floor. Beverley watched her, her mounting irritation plainly visible in every line on her face. 'Would you just leave it, Lou. Go and sit down. You know very well, it wasn't an accident.' She glared across the table at her son. 'Tim can clean up his own mess. He doesn't need you doing it for him.'

Lou stopped and scrunched the damp napkin into a tight ball with her fingers. Slowly, she stood up and cast a strained smile across the table at Tim and his father. Then silently, she went back to her seat, humiliation inscribed into every contour of her face.

Beverley turned to Patricia. 'Have the hotel arrange for your dress to be dry cleaned. Don't worry about the money; just put it on to your room bill.'

George gave a scathing laugh. 'Money is never a problem with you, is it, Beverley? Until we want to get our investment back. Then, oddly, there doesn't seem to be enough of it.'

'George!' Patricia scowled at her husband. 'This is hardly the time.'

'Then when *is* the right time? Every time I raise the subject, you and your brother shut me down.' George threw a sharp glance across the table at John Marsters. 'We have to settle on the house in two weeks and if we don't, we lose our deposit.'

Patricia pursed her lips in irritation. 'We have the option of bridging finance.'

George crossed his arms tightly over his chest. 'I am not paying for bridging finance when we have got the money to settle.'

Beverley cast an uncomfortable glance along the table towards Peyton. 'Why don't we leave this discussion until tomorrow, George? We're here to celebrate James and Peyton getting married; let's not mar the evening with unpleasantness.'

George drew a deep breath. 'I am not marring it with unpleasantness; I am just stating the facts. And the facts are that you promised us our money back and we haven't got it. I'm not going to wait any longer. I want it returned.'

Patricia gave him a stern frown. 'Keep your voice down, George! We don't need everybody hearing this.'

'I don't care who hears it. I want to get an answer.'

Beverley leaned forward with one elbow resting on the arm of her chair, the tension in her hunched shoulders belying the calmness in her voice. 'We have already given you an answer, George. If you were to take your money out now, we would have to find another investor to replace you. Doing that, at this late a stage, is not feasible. We can't offer the same favourable terms that we offered to you, to a new investor. It wouldn't be fair to everyone else in the deal. So given that you have committed to buying this property, the only solution is for you to take out bridging finance for a few weeks, until everything is concluded. The cost will be infinitesimal in the scheme of things.'

'It might be infinitesimal to you, but it is not to me.' George banged his clenched fist down hard, rattling the crockery.

The other guests turned to look at him, their halted conversations hanging unfinished in the awkward silence.

Patricia glared at her husband. 'For goodness' sake! What has got into you?'

To Victoria's surprise, George, for once, ignored his wife. He seemed so mild-mannered—this situation had clearly riled him up. Either that or he had enjoyed a few too many glasses of champagne.

James raised his hand to summon a waiter. 'Come on, George. Let's have another drink and park this discussion until tomorrow. There's no point ruining dinner. And it's a public holiday in the US, there is nothing we can do tonight, anyway.'

George shook his head. 'There's always an excuse, isn't there? In the meantime, I'm expected to pay exorbitant rates for bridging finance. It's absolute madness.' He looked towards Peyton's grandparents at the far end of the table. 'Is this something you would ever have suggested to one of your clients, Bill?'

Bill raised his bushy eyebrows above the tortoise-shell rim of his glasses. 'I'm not sure this is a discussion we ought to be having over dinner. And it's a little hard for to me to answer without knowing any of the details. I never like to pay interest myself, as a general rule, but—'

'Exactly my view!' George exclaimed. 'I haven't borrowed money from a bank in twenty years and I am not about to start now. And if I need to get lawyers involved, I will.'

James gave an exasperated sigh. 'What is that going to achieve, George? We have already got a clear legal agreement with you in place. You can go through it with Nick again, if you want to. But there is nothing your lawyer, or any of us, can do to hurry this up. We told you right at the beginning that this was a big deal with a lot of heavy-hitting investors involved, from across the globe. It was never a standard investment opportunity. We've got members of the Saudi royal family with an interest in this. It is not something that is open to just anybody.

And when we're dealing at this level, you have got to understand we are not in a position to rush things.'

'I am not asking you to rush things. I just want you to stick to our original timetable. If you can't do that, I'll have no choice but to take legal action.'

Nick placed his champagne flute down on the table. 'George, there is nothing that can be done from a legal perspective to move things along any quicker. There is no specific timeline in the agreement you signed. I believe we went through all of that with you, at the time. And don't forget there are preemptive rights within this deal applicable to existing investors, which makes it very complex to bring in a substitute investor at this late stage. But if you would like to, we can get together tomorrow and I can take you through all of this again.'

The colour rose on George's freckled, yellow complexion. 'I don't need to go through preemptive rights or any of the other fancy legal terminology again. You told me—' he pointed an accusing finger at John. 'That we would have our money, weeks ago. And now we haven't got it and you're trying to pull the wool over our eyes with more excuses.'

Tim slumped back in his chair. 'That's how the finance industry works, isn't it? If they didn't pull the wool over your eyes, how would they feed their corruption and greed? Of course, they don't call it that. They don't call it "theft", which is what it is. They call it "the creation of wealth". But they only create it for themselves.'

James glared at his brother. 'For Christ's sake, Tim, would you shut up! You don't know anything about the finance industry.'

'I know as much as you do. Take all the money you can and don't worry about the people who might lose their houses and jobs because of your greed. And you know you'll never be held accountable, because financial institutions are protected by corrupt governments who are only interested in sharing the profits.'

Isabelle stirred in the seat beside Victoria. She raised one thinly drawn eyebrow. 'There are many examples of financiers being sent to prison. The system is not quite so inept as you believe.'

Tim stared at her. 'Yeah, well, not enough of them. There should be a lot more in prison.'

'Tim, that is enough,' Beverley snapped. 'This is not a conversation we need to be having over dinner.'

George gave a harsh, dry laugh. 'That's right, Beverley, shut everyone down, just like you usually do.'

'George!' Patricia turned sharply to her husband. 'That is no way to speak to Beverley.'

The sudden loud clang of Zara's champagne flute, knocking against a porcelain side plate brought the arguments around the table to an abrupt halt. She sat frozen in her seat, her hand still clasped around the glass, staring at the bracelet on her wrist. 'One of the yellow diamonds is missing!'

She began frantically searching amongst the purple folds of her chiffon dress and then pushed her chair back to search the floor around her feet. 'Tim, can you move your chair so I can look under the table?'

Tim rolled his eyes. 'Why would it be under the table? You could have lost it anywhere.'

'Then I'll look everywhere!' Zara got down on to her hands and knees. 'Move!'

Grudgingly, Tim shifted his chair out of her way and sat watching her with his arms folded over his chest.

James glared at his brother. 'You could get up and help her, Tim, instead of sitting there like a moron.'

Tim tightened his folded arms. 'Why don't *you* get up and help, if you're so worried about her precious diamond.'

Zara stood up. She looked across the table at James with tears welling in her eyes. 'I can't find it.'

James rose from his seat 'Why don't we have a look in the bar, it might have fallen out in there?' He threw a caustic glance across at his brother. 'Are you going to come and help?'

Tim sat back in his chair. 'Why don't you get the staff to go and look for it? Isn't that what you're paying them for? To run around after you?'

'Tim, for goodness' sake!' Beverley's sharp words cut across the table. But they faded into the background, as Victoria's attention was drawn to Isabelle, standing up beside her.

Isabelle leaned forward, reaching out for her clutch bag and the packet of Gauloises Blondes she had left lying on the table. 'I am going outside for a cigarette, if you wish to join me.' She glanced across at the warring factions. 'It might be more peaceful than staying in here.'

Victoria smiled. 'Thank you, Isabelle, but I think I'll stay put. I'm rather hoping they will feed us soon.'

Isabelle threw a sardonic glance down at Peyton. 'Is it possible to enjoy good food in this environment?'

Peyton glared at her godmother. 'Isabelle!'

'My dear, a life of indigestion might suit you. But there is no reason for the rest of us to endure it.' Isabelle popped the Gauloises into her clutch and cast a glance towards Curtis. 'Especially when there are alternatives.' She snapped the clasp of her handbag closed and left the table.

Peyton shook her head at Victoria. 'I swear, she never gives up.'

Victoria smiled. 'Tenacity is one of her strong points.'

'Tell me about it. I just wish she would leave it in the boardroom.' Peyton glanced towards the far end of the restaurant. 'And now here's the food arriving, just as she disappears. That is so typical of her.'

In a highly choreographed formation, a troupe of waiters approached, parting, liked synchronized swimmers, as soon as the first waiter reached the head of the table. He paused beside Kate de Brouwer, a silver tray held in the palm of his hand, high above his head. With a broad sweep of his arm, he lifted a large white plate from the tray and deposited it in front of Kate. 'The tomato myriad for you, Mrs de Brouwer.'

The maître d'hôtel glided along the table and swooped in beside Victoria. 'For you, Miss West, the brown crab with creamy dill and fine mikan jelly. And for Madame Sauveterre—' he swung around to the empty chair beside Victoria, poised to serve a plate of Quail Sausage with Parsnip Véloute.

'You can leave it for her,' Victoria said. 'She's not far away.'

The maître d'hôtel bowed and lowered the plate into position, adjusting it minutely to ensure it sat in the middle of the place setting. He stepped back and inclined his head towards Victoria. 'Bon appétit.'

With the dexterity of a skilled juggler, he navigated the rest of the table, firing off instructions to his staff. 'The crab, gluten-free, for Miss Avery-Smythe . . . and for Mrs Marsters, the crab *without* peanut oil . . . and the crab with no sauce for Mrs Helstone . . .'

Victoria leaned back in her chair, smiling at the performance and enjoying the relative silence that had now settled over the table. The flurry of activity had brought the arguments to a halt. Although, she wondered how long the peaceful hiatus would last. Probably not very long.

Her gaze fell on her plate and the small, perfectly arranged portions of crab, the delicate coating of creamy dill sauce and the tiny orange droplets of mikan jelly, arranged in a fan-like pattern around the edge. Unlike Isabelle, the family squabbling hadn't dampened her appetite. If anything, the arguments had made her realize just how hungry she was. Nonetheless, she wasn't sure she would be able to endure another four courses.

She sank her fork into the crab's firm flesh and began to contemplate how she might conjure up an early exit.

Eighteen

Victoria rolled over, luxuriating in the softness of her enormous bed. Reluctantly, she opened her eyes. It was morning; daylight was creeping under the curtains and spreading its tentacles across the wooden floorboards. She reached out for the iPhone she had left on the bedside table, the night before. Eleven o'clock. That meant breakfast was over. Not that she needed any; she had eaten enough at dinner to cover both meals and probably, lunch as well. The food was the only part of the evening that had been pleasant. She knew weddings had a tendency to bring out the worst in people, but the arguments over dinner had been extraordinary. She was heartily glad it was over—although worried for Peyton. She couldn't help but feel uneasy for her, given everything she had heard.

She turned onto her back and gazed up at the wooden ceiling fan whirring effortlessly above her, torn between her desire for more sleep and her longing for the sunshine and to be revived by the cool water in the hotel's gorgeous swimming pool.

She played with the choice for a moment; then threw off the sheets and slipped her feet into the navy blue slippers that had been laid out on the carpet beside the bed, on a mat of starched, white linen.

She padded through to the bathroom to freshen up, then went around to the closet and opened the suitcase that she hadn't had time to unpack. She pulled out a white bikini and a matching kaftan. Her mind was made up; she would spend the afternoon relaxing by the pool. She scarcely ever had the time to laze in the sun, and when she did get the chance, it was always pure heaven. And she could do with some relaxation—Beverley Marsters had announced that she and John were hosting yet another dinner that evening, for the wedding guests. It was to be a Singaporean buffet in their suite.

Victoria could think of very little that she would enjoy less, having endured the endless bickering on just the previous evening. Still, it would give her the chance to spend some more time with Peyton. They had seen so little of each other in recent years.

She dug around in her suitcase for a pair of red sandals, eventually finding them buried right at the bottom. She threw them down onto the wooden floorboards, and slipping her feet out of the hotel slippers, slid them on. She continued searching for her book. She wanted to read the diaries of Gertrude Bell before she left Singapore. Her next contract was in the Middle East and the region fascinated and confounded her. Many of her friends there still spoke of Gertrude with pride and fondness. They considered her to be one of them and Victoria was intrigued to know more about this adventurous Englishwoman who, as Churchill's advisor, was essentially the architect of modern Iraq. Although she wondered what Gertrude would make of it now, in its current state of upheaval.

She found the book and threw it into her tote bag; then hunted around until she found her straw sunhat. It was badly squashed and she had to stretch it back into shape. She briefly considered unpacking the rest of her clothes, but as everything was going to need ironing anyway, she left them for the butler to deal with, and made her way back around into the bedroom. She picked the iPad up and opened the curtains. The bright, white light of the late morning sun poured in through the French windows and across the narrow corridor separating her bedroom from the rest of the suite. The sunny, almost cloudless morning, spurred her on. She felt suddenly alive in the glorious sunshine.

Stepping out into the corridor, she made her way along to her living room. The strong perfume of frangipani flowers filled the air. She smiled at the huge floral display at the centre of the large coffee table, with the little note from Mario sitting beside it. He certainly knew how to be charming. And it was very kind of him to give her a

Presidential Suite; but she was rattling around in it. Most of the living spaces, she hadn't even walked into. It would have been much better suited for a guest who wanted to throw parties. Someone who would actually *use* the dining room. Unfortunately, all she wanted to do was sleep and get away from the world.

She switched the 'Do Not Disturb' light off and moved into the entrance foyer and unhinged the latch on the front door.

Outside on the landing, the bright morning sunlight streamed in through the French windows, bathing the wooden floorboards and polished mahogany furniture in a haze of white. The dazzling brightness caught the green fronds of a kentia palm, which was sitting in a large ceramic Ming pot, giving it an almost translucent appearance.

Victoria followed the wooden landing around the edges of the magnificent, pillared atrium towards the Grand Staircase. Sweeping majestically up through the centre of the hotel, its ornate, polished railings and brass carpet rods gleamed in the slanting rays of the morning sun, as it filtered in though the enormous skylight.

She mounted the stairs to the third floor, where she passed through the gym to a single door at the far end. Stepping out into the warmth of the terrace, she felt the heat from the sun burn into her olive skin.

She picked a bottle of sunscreen out of the wicker basket at the entrance and chose a lounger at the far end of the terrace, partially shaded by a large umbrella and a flowering red frangipani tree. A fresh beige and white striped towel lay draped over the lounger's thick cushions. She threw her kaftan and tote bag down on top of it and slipped her sandals behind the black-and-white-striped side-table.

She made her way around to the deepest part of the pool and stood for a moment on the edge. The mirrored image of the surrounding skyscrapers and the hotel's terracotta roof shimmered in front of her. The reflection was unbroken, except where small puffs of wind ruffled the surface and the images crinkled in the disturbed water.

She arched her body back and made a shallow dive. The blue water rippled in her wake, moving out towards the edges of the pool.

She stayed beneath the surface for as long as she could, moving with powerful strokes and allowing the cool water to comb over her skin.

When she reached the far end, she gently broke the surface and pushed herself away from the edge with a small kick. She stretched her arms out wide and floated, gazing up at the hazy blue sky. The water cushioned her body and she closed her eyes, enjoying the dense silence of the water bubbling in her ears.

Slowly, she let her body sink. Then she flipped over and with two firm kicks propelled herself to the ladder at the side of the pool. As she put her foot on to the first rung, she noticed a woman, sitting a little further along the terrace, watching her. She had a voluptuous figure and wore a long sundress in muted shades of blue and green, tied halter style at her neck. A pair of large dark glasses and a floppy sunhat shaded her face, but when she smiled, Victoria recognized Kate de Brouwer.

She climbed up the ladder and walked along the terrace towards her. The morning sun bore down on the grey tiles and the searing heat tingled on the soles of her feet. She skipped quickly across to the shade of Kate's large, sun umbrella and the solace of the cooler tiles beneath it. As she ducked under the canopy, Kate attempted to conceal the chocolate wrapper she was holding underneath a *Vogue* magazine, lying on the towel beside her.

Victoria cast a quick glance down at the corner of red foil still visible and smiled. 'Good morning, Kate—or is it afternoon, already? My body has no idea what time zone it's in.'

Seeing that she had been caught, Kate licked the remains of the chocolate from her fingers and laughed. She looked at her watch. 'It's still morning—just. It's coming up to a quarter to twelve.'

Victoria wrung the water out of her long hair. 'Have you been in for a swim yet? It's beautiful.'

'No, I haven't. I didn't bring a swimsuit. I've put on so much weight lately; I couldn't bear the thought of squeezing into one.' Kate looked enviously at Victoria in her white bikini. 'If I had a body like yours, I wouldn't be worried. But I need to lose some of this.' She grabbed a handful of fat around her waist. 'That's the problem with living in London; there never seems to be enough time to exercise.' She glanced at the crumpled Lindt wrapper poking out from beneath the magazine. 'Mind you, eating chocolate all morning isn't going to help either, is it? I just can't seem to stop myself.'

Victoria smiled. 'I wouldn't worry about a few extra pounds if I were you, the pool is far too good to miss in this heat.'

'I'm sure you're right. But I don't think I have the energy to go into town to buy something to wear. Not that they'd have anything in my size anyway, all the women here are so petite. I don't think they sell anything over a size ten. I think I'll just stay here under the umbrella and read my magazine. Besides, I've just ordered a glass of champagne.'

'That sounds like an equally good plan; enjoy! And I'll see you a bit later in John and Beverley's suite for dinner.'

Victoria returned to her own lounger and smoothed the striped towel over the cushions. She took a long drink from the bottle of cold water a waiter had left on the side-table for her and lay back, letting the midday heat soak into her wet body. She closed her eyes.

The warmth of the sun cosseted her and she pushed all thoughts of work and the wedding from her mind, thinking of nothing but the comforting blanket of heat that was wrapping itself around her. Slowly, she fell into a lovely half-sleep, vaguely aware of the frangipani trees shifting in the breeze behind her and the odd, distant scrape of a sun lounger on the terrace tiles. Occasionally, there was the hushed voice of a waiter taking an order for drinks. But nothing disturbed her rest, until she heard someone calling her name.

She lifted her sunhat and saw Peyton, flushed and agitated, rushing across the terrace towards her. 'Oh Victoria, thank God you're here! Something awful has happened!'

As Peyton spoke, her face, naturally pale, had turned deathly white and she was trembling violently. Certain she was going to faint, Victoria jumped up from the lounger and took hold of her. She held her upright. 'What is it, Peyton? What's happened?'

Peyton threw a frantic glance around the terrace. A waiter was standing a few metres away, poised over a middle-aged couple in bathing suits, relaxing on the same sun lounger Kate had occupied earlier. She must have left, while Victoria was asleep. The waiter had two Singapore Slings—one was sitting on a silver tray that he held in his left hand, and the other was in his right hand, suspended in mid-air, with a thin slice of pineapple and a red maraschino cherry perched precariously on the side of the glass. His hand was frozen and grasped around the pink cocktail, as he looked across the terrace at Peyton, in unconcealed alarm.

She turned from him and wrapped both hands tightly around Victoria's upper arm. She cast another agitated glance over her shoulder; then drew Victoria away to the far edge of the terrace, beyond the sun loungers. Victoria could feel the sharp edges of Peyton's fingernails digging into her skin. She gently prised them off and took a firm hold of Peyton's hands. They were stone cold, even in the midday heat. 'What is it, Peyton? Tell me. What's happened?'

Peyton stared at Victoria in a frightened, bewildered manner. Victoria could feel her hands quivering as she spoke. 'I don't know—I don't know what to do, Victoria. None of it makes any sense.'

'None of what makes any sense? What's happened?'

'It's James—' Peyton clasped her hand over her mouth to stifle a sob. 'Oh God! I don't understand how it could have happened. It's not possible.'

'What isn't possible? Has something happened to James?'

Peyton nodded. 'We got a message—' Her voice was low and stifled, barely above a whisper. 'But it doesn't make any sense. James was supposed to be at a meeting, only he—'

'Only he, what?' Victoria waited for Peyton to speak. In the blistering heat, she could feel the last vestiges of water evaporating from her bikini, and the scorching tiles burning beneath her feet. 'Peyton, you have got to tell me. I can't help you, unless you do.'

Peyton grasped hold of Victoria's hands, her face still a white mask. 'He never came back. We were supposed to meet, but he never turned up and then we got the message—' Sobs welled up in her throat. 'Oh God, Victoria, it's so horrible. I don't know what to do.'

'Tell me about the message. What did it say?'

Peyton fumbled in her pocket. 'Here. Read it.' She thrust a silver iPhone at Victoria. On the screen, there was a message.

I have James. Don't contact the police or go public. If you do, I'll kill him. Wait for my next instructions and then do exactly as I tell you.

Nineteen

Victoria lifted her gaze from the message on the phone's screen, her face expressionless. She quickly returned to her lounger, slipped on her sandals and kaftan, gathered up her other belongings and told Peyton to follow her inside. She didn't speak again until the two women were seated alone in her suite.

'When did you receive this message?' Victoria asked.

'About half an hour ago. I came straight out to look for you,' Peyton answered.

Victoria glanced across at the clock on the bookshelf. It had just gone one thirty. 'You're sure this isn't someone playing a practical joke?'

Peyton shook her head vigorously. 'No. James should have been back here, over an hour ago. And that's his iPhone. He would never have given it up to anyone unless he had to.'

'Then how did you get hold of it?'

'It was delivered by room service.'

Victoria fixed her eyes on Peyton. She took hold of her by the shoulders and spoke firmly. 'Peyton, you're not making any sense. Start at the beginning and tell me exactly what happened.'

Peyton took a deep, unsteady breath. 'I'd booked to spend this morning in the spa, so James decided to go downtown for a meeting. But there was some confusion over my booking and I left the spa an hour earlier than I was supposed to. On the way back to our suite, I bumped into James on the staircase. He was rushing out to his second meeting—he'd had to come back to the hotel because he'd forgotten some papers. But he said he'd be back by twelve or just after. We were supposed to meet in his parents' room at midday, so we could go over a few details for the wedding tomorrow. But at one o'clock, James hadn't turned up and we were just about to call him when room service arrived at the door. Only, John and Beverley hadn't ordered anything and John was explaining that to the butler when Beverley noticed an envelope on the trolley, addressed to them. We thought it must have had something to do with the wedding, so John signed for it. Then she opened the envelope and found James' phone, with a note saying to turn it on. Which we did and—'

Peyton's strength suddenly failed her. 'Oh God Victoria,' she cried, in a wretched, choked voice. 'What am I going to do? What if they hurt him?'

Victoria put her arm round Peyton and let her cry while she puzzled over the strange delivery of the kidnapper's message. Why the phone? Why the room service trolley?

Peyton took a tissue from her pocket and dabbed at her tears. Her sobs gradually became quieter. 'Crying isn't much use, is it? It's not going to help us find James.'

Victoria shook her head. 'No, it isn't.' She paused and considered her friend for a moment. 'Did you have any idea something like this might happen?'

Peyton stared at Victoria blankly. 'No. None.'

'You can't think of anyone who might be behind it?'

'No. I can't imagine anyone doing something like this.'

Victoria gave a small, puzzled frown. 'Especially here in Singapore.'

Peyton looked at her through her tears. 'Why do you say that?'

'This is a small country with a lot of surveillance. And the penalties for kidnapping are a lot harsher here than in most places; it still carries the death penalty. You're also only here for a week; it didn't give the kidnapper much time to—' Victoria broke off. Peyton was no longer paying any attention to her. She seemed distracted. 'What is it?'

Peyton made as if to speak, but stopped herself. Her forehead creased into a frown. She stared at her hands, twisting her engagement ring round and round on her finger.

'Peyton, what is it?' Victoria said, more firmly. 'You need to tell me.'

Peyton stared at Victoria for a moment before answering. 'I—I got a letter last week, telling me not to come here and marry James. I thought it was from an ex-girlfriend or something.' Her eyes filled with tears again. 'Oh God, this is a nightmare.'

'Do you still have the letter?'

Peyton nodded. 'I've got it with me; it's in my suitcase. I was going to talk to James about it. But it seemed so stupid, I kept putting it off. Shall I go and get it?'

'Yes, I'd like to see it.'

Peyton rose unsteadily to her feet. She pulled her light, cotton jacket tightly over her shoulders.

'Here, take this.' Victoria took her room key from the coffee table and handed it to Peyton.

Peyton tucked it in her jacket pocket. 'I'll be back in a minute.'

As the door closed behind Peyton, a shiver ran through Victoria. She crossed to the French doors and flung them open, feeling the instant pleasure of the hot, afternoon humidity on her skin. She walked over and stood in the band of sunshine bathing the edge of the balcony. The rays pierced the light cotton of her kaftan and for a brief moment, she indulged in the untainted pleasure of it. Then, snippets of the previous evening began to cloud her mind. What exactly had been said which had made her feel so uncomfortable? And could any of it have been a precursor to a kidnapping? It seemed preposterous. Nonetheless, she began to sift through the conversations as best as she could remember them. George Helstone had been in a heated debate with Beverley over money—probably fuelled by a few too many glasses of champagne. There was mention of a payment that was due and a property that George needed to settle on. Beverley had told him it would be difficult to pull his investment out. Nick got involved. George accused him of using technical language to pull the wool over his eyes. Then Tim said something about banks being corrupt. He and James argued. And there was something odd about what Isabelle had said. What was it? Victoria leaned on the thick, white, concrete balustrade and tried to remember. It was something she said to Tim, just before Beverley cut him off.

The lock clicked in the front door, but Victoria didn't move. She stayed out on the balcony, trying to remember what it was that Isabelle had said. She was still grasping for it, when Peyton appeared at her side. She stared at Victoria with a fixed, glazed expression. In her hand, she held a bright green envelope: the sort that might be sold with a cheap greeting card. Her hand trembled as she passed it to Victoria.

Victoria cast a cursory glance at the New York postmark; then extracted a carefully folded sheet of white copy paper from inside. She opened it out and laid it flat on top of the concrete balustrade. There was no signature, just three typewritten lines in the centre of the page, printed in a large serif face.

Next week you are to marry James Winstanley. I am writing to warn you against it. Don't go to Singapore. James doesn't love you—he's never loved you. Take this warning before it's too late.

Twenty

Victoria finished reading the note and slowly re-folded it. Peyton searched her face, trying to guess her opinion of it. 'Do you think it has anything to do with—' she hesitated, as if she couldn't bear to utter the next words: 'with the other message?'

'I don't know. But it does seem like a strange coincidence.' Victoria turned the envelope over. 'It's addressed to your California office. But I thought you were working out of London now?'

'I am, I moved my office there, a few months ago, to be with James. But with the sale of the company going through, I've spent the last few weeks back in California, helping with the handover.'

Victoria nodded slowly. 'So whoever sent you this, must have known you were going to be in California, last week. And knew you were coming here to get married this week.' She paused. 'As did the kidnapper.'

'But the only people we told about the wedding, were the people we invited and you were all sworn to secrecy.'

'We were. But it looks as if one of us has let the cat out of the bag. Unless there's someone else James confided in, without telling you?'

Peyton shook her head. 'No, he wouldn't have done that. He was the one who wanted to keep it quiet. Ever since the company sale was announced, the media have been hounding me and it's been driving him insane. I did my best to keep him out of everything, but he wanted to make sure they didn't find out about the wedding and follow us down here. That's why we kept it so small and only invited the people closest to us, who we could trust.'

'In which case, one of the wedding guests very likely knows the person who wrote this letter. Or—' Victoria paused to consider the alternative. 'One of them wrote it themselves.'

Peyton's eyes grew wide. 'One of the wedding guests?'

Victoria shrugged. 'It's a possibility. Did any of them know you were in California, last week?'

'Yes, I emailed everyone to tell them I'd be in the States until the wedding and that I'd see them here in Singapore.'

'In which case, one of them could have written it.' Victoria picked up the letter and reread the last words. 'Have you ever doubted his love for you?'

Peyton stared at Victoria. 'What do you mean?'

'Is there any truth to the letter? Have you ever had a reason to doubt James' love for you?'

The blood surged back into Peyton's pale cheeks. 'Of course, I haven't.' She spoke quickly and fiercely. Victoria knew the tone well. It was her pride on the attack. Peyton had always had a quick temper in response to any criticism of her judgement.

But this was no time for delicacy. If the kidnapper's note was to be believed, James was in grave danger. Victoria held up the letter. 'You asked me if I thought this had anything to do with the kidnapper's message. I can only give you an answer on that if I have all the facts. That's why I asked.'

Peyton sank down into the rattan armchair. She began to pick at the red polish on her nails. 'There was one time. But it was just me overthinking everything like I usually do.'

'Had something happened?'

'It was nothing serious. It was just something Zara said, one day, when we were with her and Tim. I can't remember exactly what it was, but I got the impression that she liked James. And the way he answered her, it crossed my mind that he might prefer to be dating somebody younger. It was stupid. I told James about it afterwards and he just laughed. He said she wasn't his type at all.' Peyton buried her face in her hands. 'I don't know why I'm mentioning any of this; it's got nothing to do with anything.' She looked up at Victoria, her blue eyes swimming with tears. 'Except, I don't know what to do. I just want to get him back.'

Victoria crouched down beside her and rested her hand on Peyton's knee. 'I know. That's why it's important you tell me everything—even if it seems irrelevant. Sometimes, our intuition is our best guide. Zara could have sent you the letter, even if there is nothing between her and James.'

Peyton sniffed back her tears. 'But why would she? I mean, anybody could have written the letter. Someone could have hacked into my emails or phone messages to get the information.'

Victoria raised an eyebrow. 'Peyton, your phone and company emails are more secure than the vaults in the Bank of England.'

Peyton gave a feeble smile. 'They're not impenetrable.'

'Maybe not to a sophisticated hacker.' Victoria looked down at the cheap, green envelope and sheet of photocopying paper. 'But I don't think the person we're dealing with here, falls into that category. If they knew how to disguise their identity online well enough to hack into your emails, I'm sure they would have sent you an electronic message—not gone into a stationery shop and bought a stamp and an envelope.'

There was a moment's dead silence.

'What about the other message?' Peyton asked. 'Do you think it's the same person that sent both?'

'That depends on whether the kidnapper had a reason for choosing Singapore for the kidnapping. If they did, then it doesn't make sense that they sent you a letter to try and stop you from coming here. But if they didn't, then it's possible it is the same person.' Victoria picked up the letter. 'Either way, I'd say there's a good chance that James knows his kidnapper. Which means, for his safety, we need to get the police involved as soon as possible.'

Peyton sat bolt upright, her face frozen with panic. 'But Victoria, we can't. They said they'd kill James if we called the police.'

'Peyton, if James can identify his kidnapper, then there's no incentive for them to release him alive. He needs to be found before anything happens.'

A pleading fear crept into Peyton's voice. 'Can't you find him without involving the police?'

'Peyton—'

Peyton took hold of Victoria's arm. She gripped it so tightly Victoria could almost feel it bruising. 'I know it's a lot to ask. But Victoria, I'm scared. I love James so much, I don't know what I'd do if anything happened to him.'

Victoria took Peyton's hands and gently loosened the bruising fingers. She held them in her own and watched Peyton in silence for a moment, not knowing what answer to give. Dealing with governments was one thing. Especially now that she was self-employed, she could pick and choose the jobs she took on. She wasn't obligated to say yes to anyone. But this was a whole different matter. This was her oldest friend asking her for help.

A tear rolled down Peyton's pale cheek. Her helplessness struck Victoria to the core.

She moved away along the balcony and looked out across the courtyard to the shaded, wooden verandahs on the other side. Bulbous grey clouds were beginning to drift over the city. The feathered edges briefly obscured the sun and a dull shadow passed over the hotel. Victoria slowly turned her head.

'There are no guarantees that I'll find him in time,' she said at last.

Peyton moved swiftly to Victoria's side. 'I know, but at least I'll know no one else could have found him, either.' She gave a weak, encouraging smile. 'I know you, Victoria. I've known you since we were twelve years old. And I know you've got a better chance of finding James than the police.'

She held Victoria's gaze and Victoria slowly nodded. She couldn't deny Peyton was right.

'All right,' she said. Yet, it was with a troubled mind that she agreed.

Twenty-One

The afternoon heat was beginning to get more overbearing as the clouds drew closer together, smothering the city in a blanket of humidity. Victoria could feel the soft, cotton folds of her kaftan starting to cling uncomfortably to the moisture on her skin. She picked up the anonymous letter and green envelope from the table. 'Let's move back inside. It's getting too hot out here.'

Once seated amongst the rust coloured cushions in the living room of her suite, Victoria's mind began to race through what she needed to do next. 'The message you received on James' phone, was it an SMS?'

Peyton shook her head. 'No it was a Privatechat message. It's a new business app we've been trialling.'

'Trialling?' Victoria raised her eyebrows. 'You mean it's not available to the public?'

'Not yet, it'll be going live in about a month.'

'Does that mean we're able to trace where the message came from?'

'I'm afraid not. That's the whole idea behind the new platform; the data can't be traced or stored. In the conventional sense, these messages don't exist. It's essentially a secure form of social media for businesses to help them prevent corporate theft.'

'So who has access to the app at the moment?'

'We've got a thousand people taking part in the trial. James is one of them.'

'So whoever sent the message to his phone must be taking part in the trial as well?'

'Possibly. Or if they had James' laptop—' Peyton clamped both hands over her mouth. 'Oh God!' She closed her eyes and tried to hold back her tears. 'I'm so sorry. I'm trying to hold it together.'

'I know you are, Peyton, and you're doing a good job. I understand how difficult this is. But I do need you to stay focused. If I'm to get James back to you, I need to find him quickly. Now, can you tell me about the wedding guests; are any of them involved in the trial?'

Peyton swallowed. 'Yes, we set everyone up on it, except Beverley and Patricia—and you, but I know you're too busy.'

'Why not Beverley and Patricia?'

'Beverley thinks social networking is a waste of time and Patricia can't even use a mobile phone.'

'Ah.' Victoria gave a light laugh. 'The technical illiterati.'

She fell silent. The facts, such as they were, began to turn over in her mind.

The kidnapper had clearly known James was going to be in Singapore and also knew that he was getting married at Raffles Hotel. They knew his parents were here and also knew which room they were staying in. They knew Peyton was going to be in their room at one o'clock. They knew James was using Privatechat and probably knew he had a meeting, that morning, which he would be travelling alone to. They also somehow managed to get their message onto a room service trolley inside Raffles. In fact, Victoria reflected, the whole thing had been very well planned-out and executed. And it was very likely that somebody close to James was involved—possibly one of the wedding guests. She gave a small shudder. It was impossible not to think the worst.

'Tell me about this morning,' Victoria said. 'What time did James leave for his meetings?'

'He was planning to leave here just before nine. I went across to the arcade at a quarter to, for my spa appointment, and he was packing everything up then, getting ready to leave.'

'Do you know who his appointment was with?'

'I'm not sure, exactly. I think it was a new client. But I could ask Beverley if you want, I'm sure she'll know.'

'Yes, that would be good. What about the other guests, did you see anyone else this morning?'

'We had breakfast with Beverley, John and Lou. They were heading off straight afterwards to Sentosa.'

'Lou is their secretary, isn't she? The woman with the black bob?'

Peyton nodded. 'Yes—although she's a bit more than a secretary. She basically runs the office for them.'

'And did you see anyone else?'

'Tim and Zara joined us at breakfast; they were running a bit late. Nick and Kate were there as well, although they left before us. Then we saw Nick again as were leaving the Tiffin Room. That would have been about eight thirty. He was heading out to play golf. Kate wasn't with him; he said she was going shopping.'

Victoria raised a curious eyebrow. 'Shopping?'

'Yes, Nick said he didn't want to go with her; that's why he booked himself a golf game.' Peyton paused and looked more closely at Victoria. 'Why?'

Victoria gave her head a small shake. 'Oh, it's nothing. I just saw Kate up at the pool, earlier. She said she didn't have the energy to go into town for shopping.'

'I guess she must have changed her mind. It is pretty hot.'

'Yes, I suppose she must have.'

The two friends lapsed into silence.

Victoria stood up and ambled over to the French doors. Her gaze wandered down into the Palm Courtyard. Not a soul stirred, aside from a few pigeons lazily pecking the grass in the tall shadows of the palm trees. She leaned against the open doorway. The heat was building and there wasn't a breath of wind to drive it away. In the stillness, Victoria could just make out the chinking of china drifting up from the La Dame de Pic below.

She looked out across the courtyard to the frangipani trees on the other side, bursting with delicate white flowers. She closed her eyes and inhaled their rich, sweet scent. Then she let out an involuntary sigh and her gaze shifted to the dark clouds drifting closer to the city.

She thought back to Kate de Brouwer sitting on the terrace beside the pool. Why had she told two different stories about going shopping? Had she changed her mind? Or had she never intended to go and had lied to her husband? But why would she lie about wanting to spend the morning by the pool? Maybe he had misunderstood her plans. Perhaps, he was so keen to get out on the golf course, he didn't pay any attention to what his wife planned to do.

Victoria cast a final glance at the darkening sky and then abruptly turned her back on the courtyard. Whatever the situation, it was time to get some answers.

Twenty-Two

Peyton stopped in front of the high, white, wooden door of John and Beverley's suite. She turned to Victoria. 'Are you sure you don't want me to come with you to talk to Kate?'

'No, you stay here. It's important that you go through James' phone. There could be something on there that'll give us a lead. And I want you to spend some time with Beverley. If there is something going on at the office, she'll be more open about it if it's just the two of you.'

'You don't think this has got anything to do with James' work?'

'I have no idea what's behind it. Which is why I want to consider every possibility. This could be from a financial deal that went wrong. People can be very bitter if they lose money. James' uncle was certainly angry, last night, about a payment he thought he was due.'

Peyton stared at Victoria. 'You don't think George is involved?'

'I'm not ruling anyone out, at the moment. Not until we get some more information. That's why I need you to help me.'

Peyton took a deep breath. 'I'll do my best. But I just can't believe someone we know could have planned this.' Tears welled up in Peyton's eyes. 'I mean, who would do this? It's so cruel.' Her voice choked as she tried to stifle a sob. She wiped her eyes with the back of her hand. 'I just want everything to go back to the way it was.'

Victoria took a clean tissue from her pocket. 'I know, Peyton. And I do understand what you're going through. When something awful like this happens, you just want the world to stop spinning and turn backwards.'

Peyton nodded. 'Yesterday, everything was so perfect. And today—' her voice sank. She pressed her lips together and sniffed back tears. 'I just want this nightmare to end.'

Victoria put a comforting arm around Peyton's shoulders. 'It'll be over, soon.'

'Do you think he'll be okay? I mean, what if the kidnapper—' Peyton's tears began to flow.

Victoria drew her closer and waited until her sobs had quietened. 'Don't torture yourself, Peyton. Let's focus on finding James. Try to put everything else out of your mind, until then.'

Peyton nodded, wiping her eyes and nose with the tissue. 'I will. It's just so hard not knowing.'

Victoria pushed a few loose strands of blonde hair back from Peyton's face. 'Try to stay strong. We'll know everything, soon enough.' She gave Peyton another minute to compose herself. 'Do you feel ready?'

Peyton brushed away the last of her tears. 'Yes. But can you come in for a minute? Just to get the conversation started?'

'Of course, I can. I'll stay for as long as you want me to.'

Victoria gave Peyton another moment to dab away the tear stains; then she reached out for the doorbell.

At almost the same instant, the door swung open and Beverley Marsters appeared on the threshold. She took one look at Peyton and enveloped her future daughter-in-law in her arms. 'Oh, Peyton. Have any more messages arrived?'

Peyton buried her face in the collar of Beverley's pale green silk blouse. She shook her head, replying in a barely audible whisper. 'No, there hasn't been anything else.'

For a minute, Beverley kept a fast hold of Peyton; then very slowly, she disengaged herself. As she stepped away and held Peyton at arm's length, her gaze fell on Victoria.

Victoria was struck by the extraordinary change in her. Without the softening effect of makeup, Beverley's face appeared lined and hard. Her eyes were dull and her cheeks, sunken and colourless. There was no trace of vitality left in her; the strength and self-assurance Victoria had seen the previous evening had entirely vanished. She seemed weighed down by grief.

Beverley acknowledged Victoria's presence with a pained smile. 'Come in, both of you. Let's get off the landing.'

As Victoria passed into the foyer she stopped and took hold of Beverley's cold hands into her own. They shook a little in her grasp. 'I am so sorry to hear about what's happened, Beverley. I know how close you and James are. Please, if there is anything I can do . . .' She let her voice trail off.

Beverley gave Victoria's hands a small squeeze. 'Thank you Victoria, that's very kind of you. But I just don't know what we can do, until we know what the kidnapper wants. Given the threats they've made, Peyton thinks we shouldn't call the police just yet.'

Victoria nodded. 'Yes, Peyton mentioned that to me.'

The three women moved in silence into the parlour. Beverley withdrew to a two-seater sofa against the far wall, where she had obviously been sitting, before Victoria and Peyton arrived. Her phone, laptop and some papers were strewn around on the blue, velvet cushions. She busied herself gathering them up, while the two friends looked on. 'I'm in a bit of disarray, but please, come in and sit down while I get rid of all this.' She piled her litter on top of the laptop and took it all into the bedroom.

Peyton sat on one of the cleared cushions, curling her legs up in front of her. She pulled James' phone out of her jacket pocket and absently turned it over in her hands, while she waited for Beverley to return. Her fingers stopped fidgeting the instant Beverley reappeared in the doorway. 'Victoria thinks it might be a good idea if we go through James' phone. Just in case there's something in here that might give us a clue.'

Beverley came back into the room and sat down beside Peyton on the sofa, her tired gaze shifting from Peyton to Victoria. 'Yes, I suppose that is a good idea. Although, I don't know that we'll find very much. If James had received a threat or anything like that, he would have mentioned it.'

Victoria lowered herself into an armchair, facing Beverley. 'It might not necessarily be a threat. It could be a misunderstanding that got out of hand, or a business problem that escalated. From everything Peyton has said, it sounds like James might know the person who's behind it.'

Beverley stared at Victoria. 'Why do you say that?'

'Because the kidnapper knew you were all in Singapore and Peyton said only the wedding guests had been told that you would be coming here. They also sent the message to James' phone via Privatechat, which isn't a publicly available platform. And—' Victoria pointed to the small, round dining table by the entrance foyer. 'They knew that Peyton was going to be in this room at one o'clock, when they sent the delivery. There are three place settings.'

Beverley followed Victoria's gaze across to the table. The deep lines on her forehead creased into a bewildered frown. 'But it doesn't make any sense. Who could it be? James doesn't know anyone who would do something like this. And why—what intentions could they have?'

'Maybe there's a disgruntled client or something that you don't know about?'

'James wouldn't keep something like that from me. And I don't believe it's someone he knows. Everyone loves James.'

'Someone wrote to Peyton warning her not to come here and marry him,' Victoria said.

What little colour remained in Beverley's face drained in an instant. 'Who wrote to her?'

'We don't know; the letter wasn't signed.'

'What did it say?'

'It said James doesn't love her and she should take the warning before it's too late.'

Beverley stared at Victoria with every appearance of being dumbfounded. 'But he adores her. Why would anyone—'

At that instant, the front door flew open and John Marsters hurtled into the parlour, his white cotton shirt wet with perspiration. 'I've talked to concierge and the front desk; nobody has seen anything. But Nigel Delamore's just been on the phone. I don't know what we're going to do—' He came to an abrupt halt, almost tripping over the armchair Victoria was sitting in. He cast a startled glance at her. 'Oh, I'm sorry, please forgive me for barging in like this. I— I didn't realize there was anyone here.'

He ran his plump fingers around inside the collar of his white polo shirt, lifting it away from the hair on his neck. The ribbed fabric on the inside was faintly discoloured with yellow sweat. His gaze shifted uncertainly to Peyton and then to his wife.

Beverley stood up and made her way across the room towards him. 'What did they say down at Reception?'

'Oh, nothing really. They have no recollection of seeing James— neither first thing this morning nor around the time that Peyton saw him.'

Victoria turned to Peyton. 'What time was it, exactly, when you saw him?'

'It was just before eleven.'

'So he left the hotel at eleven and then you got the message from the kidnapper at one?'

Peyton nodded. 'Yes.'

'And no one saw him again after that?'

Peyton shook her head. 'I didn't. I went next-door, into the arcade to do some shopping and John and Beverley were still on Sentosa Island with Lou. We all got back here just before twelve.'

Victoria leaned back in her armchair. The kidnapper certainly operated with speed. And yet, they couldn't have predicted James would forget his papers and come back to the hotel for them. 'Who did James meet with, this morning?'

John rubbed his fingers over his unshaven jaw. 'His first meeting was with a local hedge fund company that we're looking at doing some business with. I don't know much about his second meeting. It was with a new client he was pursuing.'

Victoria nodded. It seemed unlikely that either of his meetings had anything to do with his disappearance. Neither of them would have known him well enough. In which case, the kidnapper either took an extraordinary chance when they happened upon him or they had been following him, waiting for their opportunity. Or more likely, they were close enough to James—or in contact with someone close enough to him—to know what meetings he had that morning. Whichever scenario it was, given the speed at which everything happened, there had to be more than one person involved—and there was every likelihood at least one of those people was a wedding guest. A stranger couldn't possibly have had all the necessary information required to pull off this kidnapping.

She made her way, mentally, around the dinner table from the previous evening, considering each guest in turn. Given the arguments that had taken place, nothing seemed beyond the realm of possibility. But which of them was capable of it? It was a daring plan. She was beginning to think about each of the differing personalities, when her attention was brought sharply back into the room by the sound of a single, loud chime ringing out from James' mobile phone.

Peyton froze. A mortal dread swept across her face and she stared at Victoria, as if paralyzed by fear. A second chime startled her out of her trance; she swung her legs off the sofa and grabbed the phone from the coffee table.

'Oh God.' Her hand flew up to her mouth. 'There's another message.'

Twenty-Three

Peyton sat in rigid silence on the edge of the sofa with her fingers gripped tightly around the phone's silver casing. Her breath came in shallow, rapid pants.

Victoria rushed over to her. 'What does it say?'

For a moment, Peyton stared blankly at the screen with a ghostlike stillness on her face. Then she handed the phone to Victoria. Her hands were trembling. 'You look at it, I can't.'

Victoria took the phone and read the message: 'If you want to see James alive again, transfer ten million US dollars to each of the following bank accounts. You have twenty-four hours.' Victoria checked the time; it was 2.26 p.m. She looked up. 'There are three Eastern European banks and three Central American ones, all under company names.' She looked again at the bank account details; then handed the phone back to Peyton. 'Whoever is behind this, either does a great deal of money-laundering or they've been planning James' kidnapping for some time.'

John lowered himself into an armchair. He looked at Beverley with an expression of blank astonishment. '60 million dollars!'

For a moment, nobody said anything. The silence was shattered by another loud chime from James' iPhone.

Peyton started and stared at the screen with a look of terror in her eyes. Letting out a gasp, she threw the phone down on to the table, as it if had suddenly caught fire. It hit the edge of the porcelain fruit bowl and fell with a noisy clatter on to the floorboards. Peyton's face had turned a ghastly shade of grey.

Victoria bent down and picked the phone up from the floor. She read the message still displayed on the screen.

'Remember, Peyton, we're watching you. We know John and Beverley are there. Beverley is wearing a green shirt—'

'Oh, dear God!' Beverley's hand reached up to the open neck of her blouse. Her eyes darted across to the windows.

'There's more,' Victoria said, 'So don't try anything stupid or your fiancé dies. You have twenty-four hours. And just in case you're missing him, he's sent you a message.'

Beverley started forward. 'There's a message from James?'

Peyton pushed herself upright with both hands pressing into the cushions on the sofa. She stared at Victoria, her face pale and immobile as a marble statue. 'What does he say?'

Victoria scrolled down to the audio recording. She pressed play and after a couple of moments, the awful stillness in the room was broken by the sound of James' muffled voice bursting from the handset. 'Peyton, please, just pay them what they want or they'll kill me—' After a brief moment of background static, the recording ended.

Peyton clamped both hands over her mouth. She slumped into the back of the sofa. 'He's alive! Oh thank God!' She began to cry in loud, gasping sobs.

Beverley went and sat beside her. She put both arms around Peyton and pulled her in close. For the first time, Victoria saw Beverley's composure give way. Tears welled up in her eyes. 'We'll get him back safely, Peyton, don't worry.'

John sat stiffly in his chair, watching his wife cradle Peyton. 'What are we going to do? Are we going to pay the ransom?'

Beverley lifted her head; her cheeks were wet with tears. She let out an anguished sigh. 'We have to do something. If they're watching us, we can't get in touch with the police. We know he's safe now—I couldn't bear letting anything happen to him.' She turned to Peyton. 'Perhaps, we should pay the ransom.'

Peyton looked helplessly across to Victoria. 'I'm not sure—what do you think?'

Victoria walked over to the French doors and looked out into the courtyard. The Bar and Billiard Room was too low to have a sight line into the Marsters' suite and a thick canopy of travellers' palms and frangipani trees blocked any view from the hotel opposite. The balcony faced a row of suites overlooking the fountain, but the panes on the doors were small; there was no way anyone could see into the Marsters' suite from outside. She stepped away from the window and turned to face Beverley. 'Do you have 60 million dollars?'

Beverley cast a glance across at her husband. 'We could get it, I suppose—although I'm not sure if it would be possible to do so within twenty-four hours.'

'What about you, Peyton?' Victoria asked. 'Could you raise it?'

Peyton nodded. 'Yes, I got almost a hundred million in cash, as part of the company sale.'

'A hundred million?' Victoria frowned. 'When did you get the payment?'

'It came through last Thursday.'

'Last Thursday?' Victoria leaned against the arm of the sofa. A hundred million dollar payout last week and a 60-million-dollar ransom demand this week. The kidnapper either had a thorough knowledge of Peyton's business affairs or a very poor knowledge of the Marsters'. Either way, whoever it was, was very likely close enough to them to know what they did next. Which meant if Victoria was to have the full twenty-four hours to find James, the kidnapper needed to think they were going to get their money.

'It might be a good idea for you to talk to your bank,' Victoria said. 'Ask them how quickly large sums of money can be transferred, and if you need to be there in person to authorise it.'

Peyton's eyes shifted uncertainly from Victoria to Beverley. 'I could go over there now, but—'

'Now?' Victoria said. 'You mean your bank is here in Singapore?'

'Yes. It's all a bit complicated; everything's been set up in an offshore structure for tax reasons. But the bank account is here.'

Victoria slowly nodded. 'I think going to see your bank would be a good idea. We need to find out if the amount of money the kidnapper wants *can* be transferred within twenty-four hours to the bank accounts they've given you. Then we'll at least know if it's possible to pay the ransom by the deadline.'

'I think that's a very good suggestion,' Beverley said. 'We should check that from our end as well. I'll talk with our bankers in London, and Peyton, if you talk to your bank here, we'll know where we stand. Of course, John and I will cover any ransom payment. It's just a question of what we can arrange from here, in such a short span of time.'

'I really don't see how we can arrange anything within twenty-four hours,' John said, shortly. 'All our money is tied up—'

'Why don't we just wait and see.' There was an undertone of irritation in Beverley's voice. 'There's no point assuming anything until I've spoken to the bank.'

Victoria nodded. 'I think you're right, Beverley. Let's get all the information together and then we can make a plan. Would you like me to come to the bank with you, Peyton, while Beverley and John stay here and get in touch with London?'

Peyton hesitated uncertainly. 'Sure, if you think we're going to need to pay the ransom?'

Beverley laid her hand gently on top of Peyton's. 'I don't see what other options we have, Peyton. If we can't call the police, what can we do? How are we going to get James back?'

'We should at least talk to your bank,' Victoria said, firmly. 'Then we'll know where we stand. Once we know about the money, we can work out what to do next.'

Beverley gave Peyton's hand a comforting squeeze. 'I agree with Victoria. The money is the most important thing. I'm sure if the kidnapper knows we're taking them seriously and knows we're going to pay, they'll keep James safe.'

Peyton nodded at Victoria. 'Okay then, I guess we should go.'

Victoria smiled. She was grateful for Peyton's trust in her, despite her obvious confusion. She would explain everything to her, as soon as they were outside and on their own.

Twenty-Four

Victoria closed the door behind her and Peyton, pausing for a moment on the landing. It was mid-afternoon and there was no one about. Just the occasional murmuring voice drifted up through the atrium, humming through the hushed silence. The calm orderliness of the hotel was starkly at odds with the myriad thoughts that were running through Victoria's mind. She linked her arm through Peyton's and drew her quickly away, along the landing.

As soon as they were far enough from John and Beverley's suite to not be overheard, Peyton pulled on Victoria's arm to slow her down. She spoke in a low voice. 'I don't understand what we're doing. If we pay the ransom, how can we be sure we're going to get James back? Remember, you said if James knows the kidnapper, there's no reason for them to release him alive?'

'We're not going to pay the ransom,' Victoria said. 'But we need to buy ourselves time to find James. Which means the kidnapper needs to think you're going to pay it.'

Peyton cast a quick, nervous glance behind them. 'Do you think they really are watching us?'

'Possibly.' Victoria hastened Peyton on towards the Grand Staircase. On the top step, she paused. 'Which of the wedding guests knew you had a bank account in Singapore?'

'I don't know, I—I remember talking to Curtis about it . . . and Isabelle. I discussed it with John and Beverley, of course, given their financial background and—well, I guess Lou would have known because Nick got her to send through some paperwork. As for the others—I don't know; I—I didn't make a secret of it. It was such a pain in the neck setting everything up. I know I complained about it a lot. Plus I had to fly down here twice, because there was a mistake in the first lot of paperwork. The whole thing ended up being such a huge hassle, I wish I'd never got involved.' Peyton paused and frowned. 'You don't really think one of the wedding guests is involved, do you? I mean—they're all just ordinary people; they're not criminals.'

'Why did Nick send you some paperwork? Did he help you set up the bank account?'

'Yes. He's been James' attorney forever, so I trust him. He put me in touch with the bank and handled most of the admin. He suggested I set up a company in Belize and have my bank account here in Singapore. He does a lot of work with offshore companies, so he knows how to structure everything. He's done it for a lot of James' wealthy clients, that's why James recommended him to me.'

'So Nick would have known how much money you were getting and when you were getting it.'

'Yes, of course. But Victoria, he couldn't have had anything to do with it, he's a good friend.'

Victoria started down the staircase. 'So are all the wedding guests. What about Lou, does she work for Nick as well?'

'Not exactly—she's a sort of office manager-cum-secretary for James, John and Beverley, but because Nick does so much work with them, she often helps him out, as well. She basically looks after everyone. But Lou wouldn't be involved; she's known Beverley since they were kids. They went to school together. And she's worked for Beverley for forty years now.'

'Is it just the five of them in the business?'

'Yes, although Nick isn't part of the company. He just spends a lot of time working out of their offices. I think they're his biggest client now.'

'What does James' company do exactly?'

'They're a financial investment firm; that's about all I know. But they seem to be doing pretty well; they've got a lot of big clients. And Beverley works hard; she's always up late at night. She's got a big deal going through at the moment with some company in the US. Which is why they're all so stressed out.'

'What about Nick, who does he work for?'

'He works for himself. He set up his own legal practice around the time James met him. James used to work with Nick's wife, Kate—that's how they got to know each other. And when Nick went out on his own, James was keen to support him.'

'How long ago was that?'

'About five years, I think.'

'And what's Kate like? I've only spoken with her briefly.'

'She's lovely. She runs a big hedge fund company in London. She's quite successful from what James says. Although she hasn't been herself lately—I think she and Nick might be having some problems.'

'What sort of problems?'

'I don't know, they just seem to have been arguing a lot more lately. Kate is quite insecure; she's always worried about her weight or jealous when Nick talks to other women. Which is crazy because she's gorgeous. And Nick's hardly the sort to have an affair.'

'What about financial problems?'

'I don't think they'd have any; they both earn good money. And they've just bought a new house in Hampstead. That's near where you live, isn't it?'

'Yes, it's not too far away. It also happens to be one of the most expensive areas in London.'

The two friends walked on down the staircase in silence. Victoria was mulling over what she needed to do next. She had to talk to Mario about viewing the hotel's CCTV footage. That would clear up the issue of where Kate spent the morning and she could see if anyone followed James when he left the hotel. But as she only had twenty-four hours, she also needed to check the municipality cameras. That would be the fastest way of finding James. But she couldn't do that without involving the police. However . . . the Prime Minister did owe her a favour after the Chinese debacle, last year. She would give him a call. He could get things done *and* keep everything discreet.

She and Peyton reached the bottom of the staircase. They stepped from the runner of thick charcoal-grey carpet, onto the cool, white marbled floor of the lobby. Victoria was still thinking of her last visit to Raffles and how lucky she had been to resolve everything so neatly, when she felt the pressure of Peyton's hand on her arm.

'That's Nick and Kate sitting over there,' Peyton whispered.

Victoria followed her gaze across the lobby to where Nick and Kate de Brouwer were seated, having afternoon tea. Kate was wearing a long-sleeved, tight-fitting t-shirt in vibrant coral with a plunging neckline that exaggerated her full and sensuous figure. Nick sat hunched over the table opposite her. Victoria smiled. He looked exactly like the City lawyer that he was, with his shaved head, designer jeans and black sports jacket. Sitting on a silver stand beside them, a bottle of Billecart Salmon was chilling in a champagne bucket.

Nick seemed to sense he was being watched and looked up.

'Should we go over?' Peyton asked.

Victoria hesitated. 'It might be better if I go over alone. I think I'll get more out of them without you there.'

'But what about the bank?'

'How do you feel about going by yourself?'

Peyton's eyes widened. 'What if the kidnapper follows me?'

'They won't do anything to you,' Victoria said. 'They want your money. But if you don't feel comfortable, then you should go with someone. What about Eleanor and Bill, where are they?'

'They went down to Orchard Road; Granny wanted to buy some gifts for taking home with them. I could call them and pick them up on my way.'

Victoria smiled. 'That's a good idea; why don't you do that. Then I can go over and talk to Nick and Kate.'

Twenty-Five

Nick de Brouwer's cool, grey eyes followed Victoria as she crossed the lobby towards them.

Victoria smiled. 'May I join you?'

Her voice seemed to startle Nick out of his daze and he leapt to his feet. 'Oh, yes—yes, of course.' He pulled a chair across from an adjoining table and beckoned to the waitress to bring another champagne flute. 'It's nice to see you again.' He glanced across to the other side of the lobby. 'Is Peyton not going to join us?'

Victoria shook her head as she lowered herself into the burgundy armchair. 'I'm afraid something has happened. Peyton wanted me to come and tell you.'

Nick's body stiffened and his grip tightened around the back of the chair. 'What is it? Is there something wrong?'

Victoria nodded. 'Yes, I'm afraid there is. It's James, unfortunately. He didn't come back to the hotel, this afternoon and Peyton has received a message that suggests he's been kidnapped.'

Kate sat bolt upright. With both hands pressing down on the padded arms of her chair, she stared at Victoria. 'James? Kidnapped?'

Nick sank into his seat as if in a stupor. 'Kidnapped?'

'Yes. I'm sorry to be the one to break the news to you. But it does seem to be the case. James had two meetings in town this morning and he was due back here at midday; but at one o'clock, Peyton received a ransom demand.'

'But James only—' Kate stopped; her face turned deathly white. 'Oh my God.'

97

Nick leaned forward. The palms of his hands pressed on his knees. 'How—how did it happen?'

'I don't know,' Victoria said. 'All we know at this stage is that the kidnapper is asking for a 60-million-dollar ransom.'

'60 million!' Nick stared at Victoria with an expression of absolute astonishment. 'But James doesn't have that sort of money.'

'Peyton does,' Victoria said. 'As you know, she received a hundred million in cash last week.'

Nick slumped back in his chair and ran a hand over his shaved head. 'Jesus.'

A deep frown creased his forehead. For a moment, he sat silent and motionless, staring at the white border pattern on the small table in front of him. His eyes flitted rapidly from side to side, as if he were trying to make sense of what he had just been told. Slowly, his hand shifted to the stubble on his chin and his thumb and forefinger absently pulled at his lower lip.

Victoria took in his glittering Rolex watch, his Ermenegildo Zegna jacket, his Porsche sunglasses and the Billecart Salmon in his champagne flute, waiting to be drunk. There was no doubt Nick enjoyed the trappings of wealth. But did he enjoy them enough to risk his neck for a kidnapping?

Victoria rested her elbow on the arm of the chair and leaned towards him. 'Does the name Nigel Delamore mean anything to you?'

As soon as she uttered the words, she noticed a change in Nick's expression. The confusion disappeared and his eyes became more attentive, and perhaps, a little wary. 'Why do you ask that?'

'John Marsters received a call from him, earlier. He seemed quite disturbed by it.'

'Why, what did John say?'

'He didn't, but I wondered if it might have something to do with the kidnapping. Do you know who Nigel Delamore is?'

For a moment longer than necessary, Nick stared at Victoria. Then he spoke quickly, his words tumbling out on top of each other.

'I've heard John mention the name. I don't know anything about him, though. You'd really need to talk to John.' His words petered out and he gave an awkward cough. 'But what about Peyton, how is she? She must be terribly upset. James kidnapped—and on the eve of their wedding!'

'Yes, she's absolutely devastated. As I'm sure you can imagine, she's taking it very hard. But she has gone to the bank with her grandparents to talk to them about transferring the ransom money.'

Kate's eyes widened. 'Is she going to pay it?'

'She's checking if the transfers can be done in time. The kidnapper has only given her twenty-four hours. We have no idea if that sort of money can be transferred so quickly into offshore accounts.'

Kate gave a small shrug. 'Of course, it can be. That sort of money gets transferred around the world every day.'

'But how can they be sure that if they pay the money that James will be released? I mean—' There was a momentary flush on Nick's long, thin face. 'It doesn't always happen, does it? Sometimes, the victims aren't even alive when they're doing the negotiations.'

'I imagine that's something the family will need to discuss with the kidnapper,' Victoria said. 'But they did send a recorded message from James, about half an hour ago.'

Kate sat forward on to the edge of her chair. 'Half an hour ago? How was he—did he sound—I mean, had they—had they hurt him? Was he okay?'

'It's very hard to say; it was a short message. His voice sounded strained, but he was certainly able to talk. Of course, we don't know when the recording was done. It is possible something has happened to him since.'

Kate fell back in her chair and stared at the champagne flute sitting on the table in front of her. She sat quite still, with just her chest moving with each shallow intake of breath.

Victoria watched her and Nick carefully, as she asked her next question. 'Did either of you send a letter to Peyton last week?'

'A letter?' Kate said. 'What sort of letter?'

'Someone wrote to Peyton, warning her not to come here and marry James. The letter wasn't signed, but it was postmarked New York.'

Kate cast a quick glance across at her husband. 'Neither of us were in New York, last week. And why would we send it? It sounds like an ex-girlfriend or something.'

'Yes, except whoever wrote it knew about the wedding. And the only people James and Peyton told were those of us invited, and we were all sworn to secrecy.'

'I guess some people aren't very good at keeping secrets.' Kate turned to Nick. 'We should go up and see John and Beverley. There might be something they need you to do.'

'Oh, yes, I suppose we should.' Nick stood up and held out his hand to Victoria. 'Thank you for coming to tell us. And please, when you see Peyton, tell her we're thinking of her and are here, if there's anything we can do.' He placed his left hand on top of Victoria's. 'I suppose we'll see you both at dinner, won't we?'

'I think the dinner tonight will be cancelled, Nick.' Kate directed a small, curt nod at Victoria. 'But I'm sure we'll see you again before we leave.'

She brushed past Victoria as she made her way out from behind the small table; the rich, warm scent of her Chanel No. 5 filling the air between them.

Twenty-Six

Victoria watched Nick and Kate's retreating figures, until they disappeared behind the Grand Staircase towards the lifts. Then she brought her attention back into the lobby and to the waitress, who had arrived to clear away the champagne flutes, the half-empty cake stand and the untouched pots of tea. As the waitress picked up the small leather bill folder from Nick's side of the table, Victoria was surprised to see the corner of a fifty-dollar note protruding from the top. It was a large tip coming from an Englishman.

The waitress stood back, balancing the silver serving tray on her left hand. 'Is there anything I can get for you, Miss West?'

Victoria smiled. 'No, thank you, Charlene.'

Charlene inclined her head with a small nod and reached out for the silver champagne bucket. She lifted it from the stand and was turning to go, when Victoria stopped her. 'The couple who were just here; had they been here long before I arrived?'

'About an hour.' Charlene nodded at the bottle of Billecart Salmon in the champagne bucket. 'This was their second bottle.'

Victoria looked at the empty bottle. The de Brouwers were clearly not light drinkers—which might go some way in explaining the arguments Peyton said they had been having, recently. 'Did you notice if either of them used a mobile phone or laptop while they were here?'

'Yes, they were both on their phones.' Charlene paused and lowered her voice. 'At least, they were when they weren't arguing.'

Victoria raised her eyebrows. She knew the staff weren't encouraged to gossip, but she had come to know Charlene well, during her last visit. 'What were they arguing about?'

'Mr de Brouwer's work, from what I could understand. His wife wants him to find another job. But he said he knew what he was doing and she should stop nagging him about it.'

Victoria nodded. 'I see. Thank you, Charlene.'

She leaned back in her chair and thought over everything Nick and Kate had said. It was certainly possible there was something going on at the office. Nick seemed worried about the phone call from Nigel Delamore and Kate was keen to get him upstairs to talk to John and Beverley. Plus, Nick clearly had his own financial troubles.

She reached inside her tote bag and searched around for her phone. It was 3.11 p.m. They still had over twenty-three hours until the kidnapper's deadline; it was enough time to get James' company and Nick checked out. So long as she could get hold of the fabulous Bee. Bee was a magician when it came to getting information quickly. Although how she managed it, Victoria had no idea, even after ten years of working with her. But that's what made them such a great team. They could get on with an assignment without meddling in each other's business.

She opened the world clock on her phone. It was nine in the morning in Greece. A bit early for Bee, but she had no time to waste.

She scrolled through her contacts, imagining Bee asleep in some gorgeous hotel, overlooking the Mediterranean. Victoria began to wish she had taken Bee up on her offer and gone with her. The idea of lazing in the hot sun in southern Greece, eating grilled fish with fried haloumi and a fresh tomato salad at some charming little seaside taverna, was a lot more appealing than being stuck in Singapore at a wedding that wasn't going to happen, with a kidnapped groom and a distraught bride, who wanted her to find him.

It took Victoria a few attempts to get through to Bee's mobile; even then, when she finally got a connection, it only spluttered intermittently. Bee was obviously off the beaten track. She made one more attempt. The line clicked through, then died out briefly, before crackling back to life again and finally, going completely silent. Victoria was about to hang up when another ring spluttered lamely down the line, followed by a click and a loud whistle, then Bee's voice shouting over the appalling, high-pitched static, 'Victoria!'

Victoria held the phone away from her ear. 'Bee, where are you? You sound like you're in an Arctic blizzard.'

'I'm in Greece, on the back of a motorbike,' Bee shouted back. 'Hold on, I'll get Nikos to pull over.'

Victoria smiled as a loud exchange of Greek erupted from the phone; Bee had an irrepressible appetite for young Mediterranean men.

After a few minutes, the sound of rushing wind slowly abated and she began to be able to make out the sound of a motorbike, rumbling to a stop. The engine switched off and for a moment, there was dead silence before she heard Bee's voice again. 'Sorry about that, I can hear you now. We're in the mountains in Mani, exploring some of the old watchtowers. What are you up to? I thought you were at the wedding in Singapore.'

'I am, I arrived yesterday.'

'And how is it? Are you bored yet?'

'I wish I was,' Victoria said. 'Unfortunately, the way things are going, it doesn't look like there'll be any chance of that.'

'Why, are they having a few dramas? It always happens at weddings; I don't know why people bother with them.'

Victoria laughed. 'This one is a little more dramatic than most. Someone has kidnapped the groom.'

'Kidnapped him? You're kidding me!'

'I wish I was.'

'Bloody hell!'

'And even worse, I've agreed to find him. Which means I'm going to need your help. If you think you can tear yourself away from Nikos.'

There was a loud burst of laughter from the other end of the line. 'I could do with an intellectual challenge. What do you need?'

'I need you to do some research on the groom's company. His name is James Winstanley and he's a partner in an investment company in

London, called Winstanley & Marsters. He owns it with his mother
and stepfather, John and Beverley Marsters. I'll put all this in an email
to you, but there could be something going on there, that might be a
link to the kidnapping. Could you check it out for me? Could you also
see if you can get anything on a Nigel Delamore? He made a phone call
to John Marsters, this afternoon. I'll get John's mobile number and put
that in the email as well.'

'Sure, that all seems straightforward. Anything else?'

'Yes. I'll send you details of the bank accounts the kidnapper wants
the money deposited into. Can you see if you can find out who's
behind them? Could you also do a bit of digging on a Nick and Kate de
Brouwer? Nick is Peyton's lawyer. He also works with James. I get the
feeling he and his wife know something about the company they're not
letting on. I'll put whatever information I've got on them in the email.'

'Sounds good; is that it?'

'Yes, it is for now. I'll let you know if I think of anything else.'

Twenty-Seven

Victoria ended the phone call and leaned back in her armchair to gather her thoughts. While Bee got on with investigating James' company, she needed to get on with the more urgent task of finding his current whereabouts. To do that, she needed to go through the hotel's CCTV footage and get the police to check the municipality cameras. As long as she didn't tell anyone she was getting the police involved, there was no way the kidnapper would find out. She wouldn't even tell Peyton. Which meant her first job was to call the Prime Minister. Having his authority was the only way she would be able to keep everything discreet.

As she thought over her best strategy for the phone call, her gaze strayed across to the high, arched bookcase inside the Writers Bar. Ornate bottles of the world's most expensive whiskeys gleamed on the mahogany shelves. Delicate, brass reading lamps cast a soft light over the rows of books by Somerset Maugham, Rudyard Kipling and a host of other literary greats that had passed over the hallowed threshold. Her gaze drifted down to the old Imperial typewriter and antique writing desk. Raffles must have been quite the place, back in its heyday, when these renowned writers frequented the bar. How right Maugham had been, when he wrote, 'Raffles stands for all the fables of the exotic East'. Victoria was thinking there was still something intangibly wonderful about the place, when her attention was aroused by a shrill, officious voice in the lobby behind her.

'Nick said she was sitting in the lobby, George, not in the restaurant. I don't know why you don't listen to people. What would she be doing sitting in the restaurant at this time of day? Look, that's her over there.'

Victoria turned to see the sturdy figure of Patricia Helstone marching across the lobby towards her, with her head bent forward like a charging bull's and a dogged frown imprinted on her forehead. She was wearing a knee-length dress in mauve silk, with a matching short-sleeved cardigan that fitted snugly over her upper arms and shoulders, but fell in long, voluminous folds over her protruding bust. In her left hand, she carried a Raffles Boutique shopping bag, which she swung determinedly at her side, as if she were about to launch a ten-pin bowling ball. Victoria smiled to herself. She could see why Peyton had felt obliged to invite James' aunt to the wedding. She wasn't a woman to take a rebuff in good grace.

Patricia's husband followed meekly in her wake. His face wore the same placid expression Victoria had noticed during drinks, the previous evening, with a half-smile playing on his lips. His expression gave little away. A symptom, Victoria suspected, of being married to Patricia. He had no doubt become accustomed to keeping his thoughts to himself—apart from when he'd had a few drinks!

Victoria thought back to his outburst during dinner. She couldn't blame him for it—being married into such a family would test anyone's patience. The only surprise was that he didn't explode more often.

She liked George. They had only spoken briefly at dinner, but he seemed to be a very thoughtful, well-read man with a great sense of humour. A bit old-fashioned perhaps, Victoria thought, as she took in the socks and sandals poking out from beneath his grey slacks, but that was part of his charm. He didn't care what anyone thought about him, so long as he was comfortable.

Patricia stalked past the entrance to the Writers Bar and bore down on Victoria with an accusatory glare. 'We've just bumped into Nick. Is this true what he's saying about James? About there having been a kidnapping?'

Victoria rose from her seat. 'Yes, I'm afraid it is.'

Patricia plumped herself down heavily on to the seat opposite Victoria. 'I don't understand why John hasn't come and said something to us.'

George stepped forward, extending his hand towards Victoria with an apologetic smile. 'It's a pleasure to see you again.' He glanced down at his wife. 'I'm afraid the news has come as a bit of a shock.'

Victoria smiled, returning his handshake. She wondered how often George had to step in to make up for his wife's lack of manners. 'Of course, I completely understand. It's come as a shock to all of us.'

Patricia leaned forward, her forearms pressing firmly down on the slender curved arms of her chair. 'Fancy John not saying anything to us! When did this happen?'

Victoria resumed her seat. 'I don't know, exactly. Peyton saw James as he was leaving the hotel for a meeting at about eleven, so I imagine it happened shortly after that.'

'But we saw John and Beverley just before lunch! They didn't mention anything.'

'They only received the ransom demand about an hour ago.'

'An hour ago?' Patricia's voice rose in pitch. 'But John knew we were here in the hotel! Why couldn't he have come and found us?'

George lowered himself into the vacant chair beside Victoria. 'You said there's been a ransom demand?'

'Yes, the kidnapper is asking for 60 million dollars.'

'60 million dollars!' Patricia repeated the words as if her ears had deceived her. 'Who on earth can afford to pay that?'

George turned slowly to look at his wife. 'Your brother is getting four hundred and fifty million from his Bankcorp deal, isn't he?' Then he added, almost to himself, 'If it ever turns up.'

Patricia stopped in her tracks and stared at George. 'That is hardly something we should be discussing in front of Victoria. The details are confidential; John has been through all of that with you. And as Beverley and James explained, last night, it's very complex. Which is why it's taking time.'

'It's only complex because your brother is dealing with it. Financial investments are usually quite straightforward.'

'Oh for goodness' sake, George, let's not go through all of that again. We've got far more important things to think about now, given this dreadful business with James.' Patricia folded her arms across her broad bosom and fixed her eyes on Victoria. 'Do you know, I said to James it wasn't a good idea coming to Singapore for the wedding? It was ridiculous expecting everyone to travel all this way. But he gets these silly ideas in his head and you can't shift them. And now, look what's happened. I don't know why he wanted to come here. This sort of thing happens in these types of places, all the time.'

George gave his head a small shake. 'Not in Singapore, Patricia. This country has one of the lowest crime rates in the world.'

Patricia showed no sign of having heard her husband. Her attention was fixed on something behind him in the lobby. 'George, isn't that Tim and Zara over there? They must have come back from their shopping. We should call them over. They've been out, they won't have heard what's happened.'

Patricia waved furiously at the young couple sauntering through the lobby, towards the staircase. Much to Victoria's amusement, they did their best to ignore her.

'George, you'll have to go over and get them, they aren't looking at me.'

Obediently, George rose from his chair and returned with the young couple. Zara's pale face lost every vestige of colour as he told them the news.

'Isn't it dreadful?' Patricia said, before either of them could utter a word. 'Fancy someone doing this to James!'

'But how?' Zara asked, her face still white as a sheet. 'What happened? How do you know he's been kidnapped?'

'None of us know what happened!' Patricia said. 'James went off to a meeting and the next thing, there's a ransom demand from the kidnapper.'

'But when did it happen?' Tim said, frowning at Victoria. 'We just saw James, this morning.'

'We don't know when it happened, exactly,' Victoria said. 'James had a meeting at eleven o'clock; we're assuming he was kidnapped on his way to it.'

Zara stared at Victoria; her huge, round eyes didn't blink. 'At eleven o'clock?'

'Yes, that's right. And then, Peyton received a message from the kidnapper at one o'clock, followed by a ransom demand, just before three.'

Tim's eyes gaped. 'A ransom demand? What did it say? What does the kidnapper want?'

'They're asking for money,' Victoria said.

'60 million dollars!' Patricia added. 'Can you believe it? They must think we're made of money!'

'60 million?' Tim stared at Patricia in blind amazement.

'Yes, isn't it ridiculous!' Patricia let out a heavy sigh and shook her head. 'I don't know what possessed James to want to come here. I said to him, didn't I, George, that we should have had the wedding in England? It would have been lovely and they could have invited so many more people. But he got some silly idea about keeping it all a secret and coming down here, instead. Well, I was never comfortable with it. I mean, it's not like home; anything can happen in these foreign countries. There was that diplomat, just last week, that got kidnapped. They found his body, a few days later.'

A small cry escaped from Zara and she quickly clamped both hands over her mouth. 'Do you think something like that could have happened to James?'

'I'm sure he'll be fine,' George said. 'The kidnapping Patricia is talking about was in the Philippines and not here in Singapore.'

Tears began to well up in Zara's eyes. 'But what if something has already happened to him?'

'Oh for God's sake, Zara,' Tim said, sharply. 'Stop being so melodramatic.'

Zara's face flushed deeply. 'I'm not being melodramatic. Your brother's been kidnapped; I'm concerned about him, that's all. Clearly, a lot more than you are.'

'Of course I'm concerned, but we're not going to find him by being melodramatic. We need to be practical.'

'Well, what's being done?' Zara turned back to Patricia. 'Has someone called the police?'

'I have no idea,' Patricia said, in a piqued tone. 'John and Beverley haven't bothered to come and tell us anything, so we're completely in the dark.'

'Well, shouldn't we go and find them, then?' Zara responded. 'Does anyone know where they are?'

Victoria nodded her head. 'I think they're still up in their suite. They were going to call their bank about the ransom money.'

Zara's eyes widened. 'Are they going to pay it?'

'I imagine they'll have to,' Victoria said. 'The kidnapper has threatened to kill James, if they call the police.'

Zara took a sharp intake of breath. 'Oh my God! They've threatened to kill him?'

Tim glared at her. 'Zara!'

A flash of anger blazed in Zara's eyes. 'Doesn't it worry you that your brother has been kidnapped; that he's being held for ransom by— by God knows who? He could be dead, for all you'd care.'

'He's not dead! If the kidnapper wants money, they're not going to kill him. So stop being such a drama queen.'

'I'm not being a drama queen; I'm concerned about your brother. Not that you would know what that's like. All you have ever done is mock him and his success—as if you were so much better than he is. Has it ever occurred to you why people like James more than you? Well, let me tell you. It's because he actually cares about others. He's considerate and thoughtful—not selfish, like you. All you ever do is talk about yourself and your stupid beliefs, as if other people's opinions don't matter.' Zara hoisted her handbag angrily over one shoulder and turned away. 'I'm going upstairs to find your parents.'

Tim watched her for a moment with an expression of blank surprise plastered on his face. Then, shaking his head, as if not understanding what he had done wrong, he thrust his hands into the pockets of his shorts and strode after her.

Twenty-Eight

Victoria paused beside the large floral display in the middle of the lobby and watched as Patricia followed Tim, pushing past an elderly couple lingering in the small, elegant lounge behind the Grand Staircase. She was still talking at George and Victoria wondered how such an intelligent man managed to put up with a wife like Patricia. Perhaps, over the years, he had become immune to her high-pitched voice and constant chattering. It was hard to imagine, though—she had given Victoria a headache and she had only been with her for ten minutes, not forty years.

She placed her tote bag down on to the glass top of the table beside her. She couldn't help but feel jarred by Patricia's truculent manner. Everything about her was at such odds with the calm elegance of the hotel. Victoria drew in a breath and to clear her mind, she took a moment to enjoy the simple beauty of the antique table her bag was resting on. Chunky Chinese carvings framed the top of the wooden legs, which sat on the thick pile of a carpet, woven with bold patterns of cream and gold palm fronds. Atop the table was a huge round bowl of bright, tropical flowers, standing almost as tall as Victoria, in a large blue and white Ming vase. The imposing display was magnificent and emitted the most wonderful fragrance.

Victoria took a small bottle of Raffles Hotel water from her bag. The diamond pattern in the thin plastic crinkled between her fingers as she threw her head back and took a long draught from it. She let the cool water rest in her dry mouth as she looked up at the majestic, sculptured columns rising through the towering, white atrium above her and the exquisite, crystal chandelier, hanging like a spider at the end of a long, delicate, silver thread.

She drained the last drop of water and placed the empty bottle back in her bag. Then for a moment, she just stood motionless, with her hand resting on her bag, letting the peacefulness of the hotel wash over her. She looked across the lobby towards the French doors. Afternoon tea was still in full-swing. Waiters glided effortlessly amongst the tables holding aloft three-tiered, silver cake stands, laden with delicate sweets, scones and finger sandwiches. Almost every seat was taken and the quiet hum of happy chatter drifted out across the lobby, towards her. The cheerful buzz momentarily soothed her troubled mind.

She pushed aside the inevitable conclusions from Zara's outburst and was about to step across the lobby to find Mario, when Peyton's grandmother walked in through the main doors. Eleanor's petite figure was immaculate in a pair of simple, black trousers with a plain, white, cotton shirt and a single string of pearls around her neck. Her makeup was flawless and in each ear, she wore a large pearl earring. Not a strand of her short blonde hair was out of place. Victoria thought how amazing she looked for eighty-nine; even the pearl handle of her walking stick matched her outfit. But as she approached, Victoria could see her usually lively, smiling face was clouded with anxiety.

Eleanor rushed over and placed her delicate hand into Victoria's. It trembled a little in Victoria's grasp. 'We have just seen Peyton. She has told us what's happened.'

'Is Bill not with you?' Victoria asked.

'No, he has gone to the bank with Peyton. I had an arrangement to meet Lou for coffee at four o'clock, so I thought I had better come back here. I was also hoping to have a word with you.' Eleanor linked her arm through Victoria's and the two women moved slowly towards the small guest lounge behind the Grand Staircase. 'Peyton tells me you think one of the wedding guests could be behind the kidnapping.'

'I think it's very likely one of them is involved.'

Eleanor nodded. 'I'm inclined to agree with you. From what Peyton has said, I can't see any other way the kidnapper possibly could know as much as they do.' She paused beside a curved, cream sofa. 'Do you mind if we sit for a minute? I'm eighty-nine now, Victoria, I can't stay on my feet for too long.' She lowered herself down with the help of her elegant, brass walking stick. 'So tell me what you think. Do you have any idea which guest could be involved?'

'I haven't spoken to everyone about the kidnapping as yet, so I can't discount anybody at this stage.'

Eleanor's face warmed into a smile. 'You play your cards close to your chest, Victoria, and I admire you for that. We live in a world plagued with too much sharing. So I won't ask you anything else, other than what you would like me to do to help. Perhaps, I can ask some questions you can't. People don't take much notice of little old ladies.'

Victoria smiled at the thought of anyone taking Eleanor for a 'little old lady'. Her mind was as sharp as a bacon slicer. But she did make a good point.

'I would like to know a bit more about this investment company James owns with John and Beverley. George certainly didn't seem happy with them, last night. There might be something there that will give us a lead. I'd also like to find out who Nigel Delamore is. John received a call from him, earlier, and he seemed quite flustered by it. The name also disturbed Nick, when I mentioned it to him.'

'Then let me see what I can find out.' Eleanor glanced at her watch. 'I'm having coffee with Lou in fifteen minutes. She's worked as Beverley's office manager for the past forty years. If anyone knows what is going on in that company, she does. She's like a sister to Beverley and she treats James like the son she never had.'

'What do you think of James? You didn't say much about him, last night.'

Eleanor gave a small shrug. 'We haven't spent a lot of time with James. But in some ways, I think he is a bit like Bill was, in his younger days: handsome, charming and frightfully ambitious. Do you know Bill knew his father? He consulted for him when they were setting up an office in New York. They got on together very well. Bill would have enjoyed meeting Roger again. But sadly, he and James have been estranged for some time.'

'What happened there? Peyton hasn't told me much.'

'I don't think James talks a lot about him; there's still a lot of bitterness on his side. When Beverley became pregnant, Roger left her; he didn't want anything to do with the child. Reading between the lines, I don't think Beverley was quite the right pedigree for the Winstanleys. They're a very old, wealthy English family who have been in the banking business since the eighteenth century.'

'What's Beverley's background?'

'She's from Hertfordshire, I believe. That's in the South of England, isn't it? She's got an elderly mother who still lives there—a retired schoolteacher. Her father was a university professor of history, I think. So a perfectly respectable family, but perhaps not high-class enough for the Winstanley's. Roger was also quite a bit older than Beverley.'

'So what did they do? Did they pay her off to keep her quiet?'

'Not a cent, apparently, and she didn't have the money to take them to court. She was only eighteen at the time; Roger was thirty. Her own family refused to help; they weren't happy about her being pregnant out of wedlock. So she put herself through night school and worked her way into the finance business. By all accounts, she's done very well out of it—she's even had a couple of books published on the subject. She's quite an extraordinary woman, building a business from nothing and raising a child on her own; which wouldn't have been easy, forty-six years ago.'

'What about John, when did he come on the scene?'

'Not until James was twenty-two. He's an odd chap and according to Bill, not very knowledgeable about the financial world. But I think that suits Beverley—she likes being in control.' Eleanor checked her watch. 'Well, my dear, I'd better not miss my appointment for coffee with Lou. We don't have any time to waste.' She pushed herself up off the sofa. Then paused, with both hands resting on the top of her walking stick. 'I wonder what Beverley's plans are for the dinner we were all to have together, this evening? I might have a word with her. I think it would be a good idea if it went ahead. It would give us the opportunity to see everyone together and possibly sniff out the guilty party.'

Victoria laughed. 'You sound like you're writing the dénouement to one of your novels.'

Eleanor gave her a mischievous smile. 'I have never found any harm in setting a cat amongst the pigeons. It is surprising what you can discover.'

Twenty-Nine

Victoria paused in front of Mario's office. His door stood a little ajar and slipped open even further, when she gave it a gentle tap.

Mario glanced up from his laptop, and in the next instant, was on the other side of the table, pulling a chair out for Victoria with a grand, chivalrous gesture. 'Please come and sit. How is your American friend, Miss Latchmore? I understand from my staff that she was a little upset at the pool, earlier. I trust she has no reason to complain about her stay at Raffles Hotel.'

Victoria smiled and lowered herself into the chair that he held out for her. 'No, there's absolutely nothing wrong with the hotel.'

Mario's features relaxed and he gave a heavy sigh of relief. 'Ah, that is good to hear. She is a very important guest to us. We enjoy having her here.' He sat on the edge of his desk and considered Victoria for a moment. 'But there is still, perhaps, something I can help with?'

Victoria nodded. 'Yes, there is something you could help me with. As you know, Peyton – Miss Latchmore – is due to get married here, tomorrow. Unfortunately, there is a bit of a problem.'

Mario frowned. 'I am sorry to hear that. Is there some way in which I can assist you?'

'Yes, there is. Which is why I came to see you. Peyton's fiancé, James Winstanley, left their suite at eleven o'clock, this morning. He hasn't been seen since. He appears to be missing—very likely kidnapped.'

Mario's eyes grew round as two large saucers, and before Victoria could say another word, he was on his feet and his office door was securely shut.

'Kidnapped?' he said. 'From here at Raffles Hotel?'

Victoria shifted around in her seat. 'I don't know where he was taken from. It's more likely it happened en route to a meeting he had this morning. But the kidnapper has made threats and the family don't want to get the police involved; so I've offered Peyton my help—although I would prefer that to stay between you and I.'

'Yes, yes, of course.' Mario frowned. 'But it is, perhaps, unwise for the police not to be involved. A situation like this could turn very dangerous.'

Victoria smiled. 'I will be getting the authorities involved, but not officially—at least not as far as the family is concerned. I don't want to run the risk of the kidnapper finding out. The fewer the people who know I'm talking to the police, the better.'

'Oh yes, of course. Needless to say, you can rely on my discretion. I have not forgotten the favour you did us, Miss West.' Mario strode across to the other side of the office with his head bowed in deep thought. 'It is most extraordinary—a kidnapping, here in Singapore and at Raffles Hotel. *È assurdo, come è possibile!*' He flung himself back down in his chair; then sat up almost immediately and leaned forward, his hands clasped together with his elbows resting on the desk. 'But please, tell me, what is it you need from me?'

'I need to check the security camera footage from this morning. James left the hotel around eleven. I need to know exactly what time he left and if he left alone. Also, the kidnapper's message was delivered on a room service trolley to the Marsters' suite at one o'clock this afternoon. I'd like to talk to the butler who delivered it and to the person who answered the phone call. I'd also like to see if there is any camera footage of the trolley, to see how the envelope got on there.'

Mario leapt to his feet, banging both hands down hard on the desk. 'Delivered on one of our room service trolleys? But this is intolerable! Let us go directly to the kitchen and speak with the staff. I regret that many of the cameras within the hotel are not currently working—they are being upgraded, as part of our ongoing restoration work. But my staff are most reliable and they will inform us exactly what happened.

Of course, the external cameras are in place and some within the hotel are working. I will go through those myself—that way I can be assured nothing is missed.'

Victoria smiled at Mario's unblushing confidence in himself. But she knew from experience that his immodesty wasn't misplaced—throughout the Chinese debacle, he had proven himself to be a valuable ally. She was quite sure she would be able to rely on him again.

Thirty

Mario pushed open the swing doors of the kitchen and the warm, homely smell of freshly baked scones engulfed Victoria. She hadn't eaten since dinner the previous evening and the delicious aroma made her feel ravenous.

Mario gently placed his hand behind her elbow and guided her, with an outstretched arm, towards a young butler waiting beside the stainless steel shelving. He was probably no more than about twenty, with a cheerful, round face and broad smile.

'Julien, this is Miss West,' Mario said. 'She has some questions to ask you about the room service delivery you made to Mr and Mrs Marsters in the Padang Suite, this afternoon. Please provide her all the assistance you can.' He turned to Victoria. 'I shall get started on the other tasks we discussed, we have no time to lose.'

With a polite bow, Mario removed himself from the kitchen. Julien turned to Victoria with a friendly, professional demeanour and an expression that suggested he was eager to help.

'I understand you made the room service delivery as well as took the call for it,' Victoria said.

'Yes, that's right, Miss West, I did.'

'Can you tell me who made the call and what time you received it?'

'I believe it was Mr Marsters. It was about midday and he called from outside; he said he'd forgotten to place the order before he left the hotel.'

'Did he give you a time when he wanted the order to be delivered?'

'Yes, he asked for it to be delivered at one o'clock, which I did.'

'Did you take note of the phone number he called you from?'

'No, the number was withheld. I did ask him for a contact, but he said I'd be able to reach him in his suite.'

'Do you remember what his voice sounded like? Did he have an accent?'

'I think he was English. Although, I don't remember there being anything especially distinctive about his accent; it wasn't very strong.'

'What about his age, do you have any idea how old the caller was?'

'It's very hard to say. If I had to guess, I'd say middle-aged.'

'When you made the delivery, I understand there was an envelope found on the trolley.'

'Yes, there was, which was very odd because I have no idea how it got there. I packed the trolley myself and I checked everything thoroughly before I left the kitchen, to make sure it was all in order. There was definitely no envelope on the trolley at that point. And I can't think how it got there between the kitchen and the Marsters' suite. If someone had put it there, I would have seen them.'

'Did you pass anyone on your way to their suite, or did you leave the trolley unattended, anywhere?'

'No, it was very quiet in the hotel and I went straight to their suite. When I got there, I left the trolley right beside me, next to the front door. But then, while I was talking to Mr Marsters, Mrs Marsters went out on to the landing and she saw it sitting on top of the trolley.'

'Was there anyone nearby, then? The Marsters' suite is very close to the staircase.'

Julien paused and thought for a moment. 'There was one gentleman on the staircase; he was looking for the gym. I did stop and show him the way. But the trolley was behind me, the whole time so there is no way he could have put anything on it. And I only spoke with him very briefly.'

'Do you remember what the man looked like?'

'Yes, he was medium height and slim with blond hair. He looked quite fit, a bit like a surfer. He had an American accent and I'd say he was in his mid-thirties. I didn't get his name though, I'm sorry.'

Victoria smiled. 'That's all right, Julien, it's not important.'

She knew exactly who the man was. It could only be Curtis Butland—there was very little chance of two hotel guests fitting the description of Peyton's business partner. It was time she went and had a word with him.

Thirty-One

Victoria was deep in thought about Curtis as she stepped from the austerity of the service elevator into the simple elegance of the second floor landing. She turned immediately towards the atrium and walked quickly along the wooden landing that led to the Grand Staircase.

She found it hard to believe that Curtis was involved in the kidnapping. He had always seemed to her to be someone at peace with himself and the world. And money had never been a motivator for him. But then again, it was as clear to her as it was to everyone else, that his feelings for Peyton were not purely platonic. And sometimes, love did drive people to do odd things.

She was thinking of Curtis and his feelings towards Peyton, when a woman, walking along the landing in front of her, caught her attention. She was wearing an exquisite grey pinstripe trouser suit with a matching hat that towered above her head like the turban of an Ottoman ruler. Beneath it, the woman's long, platinum blonde hair fell in waves over her shoulders. Her lips were coloured with a shock of bright red lipstick. Victoria smiled at the sight of Peyton's godmother. At seventy-one years old, Isabelle Sauveterre still looked as fabulous as ever. There was something about French women—they managed to age with style. Victoria was pleased Isabelle had never had any work done. She had such a characterful face; it would be a shame to take any of that away.

Isabelle embraced Victoria warmly; then held her at arm's length and looked her over from head to foot. 'I should have you on the catwalk; you would be a sensation.'

Victoria laughed. 'I think I'm a bit old to be one of your models, Isabelle.'

'Nonsense! Women become more attractive as they get older. And you have something else as well—you have style.' Isabelle took Victoria by the arm. 'Come, let us go to my room, we can talk there. I still have work to finish on Peyton's wedding dress.'

Victoria fell into step beside her. 'I'm not sure there's going to be a wedding, Isabelle.'

Isabelle stopped abruptly, a few paces from the door of her suite. She turned to look at Victoria. 'Has Peyton seen sense, at last, and called it off?'

'Not exactly. It's a bit more serious than that, I'm afraid. James has been kidnapped.'

Isabelle drew back a step. 'Kidnapped? Well that *is* something I didn't expect.'

Victoria frowned. 'But you expected something?'

'I expected Peyton to see sense.'

Isabelle opened the door to her suite. She placed her handbag down on the coffee table and slowly unbuttoned her grey jacket. She laid it over the back of the sofa, then took up a box of Gauloises Blondes from the coffee table and placed a cigarette between her lips. Stepping out onto the balcony, she drew in a deep lungful of smoke and let it pour slowly out of her mouth. With a steady hand, she tossed the gold lighter down onto a table and stood – framed between two large, white, arched columns – looking back at Victoria. 'So, who has kidnapped him?'

Victoria shrugged. 'Your guess is as good as mine.'

'Has Peyton called the police?'

'No, the kidnapper has threatened to kill James if anyone does that.'

Isabelle leaned against the thick, white, concrete balustrade that fringed the balcony and took another long draw on her cigarette. 'Then the best thing she can do is leave him where he is.'

Victoria was startled by the sudden savagery in Isabelle's tone. 'What do you mean by that?'

'I mean she is better off without him.'

'You would rather he were dead than with Peyton?'

'I would rather he had never met Peyton.'

'You don't like him?'

'No, he is conceited and arrogant, with absolutely no reason to be either. He is handsome and charming, of course, but they are two of the worst reasons to marry a man.'

'But hardly sufficient reasons to condemn him to death.'

'If Peyton goes ahead with this marriage, James will destroy her happiness. You do not know him like I do, Victoria.'

Victoria stepped out onto the balcony and stood, for a moment, behind one of the rattan armchairs. 'Does Peyton know how you feel?'

'Of course, but she is not interested in my opinion. When people are in love, they will not listen to anything they do not want to hear.' Isabelle crossed over to the small, wooden table in front of Victoria and flicked a long stem of ash into a glass ashtray, sitting in one corner. 'So what does the kidnapper want?'

'60 million dollars.'

Isabelle arched her thin, carefully drawn eyebrows. 'And I suppose Peyton will be foolish enough to give it to them. The Marsters don't have that sort of money and the Winstanleys would only pay to have James kept out of the way.'

'Surely, they don't dislike him that much. He is their own flesh and blood.'

Isabelle ground the stub of her cigarette into the ashtray and sat down. Her thin, delicate body looked almost childlike against the armchair's high, rattan backrest. But as she spoke, her dark eyes glittered with ferocious energy. 'Roger Winstanley has disowned his son for good reason. You have undoubtedly heard of him; he is well-known in England, where the family owns and runs a private bank. He and Beverley had an affair when she was young and she fell pregnant. Roger was married at the time, with two young children, and Beverley blackmailed him, threatening to expose Roger as James' father if he didn't pay her. Forty-six years ago, things weren't as they are now and the Winstanleys did not want Roger's reputation and marriage destroyed by an illegitimate child. So they paid what she asked and until recently, Beverley had kept her side of the bargain. But two years ago, James changed his name to Winstanley and started using it to attract investors. More recently, he has threatened to make a claim on the Winstanley inheritance. Naturally, their lawyers are fighting it and are trying to protect the family name. Any connection between their business and Beverley's, would prove disastrous.'

'Why is that?'

'Beverley has been declared bankrupt twice. She isn't someone the Winstanleys can afford to be associated with. Their reputation has been established since the eighteenth century. A lot of respected families and high net-worth individuals bank with them.'

Victoria sank slowly down onto the arm of the rattan chair opposite Isabelle. 'Do you think they could be behind the kidnapping?'

Isabelle took another cigarette from the packet. She shook her head, inhaling a thick lungful of Gauloises. 'I would be surprised if they were. They are ruthless people, but kidnapping isn't their style. If their lawyers can't stop Beverley and James, then they'll use their influence with the regulators to have them put out of business.'

'Can they do that?'

Isabelle shrugged. 'I would not put anything past them, when it comes to protecting their business and their reputation. Roger has warned James and Beverley, but they have chosen to ignore him.'

Victoria stood up and moved away from the cigarette smoke. 'How do you know all of this?'

Isabelle exhaled a long, slow coil of smoke and watched it drift out over the balcony until it disappeared into the thick, brooding air. All trace of the sun had disappeared; just a gloomy half-light engulfed the courtyard now, suffocating it in a haze of humidity.

Isabelle turned her head slowly to look at Victoria. 'I have a long history with the family,' she said. 'Roger and I are lovers.'

Thirty-Two

Victoria withdrew to the far side of the balcony and stood in silence, gazing out at the bloated underbellies of the clouds gathering over the city. She rubbed her temples. She could feel the pressure of her headache building. The oppressive heat and lack of food were beginning to take their toll. But there was no time to dwell on her own discomfort, so she pushed the pain away and turned round slowly to face Isabelle. 'Does Peyton know about you and Roger?'

'No and I do not want her to.' Isabelle stood up and moved across to the other side of the balcony. She stood there with her back to Victoria, looking out over the courtyard. 'Peyton is behaving like a schoolgirl. She is in love with the idea of being in love. And James is very good at saying all the right things to her. But in the end, he will break her heart. He is a cold and ruthless man. I have seen how he has behaved towards his father. Peyton does not know this side of him, but she will discover it if she marries him. Of that, we can be certain. And that is why I do not want her to marry him. It has got nothing to do with Roger, but Peyton will think it does, if she comes to know of my relationship with him.' Isabelle returned to her chair. 'If Peyton could only see sense, she would see this kidnapping as a warning. The kidnapper is doing her a favour.'

'Not if you don't think she should be marrying him. The thought of losing James has made her fall even deeper in love. She's prepared to do anything to get him back.'

'Then she is a fool.' Isabelle leaned her head against the backrest of her armchair. 'I don't know why she cannot see that she can do much better than James.'

Victoria smiled. 'You mean, by marrying Curtis?'

'Yes, why not? He is in love with her.'

'Yes, but she isn't in love with him. And it takes two to make a marriage.'

Isabelle nodded slowly. She held the smouldering cigarette between her two thin fingers and caressed the end of the stub with her thumb. Her gaze drifted out beyond the balcony and she answered in a voice so low and melancholy that Victoria struggled to hear it. 'Yes. You are right, it does.'

Isabelle remained motionless, her unseeing eyes staring out across the courtyard as the cigarette burned slowly. The orange glow almost reached her fingers.

A chime from the doorbell jolted her out of her reverie. Isabelle's statue-like figure came back to life in an instant and her face regained its animation. 'Ah, that would be Curtis. He has come to try on his suit.'

She extinguished her cigarette in the ashtray and walked quickly from the balcony, into the half-darkness of the still-curtained living room.

When Isabelle returned with Curtis, Victoria was pleased to see him back as his old self in a pair of shorts and a faded blue t-shirt, his blond hair uncombed and looking desperately in need of a cut. He seemed a lot more comfortable than he had, the previous evening, in a dinner suit—and younger. In the suit, he had looked every day of his thirty-four years, whereas in shorts and a t-shirt, he didn't look much more than about twenty-eight.

He smiled when he saw Victoria. 'Hey, how are you doing?'

Victoria flinched at the question. 'I wish I could say "well", but unfortunately, we've had some bad news this afternoon. I've just been telling Isabelle.'

The smile on Curtis' face vanished. 'What's happened? It's not Peyton, is it?'

'No, it is not Peyton.' Isabelle strode past him out onto the balcony. 'It is that fool she wishes to marry.'

Curtis frowned at Victoria. 'James?'

Victoria nodded. 'Yes; he was due back at the hotel around midday, but he never showed up. An hour later, his parents received a message telling them James had been kidnapped.'

Curtis' eyes widened. 'Kidnapped? You're kidding me!'

'I wish I was,' Victoria said. 'But the kidnapper sent a voice recording from James. It seems to be genuine.'

Curtis inhaled a sharp breath; then puffing out his lips, he slowly exhaled. 'Wow, that's pretty full-on.' He followed Isabelle out onto the balcony. 'How did it happen?'

Victoria shrugged. 'We have no idea. James left for a meeting at eleven o'clock this morning and didn't come back. At about two thirty, his parents received a ransom demand and have been given twenty-four hours to pay the money.' She glanced at the clock on Isabelle's writing desk. It was almost a quarter to five. 'That was over two hours ago, which means they now have less than twenty-two hours to pay it.'

'Are they going to?'

'It doesn't look as if the Marsters will be able to pay it in time. But Peyton can.'

'And will she?'

'Of course, she will.' Isabelle threw herself down on to the sofa. She reached out for the box of Gauloise Blondes on the side table. 'If she is foolish enough to marry him, she will be foolish enough to pay the ransom.'

Victoria smiled. She could see Curtis was surprised by Isabelle's callous outburst. 'As you can see, Curtis, Isabelle doesn't think much of James.' She fixed her gaze on Curtis and watched him carefully. 'What about you? What do you think of him?'

The muscles in Curtis' face tightened. He turned from Victoria and walked across to the sofa. 'Not that much, I guess; he seems like a bit of a jerk to me.'

'In what way?'

Curtis shrugged. 'I don't know. I guess it's just the way he fawns all over Peyton, when they're together. He treats her like a princess and she laps it up. But he can be a total bastard, as well. I've seen that side of him.'

'Have you seen anything that might make him a target for kidnapping?'

'Nothing specific, although he does like to throw his money around. I guess people like that can be a target if someone sees them doing it. They were in the casino at Sentosa, a couple of nights ago, in the high rollers' room; maybe someone saw them there and thought they'd take a chance.'

Victoria shook her head. 'I don't think this was a spontaneous kidnapping. From everything Peyton has told me, it sounds like it was well planned-out. Plus they're using Privatechat to send messages to James' phone.'

Curtis lifted his eyebrows. 'Privatechat?'

'Yes, but Peyton says there's no way of tracing where the messages came from.'

'There's not, really. Although, if we could hack into his account, we could build something in, which would tell us where future messages come from. Assuming they're being sent from a device with GPS capability.'

Victoria thought about the suggestion for a moment. 'It could be worth trying, if you think it's possible. Would you be able to do it, or would you need someone else in your company to get involved?'

'I could give it a shot. I was involved with the build. Although, we did make the system pretty secure.'

'And then what?' Isabelle asked. 'Peyton doesn't want to get the police involved because they have threatened to kill James. So what do *we* do with the information—go and track down the kidnapper ourselves?'

Victoria gave her a half-smile. 'Why not? Then you can thank them in person for having the wedding called off.'

Thirty-Three

Peyton's grandmother slowed her pace as she turned the corner into the short, tiled walkway leading out of Raffles Arcade. She paused and glanced down at her wristwatch—delighted at eighty-nine to still be able to read the small, diamond-encrusted numbers without glasses.

Eleanor smiled to herself. It was four o'clock; she was bang on time. Cautiously, she took a few steps forward and peered out at Bridge Road. The dark, menacing clouds cast a sombre shadow across the immaculately clean street.

Eleanor took in the scene for a moment. Not observing Lou anywhere, she slipped round the corner, winding her way quickly through a group of meandering tourists, until she reached the broad verandah sheltering the sidewalk, outside Zheng He's bakery. She slowed her pace and leaning heavily on her walking cane, weaved between the tables and chairs until she reached the café's main entrance. She stood for a moment, outside; then stepped forward and pushed open the front door.

Inside, the sweet smell of pastries filled the cool air. The glass cabinets looked delightful, brimming with row upon row of delicate fruit tarts, small, intricately decorated portions of tiramisu, chocolate banana cake cut into perfect squares and wrapped in fine wax paper, almond croissants and her favourite sweet pastries filled with lychees, strawberries, raspberries and apricots. Everything looked and smelled divine, especially the aromas coming from the warmer, which was overflowing with tuna puffs, quiches, bite-size meat savouries and small frankfurters wrapped in golden pastry. Beyond the warmer, glass cake-stands lined the countertops, piled high with brightly coloured sweets and baskets of freshly baked bread, still hot from the oven.

She turned her focus from the mouth-watering array of food to the large dining room, crammed full of customers sitting at small, round, French-style tables. Almost every wooden chair in the place was taken. In the far corner, beside the French windows, Eleanor spotted Lou, sitting erect with one side of her dark bob tucked neatly behind her ear. A tourist map of Singapore laid spread out on the table in front of her, and a collection of bags from Raffles Boutique sat in an orderly row at her feet. Eleanor smiled to herself—Lou was the epitome of an efficient secretary, even when she was on holiday.

She rushed over to her in a fluster. 'Lou, I am so sorry to be late.'

Lou looked up and smiled. 'Oh, please don't worry, Eleanor, come and sit down. I've been busy planning what places I want to visit, while I'm here. Although I must say, in this heat, I don't feel inclined to rush off anywhere today. I've never felt anything like it.' Bending forward, she squinted through the window. 'It looks like it might start to rain a bit later, as well.' She gave a small laugh. 'Sorry, you must excuse me. Talking about the weather is an English pastime.' Lou paused and fixed her attention on Eleanor's face. 'Is everything all right, you seem a little flushed?'

Eleanor hurriedly stowed her walking cane against the window and sat down, her forearms resting on the table. She bent her head towards Lou and spoke in a confidential tone that was barely louder than a whisper. 'Oh Lou, the most terrible thing has happened. I've just come from Peyton. She tells me James has been kidnapped.'

Lou drew back from Eleanor. Her fingers wrapped tightly around the edge of the table. 'Kidnapped?'

'Yes and poor Peyton is so upset. The kidnapper wants a ransom payment and they've only given them twenty-four hours to pay it. She and Bill have gone downtown to her bank.' Eleanor shook her head and sighed. 'I can't believe this has happened here in Singapore, it's normally so safe!'

Lou shrank into the back of her chair. 'God Almighty! How did it happen?'

'I really don't know; it still seems too incredible to be true. Peyton said he went off to a meeting this morning at eleven o'clock and never came back from it. At one o'clock, they received a message from the kidnapper.'

For a moment, Lou neither moved nor spoke, and Eleanor reached her hand across the table and placed it on top of hers. 'I am so sorry; I know how fond you are of James.'

Lou pulled her hand away and fastened her eyes on Eleanor's face. Her voice was hoarse. 'Who would do this?'

Eleanor shook her head. 'I can't even begin to imagine; it's just too awful to think about.' She paused as if trying to recollect something. 'Peyton did mention a name though. Now, what was it? Oh golly, I should have taken more notice. She wondered if he might have had something to do with it. It was someone involved with James' company. Perhaps, you might know him. Now let me think, was it Nigel? Nigel Delaney or Dalton or something like that.'

Lou's eyes became suddenly alert. 'Nigel Delamore?'

'Yes, that was it! Do you know him?'

Lou hesitated for a moment. 'No—no, I don't. I just remember he left a message last week.'

'A message? Do you know what it was about?'

Lou began to fold up the map that was lying on the table. Her hands shook a little as she fumbled over the folds. 'No, I don't know. The message was for Beverley to call him.'

Eleanor looked up at Lou with a puzzled frown. 'How odd. Because John received a call from him, this afternoon after the kidnapping, and he seemed quite disturbed by it. I wonder what it could have been about?'

Lou stuffed the half-folded map into her handbag. 'I really don't know. But I'm sure it would have been about work. I can't imagine it would have anything to do with James.'

Eleanor sighed. 'It's just so awful not knowing where he is and not being able to do anything to help. I do hope he is all right.'

Lou hurriedly gathered her bags together and stood up. 'I really should go and find John and Beverley, they must be in a terrible state.'

Eleanor rose from the table. 'I think I might come with you. I would like to let John and Beverley know that Bill and I are here, if they need anything. I can only imagine what Beverley must be going through, right now; she and James are so close.' Eleanor leaned against the table. Tears filled her soft, blue eyes. 'I remember so clearly how I felt when my daughter was in the hospital in Kenya, after her car accident. It was the uncertainty that was so awful and being so far away from her.' She laid her hand gently on Lou's arm. 'Thank goodness, we're all here together. When Peyton was at her mother's bedside, she didn't have anyone until Bill and I could get there. And then, she had to cope with losing both of her parents. It would have been unbearable for her if she had been here alone with James, when this happened. And I know Beverley must be awfully grateful that she isn't back in England. That would have been too much for her to bear, I am sure.'

Lou rested her shopping bags on top of the table. 'I am so sorry about your daughter, Eleanor. It must have been an extremely difficult time for you. I can't even begin to imagine the pain of losing a child. I don't know how you have coped.' She pulled the strap of her handbag up over her shoulder. 'Given everything you have been through, I'm sure Beverley will be very grateful for your support.'

Lou gathered her shopping bags into one hand and with a quick glance under the table to ensure she had left nothing behind, she moved across to help Eleanor. Eleanor slipped her hand through the crook of Lou's free arm and the incongruous pair turned their steps towards the front door.

Eleanor stayed closely at Lou's side as they threaded their way through the crowded tables. 'I do hope I might be of some small comfort to her. It would be a great satisfaction to me if I could be.'

The two women stopped at the front entrance. Eleanor disengaged her arm, and Lou stepped forward to open the door. With a gracious inclination of her head, Eleanor passed through the doorway, stepping out into the furnace of afternoon heat.

Lou closed the door softly behind them. She held her arm out and Eleanor linked arms with her at the crook of her elbow. With her weight resting heavily on Lou, the two women set off into the arcade's labyrinth of walkways.

As they passed through Raffles Courtyard, Lou attempted to increase her pace. She seemed anxious for them to move more quickly. But Eleanor maintained a firm grip on her arm and held her back. She wanted to get as much information out of Lou as possible, before they reached the hotel. 'It's dreadful to think James might have had an association with the kidnapper. If he can identify them, it puts him in terrible danger. But then, the finance industry can be so volatile, can't it? I know from Bill's time on Wall Street that if a client loses money, they can become quite desperate. It's hard to comprehend what some people might be driven to do.'

Lou turned on Eleanor, her voice sharp and suspicious, 'What makes you think this has anything to do with the business?'

'Oh, I am sorry, Lou; I didn't mean to suggest that it did. But I suppose, we should look at every possibility. George certainly seemed very upset, last night, about some money he thought he was due.'

Eleanor felt Lou's arm stiffen. 'George is a nuisance. John was generous enough to help him out and he has done nothing but complain, ever since. He's been making John's life hell, over the past few months. If he *has* got anything to do with this, I hope the full force of the law comes down on him.'

'Oh, I wasn't suggesting George was involved. I was just thinking that if there is a particular client who has a reason to be disgruntled—'

'There are no clients that have any reason to be disgruntled. George doesn't know what he's talking about.' Lou stopped and hoisted the strap of her handbag firmly over her shoulder. 'I really should get up to John and Beverley as soon as possible. Perhaps, I can mention your offer of help to them for you. If they need anything, I'm sure they'll come and find you.'

'Oh yes, of course my dear; I am so sorry, I'm holding you up. You go on ahead. You'll be quite anxious to know what's happening, I'm sure. I know how close you and Beverley are. I'll follow along at my own pace.' Eleanor patted the pearl handle of her walking cane.

'Getting old is not for the faint-hearted, I can tell you. But please do give Beverley my love and tell her I'll pop along and see her soon. Now you get going, I don't want to hold you up any longer.'

A thin smile of gratitude crept on to Lou's taut lips. 'Thank you, I will tell her. I'm sure she'll appreciate it. I am so sorry to rush off. But I know how upset Beverley will be right now. I feel terrible not being with her, already. Are you quite sure you will be okay to find your way back?'

'Yes, of course, my dear. I'll be quite all right. Now you run along.'

'Thank you, Eleanor, I'll see you again very soon.' Lou gave Eleanor's hand a brief, slightly awkward squeeze; then gathering her shopping bags into a firmer grip, she rushed off along the pathway.

Eleanor watched her until she disappeared through the filigree gates into the hotel. Then, with a satisfied tap of her walking cane on the terracotta tiles, she set off at a brisk pace after her.

Thirty-Four

Curtis and Victoria made their way along the landing, leading away from Isabelle's suite. When they reached the exit to the Palm Courtyard, Curtis took hold of the large brass handle on the swing door and pulled it back for Victoria to pass through. She gave a small shudder as she stepped from the chill of the air-conditioned hotel into the sultry heat outside.

She led Curtis away from the swing doors, down a flight of stairs and out on to the broad wooden landing that fringed the inner courtyard. Victoria paused briefly, glancing over the white, concrete balustrade and across the courtyard, at the incongruous, grey skyscrapers that lay beyond. The black clouds were closing in on the city, threatening an afternoon rainstorm.

They turned into an enclosed corridor—its walls lined with photos of celebrities who had stayed at the hotel. Diana Ross, the Duke and Duchess of Cambridge and Sir Peter Jackson smiled down on them, from behind their gilt-edged frames.

Curtis ran his fingers through his shaggy, blond hair. 'You know, I was thinking about the message you said Peyton got. If the cell phone was delivered to Beverley and John's suite at one o'clock, then I reckon I saw the guy taking it there, when I was on my way up to the gym.'

Victoria turned to look at him. 'Really?'

'Yeah, I was on the staircase when I stopped this dude with a trolley to ask him for directions. It would have been around one o'clock.'

'You didn't happen to notice if there was an envelope on the trolley, did you?'

Curtis shook his head. 'I wasn't taking that much notice of it.'

'Did you see anyone go near the trolley?'

'No. The only person I saw was that old guy with the bald head. What's his name? The one with the obnoxious wife? He's James' uncle I think.'

Victoria stared at Curtis. 'George Helstone?'

'Yeah that's it, George.'

'Where did you see him? Was he near the trolley?'

'No, he was on the staircase, heading downstairs.'

Victoria nodded slowly and walked on a little way in silence. Could George be involved in the kidnapping? It seemed improbable. But then, so did everything else.

Curtis thrust his hands into the pockets of his shorts. 'Were you serious about what you said before, to Isabelle, about finding the kidnapper?'

Victoria gave a small shrug. 'Why not? I feel like we ought to be doing something.' She cast a sideways glance at Curtis. 'Although, you might prefer not to be involved, given how you feel about James.'

There was a momentary flush on Curtis' tanned face. 'I don't dislike the guy enough to wish a kidnapping on him. Anyway, what else are we going to do? We can't exactly get on a plane and leave Peyton here on her own, can we?'

Victoria's lips curved into a faint smile. 'No, we definitely can't do that. She needs all the support we can give her, right now.' She continued on, along the corridor, a little further. 'Did you mean what you said earlier about hacking into James' account?'

Curtis shrugged. 'Sure, I can give it a try.'

'How easy would it be for someone else to hack into his account— someone who didn't know anything about the app?'

'Virtually impossible. The whole system's pretty secure.'

'What if they had James' laptop with the app on it?'

Curtis paused and considered the question. 'That would make it a bit easier. If you had the physical unit, you might be able to get into the app via the history and manipulate it. But you'd have to know what you were doing. And you still wouldn't be able to see where the messages were being sent from.'

'Who came up with the idea for Privatechat?' Victoria asked.

'Peyton and I came up with the concept together. Then I built the basic platform.'

'Is that not something Peyton does?'

'She can, but she's more interested in the marketing and management side of things.'

'She was the major shareholder, wasn't she?'

Curtis hesitated for a moment. He shifted his gaze away from Victoria. 'Yeah. She had seventy percent, I had thirty.'

Victoria glanced across at Curtis, intrigued by the change of tone in his voice. 'Did that annoy you, given the final sale price?'

Curtis shrugged. 'It's the way it goes. Peyton had more money to put in at the start, so she got the bigger slice.'

'But you both put in the same amount of work to build the company up?'

Curtis kicked a dead leaf along the landing's wooden floorboards. He thrust his hands deeper into his pockets and gave another shrug. 'That doesn't count for anything when you sell.'

'Did Peyton ever suggest splitting the payout with you?'

Curtis lifted his eyes and gave a short, harsh laugh. 'James would never have let her do that.'

'Why not?'

'Because he's greedy; he's in this for all he can get.'

'You mean, from the marriage?'

'Yeah. James likes money and Peyton's got plenty of it. It's a marriage made in heaven for him.'

Victoria frowned. 'I thought James was wealthy in his own right.'

'That's what he tells everybody. He keeps talking about this big deal he's working on in the US, worth 450 million. Says he's got politicians and celebrities involved. Yet, he lets Peyton pay for everything. It's a load of crap, if you ask me.'

'Surely, Peyton would see through it, if it was?'

Curtis shrugged his shoulders. 'You'd think so. But she's been so taken in by him, she can't see it. And there's no point trying to tell her.'

Victoria smiled. 'No, you're right there. Peyton has never liked being told she's wrong. She's very proud. Still, she and I go back a long way. I'd like to do what I can, to help.'

They reached the door of Curtis' suite and Victoria looked over the balcony down at The Lawn below. The small wrought iron cabana, where James and Peyton were to have taken their wedding vows on the following morning, was already in place, decorated with grape leaves, white orchids and small green apples hanging from thin wires. The neatly clipped grass and immaculately manicured gardens stood ready for the happy occasion. Even in the dull light of the impending rainstorm, the greenery was alive in its rich colour. Victoria could have imagined nowhere more romantic for them to get married.

But now, with less than twenty-four hours to go, a black cloud hung over the wedding.

Her gaze drifted along to the pagoda at the far end of the garden, its dark wooden pillars and slanted terracotta roof framed against a backdrop of towering coconut palms and lush Heliconia bushes, with their magnificent red flowers. Stacked under the shelter of the pagoda's sloping roof were fourteen white, iron filigree chairs. At ten o'clock, the following morning, Victoria should have been sitting on one of them, with her feet resting on a bed of white rose petals. But now the chairs stood stacked in a useless pile, waiting to be removed as soon as Mario gave the word. He had been polite enough not to mention the arrangements to the family. No doubt everything would be managed in his usual, diplomatic fashion. It probably wasn't the first wedding which had to be cancelled at the last minute.

Curtis took a door key from his pocket. 'Well, I guess I better get on with it. Getting into his account might take me a while.' He pressed the card against the electronic lock on his door. 'I'll come and find you if I have any luck.'

Thirty-Five

Victoria slowly retraced her steps along the second floor landing. It was strange to hear Curtis sounding so resentful about the money. He had never shown any interest in accumulating it, before. He had only ever looked at the business as a way of funding his surfing. Still, she couldn't blame him for feeling aggrieved. He had worked at least as hard as Peyton to build the company up. In fact, Peyton had once told Victoria that without Curtis, they would have had no business. And now he had to stand by, watching the proceeds of all his hard work fall into the hands of a man he despised. It would be hard for anyone to take.

She followed the verandah back around to the corridor. Emerging on the other side, she caught a glimpse of the stooped, balding figure of James' uncle, staring at a list of suite numbers engraved on a thick brass plaque, mounted on the wall. George had his back to her, but she recognised the band of grey hair around his balding crown and the old-fashioned blue-checked shirt and grey slacks that she had seen him wearing earlier in the day. An umbrella dangled from his right arm and he had a copy of *The Straits Times* tucked under his left, along with a small, white package.

Victoria smiled as she approached him. 'It looks like you've been out and about.'

George straightened up with a start. 'Oh yes, sorry, I didn't hear you coming.' He tapped the small, white paper bag under his arm. 'I had to dash out and get some migraine pills for Patricia.' He turned back to look at the suite numbers on the wall. 'Of course, I'm now completely lost. I decided to come in using the back way, through the arcade to save walking around the front in this heat; but I seem to be going around in circles.'

'Where are you trying to get to?'

'I need to take Patricia's pills up to her in John and Beverley's suite. I've tried to get her to come back to our room and lie down, but she won't leave her brother.' He shook his head with a small, resigned sigh. 'This business with James has got everyone on edge; they're all up there fretting about what to do. Of course, I said they should call the police, but none of them want to do that. How on earth they think they're going to deal with this on their own, I have no idea.'

'Has there been any more news?'

George shook his head. 'Not that I've heard. Although, I don't suppose anything will happen now, until they hand the money over.'

'Did Beverley have any luck getting hold of her bank, do you know? She was going to call them, earlier.'

'She said they couldn't get the money together in time, but I understand Peyton has gone to see her bank, too. It all seems damned odd. They have millions to put into this Bankcorp deal, but can't find the money to get their own son back.'

'What *is* the Bankcorp deal?'

George groaned. 'It's all they ever talk about. They've got some deal in the US, they're working on; supposedly, it's worth 450 million dollars. Bankcorp is the American company coordinating it all. They talked us into investing in it. You, no doubt, heard us discussing it at dinner, last night. Anyway, they told us we could put our money in with theirs, because we didn't have enough to be sole investors. I wasn't too sure about it all. I prefer to leave my money in the bank. But Patricia was insistent. And of course, we're still waiting for the deal to come through and haven't seen any of the huge profits they keep promising us. Every time I've mentioned it, there's been a new excuse; someone was away on leave or the clearing bank in Japan was closed for a holiday. Meanwhile, here they are, living the high life as if they've got all the money in the world. That's why I got a bit angry, last night. Still, I think it was worthwhile. They're going to pay us our investment back, next week. I'd rather forgo the profits and know I've got my money secure in the bank.'

'So how does this deal work?' Victoria asked. 'What do you get out of it as an investor?'

'I'm blessed if I know; I can't seem to get a straight answer out of them. It's beginning to sound like one of John's hair-brained schemes to me.'

'Does he have a lot of those?'

'He's always working on something: a fizzy drink that'll prevent aging or a vitamin sachet that'll cure cancer. Every one is "the one that's going to be the pot of gold".'

'But they make good money out of their investment business, don't they?'

'So they say. But that's more Beverley and James' concern, than John's. He concentrates on investing in start-ups. Although, he doesn't seem to have much of a head for business, from what I can see.'

'But he works in the investment company, as well?'

'He deals with some of their clients. But what he actually does, I couldn't tell you. James and Beverley seem to run everything, along with Lou, from what I can see.'

'What about Tim—he's never joined the family business?'

George looked amused by the suggestion. 'Tim's an anti-capitalist. He thinks banks and financial institutions are driving us all towards destruction. Commercial terrorism, I think he calls it. Of course, if he had to get out there and earn his own living, I'm sure he'd have a very different view of the world.'

'Yes, I'm sure he would. I heard him talking, last night; he does seem to have a rather idealistic view of things. I'm not sure he quite understands that if you want to be philanthropic, you need to have money. I know from the charity work I do, it takes a lot of cash to have any impact. Although, I suspect Tim might be more of a Champagne socialist rather than a hands-on one.'

'Exactly; he has all of the answers but I've never seen him roll up his sleeves to be a part of the solution.' George paused and scratched the single tuft of hair sitting upright on the top of his otherwise bald crown. 'I can see problems ahead for that lad—he's got a chip on his shoulder, the size of Great Britain. Just between you and I, I think the problem comes down to Beverley. She's never given the young chap much encouragement—always putting him down and telling him he should be more like James. But he's a very different character and she can't seem to accept that.'

Victoria gave a small nod. 'I did get the impression that he and James weren't close. I can imagine Tim would find it very difficult if he were being constantly compared to his brother.'

'They don't get along at all. And it's mutual. James doesn't have much time for Tim, or his stepfather for that matter. There's a lot of friction there.' George glanced down at his watch. 'Oh my goodness, I'd better stop gossiping and get up to Patricia. She'll wonder where I've got to.' He turned again to look at the suite numbers on the wall.

Victoria smiled. 'Why don't I show you the way? I'm heading back to my room; it's very close to their suite.'

George gave a grateful sigh of relief. 'Oh, that would save me a lot of trouble, thank you.'

'It's no problem at all.' Victoria guided him towards the short staircase leading away from the landing. They mounted the few steps and pushed open the swing doors at the top.

As they stepped inside, George took a white handkerchief from his trouser pocket and wiped his freckled forehead. 'It's nice being back inside, in the cool. I'm not used to this sort of heat.'

Victoria watched him pat his face dry with the handkerchief. He was much friendlier and chattier without his wife around. As they waited for the lift, she wondered what other gossip she might be able to extract from him. 'How does Tim get along with Peyton? Have they spent much time together?'

George shook his head. 'I doubt it. A few months back, *The Guardian* published an article about how badly she treated her workers. Tim took a dislike to her, after that.'

The lift bell rang out and the doors slid open. They stepped into its mahogany-panelled interior and Victoria pressed the button for the third floor. 'Oh yes, I remember that article. Poor Peyton was very badly criticised. I think they called her "The Iron Lady", didn't they?'

'Yes, something like that, I think.'

'Then I can see why Tim has taken a dislike to her. An unflattering profile like that wouldn't have fitted with his socialist ideals.'

'I don't think running any business fits with Tim's socialist ideals.' The lift chimed as it came to a slow halt on the third floor and the polished brass doors gradually opened to reveal an enormous display of red orchids sitting atop a large, round antique table. They were the colour of ripe tomatoes with elegantly sculptured petals that seemed to fall away from their small yellow centres like the floppy ears of a Dachshund. George eyed them delightedly. 'Ah, *Renanthera kalsom*. Beautiful flowers. They had Dendrobiums up here, earlier.' He peered over the top of the orchid display. 'I know where I am now. Ridiculous getting lost, really, wasn't it?'

'Not at all,' Victoria said, as they walked the few steps towards John and Beverley's suite. 'It's easily done.'

'Well, thank you for getting me here safely. I'm sure I'll see you again very soon. Hopefully once this business is all sorted out.'

He turned from Victoria and took a step towards the door of John and Beverley's suite. He raised his forefinger and was about to press the doorbell when the door flew open and Eleanor Springfield almost collided with him. She stopped herself just in time and stared at him, startled. 'Oh, George. You gave me a fright. We were just talking about you. Patricia was wondering where you were. The poor dear has the most dreadful headache; she's having a lie down. She doesn't look at all well.'

'Oh goodness, I'd better get in there, then. I've got her migraine medication. My apologies for not stopping to chat.'

'Don't be silly,' Eleanor said. 'You go on in and see your wife. I'll catch up with you a little later, at dinner.'

Eleanor waited for George to close the door behind him, before tucking her hand through the crook of Victoria's elbow and leading her away. 'That poor man, I do feel so sorry for him. His wife is to a peaceful life what a bull is to a china shop. I'm hardly surprised she has a headache; she never stops talking. I would have ended up with one as well, if I had stayed in there any longer.'

'Just as well you escaped, then,' Victoria said. 'Because I'll need my number two spy sharp and alert, this evening, if this dinner is still on.'

'Oh, it is most definitely on. Beverley suggested it herself. She thought it would be best for Peyton if we were all together to support her. I don't imagine anyone will eat very much, but she is committed to paying for all of the food. So they may as well deliver it.'

'In that case, we'll both need to be on watch. I won't be able to keep an eye on everyone myself.'

Eleanor gave her walking stick a firm tap on the wooden floorboards and smiled. Victoria knew that mischievous smile only too well. It meant Eleanor had something up her sleeve.

'Don't you worry, my dear,' Eleanor said. 'I'll keep my wits about me.'

Thirty-Six

Victoria threw her handbag down onto the coffee table and flopped on the sofa. She stretched her long body out along its full length, laying her head back on to the soft, rust-coloured silk of the cushions. It was nice being back in the peace and quiet of her own room.

Her call to the Prime Minister had gone much better than she had anticipated. The police were now scanning the city's CCTV footage for any sign of James and talking to every taxi operator who had been in the vicinity of Raffles that morning. The Commissioner of Police had taken personal charge of the case, as a mark of gratitude for the work she did for them, the previous year. He was currently working with the Immigration and Checkpoint Authority to ascertain if James had been taken out of the country. There wasn't much more for Victoria to do now, but wait.

As she gazed up at the crystal chandelier suspended above her, thinking of James, she suddenly felt ravenously hungry. With everything that had happened, she still hadn't had a chance to eat anything. She glanced across at the small clock on the bookshelf. It was almost five thirty. There was no point ordering anything—by the time it would arrive, she would need to start getting ready for dinner.

She swung her legs off the sofa and pulled the fruit bowl towards her. She took a large, spindly, red rambutan from the top and stuck the pointed end of the fruit knife into its rubbery skin. Mario must have remembered her aversion to their blunt fruit knives, which, for as long as she could remember, had been useless for cutting through anything more challenging than soft butter.

She ran the sharp edge of the knife around the centre of the fruit, slicing through its thick skin, until she could pull it apart like a Russian doll. The slippery, white flesh sat inside, like a pearl in its shell. Popping the smooth ball into her mouth, she savoured the fruit's delicate sweetness. The scented flavour was heavenly, but it did little to satisfy her hunger.

Hunting around in the fruit bowl for something else, she passed over the apples and oranges—they were always tasteless in the tropics. Instead, she chose a small Lady Finger banana and peeled back the thin, yellow skin. She sunk her teeth into its firm flesh and sighed. To think she had been looking forward to the wedding and spending a few days with her old friend. Amazing how dramatically life could change within twenty-four hours.

Reluctantly, she picked her iPad up from the coffee table. There was no sense in wasting time; she might as well see what other information she could find for herself. She opened the Safari icon and typed Bankcorp into the search box.

She was intrigued by the 450 million-dollar deal that George had said Beverley and James were doing with them. It seemed like an extraordinarily large amount of money.

Only one company in the US came up with that name. She clicked through to their website. Louis Armstrong's 'What a wonderful world' burst forth from the speakers. She couldn't help smiling at the irony. She turned the volume down and ran her eye over the home page. A list of inspirational quotes morphed over images of gold bullion and bank notes. The clichés would have made Tony Robbins blush: 'Your wealth can only grow to the extent you do'; 'Everything you can imagine is real'; 'If something is important, even if the odds are against you, do it'; 'By changing nothing, nothing changes.'

She went up to the menu bar at the top and scrolled through to the other pages. They all made similiar claims about the firm's monetary prowess: 'financial freedom for those who want it . . . large scale investments on a global basis . . . invest in the largest and richest diamond mine on the planet . . . assets and holdings in excess of 20 billion USD . . . sole provider of 200 million USD humanitarian loan to the Country of Mauritius.

There were a couple of gold stars for awards they had won, but otherwise, just the usual generic nonsense that banks and financial institutions liked to fill their websites with.

She pressed the backspace icon and returned to her Google search. There wasn't much else on the company. A couple of consumer review sites accusing Bankcorp's owner and his glamorous wife of lies and deception, but they seemed to be venting a personal grievance. There was an old court case against the company for fraud, but that had been dismissed. Otherwise, there was nothing; they seemed to be operating in an online vacuum.

She threw the skin of her banana into a small rubbish basket and was contemplating taking a second one from the bowl, when her phone vibrated on the tabletop with a new text message. She leaned over and looked at the screen. Bee's name flashed up in bold.

The message beneath contained only a few words, but they were enough to make Victoria sit bolt upright.

'It's a Ponzi scheme, call me.'

Thirty-Seven

Victoria ended the call. She slumped into the back of the sofa, and holding the phone in both hands, stared at the black screen. She could scarcely believe what Bee had told her. A Ponzi scheme! A Ponzi scheme that Roger Winstanley knew about. Which meant Isabelle must have known about it as well and yet, she chose not to say anything. Victoria felt a surge of anger well up inside her. How could she have not said a word to Peyton?

Grabbing her tote bag from the coffee table, Victoria threw her phone into it. Conscious of little other than the outrage she felt, she slipped her white sandals back on and strode across to the console table in the corner. Snatching her room key from the small silver tray, she marched down the hallway towards the front door of her suite. She paused by the iPad to turn on the 'Do Not Disturb' light—she didn't want anyone in her room, when she returned.

Pulling the door closed behind her, she made her way along the landing, following the atrium around towards Isabelle's suite. She replayed the conversation with Bee over and over in her mind. Was she being unfair towards Isabelle? Was it in any way possible, that Isabelle didn't know about the Ponzi scheme?

Victoria came to an abrupt stop in front of Isabelle's door. It suddenly came to her. The conversation over dinner that she had been trying to recall. Tim had been talking about financial institutions being protected by corrupt governments. In response, Isabelle had said, 'There are many examples of financiers being sent to prison. The system is not quite so inept as you believe.'

149

Isabelle did know! And what's more, she fully expected the law to come down on them. Otherwise, why would she have sent Roger her email correspondence with Beverley for him to forward on to the SFO? She would only have done that because Roger would have asked for it.

Victoria felt a surge of anger boil up inside her again. She stepped forward and pressed the doorbell.

The door swung open. Isabelle stood framed in the doorway, still wearing the same pinstripe trousers and white blouse that she had been in earlier, but with the high heels and towering hat gone, she seemed much smaller and frailer.

Victoria marched inside, noticing the open bottle of Château Margaux on the side table with an empty wine glass beside it, stained on the rim with a small ring of Isabelle's red lipstick.

She stood in the middle of Isabelle's living room, facing her, making no attempt to hide her fury. 'Did you know about the Ponzi scheme?'

Isabelle hesitated. 'Ponzi scheme?'

'Yes, Ponzi scheme. An illegal scheme in which an investment company offers high returns by taking money from one investor to pay off another, without any money actually being invested—as I think you well know. But of course, when funds from new investors dry up, then everyone loses. Aside from the people running the scheme. They usually do quite well out of it, until they get caught. Did you know that's what Winstanley & Marsters were doing?'

Isabelle drew her chest up and stalked across to the bottle of red wine sitting on the side table. She snatched it up and poured out a small glass. 'I was aware Roger suspected that they were involved in a Ponzi scheme.'

Victoria looked hard at Isabelle. 'And yet you chose not to say anything to Peyton?'

Isabelle's thin fingers fidgeted with the stem of her glass. 'I was not able to say anything to Peyton. I had made a promise to Roger.'

'And that was more important to you, was it, than the promises you made to Peyton's now-deceased parents when you agreed to become her godmother?'

Isabelle turned away from Victoria. She placed the wine glass down
and reached for the packet of Gauloises Blondes lying on the small
table beside her. She placed one between her lips and strode outside
onto the balcony. With her thumb, she flicked the top off her gold
lighter. A small, yellow flame flickered to life; its long, serpent tongue
licking the end of the cigarette until the tobacco caught and the embers
glowed red with Isabelle's deep inhale of breath. She remained looking
out over the courtyard with her back to Victoria. 'If I had told Peyton,
she would have told James and that would have given them time to
hide everything.'

'Which would have ruined Roger's plan for getting as much dirt as
possible on James and his mother.'

Isabelle stiffened. She swung round and faced Victoria. Her eyes
blazed and her voice was as hard and defiant as the expression in her
eyes, 'Which would have ruined any chance for the authorities to get
the information they needed.'

'But that wasn't what motivated you, was it?' Victoria said. 'You
weren't interested in justice. You were only interested in helping
Roger prove a case against his son to preserve his own reputation.'
Victoria moved around in front of the coffee table and stood face
to face with Isabelle, feeling incensed over the contents of the email
exchange that Bee had uncovered at the SFO. 'I had a friend of mine
do some investigating. Do you know what she told me? Over four
months ago, Beverley tried to get you to invest money with her
company, Winstanley & Marsters. That was when you suspected
something was wrong, wasn't it? Because Beverley told you that any
money you invested would be safely deposited in a capital guaranteed
fund with Winstanley & Co. But you knew that wasn't true, because
Roger is the chairman of Winstanley & Co. and you knew he would
have nothing to do with Winstanley & Marsters. But instead of
taking your suspicions to the authorities or warning Peyton, you told
Roger. And for the last four months, he has had a private investigator
digging up as much dirt on their company as possible, in order to
protect himself in any future court cases that James might bring

against him, in an attempt to get hold of the family inheritance. What was he going to do, blackmail James to keep him quiet or was he banking on a convicted criminal standing no chance against the great Roger Winstanley in court? It wasn't Peyton you were interested in protecting was it—'

'I tried to stop the marriage. I did everything in my power to prevent this wedding from taking place.'

'Everything, except telling Peyton the truth.'

'What difference would it have made if I had told her about the Ponzi scheme? She wouldn't have believed me; she would have listened to James. Peyton is stubborn, you know that.'

'She would at least have been going into this wedding with her eyes wide open. As it is, she was about to go in half-blind and the responsibility for that lies on your shoulders. This Ponzi scheme potentially involves hundreds of millions of pounds. If it's true, it will be all over the media. Peyton is a successful businesswoman; she has a reputation to protect. She hasn't been *that* blinded by love.'

'I wouldn't be so sure about that. Peyton is in love with James and despite the foolishness of it, she intends to marry him. Nothing I can say is going to stop her.'

'You can hardly blame her for that, Isabelle. You're in love with James' father, and from what I can see, the two of them are cut from the same cloth.' Victoria paused. She contemplated Isabelle for a moment. 'What was your plan? Were you going to let Peyton find out about this from the media?'

'I didn't think she would marry him this quickly. I thought it would all come out, before anything happened.'

'Then it's terribly convenient for you that this kidnapping got in the way, isn't it? Because here we are, on the eve of their wedding and you've still said nothing.'

'It is better that she finds out about it from the media. She will at least believe them.' Isabelle leaned against the white frame of the French doors and took a long draw on her cigarette. 'It is only her first marriage. She can divorce him.'

'That's your solution, is it? Leave her to untangle the web of lies once it's all out in the public domain and she's being harassed by the world's media?'

Isabelle raised her chin in defiance. A deep flush of anger coloured her cheeks. 'I thought it was the best way.'

Victoria held Isabelle's gaze steadily. 'For whom, Isabelle, you or Peyton? You know as well as I do that Peyton is going to be devastated by all of this. She is a very proud woman and the last thing she will want is for the media to make a fool of her; which they will try to do, if they discover she has married a fraudster. I can't even begin to predict how Peyton is going to react, when she finds out about all of this. But I don't want her finding out about it from the media. Not in the state she is in, right now. So either you tell her before the end of the day, or I will.'

Thirty-Eight

Victoria slipped off her bathrobe and pulled on a pair of Capri pants. She had lost weight while she was away in Africa and they sat loose on her hips. But they were comfortable and the soft sheen of the burnt-orange silk felt cool on her skin. From her suitcase, she pulled out a finely woven, pale green, silk sweater. It hadn't creased and the bare midriff would be perfect for the heat. She pulled it on and grabbed a matching bright-orange cardigan as well—just in case the air-conditioning in the Marsters' suite was too cold. Then she slipped her feet into a pair of nude sandals and ran her fingers through her long, dark hair. It was nice to have finally had the chance to wash the chlorine out of it.

She put a dab of gloss on her lips and was just throwing the tube into her bag, when the telephone in her suite rang. She rushed back into the bedroom to answer it.

'Ah, Miss West, this is Mario. I am glad that I found you in your room. I have just completed a full review of the camera footage. Perhaps, if you are free, we could meet in the security office to talk through it?'

Victoria glanced at the clock on the bedside table. It was ten past seven. She still had twenty minutes before she was due at dinner. 'I can come down now, if that suits you?'

'Yes, perfectly. I shall wait for you, here.'

Mario was alone when Victoria arrived, seated in front of a blank computer screen with his back turned towards her. She tapped gently on the open door as she stepped into the room. He swivelled his chair round and sprang to his feet.

'Ah, Miss West.' He took a step forward and spread his arms towards her. 'You are looking especially beautiful. More than beautiful! You have *un non so che di affascinante*, as we say in Italian.' He held his extravagant gesture in mid-air. 'And if I am not mistaken . . .' He briefly closed his eyes and sniffed the air. 'It is Amouage that you are wearing.'

Victoria smiled. 'You have a very good memory, Mario.'

He bowed, in appreciation of the compliment. 'It is these small details that make a beautiful woman exceptional.'

As he spoke, he wheeled a chair from the other side of the small room and positioned it in front of the computer. He laid his hand gently on the small of Victoria's slender back and guided her towards it. 'Please, sit down.'

He took the chair beside her and moved the notepad he had been looking at, when Victoria walked in. Settling into his chair, he gave the wireless mouse a small jiggle and the screen in front of them sprang to life. 'Shall we look, firstly, at Mr Winstanley's movements, this morning?'

Victoria leaned towards the illuminated screen and nodded. 'Yes, that would be good.'

Mario consulted his notepad. 'You asked me to look for evidence of Mr Winstanley leaving the hotel at around eleven o'clock this morning. Unfortunately, I could find nothing. I therefore extended my search from eight o'clock this morning until one o'clock this afternoon.' Mario shifted his cursor to a small window at the bottom right of the screen and brought up an image. 'This was taken by one of our external cameras outside the lobby area this morning.' He indicated a male figure with a small circular motion of the cursor. 'As you can see, Mr Winstanley is leaving the Tiffin Room with Miss Latchmore, immediately after their breakfast.'

Victoria rested her elbows on the wooden desk and leaned closer to the screen. The enlarged image from the CCTV camera was grainy, but she could clearly see it was James and Peyton leaving the Tiffin Room, hand in hand, and walking towards the Grand Staircase. She squinted at the small timer in the corner: 08:27:17.

Mario leaned back in his chair. 'Unfortunately, this is the last image I have of Mr Winstanley.'

'Is there nothing later, that shows him leaving the hotel?'

'I am afraid not. I have checked all the cameras between this time and one o'clock this afternoon, when the kidnapper's message was received.'

'Is there any way he could have left the hotel without being captured on camera?'

Mario shook his head. 'No, all the exits and entrances into and out of the hotel are covered by our cameras.'

'And yet, nothing shows him coming back at around eleven o'clock,' Victoria said, speaking more to herself than Mario. 'Apparently, he returned to the hotel because he forgot some documents, but you're saying there is no footage of him coming or going?'

Mario shook his head. 'I have found no footage of him at all. And I have done an exhaustive search.'

Victoria had no doubt he had.

'However—' Mario's face brightened and he turned triumphantly back to face the computer screen. 'I did find some footage of Mr Winstanley from yesterday evening, which might be of some interest to you.' He double clicked on a small icon in the top left-hand corner of the desktop. Enlarging the window to fit the full width of the screen, he pressed the play button. 'It is not of the best quality, unfortunately. We have only one camera operating in the courtyard and the footage is taken at some distance.'

Victoria sat forward in her chair. At first, she could make out nothing but the distant outline of the verandah in front of the La Dame de Pic. Mario zoomed in. A figure stumbled into shot, knocking against the grey filigree gate in the corner. Victoria leaned closer. The resolution was poor, but Tim Marsters' tall, lanky figure and red hair was distinctive. Another figure came into shot and moved towards him. It looked as if they were about to have a fight. She couldn't see the face on the second figure, but she was pretty sure it was James. He moved to one side and she saw something in Tim's hand. It was a knife.

John Marsters' stocky frame then appeared rushing towards Tim. Mario zoomed out and Victoria could see Beverley standing behind her husband.

She glanced down at the timer in the corner of the screen: 18:36:14. Just after they were all due to meet in the Writers Bar for drinks. Tim and James' argument at dinner now made a lot more sense. Whatever this fight was about, it would have been fresh in their minds.

Victoria leaned back in her seat and watched the rest of the altercation unfold. James eventually turned and his face was captured by the camera. Even with the grainy footage, there was no doubting it was him. She turned to Mario. 'Can you email me this clip?'

Mario nodded. 'Yes, of course. I shall do it immediately. I did also have a little bit of luck with the room service delivery.' He turned his attention back to the screen and opened another window. 'I found this footage of Julien with the trolley in the service elevator at twelve fifty-four. That camera is now back in operation. As you can see here . . .' he enlarged the image and pointed to the top of the trolley with the nib of his pen 'there is no envelope visible, at this point. Unfortunately, once Julien left the elevator and entered the guest area of the hotel, we have no further footage.'

'But we have Julien's word that no one could have put anything on it after that.'

Mario nodded. 'That is true.' He spread his hands out in a gesture of apology. 'I am very sorry that I cannot be of more help to you.'

Victoria smiled. 'On the contrary, Mario, you have been a great help.'

Thirty-Nine

Victoria stopped in front of the Marsters' suite and pulled her phone out of her bag to check the time. She was twenty minutes late. Oh well, it couldn't be helped. She was probably still just within the zone of being fashionable and not rude.

Stepping through the front door, and across the entrance foyer, into the parlour, she was pleased to see large silver trays of hors d'oeuvres still laid out. The main buffet hadn't arrived, which meant, technically speaking, she wasn't late. Not that anyone seemed to be eating much, or drinking, for that matter. Only a couple of tamarind prawns and white radish cakes seemed to have been touched on the trays beside her. The mood was very sombre. Just a quiet, almost apologetic mumble of voices filled the room.

She stood in the doorway of the parlour, surveying the guests. Nick and Kate were standing in the opposite corner, talking with Eleanor and Bill. From the uncomfortable looks on their faces, Victoria surmised Eleanor was working hard to extract information from them.

Kate looked beautiful. She had changed into a summer dress in muted shades of blue, red and white. The colourful swirls formed a cloud-like pattern over the snugly fitted bodice and flowed with the skirt in soft, elegant folds down to her ankles. Her dark hair was loosely clipped back on the nape of her neck, revealing two long, white, teardrop earrings. The previous evening, she had worn high heels and now seemed much shorter, standing next to Nick in a pair of flat, white sandals. Nick still looked like the fashionable City lawyer on holiday, in the same pair of jeans he had been wearing earlier, but he

158

had dispensed with the black shirt and Ermenegildo Zegna jacket, and instead, was wearing a simple, short-sleeved, grey polo shirt. A pair of aviator sunglasses was perched on the top of his shaved head.

Victoria couldn't help smiling as she watched the pair's overt discomfort. They both seemed keen to escape Eleanor's clutches. Kate's attention continually drifted to other parts of the room and Nick endlessly shifted his weight from one leg to the other, gulping down large mouthfuls of red wine with each movement. Much to Victoria's amusement, Eleanor ignored their obvious disinterest and doggedly pursued a conversation with them.

Eleanor seemed to have everything under control, so Victoria took a crab cake from one of the trays of hors d'oeuvres laid out on the dining table, and made her way further into the room. In a halo of blue velvet cushions, Patricia's stout figure dominated the centre of the small space, her broad frame consuming both sides of the two-seater sofa. On her lap, an incongruously elegant plate of dumplings nestled in the folds of her green floral dress.

Standing beside Patricia, Zara looked elegant in a floaty, white, wraparound dress, the antithesis of Patricia's garish appearance. It struck Victoria as almost comical that these two women, from such opposite ends of the social spectrum, had been thrown into each other's company under such bizarre circumstances.

The high-pitched notes of Patricia's voice gradually began to rise above the general murmur in the room. 'We don't know anything at all. Poor Beverley and John are beside themselves with worry.'

Zara gathered in the pleats of her short skirt and perched on the edge of the sofa. 'But Tim said there was a message from James?'

Patricia swallowed the last morsel of a dumpling. 'Oh yes, but it didn't tell us anything. And poor Beverley was so distressed when she heard it. Can you imagine how she must have felt? You really do have to wonder what's wrong with these people. I can't think what must be going through their minds to send such a thing. I only hope it all gets sorted out, quickly. I've had one of my migraines, all afternoon, from the worry of it. George had to go out and get medication for me. Mind you, this dreadful heat doesn't help. I feel so worn out. It's hard to function properly.' Patricia gave an exhausted sigh. 'I still don't know why James wanted to come down here. And now, poor Beverley and John are having to deal with all of this on their own, in a strange country.'

'But what did James' message say?'

'I don't think he had the time to say anything much at all. That's what's been so awful. It's the lack of information.'

'But was he all right, did he sound as if he had been hurt?'

'I don't know. I certainly hope they haven't hurt him. I don't see why they would. Beverley and John have got plenty of money, they'll pay the ransom. Surely, that's all they want?'

Patricia's grating voice faded a little, as Victoria moved away to the far end of the room, helping herself to a small curry puff on the way. Patricia really was an extraordinary woman. It was hard to think of anyone who showed less interest in others, whilst at the same time, professing the most heartfelt concern.

Through the French doors, Victoria could see Isabelle on the balcony, ensconced in conversation with Curtis and George. She cut a striking figure in a pair of wide red-and-white striped trousers. Teamed, in her inimitable style, with red lace gloves, a green blouse cinched at the neck with a large black bowtie, a pair of clear plastic brogues and a black and white Panama hat, perched on the top of her peroxide blonde hair. Only Isabelle could pull off such an outlandish outfit at seventy-one years of age and look amazing.

As she turned to exhale a mouthful of smoke, her gaze briefly met Victoria's. She made no acknowledgement but slowly and pointedly turned her head away and fell back into conversation with Curtis and George.

In front of the French doors, Tim sat slumped in a tan leather armchair. The long, bony fingers of his right hand clasped a nearly full glass of white wine, while the thumb of his left furiously tapped the screen of his silver Samsung. His left leg jiggled up and down in small, rapid movements, almost keeping up with his typing.

Lou emerged from the shadows of the potted plant beside him, with a tray of hors d'oeuvres carefully balanced on her forearm. She looked smart in a simple black shirt-dress, nipped in at the waist with a thin belt. It struck Victoria that, even off duty, Lou never left her role as chief organizer of the family's affairs.

Tucking one side of her short, dark bob behind her ear, she leaned over Tim and placed a tender hand on his shoulder. 'Would you like something to eat, love?'

Tim pulled his shoulder away. 'I'm not hungry.'

Lou sat on the arm of his chair and stroked his coarse red hair. 'I know you're upset, Tim, but you haven't had anything to eat, all day. Why don't you just try to have something small?'

Tim jerked his head away from her hand, almost knocking the tray of hors d'oeuvres off her knee. 'I said I'm not hungry. Just leave me alone.' He slammed his wine glass down onto the small table beside him and hunched over his phone, typing even faster than before, with both thumbs tapping furiously on the screen.

Lou took hold of the silver tray in both hands and stood up. She watched him for a moment with affectionate, motherly concern; then with a small sigh, turned away. She made her way across to where Victoria was standing.

Victoria gave her a sympathetic smile. 'It must be very hard on him.'

Lou nodded. 'It's hit him a lot harder than he's letting on. He won't talk to any of us, he's holding it all in.'

'Are he and James close?'

'Yes, they're a close family. James always looks out for Tim. There's a very special bond between them.' Lou looked across to where Tim was sitting. The affection in her eyes surprised Victoria, given her stiff demeanour. 'He's a sensitive, young man. This is very difficult for him.' She abruptly shrugged away the sentiment and turned back to Victoria. 'Still, we have to stay positive. All this doom and gloom isn't going to bring James back.' She held out the tray of hors d'oeuvres. 'Can I offer you something to eat? There's no point having all this good food go to waste.'

Victoria took a white radish cake from the tray and a white linen napkin. 'Thank you Lou, I will. I'm starving. I haven't had a chance to eat all day.' She cast her gaze round the room. 'Is Peyton here, I haven't seen her?'

'Yes, she is. She just popped into the bathroom, a moment ago. I must say, I am so pleased we went ahead with the dinner tonight. I don't think Peyton should be left by herself, at the moment; she doesn't seem to be coping at all well.'

Just then, the shrill of the doorbell pierced the quiet hum of voices in the room. Lou started; then hurriedly put the tray of hors d'oeuvres down on to the small writing desk next to Victoria. 'That'll be dinner arriving. I'd better go and let them in.'

Victoria took another radish cake from the tray and watched Lou as she rushed over to the entrance foyer. At the same time, John dashed out from the bedroom and almost collided with her. Apologetically, he put his hand on the small of her back and gestured for her to go first. 'Sorry Lou, I'll let you get the door. I'll clear some space over here on the table.'

He moved across to the dining table and began to pile the hors d'oeuvres platters on top of each other. Balancing them precariously in the palm of one hand, he moved towards entrance foyer, and was just stepping into the pantry, when Beverley came out from the bedroom and spotted him. 'Oh John, for Heaven's sake, don't put everything on top of each other like that. Lay them out on the coffee table over there.' She pointed to the large coffee table sitting between the two blue sofas. 'People might want some more.'

With an irritable sigh, she abruptly turned away and went to join Lou at the front door. Lou had already taken charge and was directing the two butlers, dressed in immaculate suits and white gloves, towards the dining table. With large, white serving platters balanced on both arms, they passed in front of her, bringing in plate after plate filled with Singaporean curries and stir-fries. The delicious fragrances mingled and filled the room, making Victoria realize just how hungry she was.

Beverley stopped one of the butlers midway across the foyer. 'Do you not have covers to keep everything warm?'

'Oh, yes we do, Mrs Marsters, but—' he turned to look at Lou.

Lou shot a nervous glance at Beverley. 'I asked them to bring everything in without the covers. I thought it would be easier.'

'I want everything to stay hot,' Beverley said, testily. 'Put all the covers back on everything.'

Victoria could see it was going to take a little while for the food to be arranged, so she helped herself to a tamarind prawn. The flesh was perfectly firm and the flavour was delicious; it was hot and spicy and sour, all at once. She was looking for somewhere to dispose of the tail, when she caught sight of Peyton coming out of the bedroom.

Peyton looked dreadful. The strain of the past few hours was showing plainly on her face. All her usual sparkle had disappeared; her features were rigid and colourless, her eyelids puffy from crying and she seemed unable to focus on anything. Her gaze drifted vacantly over the room.

Victoria went to her and took hold of her arm. 'Peyton, you look terrible; come and sit down.'

She attempted to draw her towards an armchair, but Peyton resisted. 'I'm okay; I'm fine.'

Victoria looked at her pale face and distrait expression and raised an eyebrow.

Peyton attempted a smile. 'Honestly, I'm fine, I'll be okay.'

'You don't look fine,' Victoria said. 'You look like you're about to pass out.'

Peyton pressed the heels of her hands over her eyes. 'I'm not, I'm just exhausted.'

'Why don't you go back to your room and have a rest? Everyone will understand.'

Peyton shook her head. 'I'd rather stay here. I don't want to be on my own.'

'Then at least have something to eat. We don't want you fainting on us. Then you can tell me how you got on at the bank.'

'Oh, that went fine. Grandpa came with me. They said it's no problem to transfer the money; it can be done immediately, if we need to.' Peyton paused and Victoria was relieved to see some colour creeping back into her cheeks. 'Do you still think we should hold off making the payments?'

'Yes, I do. I just wanted to know if the bank could do it, if necessary.' Victoria gave Peyton a smile. 'Come on, let's get something to eat. It could be a long night.'

Peyton nodded. 'I'll come in a minute. I just need to get a glass of water. I've got such a headache, I haven't drunk anything all afternoon.'

'I'll put a plate together for you, then,' Victoria said. 'I want to make sure you eat something. Otherwise you'll make yourself sick.'

'I'm not sure I'm going be able to stomach anything, but I'll try.' Peyton rubbed her fingers across her forehead. 'Let me go and get something to drink, then I'll come back.'

Peyton disappeared into the pantry and Victoria ran her eye over the array of food laid out on the dining table, reading the small name tags sitting in front of each dish: claypot chicken, Malay fish curry, chilli crabs, butter prawns, coconut beef, Sichuan pork, braised ribs, Peking duck, spiced lamb, vegetable rice. It all looked and smelled delicious. She couldn't help thinking how perfect it all would have been for the celebration it had been ordered for, and how ill-suited it now appeared, for the funereal gathering that was consuming it. Not that anyone's appetite seemed to be affected by the day's events. The earlier reticence Victoria had detected in the room for enjoying any form of hospitality, seemed to have disappeared with the arrival of the buffet.

Nick held centre-court on one side of the dining table. With a large silver spoon poised over the dish of chilli crab, he took charge of serving. 'Why don't I play mum? Zara, some chilli crab for you . . . What about you, John? Beverley, here you go, I think you need to eat something. Isabelle, how about a small spoonful for you? Victoria, can I offer you some—' He dipped the spoon back into the red sauce in preparation to serve her, but Victoria shook her head.

'No, thank you, Nick. I might come back for some, a bit later.

She took two dinner plates from the pile and made a small selection of Peking duck and spiced lamb on each one. The one thing she disliked about buffets was mixing all the food together. She preferred to eat everything separately and enjoy it. Patricia, on the other hand, seemed to have no such qualms; she was piling spoonfuls of every dish on to her plate, as if she were worried they were going to run out.

Victoria took the half-empty plates and moved outside onto the balcony. Kate was standing in the doorway. She seemed preoccupied with what was going on in the room and didn't acknowledge Victoria passing in front of her. Victoria sidled by, carefully; keeping her clothing well away from the chilli crab's red sauce that had seeped out to the edges of Kate's plate. It was the same bright colour as her nail polish and would have left a nasty stain on her clothes, if she had brushed against it.

Victoria chose an armchair in the corner, as far from anyone else as she could get. She wanted some time on her own, to think. As she rolled the shredded duck and slivers of spring onion inside one of the bite-sized pancakes, she ran over everything she had learnt from Mario in the security room.

Slowly, things started to fall into place and a theory of how James had been kidnapped began to form in her mind. She still wanted to wait for the results of the police search. But if, as she suspected, they found nothing, then she would—

There was a frantic scream in the living room. Victoria threw the pancake she was rolling on to her plate and raced across to the doorway.

She was greeted by what looked like a scene from an Edvard Munch painting. Beverley was standing in the middle of the room, leaning against the blue sofa, her mouth open and her eyes wide with panic. Lou was beside her, arms outstretched. While John was on the sofa opposite watching them both, with bulging eyes and a forkful of food frozen halfway to his open mouth.

'Someone, get her adrenaline pen!' Lou cried out.

Her voice spurred John into action. He thumped his dinner plate down onto the coffee table. The knife and fork clattered noisily off the edge, smearing the wooden surface with a streak of yellow curry sauce. Then with an energy that surprised Victoria, he sprang to his feet and hurtled past Lou, into the bedroom.

Lou put her arm round Beverley and did her best to comfort her, as she might have comforted a small child, who had woken from a nightmare. 'Try to stay calm Beverley; John's gone to get your pen. You'll be okay in a minute.'

A fierce, blotchy, red rash began to spread over Beverley's face and down on to her chest. She clutched at her throat and began to scratch and claw the raw, itchy skin. Her eyes wide with panic, she started to gasp for air. She tried to speak, but her lips and tongue were swollen and her words were too slurred to be understood.

Victoria rushed over. She recognised the signs of a severe allergic reaction and knew they didn't have long to get adrenaline into her.

After what seemed like an eternity, John reappeared in the doorway, dishevelled and sweating profusely. 'I can't find the pen anywhere. It's not in her handbag or the suitcase.'

'Oh God Almighty!' Lou left Victoria supporting Beverley and ran towards the bedroom, pushing John aside to get in through the doorway.

Peyton watched from behind the dining table, her entire body frozen into inaction as she gaped in horror at the unfolding drama. Her face was a ghastly white mask. But as Beverley lurched forward in Victoria's arms, hugging on to her stomach, life seemed to surge back into Peyton. Colour flooded her cheeks and she raced into the bedroom after Lou.

'Can someone call Reception?' Victoria called out. 'Ask them if they've got an adrenaline pen. Tell them we need it urgently.'

Curtis was standing at the dining table, holding a spoon suspended over the plate of butter prawns. He quickly dropped it. The spoon missed the serving dish and clattered on to the table. A thick pool of red curry sauce spread across the white tablecloth. 'I'll go downstairs, it'll be quicker.' Without waiting for an answer, he raced into the entrance foyer and out of the front door, slamming it closed behind him.

Beverley's body convulsed in Victoria's arms and she began to vomit.

Patricia jumped up from the sofa. 'George! We need to do something! It's the nuts. She must have eaten some.'

Victoria shook her head. 'The only thing we can do is get adrenaline into her.' She looked towards the bedroom door. 'We need her EpiPen, quickly.'

'I don't know what's taking them so long!' Patricia pushed past Victoria and Beverley and headed into the bedroom. 'There's always one in Beverley's handbag!'

Victoria felt Beverley's body squirm in her arms. She was clutching her stomach and Victoria suspected that the cramps had started. She glanced across at the tan, leather armchair in front of the French doors. 'Tim, can you come and help me move your mother on to the sofa.'

Tim stared at her uncomprehendingly.

'I need you to come and help me, Tim,' Victoria said, more loudly.

The firmness in her voice seemed to rouse him from his stupor. 'Sorry, yes, of course.'

As he and Victoria manhandled Beverley, in small increments, around onto the sofa, Beverley's breathing became more and more laboured, rasping as she fought for a gulp of air. She tried to speak, but Victoria stopped her. 'Keep your energy, Beverley. We're doing everything we can.'

Beverley's face began to swell up like a balloon, until her eyes were little more than small slits. Gently, they lowered her on to the sofa and Victoria saw the rash was starting to disappear and her face was beginning to turn pale. She wouldn't last much longer without adrenaline. Victoria felt her pulse. It was extremely fast; a sign her system was starting to shut down. She knelt down beside Beverley and tried, futilely, to make her more comfortable.

Then she heard the sound of footsteps outside, thundering along the landing. The noise shook Nick out of his daze. He jumped up from where he was sitting, frozen, with his dinner plate on his lap, and rushed to the front door. As soon as he flung it open Mario and Curtis appeared, out of breath, in the entrance foyer.

Mario raced forward and quickly surveyed the room. Seeing Victoria, he dashed towards her, holding an EpiPen out in front of him.

As he approached, Victoria stood up and slowly shook her head. 'I'm afraid it's too late.'

Forty

Patricia's shrill voice broke the numb silence in the room. 'But I don't understand how this could have happened! I heard Beverley on the phone, telling them she was allergic to nuts. How could the hotel have ignored something like this? They're putting people's lives in danger!'

Mario took a little step forward, his face flushed with indignation. 'Madam, I can assure you most strongly, the hotel does not ignore requests of this sort. We have never had an error like this occur at Raffles Hotel in all the time I have been here. We have many guests with dietary requirements, including allergies, and my staff have always met, if not exceeded, our guests' expectations.'

Tim threw himself back down into the tan armchair. There was a smile of grim sarcasm on his lips. 'Well, they didn't meet them today, did they?'

John sank onto a dining chair, his face a mask of incomprehension. 'Tim, there's no need for that. We're all very upset, but this was obviously a genuine mistake.'

Mario inclined his head with a small nod of gratitude. 'It is a grave mistake that I give you my word we will get to the bottom of, Mr Marsters.'

'What's the point?' said Tim, in a tone of cool contempt. 'There's nothing to get to the bottom of. Your chefs put nuts in my mother's food and now she's dead. It's pretty simple.'

'That's enough, Tim.' John turned to his son, the leaden hue of his complexion conveying the sorrow absent in his words. 'We are all in shock, but there is no need to take your anger out on Mr Fabrizio. What has happened is not his fault.'

'Then whose fault is it?' Tim said. 'They charge a fortune to stay here and they can't even get the food right. It's not exactly value for money, is it? They should be charged with murder.'

Tim shrank moodily back into his armchair.

Eleanor's clear, measured voice broke the mute awkwardness that followed. 'It seems odd to me that no one could find any of Beverley's adrenaline pens. I would have thought she would have kept them somewhere obvious.'

'She always did,' John said, the emotion in his voice catching as he spoke. 'We put two packs in the suitcase when we left England and Bev had another pack in her handbag. I can't understand why they aren't there.'

'She must have swapped handbags,' Kate said. 'Didn't she go out, this morning?'

'We've searched all her bags.' Lou stared at John, her eyes dull with bewilderment. 'And the suitcases.'

Kate shrugged her tense shoulders. 'Then she must have moved them and not told anyone.'

Victoria was only half-listening to the buzz of conversation in the room. The rest of her attention was fixed on a dark, mahogany side table, sitting in the centre of the room, between the blue sofa and a plush velvet armchair. It was a simple, elegant table with a curved top and tapered legs that sunk deep into the blue carpet. Victoria bent down and ran her finger over a cluster of small crumbs near one of the feet.

On top of the table a thick coffee table book entitled *The Romance of the Grand Tour:100 years of Travel in South East Asia* had been pushed to one side and a glass full of white wine sat next to it, with a faint stain of pink lipstick on the rim. Underneath a plate of food, balanced on one end of the table, a few more small crumbs were visible, similar to those Victoria had found on the floor. She wetted the tip of her forefinger with her tongue and tasted one of the larger crumbs.

'Maybe Beverley left her EpiPens out somewhere,' Patricia said. 'The cleaners might have taken them when they serviced the room. They probably wouldn't have known what they were. They may not even have them here in Singapore.' She took a tissue from the bosom of her dress and dabbed at her eyes. 'It's all so upsetting; I knew we should never have come here.'

Victoria looked at the white porcelain dinner plate lying face side down on the carpet beside the table and the claypot chicken and chilli crab splayed out around it. She slowly shook her head. 'I don't think the cleaners are to blame. I think someone deliberately removed Beverley's EpiPens.'

Patricia turned to Victoria with a sour frown. 'Who on earth would do something like that? Everyone knows Beverley needs her pens, in case she has an attack!'

'Exactly,' Victoria said. 'And if they couldn't be found, then Beverley wouldn't recover from such an attack.'

Patricia stared at her, dumbfounded. 'So why would someone take them?'

'Because someone didn't want Beverley to recover from an attack.'

Patricia looked mystified. 'But why would someone in the kitchen not want Beverley to recover? It doesn't make any sense!'

'It wasn't someone in the kitchen,' Victoria said. 'It was someone in this room. Somebody put crushed nuts into Beverley's food—you can see a few crumbs lying here on top of the table and on the floor. I imagine Beverley must have left her food unattended, while she went and refilled her wine glass. I think when all the food is examined, the only traces of nuts that will be found will be in the food that was on Beverley's plate.'

Patricia drew her chin back into her neck, like a turtle retreating into its shell. 'But why on earth would anyone put nuts in Beverley's food? We all know she's allergic!'

'The nuts were put in her food because someone wanted her dead,' Victoria said. 'Beverley's death wasn't an accident. She was murdered.'

Forty-One

Victoria stood for a moment on the edge of her balcony, staring out at the black arc of the moonless sky, suspended high over the bright lights of the city's skyscrapers. She drew in a deep breath, the oppressive night air catching in her throat. How could she have been so wrong? Her mind drifted back to Beverley's contorted body lying on the sofa in the Padang Suite and the crumbs of crushed nuts on the wooden table. If it *was* murder, it blew her theory about the kidnapping completely out of the water.

She turned her back on the courtyard and glanced across the balcony, into the dining room. The Commissioner of Police sat watching her, with his elbows resting on the mahogany table and the passports of all the dinner guests laid out neatly in front of him. Light from the chandelier above, caught the puffy bags of skin beneath his eyes, casting dark, circular shadows across the tops of his cheekbones. Three distinct frown lines creased his forehead. And yet, the high arch of his brows, the thin laugh lines at the corner of his narrow eyes and the permanent upward curve of his lips gave his middle-aged face a boyish appearance—despite his thick crop of greying hair.

Victoria was pleased he had decided to personally take charge of the case and appreciated his suggestion that he use her suite as a base for his enquiries. She was keen to keep Peyton shielded from prying eyes for as long as possible.

The Commissioner raised his hands, pressing the tips of his fingers together to form a small pyramid. 'So, tell me who you think is behind this murder?'

'*Alleged* murder,' Victoria reminded him. 'We still have to prove that's what it was.'

The Commissioner folded his fingers down and drew his clasped hands closer to his face. He shifted his chin a little to one side and smiled. 'I have complete faith in your instincts, Victoria. If we hadn't listened to you this time last year, I don't believe that small problem we had with the Chinese would have gone away as quickly as it did.' He spread his thumbs wide. 'So let us assume for now that it *was* murder. You said the staff didn't go near the table, where you found the peanut crumbs; which means it had to be one of this lot, who put them into her food.' He nodded at the array of passports on the table. 'Any idea which one of them did it?'

Victoria shook her head. 'I'm afraid not. I did have some ideas on the kidnapping, but Beverley's murder has changed all of that.'

There was a light tap on the living room door. The Commissioner called over his shoulder, 'Yes?'

The door opened and a young woman entered. She held a white mask and pair of surgical gloves in her hand. 'Excuse me, sir. We've found a jar of mixed nuts in the rubbish bin in the guest bathroom and a few crumbs on the floor. We're checking for fingerprints and a match on the crumbs. We also found the EpiPens. There were four of them; all submerged in a vase of flowers in the master bedroom. We're checking the vase and table for fingerprints.'

The Commissioner nodded. 'Thank you. Let me know if you find anything else.'

The young woman left the room, quietly sliding the door closed behind her and the Commissioner turned back to Victoria. 'You see, your instincts are proving to be correct. It would seem we *are* investigating a murder. I don't imagine those nuts got into the rubbish bin or the EpiPens got into the vase by themselves.' He leaned back in his chair and tapped the tips of his fingers together. 'The question is, how does Beverley Marsters' murder tie in with her son's kidnapping?'

Victoria exhaled deeply, shaking her head. 'I have absolutely no idea. I can't see any link between the two, at all. If the kidnapper was involved and intended it to be a warning to make the ransom payment, they would surely have sent another message. Why kill her and make it look like an accident? That doesn't make any sense.'

'And yet, it seems too much of a coincidence for there not to be a link.' The Commissioner pushed his chair back and stood up, straightening the tail of his blue tie under his jacket. He moved across to the French windows. 'What about the husband? Could he be behind the murder?'

Victoria smiled. 'I don't think he'd be able to pull off a murder without the whole world knowing. He's more Johnny English than James Bond.'

The Commissioner's eyes narrowed as his lips curved upwards into a grin. 'He wouldn't be the first bumbling fool to successfully pull off a murder—which isn't to say he would get away with it. Oh, excuse me.' He pressed his hand against the breast pocket of his jacket. 'That's my phone vibrating.'

He pulled out a black Samsung and answered the call. Victoria couldn't hear the other side of the conversation, but she garnered enough from the Commissioner's side to get the general gist. 'You're quite sure? You've checked all the cameras? Absolutely nothing? What about yesterday? What time was that? Yes, if you could. No, that's all for now. I'll let you know if I need anything further.'

The Commissioner placed the phone back into his pocket and walked slowly towards the table. He stood facing Victoria with his hands resting on the back of a dining chair. 'You were quite right; there is no footage from today of James Winstanley on any of our security cameras. The last image we have of him is from yesterday afternoon. Which suggests—'

'That he is still here in the hotel.'

The Commissioner nodded. 'Precisely.' He slapped his hands decisively down on the back of the orange leather chair. 'Which means, before we do anything else, we need to go and find this young man.'

Forty-Two

Mario greeted Victoria and the Commissioner at the entrance to the Tiffin Room with a firm handshake. He summoned the maître d'hôtel. 'Yati, if you could please take care of my guests and show them to a private table. They are short of time, so if you could make them comfortable, as quickly as you can.' With a gracious bow and an outstretched arm, he gestured for Victoria and the Commissioner to follow Yati into the dining room. 'I will join you just as soon as I have the information you require. In the meantime, please enjoy our special Indian buffet as my guests.'

Yati and Mario exchanged brief nods of mutual understanding as he departed. Yati then turned to Victoria and the Commissioner with a warm smile. From her deferential manner, it was clear she had comprehended Mario's desire that his guests be treated with the utmost attention. She led them to a table in the far corner by the window, separated at a sufficient distance from the other diners for their conversation not to be overheard.

As her two charges settled into their seats, Yati removed a white napkin from the centre of Victoria's place setting and with a deft flick of her wrist, unravelled it. She laid the napkin across Victoria's lap. 'Can I offer you something to drink, Miss West?'

'A bottle of sparkling water would be wonderful, thank you Yati.'

'And for you, sir?' Yati asked, unfurling the Commissioner's napkin in the same skillful manner.

'A Coke-Cola.' The Commissioner smiled across the table at Victoria. 'Don't tell my wife, she hates me drinking the stuff.'

Victoria laughed. 'Your secrets are quite safe with me.' As soon as Yati left them, she pushed her chair back and laid her napkin on the table. 'Please excuse me if I go straight up to the buffet. I haven't had a chance to eat properly all day. If I don't get something substantial into me soon, I'm going to pass out.'

The Commissioner rose from his seat. 'I think I'll come and join you. I can't claim to have eaten as little as you, today.' He patted the small paunch that protruded from his otherwise slim figure. 'But it's not often that I get to dine at Raffles Hotel, courtesy of the management.'

Victoria smiled. 'You won't regret the extra calories; the food is very good. I can vouch for that.'

She made her way directly to the array of curries laid out on the marble display table. She took a plate from the warmer and heaped a large spoonful of steamed white rice into its centre. On either side, she added a large spoonful of Gosht Korma and Kolhapuri Baingan Masala. Everything smelled delicious, but she settled on just the two dishes, along with some freshly baked and piping hot roti.

The Commissioner filled his plate with the Dhaba Chicken Curry and a large helping of Subz Biryani, along with an enormous array of pickles and chutneys.

The drinks they had ordered were waiting on the table when they returned; the Commissioner's cola in a frosted glass filled with ice, and the bubbles in Victoria's water still fizzing, with two thin slices of lemon.

They reassumed their seats and ate for some time in silence. Victoria savoured every mouthful, briefly forgetting about the task that lay ahead of them. The roti was flaky and melted in her mouth; the lamb was so tender it almost fell apart on her fork and the eggplant in the Kolhapuri Baingan Masala had soaked up the rich flavours of coconut and sesame seed to perfection. She began to feel revived and the faint headache that had been developing all afternoon, started to slowly recede with each mouthful.

When the Commissioner finished his plate, he patted the edges of his mouth with the white napkin and glanced towards the lobby. 'I might just have time for a quick bite of dessert. Another thing my wife never lets me have. Can I get you something?'

Victoria pushed her empty dinner plate to one side. 'No, I won't have any dessert, thank you. But I might come up with you to get some more curry.'

She followed him up to the buffet table. Having not eaten properly all day, she was surprised at how hungry she still was. She filled her plate with dal and a generous helping of mixed vegetables, cooked in a delicious-sounding saffron and cashew nut sauce.

The Commissioner rejoined her at the table with a sheepish grin and a large bowl, overflowing with fried milk dumplings cooked in a saffron and sugar syrup.

He was halfway through his gulab jamun, when Mario reappeared in the dining room. He hurried across to their table, wielding a handful of printouts on sheets of white copy paper. He presented the bundle to Victoria with a triumphant flourish. 'A full list of our current guests, along with the rooms they are each occupying. And, of course, we are at your disposal, if there is any further information you require on any one of them.'

Victoria pushed her half-finished plate of dal and vegetable curry to one side and laid the sheets out in front of her. She ran her forefinger down the column of names. There was nothing of interest on the first page and she progressed onto the second. Halfway down, her finger stopped on the entry beside the Noel Coward Suite. She glanced up at Mario. 'Which is the Noel Coward Suite?'

'It is one of our personality suites. It is located in the courtyard, overlooking the fountain.'

Victoria handed the sheet across to the Commissioner. 'It's halfway down the second page.' She turned back to Mario. 'Has the room been checked into?'

Mario took the sheet from the Commissioner and traced his finger down the column of names. 'Yes, the room was checked into on Monday—two days ago. Checkout is tomorrow.'

The maître d'hôtel approached the table and handed a small slip of Raffles Hotel notepaper to Mario. He unfolded it and ran his eye over the brief contents. 'It is the answer to your other request, Miss West. There have been four rooms our housekeeping staff have been unable to service today, due to requests for privacy.' He handed the short list to Victoria. 'The Noel Coward Suite is one of them.'

The Commissioner held his spoonful of milk dumpling and sugar syrup suspended over his plate and glanced across at the note in Victoria's hands. She raised her eyes and met his gaze with a small nod.

He quickly put the spoonful of dessert into his mouth; then picked up his napkin and wiped it across his chin. 'I suppose we'd better get up there and take a look.' He folded the napkin and placed it neatly down on to the table beside his plate. Casting a wistful glance at the uneaten dumplings, he turned to Mario. 'Perhaps you would be good enough to show us the way.'

Forty-Three

Mario hastened his pace to keep up with the longer strides of Victoria and the Commissioner, as they made their way across the white, marbled floor of the lobby. He scampered on ahead and led them up the Grand Staircase to the second floor landing. Victoria and the Commissioner were ascending a few steps behind him, both lost in their own silent thoughts.

Victoria was still puzzled and frustrated. It just didn't make any sense. The kidnapping and then the murder. They had to be two pieces of the same puzzle, yet, for the life of her, she couldn't think how they fitted together or even if they fitted together at all. Why send Beverley a ransom demand and then kill her?

They reached the top of the first flight of stairs and Mario turned left, taking them towards the swing doors leading outside onto the landing. He took hold of the brass handle and pulled the door back for them to pass through. The Commissioner strode on a little way ahead and Mario slowed his pace, moving a step closer to Victoria. 'I really must thank you for everything you are doing, Miss West. Having you involved gives me great confidence that this terrible situation will be resolved quickly.' He glanced ahead at the Commissioner. 'Of course, I have complete faith in our police department, but you exonerated our chefs so quickly, I will always remain grateful to you for that. To think there was even a suggestion they were responsible for Mrs Marsters' death—it is beyond comprehension. We pride ourselves on getting these details correct. But you have proved beyond doubt that they were not responsible and that is not something we will forget quickly.'

Victoria smiled at his earnestness. 'Let us just hope everything else can be cleared up as easily.'

They made their way along the landing and Victoria removed her orange cardigan. The humidity seemed to be hanging in the air like a thick fog and the soft silk sleeves were beginning to feel claustrophobic against her skin.

She tied the cardigan around her waist. They continued walking along the landing and she let her gaze drift out over the hotel, becalmed against the night sky. There was no sign of the moon and in the blackness, the muted lighting of the hotel felt oddly serene and comforting. She looked down into the courtyard below them and smiled at the unhappy faces of the sculptured fish in the cast iron fountain. She could sympathise with them.

The Commissioner hesitated midway along the landing, and turned to look back at Mario; his erect figure framed by the black silhouette of a frangipani tree.

Mario pointed along the balcony behind the Commissioner. 'The Noel Coward Suite is behind you. It is the one with the lights showing.'

Small squares of yellow light shone through the dark, wooden frames of the suite's French windows. The other rooms along the landing were in darkness. Victoria conjectured that the occupants were still out at dinner.

She continued on, until she was standing in front of the Noel Coward Suite. The curtains were pulled tightly together and she could see nothing inside; just the bright light shining through the white netting. She turned her attention to the rectangular brass plaque on the door frame. The number '254' was etched in black, inside a small frame above the doorbell. The 'Do Not Disturb' light glowed red in the centre. There was no sound coming from inside.

She turned to Mario. 'Do you have the key?'

He nodded and fished a tan, leather keycard out of his pocket. He hesitated a moment, before handing it to her. 'Perhaps, you would prefer that I open the door?'

Victoria smiled. 'I think it might be safer if I do that—we don't know what we're going to find inside.'

She glanced across at the Commissioner. He gave her a small nod and she stepped forward to press the doorbell. They both stood for a moment in silence and listened. Still, nothing.

Carefully, Victoria placed the key on top of the circular Raffles Hotel logo above the brass door handle. The click of the lock releasing was clearly audible in the uneasy silence. She took the sleeve of her cardigan and wrapped it around the tip of the door handle, being careful to avoid disturbing any fingerprints. Then, very slowly, she pulled the lever down and pushed the door inwards. There was no resistance from inside, so she continued pushing until the door stood fully open.

She stepped into the small parlour inside the doorway. On the highly polished, round table to her left, a fruit bowl and platter of brightly coloured sweets had been pushed to one side. A laptop and black leather satchel, with a few sheets of loose paper spilling out of it, filled the cleared space. Peeping out from beneath one sheet, she noticed the shiny, black edge of a mobile phone.

Through the shuttered doorway in front of her, she could see into the brightly lit bedroom. A brown overnight bag emblazoned with Louis Vuitton motifs lay open on the wooden bench, at the foot of the bed. The bed itself was unmade, with a few items of clothing strewn on top of it. Poking out from underneath the bed was a man's black leather, lace-up shoe.

Victoria took another cautious step forward, until she was standing framed between the two white shuttered doors separating the small living room from the bedroom. The acrid, musty smell of blood reached her nostrils before her gaze fell on the full horror of what lay hidden behind the dividing wall.

A small table was overturned in the corner and lying splayed out amongst the scattered red roses and shards of glass, was the bloodied, lifeless body of James Winstanley. He was dressed in dark jeans and a blue shirt with thin white stripes. The cuffs were rolled up to just above his wrists and the neck was open, unbuttoned low on his chest. The shirt was drenched in blood. On the wooden floorboards, beside his right hand, lay a knife with blue stones embedded into the ornate handle. Its short blade was stained red with blood.

Forty-Four

Victoria crouched down over the body and looked closely at the wound in the lower part of James' neck. It was only a thin puncture but judging from the amount of blood, it had hit his carotid artery. A thick, dark pool had coagulated on the floorboards directly beneath the wound, and red flecks had spattered on to the cream walls. Death would have come within a few minutes, possibly faster. There was no doubt it had been unexpected. His final moments of horror and disbelief were stamped for all eternity onto his dead features.

The Commissioner strode across the room and stood beside Victoria, his eyes locked on to the dead body at his feet. 'Our kidnapping victim?'

Victoria pressed her hands onto her thighs and stood up. 'Yes. With a nasty looking stab wound in the neck.'

The Commissioner looked across to the half-packed bag on the bench and around at the rest of the bedroom. 'There doesn't seem to have been much of a struggle. It looks as if he was taken by surprise.'

'He's not the only one. This was the last thing I expected to find, when I came in through the door.' Victoria looked through the open shutters into the small entrance parlour. 'There doesn't seem to be any sign of a forced entry, either. Which suggests James let his killer in.'

The Commissioner absently rubbed his thumb and forefinger over his shaven jaw and nodded. 'Given the murder took place in here, he must have felt comfortable enough bringing them into the bedroom.' He crouched down beside the body with his elbows resting on his knees. 'An unusual-looking murder weapon.' He glanced up at Mario. 'Do you sell these as souvenirs in the hotel?'

Mario gingerly craned his neck over the Commissioner's shoulder. He grimaced. 'No. We don't have anything like that for sale.'

'Tim Marsters has one exactly like it,' Victoria said. 'He's James' half-brother. I remember seeing him with it, last night, just before we went in for dinner.'

The Commissioner raised his arched eyebrows. 'An unusual thing to take to dinner; I don't imagine Raffles is short of cutlery.' He moved around behind the body and surveyed the blood splatters on the wall and across the floor; then stood looking at the knife lying beside James' hand. 'I'd say he pulled that out himself, which means if our murderer was clever, they could have got away without getting any blood on them.' He went across to the half-packed overnight bag at the foot of the bed and riffled through the neatly folded clothes packed inside. Then his gaze fell on a pen lying on the floor, beneath the bench on which the Louis Vuitton bag was sitting. He bent down for a closer look. 'Mr Winstanley certainly likes his labels. And this one here, doesn't come cheap; these are a few thousand dollars each.'

Victoria went over to have a closer look at the pen. The calligraphic logo of Montegrappa was finely etched into the top of the blue cap. On a thin gold band at the bottom, the word Winstanley wrapped around the barrel with three, seemingly unrelated 'C's engraved ornately into the background. Victoria gave a wry smile. 'It's easy to have expensive taste when it's not your own money you're spending.'

The Commissioner nodded. 'Yes, money is a lot easier to part with when you haven't had to work hard for it.' He straightened up. 'Right, well, we'd better get forensics over here. The quicker we get the job done, the quicker we can have this mess cleaned up. Then I think you and I had better go and have a little chat with Tim Marsters.'

He took his phone from his pocket and moved into the parlour to make the call. Mario followed hard on his heels, his complexion still pale.

Victoria cast one more look across at the body lying on the floor, then very slowly, made her way around the rest of the bedroom. Nothing appeared to be out of place, aside from the dishevelled bed. A white duvet lay in a crumpled heap on the floor, the sheets and pillows were rumpled (interestingly on both sides) and one of the complimentary water bottles sat, half-empty, on the bedside table.

She went into the adjoining en suite. Smudges of dried, soapy water had left marks on the vanity's white marble top. But there were no personal items on display. The complimentary soap lay unwrapped in the glass dish and a wooden comb from the vanity pack sat in the bottom of the silver rubbish bin. Victoria knelt down beside it and examined three long strands of dark hair entwined in the teeth—female hair, judging by the length.

She stood up and moved across to the bathtub. Thin, soapy remnants of dried bubble bath, mixed with body hair, formed dirty clusters in the base of the tub. On a high gloss, black stool beside the bath, two champagne flutes rested beside an empty bottle of Billecart Salmon. One of the flutes had the clear markings of a woman's faded lipstick on the rim.

Beside the bath, two white towels lay in a pile on the floor, along with a Raffles Hotel robe. Victoria crouched down beside it and bent her head close. The unmistakeable scent of Chanel No. 5 lingered in the robe's silk fabric.

Forty-Five

The Commissioner walked slowly away from the Noel Coward Suite with his head bowed and his hands clasped behind his back. He glanced across at Victoria. 'Of course, Chanel No. 5 is not an unusual fragrance. I remember my wife used to wear it, around the time we got married.'

'No, it's not unusual,' Victoria agreed. 'But Kate de Brouwer is the only wedding guest I've noticed wearing it.'

'Well, it won't take too much effort to prove if it was her in the room—*if* she denies it when we interview her.' The Commissioner stretched his arm out and checked his watch. 'Given that it's now nearly midnight, I think we'll deal with Tim Marsters, then call everyone together in your suite. I'll let them know about Mr Winstanley's death tonight, but we won't start interviewing everyone until first thing in the morning. You and I need to get some sleep.'

Victoria nodded. 'Yes, my jetlag is starting to catch up with me. A good night's sleep is definitely in order. And we've found James, so we don't need to rush around looking for him, anymore. Also, I think it's going to take us a while to get to the bottom of these murders. We're going to need to pace ourselves.'

The Commissioner gave a small chuckle. 'I never thought I'd hear those words come out of your mouth.'

Victoria's lips curved into a faint, teasing smile. 'There's always a first time for everything.'

They continued on along the landing until they reached the Palm Courtyard. Victoria began to check the suite numbers beside each of the dark, wooden door frames. She consulted the note she had made on her iPhone and then glanced at the far end of the landing. 'I think Tim's room is the last one here.'

The Commissioner followed her gaze along to the last set of French windows, the darkened panes revealing no sign of life inside.

They paused briefly at the front door and listened. Hearing nothing, Victoria stepped forward and pressed the doorbell. The hollow ring echoed loudly in the still night air. They waited for a moment. Nothing stirred inside. Victoria reached out and pressed the bell again.

After a few moments, a dim light appeared behind the curtains. Then there was a loud crash.

'Shit!' In the stillness, Tim's exclamation reached Victoria and the Commissioner with extraordinary clarity.

The Commissioner grimaced. 'Do you think we woke him up?'

Victoria laughed. 'Yes, I think we might have done.'

For a moment, there was no other sound. Then the scrape of a lock turning in its metal cage broke the silence. The door swung open.

Tim Marsters stood, blinking, in the doorway. Dressed in a pair of navy boxer shorts, his pale chest and protruding ribcage looked almost ghost-like, framed against the dull light of the entrance foyer.

The Commissioner stepped forward, holding out his identification. 'Commissioner of Police, Mr Marsters. I believe you know my colleague, Miss West. Do you mind if we come in?'

Tim shrank back, darting a confused glance at Victoria. His fingers remained firmly grasped around the metal handle on the door. 'Why, what is it? What do you need to come in for?'

'We would like to speak with you for a moment, regarding your brother.'

Tim's long fingers tightened around the door handle. 'Have you found him?'

The Commissioner nodded. 'Yes, we have. But I'm afraid the news is not good, Mr Marsters. Your brother has been found murdered.'

Tim's eyes widened, his enlarged pupils adding to his spectral appearance. 'Murdered?' His pale face lost every vestige of expression as he turned his uncomprehending gaze on Victoria.

The Commissioner stepped past him, into the foyer. 'Yes, that is correct, Mr Marsters. Stabbed with a knife, which I believe, belongs to you.'

'Knife?' Tim let go of the door handle, and taking a step backwards, turned to look at the Commissioner. 'What knife? I don't know what you're talking about!'

The Commissioner took out his mobile phone from the breast pocket of his jacket. He unlocked the screen and tapped on the camera icon. 'This is your knife, is it not, Mr Marsters?' He turned the phone around so that Tim could see the bloodied image.

Tim stared at the screen. 'Yes, I have a knife like that—'

'May we see it, Mr Marsters?'

'Yes—yes, of course.' Tim felt around on the wall behind him for the light switch. 'It's in the wardrobe in the bedroom.'

They passed through the adjoining doorway and the Commissioner turned his attention to the empty bed. 'You are alone at the moment, Mr Marsters?'

Tim nodded. 'Yes, Zara is still upstairs with the family. I needed some time by myself, so I came back down here. I must have fallen asleep. I thought it was her at the door.' He scratched his thick crop of wiry, red hair as he walked, unsteadily, across to the large mahogany wardrobe.

He bent over and pulling open the low cupboard doors, reached down towards a set of three small drawers. As he pulled out the top one, his body stiffened. 'It's not here!' He stared at the empty drawer; then began frantically searching the other two. 'I don't understand. It was in here this morning—'

The Commissioner walked slowly and deliberately towards Tim. He stood with his six-foot frame looming over Tim's hunched figure. 'Perhaps, Mr Marsters, you could give us an account of your movements today.'

Tim straightened up. 'Why do you want—' He stopped abruptly, his brown eyes widened. 'You can't be suggesting I had anything to do with James' murder?' He gave a sudden, harsh laugh. 'Why would I use my own knife to kill someone? That would be pretty stupid.'

The faintest trace of a smile twitched on the Commissioner's lips. 'Murder is not an especially intelligent act, Mr Marsters. Now, perhaps you will give us an account of your movements today.'

Tim slumped down on to the bench at the end of the bed. He picked up a green t-shirt lying on the floor and pulled it on. 'We went down for breakfast at about quarter to eight and then we left again just after eight thirty. We came straight back here; then at about eleven o'clock, Zara went to the gym. She got back around midday. After that, we caught a taxi down to Orchard Road—Zara wanted to go shopping. We got back here, sometime after three, I guess, that's when we heard about the kidnapping. Then, we spent the rest of the afternoon with Mum and Dad in their suite.'

'When was the last time you saw your knife?'

Tim hesitated. 'It would have been this morning, I suppose, when I showed it to Uncle George.'

'And you kept it in this drawer?'

'Yes, but I only bought it yesterday. Zara put it in the drawer. She didn't like looking at it.'

'Has anyone been in your suite, other than yourself and Miss—' The Commissioner pulled a small notebook from his pocket and flipped it open to the front page. 'Avery-Smythe. Either after dinner in the restaurant, last night, or this morning?'

Tim nodded. 'Yes, Aunt Patricia and Uncle George came back with us after breakfast, this morning. My aunt wanted to borrow one of Zara's magazines. Then, just after that, my parents and Lou called in, on their way to Sentosa.'

'And was the knife in the drawer, this whole time?'

'No, I took it out to show Uncle George. He has a collection of Gurkha knives, so he was interested in seeing it.' Tim glanced at the phone in the Commissioner's hand. 'It's a Yingjisha knife. They're famous. Anyone who knows about knives has heard of them.'

'And where did you put the knife, once your uncle had finished looking at it? Back in the drawer?

Tim shrugged. 'I don't know, Zara might have done. I didn't see it, later on, so she probably did.'

The Commissioner moved away and stood with his back to Tim, his tall figure silhouetted against the bright light of the table lamp in the corner. He remained silent for a moment and then turned around to face Tim. 'Did you leave your suite at all, while Miss Avery-Smythe was in the gym?'

Tim shook his head. 'No, I didn't.'

Victoria moved towards the end of the bed where Tim was seated. She was intrigued. Despite the chill from the air-conditioning, a dark patch of sweat was slowly enlarging under the armpits of his t-shirt. She walked past him and sat down on the small stool in front of the dressing table. 'You and your brother had your differences, didn't you?'

Tim sat up a little straighter. 'Yes. But no more than any other family.'

'Did you ever threaten to hurt your brother?'

'No!' Tim's desperate gaze darted between Victoria and the Commissioner. 'Look, I didn't do anything, okay? I know it looks bad with my knife, but—I didn't kill anyone.'

'But you did threaten your brother with the knife, yesterday, didn't you?'

Tim's pale, freckled complexion whitened.

Victoria watched him closely. 'Your altercation with James in the courtyard, last night, was captured on camera. So you *did* threaten him and with the same knife he was murdered with.'

The colour flooded back into Tim's cheeks. 'Well—yes, but it wasn't serious. I mean . . . it was just a joke. I—I wasn't going to do anything.' His head fell into his hands. 'Jesus Christ!' He jerked his head back up and looked pleadingly at the Commissioner. 'Look, I'm telling you, I didn't do anything. You have got to believe me.'

The Commissioner replaced his phone and notebook into the breast pocket of his jacket. 'We will let the evidence speak for itself, Mr Marsters.'

Forty-Six

A shiver of pleasure ran through Victoria, as she stepped back outside onto the landing and felt the warm blanket of the humid night air envelope her. Tim's suite had been freezing. How anyone managed to sleep in such frigid conditions was beyond her.

She set off along the landing with a long, purposeful stride, the Commissioner almost having to run to keep up with her. She glanced across at him. 'Could you give me half an hour, before we call everyone together? I'd like to go and tell Peyton what's happened; I don't want her hearing about it through the grapevine. It's going to come as an awful shock to her.'

The Commissioner nodded. 'Of course. I'll go and brief my team while you're doing that. I want to get everyone's room searched tonight, just in case we can find any more fresh traces of blood.' He rested his gaze on Victoria. 'Are you quite sure you wish to tell your friend? You wouldn't rather that one of my officers broke the news to her?'

Victoria shook her head. 'Thank you, but I think she'd appreciate it if I told her.'

The Commissioner smiled. 'Yes, I'm quite sure she would. Although it won't be easy.' They reached the staircase that led down into the Palm Courtyard and the Commissioner stopped. 'Right, I'll part company with you here then and see you in your suite in about forty-five minutes?'

'Perfect.' Victoria extended her hand towards him. 'And thank you. I appreciate everything you are doing. I know how busy you are.'

The Commissioner's boyish face broke into a smile. 'The pleasure is all mine. And I am very appreciative of you taking time out of your holiday to assist me. It's not often that I get the chance to work alongside someone of your calibre. I wouldn't have missed this opportunity for the world. Besides, I'm rather enjoying being back in the cut and thrust of police-work. Being at the top of the tree now, I'm generally stuck behind a desk, most days.' He tapped his small paunch. 'And my wife tells me I need to stop sitting around so much.'

Victoria laughed. 'I'm sure she'll be very happy then, to see you back out in the field. I'll see you shortly.'

Victoria stayed on the small verandah jutting out over the courtyard and watched the Commissioner dash across the strip of green lawn towards the lobby. She needed a few moments by herself to collect her thoughts. Telling Peyton about James' death was not going to be easy and she wanted to think of the kindest way to break the awful news to her.

She settled into one of the rattan armchairs overlooking the courtyard. For a moment, she sat motionless and stared out at the night sky, thinking of nothing but the shock imprinted on James' lifeless face and the knife wound in his neck. With a heavy sigh, she leaned her head against the large, white, concrete pillar beside her.

As she stared out into the blackness, a flash of orange lightning lit up the horizon. Without thinking, she started to count. It was a habit she had got into, as a young child, when her father had told her that you could calculate how far away the lightning was, by the number of seconds it took for the thunder to arrive. Four seconds passed and a loud clap exploded above the hotel like a salvo of cannon fire.

In the midst of the short, thunderous rumble, Victoria heard a woman's startled cry behind her. She turned her head and watched two silhouettes emerge from the shadows on the landing. Light from one of the teardrop lanterns fell on them and illuminated the figures of Lou Farmer and John Marsters. Lou had one hand clasped around John's arm.

She tossed her dark bob away from her face and laughed. 'Oh my goodness, that gave me such a fright. I wasn't expecting it.'

In the still air of the impending rainstorm, her crisp voice carried over the landing with striking clarity.

John put his thick, chubby hand comfortingly on top of Lou's and smiled. 'It's this tropical climate. The electrical storms are brought on by the heat.'

Lou gave a gentle sigh. 'And it has been exceedingly hot today.

They both stopped in front of the dark, wooden door of suite 203 and stood facing each other. John took both of Lou's hands into his own. 'You mustn't worry about anything.'

'But what am I to say to the police? I imagine they will want to interview all of us, tomorrow?'

'Just tell them you didn't see anything at dinner. That's all they will be interested in.'

'But what about Tim? You know what he's like. He is bound to say something.'

'I'll have a word to him. Don't worry, Lou, Tim's a good lad. And everybody will tell the police the same thing—that you were a loyal secretary and good friend to Beverley for forty years.' John patted the back of Lou's hand. 'Now try to get some sleep. This will be all over in a couple of days and we'll be on a plane back to England.'

Even in the low evening light, Victoria could see Lou's usually placid expression was anxious.

'I do hope so,' Lou said. She unclasped the silver catch on her handbag and fished around for her key. Passing the magnetic, leather card over the lock, she paused for a moment with her hand resting on the door handle. She turned to John and smiled. 'I'll see you in the morning.'

As the door closed behind her, Victoria pulled her head back and remained perfectly still as John's slouching figure passed along the landing behind her. She watched his retreating back, until he faded into the distant shadows. Then she turned her attention back to the courtyard.

Another flash of lightning lit up the night sky, so close this time, that she could smell the sweet, pungent scent of the ozone. Then almost immediately, single, large droplets of rain began to fall. Sparkling in the lantern light, they bounced off the concrete balustrade in front of her and evaporated on the hot floorboards at her feet.

The deluge that followed, quickly engulfed the droplets. Victoria shifted her feet back as solid sheets of water started to fall, splashing on the floorboards at the front of the small verandah and drenching the courtyard, below. Victoria closed her eyes and breathed in the rain's warm, earthy smell.

Forty-Seven

Victoria stopped in front of the tall, double doors of Peyton's suite and drew in a deep breath. The intensity of her tiredness finally hit her. She felt completely drained. The last three months in Africa had been exhausting. The results were fantastic, better than she had dared to hope for. But the work had been gruelling and she was in desperate need of a break.

She had envisaged spending a week lazing by the pool on Raffles' rooftop terrace, with only her book for company. But that was no longer going to happen. Her dream of solitude was shattered and her week would now be spent solving not one, but two murders. And on top of that, she needed to tell her friend that the man she loved was dead—stabbed in the neck with his brother's knife.

There was no gentle way she had been able to think of, to break such a brutal piece of news. She would have preferred the police to do it. But she couldn't put Peyton through that. She remembered how upset Peyton had been, after her parents' car accident. The least she could do, as a friend, was be here for her when she found out about James' death.

She glanced across at the doorbell and gave a small, involuntary shrug. There was nothing to be gained by delaying; she might as well get on with it. As it was, she was probably only going to get about five hours' sleep. Cutting it any shorter would only make her feel worse.

She stepped across to the other side of the doorway and pressed the bell.

It took a few minutes before she heard any movement inside. When the door finally opened, she was relieved to see Bill's smiling face behind it.

'We thought it might be you,' he said. 'Come on in.'

Despite the warmth in Bill's greeting, Victoria could see the sadness in his eyes and her heart ached for him. She knew how much he doted on his granddaughter—he was so proud of Peyton.

Bill closed the door softly behind her. 'Is there some news?'

Victoria slowly and reluctantly nodded her head. 'Yes there is. But it's not good, I'm afraid.'

Bill rested his hand on the dark wooden top of the antique console table beside him, steadying his ninety-one-year-old frame. Yet, the gaze he fixed on Victoria was as firm and determined as she had ever known it.

'Has James been found?' he asked.

Victoria met his gaze with a small nod. 'We've found his body.'

A movement over her shoulder caught Victoria's attention. She turned and looked behind her.

Peyton stood in the hallway, both hands clasped around a glass of water. With an awful vacancy in her eyes and a terrible stillness in her voice, she repeated Victoria's last words. 'His body . . .'

The glass of water slipped from her grasp. It bounced on the thick pile of the carpet in the entrance foyer and rolled to one side, the contents spilling over the cream and beige pattern in a creeping dark stain. Peyton's eyes ceased to focus on Victoria. The colour drained from her face and her body sank heavily forward.

Victoria rushed towards her and with Bill's help, managed to catch her before she fell. Together, they manhandled Peyton's dead weight into the living room, lowering her down onto a sofa.

Eleanor hurried over and sat beside her granddaughter. Gently, she tilted Peyton's head forward until it was resting between her knees.

After a few moments, Peyton began to squirm. Eleanor rubbed her hand soothingly across Peyton's back. 'Just relax, my love, and keep your head down. You have just fainted; we need to get your blood flowing again. Take deep breaths.' She looked up at her husband. 'Bill, could you have a look in the pantry to see if there's some soda in the fridge? Her blood sugar must be low. She hasn't eaten a thing since breakfast.'

Bill gave a quick nod and disappeared with a fast, loping stride down the hallway.

Eleanor stroked Peyton's long, blonde hair and pulled it back, out of her eyes. Slowly, Peyton raised her head. Her face was ghost-pale. She shivered and Eleanor took Bill's grey blazer from the back of the sofa, laying it tenderly over her shoulders. She held the jacket in place until Bill returned to the sitting room.

'Here you go, sweetheart.' Bill tore the tab off a can of Coca-Cola and handed it to Peyton. 'Try to get some of this into you.'

Peyton took hold of the can in both hands and shakily raised it to her lips. As she sipped the sugary liquid, a hint of colour gradually began to return to her cheeks. She fell against the back of the sofa, squinting at the dim light from the table lamp. 'I don't know what happened. I've never fainted before.' She pressed the heel of her hand against her temple. 'I still feel quite light-headed.'

Eleanor soothed Peyton's hair. 'It's probably a combination of the heat, my love, and a lack of food, and all the stress you have been under.'

Peyton stared at the can of Coco-Cola she was cradling in her lap. Then very slowly, she raised her eyes and turned to look up at Victoria. 'Can you tell us what happened?'

'The police are on the scene now,' Victoria said. 'They're trying to piece everything together.'

'But what happened? How did he—' Peyton took a deep gulp of air to quell a sob rising in her throat. 'How did he die?'

Eleanor placed her hand tenderly on top of Peyton's. 'Oh, sweetheart, let's wait until you're feeling a bit stronger. Then Victoria can tell us everything.'

Peyton shook her head firmly. 'I'm okay.' There was a hint of defiance in her voice. 'I want to know.'

Victoria knew it was futile to try and avoid giving her an answer. When Peyton was determined to have something, she wouldn't give up until she'd got it.

'He was stabbed,' Victoria said. 'The wound is in his neck. It looks as if the knife hit his carotid artery. Death would have been very quick; he wouldn't have suffered.'

Peyton's fingers tightened around the red label on the can, the pressure of her grasp creating deep indentations in the aluminium. A tear rolled slowly down her cheek and dripped onto her hand. She wiped the sleeve of her blouse over her wet eyes. 'Where did you find his body?'

Victoria hesitated. Peyton was clearly in shock from the news of James' death. She didn't want to add to her distress by mentioning any details.

She decided to stick to the simple facts. Everything else could come out later, when Peyton was feeling stronger and better able to cope. 'He was found here in the hotel, in the Noel Coward Suite. We got a list of all the hotel guests from management and found the Noel Coward Suite was booked under James' name; although at this stage, we're not entirely sure why. But that was what prompted us to check the room.'

Peyton looked up. 'That was the room we had booked for James to stay in, tonight.' Tears filled her blue eyes and her words came out in short bursts, between the sobs she tried in vain to suppress. 'We thought it would be more romantic if we didn't spend the night before our wedding together.'

Victoria took a tissue from the box on the coffee table and handed it to Peyton. 'How many nights did you have the room booked for, can you remember?'

Peyton wiped her eyes and nose with the tissue. 'It was just for tonight. He was going to check into it this afternoon, after we'd met up with John and Beverley.'

Victoria moved across to the French doors and stared out into the blackness. The rain shimmered in the light from the teardrop lanterns, but beyond the balcony, she could scarcely make out anything in the haze of the downpour. She turned back to Peyton. 'James checked into the room, two days ago. Do you have any idea why he would have done that?'

Peyton shook her head. 'No, we only had it booked for tonight. Up until now, we've both been staying in here.'

Victoria nodded. She could surmise why James had extended the booking without Peyton's knowledge. But the question was: who, besides Kate de Brouwer, knew about it?

Forty-Eight

The Commissioner stood erect beside Victoria, his eyes fixed keenly on the guests assembled in her dining room. They stared at him in horrified silence. As the news of James' murder sank in, Victoria ran her gaze around the dining table, her attention moving rapidly from one face to another.

Zara had both hands clamped over her mouth with tears welling up in her eyes. She turned to Tim. 'Oh my God, they've killed him!'

John slumped heavily forward on the mahogany table. Slowly, he turned to look at Lou, his pallid face a pitted effigy of disbelief. Lou placed her hand on top of his, giving it a comforting squeeze.

Kate sat motionless in her chair. She addressed the Commissioner and yet, seemed oddly wrapped up in her own thoughts. 'Have you caught the person who did this?'

The Commissioner shook his head. 'No, not as yet.' He cast his eye over the guests. 'We are considering the possibility that whoever is behind Mr Winstanley's murder is also responsible for the murder of Mrs Marsters.'

Nick's eyes shot wide open. 'You said *we* were all under suspicion for Beverley's murder. Which means you think one of us killed James, as well?'

'One of us!' Patricia's shrill voice pierced the stillness. 'Why would one of us murder James and Beverley? That's ridiculous!'

George stiffened a little in his chair. 'I'm afraid I would have to agree with my wife, Commissioner. I think you might be barking up the wrong tree, here. It's a bit far-fetched to think anyone sitting around this table is a murderer.'

The Commissioner gave him a polite, half-smile. 'It would be nice to think that that is the case, Mr Helstone. However, it is highly improbable that an outsider put the nuts into Mrs Marsters' food, this evening. On that basis, we will need to search each of your rooms, tonight.' He paused, contemplating the startled faces turned in his direction. 'We appreciate that this is a very difficult time and everybody is tired. My staff will work as quickly as possible in order to allow you all to get some sleep. Tomorrow, I will begin interviewing each of you, individually.' He turned to Victoria. 'I believe you all know my colleague, Miss West. She has an extensive background in high-level security work and has very generously offered to work alongside me, during the investigation process.' Eight astonished faces turned from the Commissioner to look at Victoria. 'I would ask that you give her your full cooperation. And please, while our inquiries are underway, no one must leave the hotel without my personal permission—or attempt to leave the country.' He glanced at the stack of passports sitting on the marble shelf. 'We will continue to hold onto your passports and our officers will be stationed outside your rooms, overnight—'

'Outside our rooms!' Patricia's high-pitched indignation overrode the Commissioner's measured tones. 'We are hardly going to go anywhere in the middle of the night. We are not common criminals!'

Curtis shifted in his chair, wrapping his long fingers around the thin, mahogany arms. 'Perhaps they're being put there for our protection. After all, there is a murderer on the loose.'

Zara let out a small screech. 'Oh my God, I never thought about that!' Her eyes darted around the dining table. 'Do you think there's a chance they could strike again?'

Isabelle reached a languid hand out for her cigarettes. She threw a stinging glance across at James' family. 'I doubt we will be that fortunate.' She turned to face the Commissioner. 'You are welcome to begin searching my room. I have nothing to hide and I never go to bed early.'

The Commissioner extended a deferential nod in her direction. 'Thank you, Madame Sauveterre—'

He left the rest of his sentence hanging, his attention drawn to the sound of footsteps hurrying across the wooden floorboards in the entrance hall. He threw a puzzled glance at Victoria, but before she had a chance to move, the living room door flew open and Peyton appeared, flushed and agitated, in the doorway.

She stood, breathless, staring at the guests with her fists clenched and a look of fury in her eyes. 'I know one of you killed James!' Her face quivered and her voice trembled with passion. 'I loved him so much. Whichever one of you did this, I will never forgive you. I hope you hang!'

Forty-Nine

The morning sun appeared fleetingly behind the feathered edges of a raincloud and streamed into the Tiffin Room, casting long shafts of silver light over the breakfast tables.

The Commissioner dug his teaspoon into a small jar of strawberry jam and lathered it generously on to a hot, flaky croissant. He folded the soft pastry in his fingers and grinned across the table at Victoria. 'I'll have to put myself on a diet, once this case is over.' He eyed Victoria's large plate of tropical fruits. 'That's exactly what my wife would be eating; she'd never touch anything like this.'

Victoria smiled as she stabbed her fork into a thin slice of beautifully ripe papaya. 'If it makes you feel any better, I've got an omelette on the way. And then I fully intend to finish off with a plate of French cheese.'

'Oh yes, I spotted the cheeses—they were right next to the pastries.' The Commissioner added another dollop of strawberry jam to his last morsel of croissant, and popped the whole lot into his mouth.

He was dusting the buttery crumbs from his fingers when a waiter glided across the dining room towards them. With an elaborate sweep of his arm, he set a large, white dinner plate down in front of Victoria. 'Your omelette, Miss West.'

Victoria glanced down at the perfectly smooth oval shape, formed like a large madeleine cake, in the centre of her plate. The edges were browned to perfection, with sprinklings of red chilli and green coriander on the top. The mozzarella cheese was just beginning to ooze from the centre. She smiled. 'Thank you, Daniel, it looks perfect.'

The waiter inclined his head; then pivoted towards the Commissioner. 'And for you, sir.' He placed two golden waffles, dusted with icing sugar, down on the table in front him. 'The Belgian waffles.' He took a small step back from the table. 'Bon appétit.'

The Commissioner's eyes glittered. He quickly busied himself with the jug of maple syrup and the small bowl of berry compote, pouring both over his breakfast. Then, with a satisfied smile at the result, he dug his knife and fork into the crispy batter. 'This is certainly a step above the hawker stall I go to, in the mornings.'

He proceeded to eat his first triangle of waffle, washing it down with large mouthfuls of black coffee. He then began work on the second. Only when the sprig of mint from his berry compote remained, did he lay down his knife and fork.

He gave his stomach a satisfied pat and leaned back in his chair with a deep, contented sigh. 'That was delicious!'

Victoria took a sip of her cold mango juice and smiled at his empty plate. 'There is nothing quite like a good American breakfast to set you up for the day, is there?'

'There certainly isn't. Speaking of America—' the Commissioner slipped his hand inside the breast pocket of his jacket and pulled out a small notebook. 'We checked the passports of all the wedding guests and two of them could have sent that anonymous letter from New York.' He flipped his pad open to the first page. 'Zara Avery-Smythe was there for the weekend of the fourteenth and fifteenth and Nick de Brouwer arrived on the twelfth. He left again on the eighteenth.'

Victoria paused, with a forkful of omelette midway to her mouth. 'Did he? That's interesting. When I asked them about the letter, his wife said neither of them were in New York, last week.'

The Commissioner drew his arched eyebrows together. 'Is that right?' He took the napkin from his lap and dabbed the edges of his mouth. 'It seems to me Mrs de Brouwer has a few things she needs to explain to us.' He placed the napkin down on the table and looked at his watch. 'I think we might get her in for a chat first.'

Fifty

Victoria threw her handbag down onto a chair in her living room and glanced around. Housekeeping had been, while she was at breakfast. Everything looked tidy.

She walked into the dining room and opened the French doors, letting the warmth of the tropical air envelope her. She stepped outside. The rain had started falling again in earnest. But at least the downpour had taken the edge off the humidity; it was still hot, but no longer oppressive.

She stood on the balcony, gazing out at the rain. Its melodic patter shrouded the hotel in a cone of silence.

Enjoying the peaceful solitude for a moment before the Commissioner returned with Kate, her mind drifted to the pool, upstairs. She loved swimming in the rain, when it was hot—it was the ultimate tropical pleasure. It always felt exotic, yet cosy at the same time.

She pushed the thought from her mind and straightened the skirt on her Vivienne Westwood suit. It was best not to think of the things she would rather be doing than interviewing murder suspects. Especially at 9 a.m. in the morning! Still, on the upside, at least the murders happened *before* the wedding. That was one blessing. She dreaded to think of the fallout for Peyton if they had occurred *after* they'd tied the knot and had made a public announcement. The media would have had a field day.

She heard the sound of her front door close, followed by the thud of the Commissioner's heavy tread on the floorboards. Fastening the buttons on her yellow tartan jacket, she stepped back inside, closing the French doors behind her.

Kate de Brouwer entered the dining room ahead of the Commissioner. She stopped abruptly, the moment her gaze fell on Victoria.

Victoria was struck by her haggard appearance. Despite a heavy layer of makeup, Kate's usually flawless English skin looked tired, marred by red blemishes on her cheekbones and shadows under her eyes. Her dark hair hung lank and dull, over her shoulders. The candy pink of her snugly fitting t-shirt did little to brighten her worn out— and Victoria suspected, hungover—state.

The Commissioner stepped into the dining room, beside Kate. He pulled out one of the dining chairs and gestured for her to take a seat. 'Please, Mrs de Brouwer, make yourself comfortable.'

Kate stepped cautiously forward, keeping her eyes fixed on Victoria. She lowered herself into the chair.

The Commissioner moved around to the other side of the table. 'Perhaps Mrs de Brouwer, we could start with you giving us an account of your movements yesterday.'

'Of course.' Kate shifted around in her seat, so that she was facing the Commissioner. 'My husband and I went down to the Tiffin Room for breakfast, just after seven. We left at about eight and Nick went off to play a round of golf, while I returned to our suite. At about half past ten, I went up to the pool. I stayed there until just before one. I went back to our room after that, and waited for my husband to return. We then went down to the lobby together for afternoon tea, at about two. That's where we heard the news about the kidnapping. We went straight up to see John and Beverley and stayed with them in their suite until about five o'clock. Then we went back to our room to get ready for dinner. At seven thirty, we joined everybody in the Padang Suite and after that, we were escorted back to our room by the police.'

The Commissioner pulled out a chair opposite Kate and sat down. 'Did you leave the hotel at all, yesterday?'

Kate shook her head. 'No, I didn't.'

'Yet you told your husband you were going out shopping after breakfast?'

A brief flicker of uncertainty flashed in Kate's eyes. But it passed in an instant and she gave the Commissioner a small, self-assured smile. 'I was going to go out shopping. But it was so hot yesterday, I couldn't face the prospect of walking around town. So after my husband left for golf, I decided to stay here and go up to the pool, instead.'

The Commissioner's relaxed demeanour became more earnest. 'What about Mr Winstanley; did you see him at all yesterday?'

Kate nodded. 'Yes, we saw James at breakfast.'

'You didn't see him again after that?'

'No. Like I said, I went straight back to my suite after breakfast.'

The Commissioner leaned forward, his elbows resting on the table. 'I understand you spent some time with Mr Winstanley in the Noel Coward Suite yesterday. Can you tell us what time that was?'

Panic flared momentarily in Kate's eyes. She darted a watchful glance across at Victoria. 'The Noel Coward Suite?'

Victoria moved across to the dining table and sat down beside Kate. 'Yes. James' body was found in the Noel Coward Suite. It's possible you were the last person to see him alive.' She paused, smiling at Kate's resolute silence. 'I smelt your perfume in the bathrobe. We also found some long, dark hair and a ring of lipstick on one of the champagne flutes. It wouldn't be too difficult for us to run a DNA test on them. And, of course, you provided a fingerprint sample when you arrived at Changi airport. Assuming you were in the room, it won't take forensics long to confirm a match. So it would be best if you were honest with us.'

Kate's gaze darted frantically between Victoria and the Commissioner. 'I didn't kill him!'

The Commissioner gave her a dry smile. 'We are not suggesting that you did, Mrs de Brouwer, we are simply trying to gather the facts.' He leaned back in his chair, resting his elbows on the delicate mahogany arms. 'What time were you in the Noel Coward Suite with Mr Winstanley yesterday?'

Kate eyed him cautiously. 'I couldn't be sure, exactly. It was probably about nine o'clock. I left again at around ten thirty. James had to be at a meeting in Marina Bay by eleven.'

'And did you go straight up to the swimming pool, when you left him?'

'No, I went back to my room to get changed, first.'

The Commissioner rose from the table and turned to the marble shelf behind him. 'When you were in the Noel Coward Suite with Mr Winstanley, did you see this knife, at all?' He picked up a sheet of paper and placed it down in front of Kate.

She stared at the image. The silver blade and ornamental handle were smudged red with James' blood. She shuddered. 'No, I didn't.'

The Commissioner slid the sheet of paper a little to one side. 'Did your husband know you were having an affair with Mr Winstanley?'

Kate spun round to face the Commissioner. 'No, he didn't. Surely, that's not something he needs to find out about.'

The Commissioner thrust his hands into his trouser pockets and walked along to the far end of the dining table. 'Is it possible that your husband saw you with Mr Winstanley, yesterday?'

'No, he was out playing golf.' Kate stopped and stared at the Commissioner. 'Oh my God, you don't think—' she darted a horrified glance across at the image of the knife. 'You're not suggesting Nick had anything to do with this?'

The Commissioner rested his fingertips on the edge of the table. 'How long had you and Mr Winstanley been in a relationship?'

Kate gave a deep, uncomfortable sigh. 'We weren't *in* a relationship. James had been going through a tough time this year, with Peyton pushing him to get married. He wasn't sure it was the right thing to do, but he didn't want to let her down. James and I have been friends for a long time and he needed someone to talk to. I suppose one thing led to another—neither of us meant for it to happen. Then things came to a head when we got down here. James was worried about his son—'

'His son?' Victoria sat forward in her chair. 'James has a son?'

'Yes, but Peyton would never let him talk about it. So to keep the peace, we never mentioned anything around her. James was hoping she would come around, closer to the wedding. But she never did and he didn't know what to do. That's what he wanted to talk about, yesterday, and the reason I went to see him.'

'Had you and James met before in the Noel Coward Suite?' Victoria asked.

Kate nodded. 'Yes, a couple of times.'

'Did anyone else know he was using the room?'

Kate shook her head. 'Not as far as I know. He didn't want Peyton finding out he'd extended the booking.'

Victoria pushed her chair back and stood up. 'Can you tell me why you lied about Nick being in New York, last week?'

For a split second Kate froze, her eyes glued on Victoria. But she quickly covered her hesitation with a small laugh and shrugged. 'Oh—I had forgotten he went there. We've both been so tied up with work, over the last few weeks, we've scarcely had time to swap notes.'

'Yet, Nick didn't correct you when you said it?'

'We didn't think it was important. It was just about some silly letter.'

The Commissioner walked around behind Kate. 'Mrs de Brouwer, how much do you know about your husband's business dealings with Winstanley & Marsters?'

Kate's nonchalant tone became more cautious. 'In what way, do you mean?'

'Has he ever mentioned anything to you about the company being in financial problems?'

Kate shook her head. 'No, but then Nick isn't involved with the financial side of their company. He's a lawyer, not an accountant. If they were having problems in that area, I doubt he would be aware of it.'

'But surely, as a lawyer, one of his key responsibilities would be to ensure the company's affairs comply with all regulatory standards, including that of solvency and segregation of client funds. As the owner of a hedge fund company, I would have thought you would have a clear understanding of that.'

Kate's cheeks coloured. Her gaze dropped to her hands, clasped tightly in her lap. 'Yes, of course. I—I thought you were referring more to the company's day-to-day cashflow management, which would be something the accountants would handle. If it was something more serious, then yes, lawyers would likely get involved.'

The Commissioner drew his notebook across the table towards him and glanced down at his notes. 'Does the name Nigel Delamore mean anything to you?'

Kate hesitated for a moment. 'No, I don't think it does.'

'Your husband has never mentioned the name?'

'Not that I can remember. Why?'

'Nigel Delamore is employed by the Serious Fraud Office in London. There is a distinct possibility that Winstanley & Marsters is running a Ponzi scheme. Mr Delamore has been tasked with the job of investigating the allegations. I understand your husband was a little unsettled, when the name was mentioned to him, earlier.'

Kate's clasped hands tightened in her lap. She repeated the words as if to herself. 'A Ponzi scheme?'

The Commissioner raised his arched eyebrows. 'That doesn't come as a surprise to you?'

Kate glanced up at him. 'Yes—yes, of course, it does. They wouldn't be involved in something like that.'

'What about your husband? Is it something he might be involved with?'

Kate's eyes widened. 'Nick?'

'Yes. I understand he has a close working relationship with Winstanley & Marsters. A complicit lawyer would certainly be advantageous to running such a scheme.'

Kate's mouth fell open. 'Nick's not that stupid. He wouldn't get involved in something like that.'

The Commissioner smiled as he moved towards Kate. 'Let us hope for your sake, and his, that you are right.' He placed his hand on the back of her chair. 'Well thank you Mrs de Brouwer, you have been very helpful. I don't think we need to detain you any longer.'

Kate rose from her chair and turned to go. But Victoria stopped her before she reached the doorway. 'Sorry Kate, there is just one small thing I forgot to ask you. You're vegetarian, aren't you?'

Kate turned back with a puzzled frown. 'Yes, I am.'

'Do you eat seafood? Or are you a strict vegetarian?'

Kate's gaze darted between Victoria and the Commissioner. 'I don't eat seafood, no.'

Victoria smiled. 'I didn't think so. Sorry to have held you up. We'll come and find you, if there's anything else we need.'

Fifty-One

The Commissioner closed the door carefully behind Kate. With his hand still resting on the handle, he turned, with a raised eyebrow, to Victoria. 'Seafood?'

The mixture of boyish curiosity and scepticism in his voice made Victoria laugh. 'Yes, seafood. And I suspect that was one thing she wasn't lying about. Kate de Brouwer *doesn't* eat seafood.'

The Commissioner narrowed his eyes and cocked his head a little to one side. 'Is there some significance in that?'

'There could be.' Victoria walked over to the French doors and threw them open. Heat always helped her to think—her brain seemed to freeze up in the cold. 'The night I arrived, we all had dinner together in La Dame de Pic. It was a set menu that was primarily seafood. But everything they served to Kate was vegetarian. Yet last night, at the buffet dinner in John and Beverley's suite, I noticed she had chilli crab on her plate.'

The Commissioner gave a shrug. 'She might have mistaken it for something else. Perhaps she thought it was tofu. That never looks like anything in particular—it never *tastes* like anything in particular, either.'

Victoria laughed. 'I can't disagree with you, there. But unfortunately, all of the dishes had nametags on them.'

The Commissioner scratched his thick mop of neatly cropped hair. 'So you're wondering what a vegetarian was doing with chilli crab on her plate?'

'Exactly.' Victoria stepped outside onto the balcony. Her gaze drifted along to a pigeon sheltering in the corner from the rain. Its deep-throated cooing pulsated hypnotically in the stillness. She watched it for a moment, thinking back to dinner in the Marsters' suite and Kate de Brouwer standing in the doorway. As hard as she tried, she couldn't remember what other food there had been on her plate. She had only noticed the crab because of the red sauce. But Kate had seemed distracted. What had she been so preoccupied with that she hadn't noticed Victoria walking right in front of her?

Victoria turned round to face the Commissioner. 'If you wanted to put nuts in someone's food at a party, how would you go about doing it?'

The Commissioner took off his jacket and flung it over the back of an armchair. 'I suppose I would do exactly what the killer did. Have a few crushed peanuts in my pocket or in my handbag, and when the time was right, sprinkle them on the victim's food.'

'But you couldn't just sprinkle them on to the food could you? You'd have to mix them in.'

The Commissioner loosened his tie and undid the top button of his shirt. 'That would be easy enough to do with chilli crab. There's plenty of sauce to hide the crushed nuts in.'

'Except if you start playing around with somebody's food, there's a chance they'll see you.'

The Commissioner stepped out onto the balcony, rolling up the cuffs on his shirtsleeves. 'Sometimes murderers get lucky.'

'True. But what if the murderer didn't want to rely on luck? How else could they get the nuts into the victim's food?'

The Commissioner spread his arms out and shrugged. 'I have absolutely no idea.' He paused and smiled at Victoria. 'But I have a feeling you do.'

Victoria laughed. 'I've got a theory, but it's not much more than that.' She leaned against the back of one of the rattan armchairs. 'What if, instead of mixing the nuts into the food on the victim's plate, the murderer mixed the nuts into the food on their own plate and then swapped the plates over. The advantage being that if they got caught, it would be easy enough to pass it off as a simple mistake. People pick up the wrong glass all the time; why not the wrong plate?'

The lines in the Commissioner's forehead deepened. He nodded slowly. 'It's a good thought. It would be much easier to sprinkle nuts onto your own food. And as long as the two plates looked similar, switching them would be relatively simple. The killer just had to make sure they had the same food on their plate that Beverley Marsters had on hers.' He dug his hands into his trouser pockets. 'Which would explain why a committed vegetarian, such as Kate de Brouwer, would have seafood on her plate.'

'Precisely.' Victoria glanced inside at the clock on the bookshelf. 'What's the status of the Padang Suite at the moment? Has anything been moved in there?'

'No, forensics are still on the job. Nothing will have been moved as yet.'

'Then I think you and I should go over there and take a look. With a bit of luck we'll find two identical dinner plates.' Victoria lips curved into a smile. 'The killer might even have been generous enough to leave some fingerprints on them for us.'

Fifty-Two

Victoria walked through the entrance foyer of the Padang Suite into the parlour. Aside from the forensic staff conducting their painstaking search, it resembled the aftermath of a dinner party, with discarded wine glasses, napkins and dinner plates waiting to be cleared away.

She moved into the centre of the room and crouched down beside the white dinner plate on the floor, still lying face-down, where Beverley had dropped it the previous evening. Scattered chunks of congealed chicken, Chinese sausage, black mushrooms and white rice formed a messy halo around the edge. The sauce from the chilli crab had dissipated further afield and seeped into the thick pile of the blue carpet, staining the white lines of the geometric pattern red.

Using the tips of her fingernails, Victoria cautiously lifted the edge of the plate. Thick chunks of crab and pieces of coconut beef clung in a solid, coagulated mass to the underside of the porcelain. Gently, she lowered the plate back down and turned her attention to the small, wooden table beside her.

The glass of white wine, with the ring of pink lipstick on the rim, and the coffee table book, *The Romance of the Grand Tour*, hadn't shifted from where she had seen them, the night before. But there had been another plate sitting on the edge of the table which wasn't there

She stood up and cast her gaze about the room. Two dinner plates lay on a drinks trolley by the doorway, one piled high with Malay fish curry and butter prawns, the other with Sichuan pork, spiced lamb and vegetable rice.

215

She moved across to the French doors and a small writing desk tucked into the corner, with a beautiful Chinese lamp sitting in the middle; hand painted with delicate flowers in rich greens and oranges. A dinner plate sat perched precariously on the edge of the desk beside it, with spoonfuls of chilli crab, coconut beef and claypot chicken piled up in the middle. A fork lay on the plate beside the food, marked with a faint smudge of pink on the silver above the prongs. Victoria looked across to the wine glass sitting on the small, wooden table between the sofa and the velvet armchair. The ring of lipstick was the same shade of pink.

She cast her mind back to the previous evening and was trying to recall what colour lipstick each woman had been wearing, when the Commissioner strode into the room.

'Sorry about that,' he boomed. 'That was my office.' He delved into the breast pocket of his jacket and drew out his black Samsung. 'They've come across some interesting footage of Kate de Brouwer.' He began scrolling through his emails. 'She was captured by one of our security cameras on Bras Basah Road yesterday morning at 11.18 a.m., about twenty minutes before you saw her at the pool.' He turned the screen around, so Victoria could see. 'It seems she has something else to explain to us, other than a sudden liking for chilli crab.'

Victoria took the phone from the Commissioner and enlarged the image. It was clearly Kate de Brouwer standing at the intersection of Brash Basah and Beach Roads. She was wearing the same blue and green dress Victoria had seen her in, at the pool. She handed the phone back to the Commissioner. 'So she lied to us. She *did* leave the hotel yesterday.'

'It certainly looks that way.' The Commissioner returned the phone to his breast pocket. 'I've got my team looking into her exact movements, so we know where she went and what she did. We won't confront her until we've got all the information. But it is interesting that she only seems to have left the hotel briefly.'

'Just long enough to get rid of some blood-splattered clothing?' Victoria suggested.

The Commissioner smiled. 'Yes, very possibly.' He nodded at the writing desk beside Victoria. 'Have you found something?'

'Yes, I think this could be our identical dinner plate.' Victoria pointed to the fork sitting beside the food. 'There's a smudge of pink on here, which looks very much like the colour of the lipstick on the wine glass on the small, wooden table over there, between the sofa and the armchair. And if my memory serves me correctly, Beverley was wearing pink lipstick, last night.'

The Commissioner stepped forward and leaned over to get a closer look at the fork. 'We'll get them both tested for a match. And check both plates for fingerprints.' He straightened himself up. 'Of course, if Kate de Brouwer *is* our killer, and responsible for both murders, we need to ascertain how she got hold of Tim Marsters' knife.'

'Yes, I was thinking the same thing myself.' Victoria was beginning to contemplate the possibilities, when a knock on the door interrupted her thoughts.

They both turned to the young inspector standing in the doorway; her long, dark hair pulled back from her face in a neat ponytail.

The Commissioner stepped forward. 'Ah, Inspector Yew; come on in. We were just finishing up. I do hope you're having a bit more success than we are.'

The inspector entered the room and smiled, with stiff formality. 'I'm not sure about that, sir, but we have found a couple of things.' She pulled a small plastic bag from her folder. 'We found this under one of the pillows on the bed in the Noel Coward Suite. It looks like a yellow diamond, but we'll get it tested.'

The Commissioner took the bag from her and squinted at the large stone inside.

The inspector consulted her phone. 'We've checked with housekeeping and the sheets were last changed two days ago, on Tuesday morning. They didn't service the room yesterday on account of the 'Do Not Disturb' light being on.'

The Commissioner handed the bag to Victoria. 'Could belong to Kate de Brouwer.'

Victoria took the bag from him and scrutinised the diamond inside. 'I think you'll find that it belongs to Zara Avery-Smythe. She noticed a yellow diamond like this one, missing from her bracelet at dinner, on Tuesday evening. She was very upset about it.'

The Commissioner fixed a puzzled frown on the plastic bag. 'How would a diamond from her bracelet have ended up under a pillow in the Noel Coward Suite?'

Victoria raised an eyebrow at him.

The Commissioner's eyes widened. 'Surely, he hasn't had *both* women in there. He's only been in the country, a few days!'

Victoria smiled. 'I think James Winstanley had many faults, but I don't think being slow with women was one of them.'

The Commissioner gave a wry smile. Then he paused, drumming his fingers on the arm of the sofa. 'I suppose it does open up the possibility that this was a crime of passion. Kate de Brouwer or Zara Avery-Smythe might have gone into the affair with Mr Winstanley having unrealistic expectations; then felt aggrieved, when things didn't work out the way they expected. "Heav'n has no rage like love to hatred turn'd, nor hell a fury like a woman scorn'd."'

Victoria smiled. 'You know your Restoration drama. And Congreve probably was quite right. But I wouldn't discount the wrath of a betrayed husband or boyfriend. I can't see Nick or Tim being very happy about Kate or Zara having an affair with James. Although, I have no idea how that theory links in with Beverley's murder.'

'She may have known something, without being aware of it and the killer had to get her out of the way before the body was discovered and she put two and two together.' The Commissioner stepped away from the sofa. 'Or perhaps, she and her son were the original targets. Tim Marsters was very bitter towards the two of them. And if Nick de Brouwer is party to this Ponzi scheme, both Beverley Marsters and James Winstanley would have been aware of it. Removing them as witnesses to his involvement would be advantageous to him, if the whole business ended up in court.' The Commissioner turned to the inspector. 'I don't suppose you found the murderer's fingerprints on the knife?'

Inspector Yew shook her head. 'I'm afraid not, sir. There are no fingerprints on the knife at all; it must have been wiped clean. However, we have found something quite interesting with regards to Tim Marsters. We have found small traces of blood in the room he shares with Miss Avery-Smythe. I've asked for the samples to be tested, to see if there's a match with Mr Winstanley's.'

'Interesting. Let me know as soon as you get an answer on that.'

'I will, sir.' The Inspector consulted her phone again. 'Also, the pathologist has given us a very rough approximation of the time of death. Mr Winstanley was likely killed yesterday between eleven o'clock in the morning and one o'clock in the afternoon.'

The Commissioner glanced across at Victoria. 'About the time Zara Avery-Smythe left her suite to go to the gym.' His gaze fell to the plastic bag containing the yellow diamond. 'She knew about the Noel Coward Suite and she had access to the knife.'

Fifty-Three

Zara's slender hands trembled as she took the small plastic bag from the Commissioner. She fingered the diamond inside with the tips of her coral nails. Handing the bag back, she cast an anxious glance from the Commissioner to Victoria. 'Yes, I'm sure it's mine. Where was it found?'

The Commissioner straightened his tie and moved away from the dining table. He placed the plastic bag down on the sideboard and turned back to face Zara. 'It was found under a pillow on the bed in the Noel Coward Suite.'

Zara's eyes grew wide and her mouth fell open. A deep flush spread over her pale face, burning her cheeks blood red—her guilt inscribed into every crimson pore. She gaped at the Commissioner in mortified silence.

His expression softened. 'Perhaps, Miss Avery-Smythe, you could tell us when you were in the Noel Coward Suite?'

Zara's huge, round, unblinking eyes filled with terror. 'I—' Her voice failed her. She turned to Victoria in mute trepidation, unwilling or unable to say anything further. Victoria wasn't sure which.

The Commissioner picked up the image of the bloodied knife and laid it down in front of Zara. 'Do you recognise this?'

Zara let out a small gasp, clamping her hand over her mouth. 'That's Tim's knife.'

The Commissioner moved the sheet of paper a little closer to Zara. 'James Winstanley was discovered murdered in the Noel Coward Suite.' He tapped his forefinger on the image. 'This knife was found beside his body. Do you have any idea how it got there?'

Zara darted a horrified glance from the Commissioner to Victoria. Fear seemed to have struck her dumb.

Victoria went and sat down beside her. 'Zara, it's very important that you tell us everything you know. We'll get to the truth, eventually. But it would be much better if you told us what happened. We know it's difficult, so just try your best.'

Tears flooded Zara's eyes, but she swallowed them back and nodded. 'I went to see James, yesterday. I wanted to give him the knife.' She glanced down at the photo lying on the table. The tears she had been trying to hold back burst from her and she began to sob loudly.

Victoria took a tissue from the box on the table and handed it to her. 'Why did you want to give James the knife?'

'I'm not sure. I—' Zara wiped her wet eyes with the tissue, leaving a streak of black mascara on her cheekbone. 'I was worried about Tim. I thought—' she sniffed back fresh tears. 'I don't know—I thought he might do something stupid.'

'What sort of thing did you think he might do?'

Zara started to twist the tissue around her finger. 'James said I was being silly. He said Tim wouldn't do anything. But—I don't know— it's just . . . Tim kept saying how the knife could kill someone and he said James wouldn't believe him. I thought—I thought, maybe, Tim wanted to prove him wrong.'

'Did Tim know you had taken the knife?'

Zara shook her head. 'No. I took it out of the drawer while he was in the bathroom. I went straight to James with it—but I told Tim I was going to the gym.'

'How long did you spend with James yesterday?'

Zara twisted the tissue into a tight knot on her finger. 'Not very long. James said he was running late for a meeting and had to rush off. I only stayed for about five minutes. After that, I went to the gym.'

'What time was this?'

'It was just before eleven. I got back to our room at midday. I remember because Tim said we'd wasted the whole morning.'

'Is it possible that he saw you leaving the Noel Coward Suite?'

'No, he stayed in our room while I was out. He was asleep when I got back.'

Victoria stood up. She took the photo of the knife from the table and went across to the marble shelf with it. 'Other than yesterday, were there any other times you went to visit James in the Noel Coward Suite?'

Zara fixed her gaze on the tissue twisted around her finger. 'I went to see him on Tuesday afternoon, while Tim was at the museum with his father.'

'Do you think that's when you might have lost the diamond?'

Zara's long, red hair hung forward, partially covering her face, but Victoria could see her blushing cheeks beneath it. She gave a small, self-conscious nod. 'Yes, I suppose it must have been.'

'Is it possible Tim knew you and James were involved?'

Zara raised her head. A sad, bitter smile crept on to her lips. 'No, he was always too tied up with himself to worry about what I was doing.'

Victoria placed the photo of the murder weapon down on the marble shelf and went back to the dining table. 'When you were in New York, last week, did you send a letter to Peyton?'

Zara's restless fingers stopped playing with the tissue. 'A letter?'

'Yes. Someone sent an anonymous letter to Peyton, warning her not to come here and marry James. It was postmarked New York. Did you send it?'

Zara shook her head. 'No. I didn't. I'm sorry, it's the first I've heard about it.'

Victoria smiled. 'There's no need to apologise. You've been very helpful, Zara, thank you.' She cast a quick glance across at the Commissioner. 'I don't think we have any other questions for you, at the moment.' Stepping forward, Victoria gestured towards the doorway. 'Why don't I show you out?'

Zara rose from her seat. She cast an awkward, uncertain smile across at the Commissioner and then followed Victoria into the living room.

The sergeant seated in the entrance foyer jumped up as they approached, thrusting his mobile phone into his pocket. Victoria inclined her head in his direction. 'Sergeant Tong will show you back. We'll come and find you, if we need anything further.'

She closed the door behind Zara and slowly retraced her steps back along the short hallway to the living room, thinking over Zara's explanation of the knife. If what she said were true, it opened up a raft of new possibilities.

When she emerged from the hallway, she found the Commissioner settled back into the living room's long sofa, his feet propped up on the coffee table and his clasped hands resting on his stomach. 'What did you make of Miss Avery-Smythe?'

Victoria went across to the minibar and took out two bottles of cold mineral water. She handed one to the Commissioner. 'She was embarrassed, but I'm not sure if that was because she was having an affair or because she had committed a murder and thought we'd caught her out.'

'Or both,' the Commissioner suggested.

Victoria kicked off her black heels and sank down into the chair, tucking one leg up on to the soft, cream cushion. 'The timing on the diamond fits. If the sheets were changed two days ago, on Tuesday morning, and she lost it while she was in bed with James on Tuesday afternoon, then it makes sense that no one found it until forensics went in there, last night. The afternoon service wouldn't have been done on Tuesday, because James was in the room with Zara. He would have then spent that night with Peyton in the Presidential Suite, and not gone back into the Noel Coward Suite until yesterday morning, when he met Kate. He would have missed yesterday morning's service because he was with her. And they were in the bathtub together, so they probably never made it into the bed, which means he wouldn't have found it. And if he had, I'm sure he would have returned it to Zara. Then, the afternoon service didn't happen yesterday because the killer had turned on the 'Do Not Disturb' light.' Victoria leaned back in her chair. 'I am intrigued by her explanation of the knife, though. If she's telling the truth and she did leave it with James, then your theory about it being a crime of passion could be correct. It would rule out a pre-planned murder. The killer wouldn't have known they were going to find a knife in the room.'

'Unless, the killer was Tim Marsters—he may have seen her take it out of the wardrobe without her realizing it.'

'True. And given how readily Zara blushes, I don't imagine she's the best liar in the world. He might have had an inkling that something was going on between her and his brother.'

'In which case, he could have followed her. We only have his word for it that he didn't leave their suite, while she was at the gym. She didn't get back until midday; that would have given him enough time. And forensics have found traces of blood in their suite.'

'Yes; and if that matches James' blood, it'll be pretty damning evidence.'

Victoria unscrewed the cap on her water bottle and raised it to her lips. As she tipped her head back to take a sip, her iPhone began to vibrate on the wooden coffee table in front of her. Bee's name flashed up on the illuminated screen.

Victoria swallowed her mouthful and glanced across at the Commissioner. 'Excuse me as I take this; it's my colleague. She could have some more information for us.'

Fifty-Four

Victoria stepped outside onto the balcony to answer the call. She didn't speak immediately, but remained silent for a moment, listening to the soft opera music wafting down the line. After a few seconds, she decided. 'Mozart!'

A burst of laughter erupted from Bee at the other end. 'Very good, Victoria, I'm impressed. You're learning, at last.'

Victoria shifted one of the rattan chairs on the balcony further back under the verandah, away from the persistent downpour still saturating the courtyard. She threw herself down on to the soft grey cushion and laughed. 'It's not hard, you always listen to the same things.'

'Of course I do, I like to make it easy for you.' The music reached its crescendo in the background. 'So how's it all going down there?'

'Well, we've still only got two dead bodies, so not too bad, I guess, all things considered.'

Another burst of Bee's raucous laughter exploded from the phone. 'Christ, what a debacle! And I'm afraid it gets worse. I've done a bit of research on Nick de Brouwer for you. You said he was acting for Peyton as well as Winstanley & Marsters. I hope he wasn't holding any funds for her, because three weeks ago, he cleared out his Client Money Account. There were six million quid in there—money he was holding for a variety of his clients, by the look of things. He transferred the lot to Winstanley & Marsters. At around the same time, they transferred ten million dollars to Bankcorp in the US.'

Victoria leaned back in her armchair. 'That's interesting. They are the company Winstanley & Marsters are supposedly doing some big deal with. It's worth 450 million dollars, apparently. Although I find that hard to believe—it seems like a ridiculously large amount of money.'

'It certainly does. And not the sort of money Bankcorp would be capable of coming up with. I did a bit of research on them—they're pretty dodgy. There's an arrest warrant out for the husband and wife who run the show, but they seem to have scarpered.' Bee gave a small chuckle. 'It looks like Winstanley & Marsters have had the money stolen from them, that they stole from their clients. That's karma for you. But needless to say, if everything turns out to be as bad as it looks, then Nick de Brouwer is unlikely to see any of his clients' funds again. I'd say that six million quid has been completely lost.'

Victoria frowned. 'Yes, it certainly sounds like it. And that fits with an argument I overheard him having with his wife, on the night I arrived. She was suggesting he was in financial trouble.'

'I'd say that's an understatement. He'll be heading straight to jail, if he doesn't find six million quid in a hurry. His wife sounds pretty smart, though. I did a quick background check on her.' Victoria could hear Bee tapping on her keyboard in the background. 'She runs a successful hedge fund company in the City. And from what I can see, she keeps all her money and assets in a trust, separate from her husband. He has no financial interest in the place they've just bought in Hampstead. Perhaps, she knows he's dodgy.'

'Very likely—although she's playing her cards close; she didn't give much away, when we interviewed her.'

Bee laughed. 'I don't blame her. I'd be keeping my distance from a husband like that, as well. The last thing she needs is his downfall ruining her reputation.'

'Exactly.' Victoria tucked her legs up on to the chair. 'Which does make me wonder if she's trying to prevent his downfall. She's lied to us about a few things, one of which suggests she's trying to protect him.'

'I wouldn't waste my time trying to protect a husband like that; he's not even cute! Still, I suppose our choices are dictated by our options. Maybe in the financial circles she mixes in, there aren't too many better ones.'

'I don't think there can be; she's been having an affair with James, as well.'

'There you go; case in point. They're probably all as bad as each other. Oh, I got into James' Privatechat account for you, too. It isn't quite the impenetrable fortress they seem to think it is. I'll send you a link now, so you can have a look at what's in there. But interestingly, there seem to have been a few messages deleted in the last twelve hours. Which suggests I'm not the only one who's been looking at his account.'

'Is that right?' Victoria sat forward. 'I wonder who else has been.' She unfurled her legs and placed her feet back down onto the balcony's wooden floorboards. 'How easy was it to get into?'

'It was hard, but not impossible. I will give them credit for the set up. I haven't come across anything like it before.'

'Who would have been able to hack into it then, do you think?'

'It would either have to be someone very highly trained or someone involved in setting it up who knew what they were doing.'

'Someone like Curtis, maybe? How long do you think it would have taken him to get in?'

'Given that he helped build the system, I'd say three to four hours, maybe a bit longer.'

'Then I'd put my money on it being him. It's strange he hasn't said anything though, because we talked about it and I would have expected him to come and tell me, if he got in.' She pushed herself up out of the chair. 'I suppose I had better go and have a chat with him.'

There was a clank of china on the other end of the line, followed by Bee's clear voice. 'Then I'll let you get on with it, while I get on with my bowl of yoghurt and fresh figs.'

Victoria smiled, imagining Bee relaxing on her balcony, overlooking the Mediterranean, eating fresh figs. What she wouldn't have given to be doing the same thing herself! 'That sounds divine, Bee. Enjoy. I'll talk to you soon.'

Fifty-Five

Curtis ran his fingers through his messy blond hair. Victoria could see he was uncomfortable. His gaze shifted uneasily between her and the Commissioner. 'Yeah, I did manage to get into his account. But it was after midnight. I didn't think you guys would appreciate me coming to tell you about it, then.'

The Commissioner leaned against the marble shelf with his arms crossed and his gaze fixed firmly on Curtis. 'Mr Butland, we gathered everybody together at one o'clock, this morning. What prevented you mentioning it to us, then?'

Curtis tightened his grip on the arms of his chair. 'You said you wanted to interview us all separately, today. I figured we would discuss it then.'

Victoria left her position beside the French doors and moved across to the dining table. She was intrigued by his obvious discomfort. The day before, he had been eager to help and now he was being decidedly unhelpful, evasive, even. He was clearly trying to conceal something and she wanted to know what that was. 'Curtis, can you tell us about the messages deleted from James' account?'

For a moment, Curtis sat motionless, staring at Victoria. His furtive eyes scrutinised her face. 'How do you know about those?'

Victoria smiled. 'It's our job; it's what we do for a living. Now my guess is that you were going to wait until after midday before you came and spoke to us, because as I understand it, your platform has been designed to remove any trace of a deleted message after twelve hours. And because there's no way of telling exactly when a message was deleted, you were going to play it safe.'

The tension drained from Curtis' body. With a heavy, defeated sigh, he slumped in his chair, leaning his head against the leather backrest. 'Okay, you got me. That is exactly what I was going to do.' Slowly, he brought his head forward. 'I am so sorry, Victoria. I should have come and told you. I was stupid.'

Victoria pulled a dining chair out from the table and sat down. 'Why did you delete the messages? What was in them?'

Curtis' eyes widened. 'I have no idea; *I* didn't delete them.'

'You didn't?' Victoria darted a puzzled glance across at the Commissioner. 'Then who did?'

Curtis shrugged. 'I honestly don't know, but I assume it was Peyton.'

Victoria sat forward in her chair. 'Peyton?'

Curtis nodded. 'Yeah. After you and I spoke yesterday, I started trying to get into his account, but I hadn't cracked it by dinner-time, so I decided to have another go after dinner. Then everything happened with Beverley and I ended up staying with Peyton and her grandparents, until about eleven thirty. When I left, I told them I'd been trying to get into the backend of his account, and I was going to have another go. Peyton acted kind of weird then; but I put that down to everything that had happened. Anyway, it took me about another hour to get in, and when I did, I noticed some messages had been deleted from there. I figured Peyton must have had his password, and after I left her, she went into his account. I thought maybe there was something in there that she didn't want anyone to see – something personal – so she went and deleted it.'

Victoria stared at him. 'Curtis, this is a double-murder investigation. Withholding evidence from the police is a criminal offence. This is serious; you must have known that. Why didn't you come and tell us any of this?'

Curtis pushed his long fringe from his eyes. 'I figured if Peyton hadn't told you, it wasn't my place to say anything. She and I have known each other for almost fifteen years. If her fiancé had been murdered and she went into his account and deleted something, she wouldn't have done it lightly. I don't know what was in there; it could have been photos or something else that was personal. But whatever it was, she obviously didn't want any of us to know about it. It wouldn't have been anything criminal. She wouldn't have even thought about that.' He leaned his head against the back of the chair and gave a heavy sigh. 'You know, Victoria, she's been through enough. I guess I just wanted to protect her from any more questions. The faster she gets over James, the better. And there was nothing in the account that was vitally important.'

The Commissioner moved across to the dining table. Placing both hands firmly down on the polished mahogany top, he leaned forward towards Curtis. 'Mr Butland, it is admirable that you wish to protect your friend. But withholding information from the police is a serious matter, whether you believe it is important or not. We have seen what is in the account and have made our own judgement on that, but you are a suspect in the murder of James Winstanley and Beverley Marsters, and it is on that basis, that you are being questioned. If there is any other information you have not told us, I would strongly advise you to share it with us now. And please, let me remind you, the maximum sentence for murder in this country is death by hanging. It is not in your best interests, or in Miss Latchmore's, for you to withhold anything that is likely to interfere with our investigation.'

Fifty-Six

The Commissioner stood at the French doors, gazing out at the torrents of rain still falling in the courtyard. It amazed Victoria just how much water Singapore managed to absorb during such downpours. It always seemed as if they would never end; and then suddenly, the sun would break through and the freshly soaked city would bake under its scorching rays—refreshed by the deluge.

But today, the gloomy haze cloaking the city stubbornly refused to lift. A glimpse of the blue sky hidden behind the rain clouds remained a distant hope. And yet, Victoria knew that a breakthrough would eventually come. It always did.

The Commissioner turned away from the French doors to face her. 'I'm sure you won't want to think about this, but we do have to look at the possibility that your friend, Miss Latchmore, deleted those messages. I appreciate we only have Mr Butland's word at this point and he could very well be lying to protect himself, but it is something we do need to consider. If there are things she deleted, then it's possible she deleted them because they pointed the finger of suspicion towards her. She could have found out about her fiancé's affairs or the Ponzi scheme or him lying about his wealth. Any one of those reasons could have caused her to act in the heat of the moment and then attempt to cover her tracks.'

Victoria shook her head. She knew the Commissioner was right; they did have to consider Peyton as a suspect, but there was no way she could believe Peyton was behind the murders. 'I've known her since we were teenagers. She wouldn't kill someone out of jealousy or anger. That is not who she is.'

'Love can make people do very odd things. My wife tells me I'm evidence of that. Apparently there was no rational reason for marrying me.'

Victoria smiled. 'I'm sure there would be no rational reason for murdering you, either. Which is why I can't believe Peyton is our killer. She's too pragmatic. She wouldn't ruin her own life because her fiancé was unfaithful or had lied to her.'

'What about those deleted messages?'

'If there was something personal on there, then yes, I could see Peyton deleting them. She isn't stupid, but she is proud. She would be terrified of the press getting hold of anything. And she wouldn't want any of us seeing it either, especially Curtis.'

'Then why share something so personal on a business platform?'

'Because it was supposed to be completely secure. That's the whole point of Privatechat. Even the company can't access the messages.'

The Commissioner frowned. 'The perfect platform for criminals.' He sank down into a chair at the end of the table and pulled his notebook towards him. 'So where does this leave us? Putting your friend to one side for the moment, I can't say I would put murder past anyone, so far. Curtis Butland, Kate de Brouwer, Zara Avery-Smythe and Tim Marsters all have credible motives. And that's without considering the other—' He paused and looked down at his notes. 'Eight suspects.'

'Nine,' Victoria corrected him. 'You mustn't forget me.'

A sparkle of wry amusement lit up the Commissioner's face. 'I think if you were the guilty party, you'd be well out of the country by now and we'd be investigating an "unfortunate accident", not a murder.' He stretched his arm out and tapped his forefinger on the glass face of his Omega watch. 'I suppose we had better get a few more interviews in, before we break for lunch. What do you think?'

Victoria smiled. It was only 11.45 a.m.; she didn't feel in the slightest bit hungry after their enormous breakfast. 'I think that is an excellent plan.' She nodded at the list of suspects jotted down in the Commissioner's notebook. 'Who would you like to tackle next?'

'How about the lawyer, Nick de Brouwer? If he's in as much financial trouble as your colleague suggests, then he'd have had a very good reason for wanting to get his hands on the 60 million dollars. His golfing alibi might take him out of the running for James Winstanley's murder. But he and his wife could be in it together.'

As if reading the Commissioner's thoughts, Sergeant Tong poked his head into the living room, his earnest young face silently apologising for the intrusion. 'Excuse me, sir, Inspector Yew is wondering if it would be a convenient time for her to speak with you?'

The Commissioner nodded. 'Yes, of course, send her in. And then we'd like to have a chat with Nick de Brouwer.'

Sergeant Tong gave a small bow of acknowledgement. 'No problem at all. I'll go and get him.'

He stepped back into the entrance hall, making way for the inspector to pass. She smiled at Victoria and the Commissioner as she strode into the room. 'My apologies for interrupting again, so soon.'

'Not at all.' The Commissioner gestured to the chair opposite him. 'Please, take a seat.'

'Thank you, sir.' The inspector laid her phone down on the table. 'We've checked both dinner plates that you indicated for fingerprints.' She glanced across at Victoria. 'As you predicted, Beverley Marsters' prints are on both of them; although on one, some are a little smudged. But I'm sorry to say, there are no other prints on either plate.'

The Commissioner frowned. 'That seems odd.' He turned to Victoria. 'I suppose our killer could have used a napkin to handle them. I seem to remember there were a few in the room. It would explain the smudged fingerprints.'

'It would discount Kate de Brouwer though,' Victoria said. 'I noticed her nail polish while she was holding the plate. If she'd been holding it with a napkin, I wouldn't have been able to see her fingernails.'

Fifty-Seven

Sergeant Tong stood with his legs astride, in the middle of the living room. His stocky, muscular frame looked oddly out of place in the refined elegance of the Presidential Suite. He leaned forward, rising a little on his toes, and addressed himself with great earnestness, to both Victoria and the Commissioner. 'There is a lady here who wishes to speak with you. A Mrs—' He raised both hands and stared hard at the business card he was holding. 'Sav—Sov—Suvy—'

'Sauveterre?' Victoria suggested.

Relief spread over the sergeant's young face. 'Yes, that was it, Sauveterre. She's—' he squinted again at the business card. 'Her address is in Paris. I think she could be French.'

A smile crept on to the Commissioner's lips. 'Very good detection, Sergeant.' He paused, looking expectantly at the young man. But Sergeant Tong remained firmly planted beside the sofa. 'Perhaps, you would be good enough to show the French lady in?'

'Oh, yes, of course, sir.' Sergeant Tong pointed uncertainly over his shoulder. 'Shall I ask Mr de Brouwer to wait?'

The Commissioner nodded. 'Yes. Ask him to take a seat in the foyer.'

In sharp contrast to the sergeant's incongruous appearance, Isabelle appeared in the dining room looking very much at home. Despite her tiny frame and limbs that looked as if they would snap at any moment, she filled the large room, looking almost regal in a royal blue coat made of cotton tweed. Beneath the coat, she wore a pair of loose, white pants and a fine linen sweater, knitted in a zigzag pattern of black, royal blue and white. Her waist was adorned with a belt of shimmering glass pearls, locked together by the distinctive interlinking 'S's of her logo. Long strings of glass pearls and blue crystals hung round her neck. Perched on her head, atop her long, peroxide blonde hair, she wore a blue tweed beret, sitting low, just above the thin line of her pencilled eyebrows. A pair of white Mary Jane style shoes completed the outfit.

The Commissioner extended his hand towards her. 'Madame Sauveterre, you look absolutely stunning. My wife is a huge fan of your clothing. She tells me as soon the children are off our hands and we stop spending money on them, she is going to treat herself to an Isabelle Sauveterre outfit.' He spread his hands out and cast a rueful glance down at his grey suit. 'Unfortunately, I am not a follower of fashion myself, as you can see.'

Isabelle gave a dismissive, and distinctly French, puff of her lips. 'Pfff—it is not necessary to follow fashion, in order to have style. To stand out, one must have confidence and humility. *That* is the essence of style.' She ran a critical eye over the Commissioner's finely striped suit. 'The clothes, we can change. The person who wears them, unfortunately, we cannot.' She looked enquiringly at him. 'Tell me about your wife.'

The Commissioner's face lit up into a proud smile. 'My wife has style. Although she's a captain for Singapore Airlines, so she lives in a uniform at work—as do I, usually. But when we go out, she likes to dress up.'

Isabelle gave a quick, approving nod. 'Then we shall get your wife in for a fitting. It is important for strong and successful women to dress well.' She cast a reproachful glance at Victoria's Vivienne Westwood suit, before waving a thin, heavily ringed hand in the direction of the hallway. 'Your officer has my card. Tell your wife to phone me. I shall be in the country until we are permitted to leave. Are we getting any closer to that?'

The Commissioner gave an apologetic shake of his head. 'We don't have a resolution as yet, I'm afraid, but we are working day and night to solve the case as quickly as we can. Rest assured, Madame Sauveterre, every resource at our disposal is being used.'

Isabelle's thinly pencilled eyebrows rose with haughty indifference. 'I should think your resources could be put to better use, elsewhere. Whoever the murderer is, they have done us all a favour. The world is a better place, Commissioner, without my goddaughter's fiancé and his mother. I should not waste my time trying to catch their killer.'

A glint of amusement sparkled in the Commissioner's eyes. 'Unfortunately, Madame, if we ignored the crimes committed against people we didn't like, I fear we would have a very idle police force.'

Isabelle raised her chin. 'And a more efficient one.'

The Commissioner's cheerful face broadened into a grin. 'Ah, yes, of course, the French enthusiasm for giving power to the people. *Vive la Revolution!* But I think if we are to learn anything from 1789, it is that the people are a little blood-thirstier than we give them credit for. We currently have two dead bodies. I am not keen to increase the number.'

'Perhaps, then it would be better to allow us all to leave the country.'

The Commissioner inclined his head into a thoughtful nod. 'That would potentially stop our killer striking again—in Singapore, at least. But I would not want us getting a reputation as a place to visit if you want to get away with murder. We pride ourselves on our low crime rate.'

'In that case I shall let you to get on with your job.' Despite the charm of Isabelle's thick French accent, there was a sharp edge of reproach in the deep, gravelly tone of her voice. 'I must get on with my work, also. I have an appointment at my shop in Takashimaya with a client. Do I have your permission to leave the hotel, or am I to be imprisoned here?'

The Commissioner bowed his head. 'Madame Sauveterre, in your case, I am happy to make an exception; you are very welcome to leave.' He bent his head a little closer; a faint hint of a conspiratorial smile hovered on his lips. 'So long as of course, you would be happy for Sergeant Tong to accompany you. Perhaps, when you return, we can have a word with you regarding the events at dinner, yesterday evening. And I would be interested in your thoughts regarding James Winstanley's murder.'

'My thoughts regarding his murder are very straightforward, Commissioner. It is a blessing for my goddaughter and I have no interest in discovering who is behind it.'

The Commissioner rested a thoughtful gaze on Isabelle. 'Even if that person is your goddaughter?'

'My goddaughter!' Isabelle glowered at the Commissioner in a manner that suggested he had taken leave of his senses. 'That is a ridiculous suggestion.' She drew herself up with imperious disdain. 'My goddaughter is an extraordinarily clever and successful businesswoman. She has succeeded where others have failed, because she is resilient and does not suffer fools. But I can assure you, she is not a murderer. *That,* she does not have in her.'

Fifty-Eight

Victoria watched Sergeant Tong lead Isabelle towards the front door. A more disparate pair, it wasn't possible to imagine, and yet, the sergeant's simple civility seemed to please Isabelle. She allowed herself to be guided by his sturdy hand resting on the back of her tweed coat—the cost of which would have been his entire year's salary, if not two.

As the door closed behind them, Victoria heard her phone vibrating. She rushed across to the coffee table, and seeing Bee's name on the screen, answered it.

Bee's cheerful voice immediately lifted her spirits. 'Hey, Victoria. I've got that information for you on these offshore bank accounts you gave me. Your suspicions were absolutely correct.'

Victoria sank down on to the sofa. 'Unbelievable. The absolute brazen nerve.'

'It gets worse,' Bee said. 'It turns out that the delightful James Winstanley is also married—or at least *was*, before he died.'

'Married? You are kidding me.'

'No, I'm not. He got married under the name of James Bradford, his mother's maiden name, eleven years ago in Brazil. His wife still lives there with their son, a ten-year-old by the name of Paulo.'

Victoria stared out into the rain-soaked courtyard, letting the news sink in. James was certainly no angel, but she didn't have him pegged as a bigamist. 'You're quite sure there hasn't been a divorce filed in some obscure courthouse in a small town, somewhere in the countryside?'

'Absolutely sure; it's still stuck in the courts. His wife wants a larger portion of his assets and is refusing to divorce him until she gets it. Ironically, another hearing is scheduled for this week.'

Victoria gave a dry laugh. 'She's going to be mortally disappointed then, isn't she? But it does explain why James wanted to keep the wedding quiet. I don't imagine he wanted his wife getting wind of it.'

'No, that would have been a disaster for him. Still, on the bright side, keeping the marriage quiet means Peyton doesn't have a PR disaster on her hands, on top of everything else. She should be sending the killer a thank you note. Speaking of which, how are you getting on, are you any closer to finding them?'

Victoria leaned her head against the back of the sofa. 'No, not as yet. And I'm not sure if this information you've just given me is a help or hindrance.'

Fifty-Nine

Nick de Brouwer's shrewd gaze watched Victoria as the Commissioner ushered him into her dining room. 'Our apologies for keeping you waiting, Mr de Brouwer. Please come on in and take a seat.' The Commissioner drew out one of the dining chairs on the far side of the table and waved towards the chair opposite. 'We'll try to be as brief as we can.'

Victoria could see from the hastiness of the Commissioner's actions that his mind was already focussed on lunch. Nick scarcely had time to sit down, before he launched into his first question. 'I see you were in New York, last week, Mr de Brouwer. Did you send a letter to Miss Latchmore while you were there?'

Nick settled comfortably into his chair and shook his head. 'A letter? Not that I can recall.'

The Commissioner swivelled round and reached out for the green envelope sitting on the marble shelf behind him. He placed it on the table and slid it across to Nick. 'This doesn't look familiar?'

Nick picked up the envelope and gave both sides a cursory glance. He shook his head, pushing it back towards the Commissioner. 'No, I can't say that it does.'

The Commissioner smiled. He reached across the table and took the envelope back. 'I understand you played golf yesterday. Which course were you playing at?'

Nick ran his hand over his shaved head and down around the back of his neck, massaging the muscles inside the collar of his black polo shirt. Victoria noted the iconic Gucci stripes and distinctive XXV logo emblazoned on the sleeve. He certainly enjoyed expensive labels. 'I went across to Sentosa. I was lucky enough to get a slot at the last minute.'

The Commissioner leaned back in his chair. 'That's a challenging course.'

Nick gave a light, amiable laugh. 'It certainly can be. Although I got forty Stablefords yesterday—but I think that was more luck, than anything else.'

'What time did you return to the hotel, after your game?'

'It must have been around two, I suppose. I didn't hang around in the clubhouse; I came straight back here. Kate and I had made plans to have afternoon tea, together.'

The Commissioner returned the green envelope to the marble shelf. Then swivelled back round to face Nick. 'Can you tell us about your relationship with James Winstanley and Beverley Marsters?'

'Sure.' Nick spread his elbows out to rest on the arms of his chair and casually crossed one leg over the other. 'I've been their lawyer for about five years now—both in a personal and business capacity. We get on well. Of course we've had the odd difference of opinion, over the years, but—' he gave another affable laugh. 'Who hasn't?'

The Commissioner kept a steady gaze fixed on Nick. 'Have your differences of opinion stretched to the financial management of their company?'

Nick seemed to be ready for the question. He didn't flinch. His answer came slick and fast. 'I don't get involved in that side of things; I leave that to the bean counters.'

'Can you tell us exactly what your role entails then, Mr de Brouwer?'

'I cover pretty much everything for them, from a legal perspective. It can range from dealing with compliance issues to settling transactions, to looking over investment statements or dealing with the regulator. Generally, my role is to make sure everything complies with Securities regulations—which in Britain, these days, can be a bit of a minefield.'

'I assume then that you are aware that Winstanley & Marsters is being investigated by the Serious Fraud Office in London?'

Victoria watched Nick closely to see his reaction; but barely a muscle on his face moved. He shook his head. 'No, I'm not aware of that. What are the charges against them?'

'There has been a suggestion they are running a Ponzi scheme.'

Nick raised his eyebrows and let out a low whistle. 'That's not good. I had no idea about that.'

The Commissioner frowned. 'I would have thought that as their lawyer, it was your responsibility to stay on top of regulatory requirements?'

Nick spread his hands out wide in a gesture of innocence. 'As a lawyer, we can only advise our clients based on the information we are given. Unfortunately, if that's not accurate, there is not a lot we can do.'

'I presume that lack of oversight does not extend to your own business, Mr de Brouwer.' The Commissioner fixed his gaze firmly on Nick. 'I understand from our British counterparts, that you are also under investigation, for some financial dealings you have had with the company.'

Nick gave a harsh, and unnecessarily loud, laugh. 'Why on earth would they be investigating me? I don't know anything about the Ponzi scheme!'

'I believe they are interested in the six million pounds you transferred out of your Client Money account. I'm sure, as a lawyer, you realize that is illegal.'

Behind Nick's suntan, the colour drained from his face. For a moment, he remained frozen, staring at the Commissioner, his enlarged pupils adding to his dazed appearance. But he quickly recovered his equilibrium and responded in a confident, assertive tone, such as a lawyer might use, when addressing a jury. 'I don't see what that has got to do with this investigation.'

The Commissioner placed his clasped hands down on the dining table and leaned forward. 'With six million pounds missing from your Client Money account, you would seem to be in need of a large amount of cash, Mr de Brouwer, if you are to avoid a lengthy jail sentence. The perfect motive, perhaps, for trying to defraud Miss Latchmore out of 60 million dollars.'

'Jesus Christ!' Nick fell back in his chair. 'You can't seriously be suggesting that I was James' kidnapper. Why would I have murdered him? Why would I have murdered Beverley? I'm not stupid; I know the death penalty exists here.'

'Perhaps, that is why you wrote to Miss Latchmore. Perhaps your intention was not to carry the kidnapping out here in Singapore.'

Nick lurched forward, his dark eyes pleading with the Commissioner. 'I didn't write to her because of that. I didn't know anything about the kidnapping. I wrote to her because I—oh Jesus!' He fell back in his seat, pressing the heels of his hands against his temples. He stared, wide-eyed at the dining table. Then, running his hands down over his face, he sat forward. 'Look, I didn't have anything to do with the murders or the kidnapping. I wrote to Peyton because I thought she was making a mistake by marrying James—that was all. I'd worked with James for five years, I knew what he was like and frankly, I thought Peyton was too good for him. She's a beautiful woman and a lovely person. I knew if the marriage went ahead, she would regret it. James was only interested in her money.' He threw himself back, slapping his hand down on to the tabletop. 'Christ! If it's the murders you're trying to solve, it's Lou and John you should be talking to, not me.'

The Commissioner raised an eyebrow. 'Why should we be talking to them about the murders?'

'Because they wanted her dead.'

'You mean Mrs Marsters?'

'Yes.' Nick scratched his unshaven jaw and wiped the perspiration gathering on his temples. 'Just before we left London, I overheard Beverley giving Lou a dressing down. As soon as she left the office, Lou told John that she couldn't put up with it any more. She said she wished Beverley hadn't recovered from the pneumonia she'd had, because they would all be a lot better off without her. John told her not to worry; he said it would all be over soon.' Nick ran his hand around the back of his head. 'If you don't believe me, ask Tim. He was in the room with them.'

The Commissioner gave a small nod. 'We'll be sure to do that, Mr de Brouwer, thank you. Is there anything else you would care to share with us? Any other conversations you might have overheard?

Nick shifted uncomfortably in his seat. 'Nothing I want to talk about without a lawyer present.'

Sixty

Victoria pushed her chair back and stood up. She needed to get her body moving. The last four interviews had been interminable! And from what she could see, had got them no further ahead. She reached her long arms up over her head and interlacing her fingers together, inverted her hands and stretched them towards the ceiling. No wonder cats stretch when they wake up; it was a lovely feeling when your body has been constrained. The dining chair had been comfortable for the first half an hour, but her back muscles weren't thanking her for the last hour and a half!

She stretched her arms out sideways, sneaking in a silent yawn while the Commissioner was busy arranging his notes. Never had she been more grateful that she had chosen a career in the Secret Service, rather than the police force. The endless interviews and minutiae of detective work would have driven her mad. She lowered her arms and bent forward. She'd love to do a yoga class – or visit the gym, at the very least. But they still had three more interviews to go; one of which was Peyton. Perhaps, she should suggest a lunch break first. She would like some time to think through the best strategy with Peyton.

She also needed to clear her head from their interview with Patricia. Never had she met anyone who took such a morbid interest in the suffering of others. Her professions of sympathy would make Mother Teresa look insincere. Yet Victoria couldn't help feeling that her macabre fascination was more a desire to fill her own empty existence with chatter, than out of any genuine concern. She pressed her hands down flat on the floor, giving her hamstrings an extra stretch.

Slowly, she unfurled herself, as the Commissioner glanced up from his notebook. He placed his pen down on the table and shook his head. 'Well, I'm not sure if we gained anything from that lot.' He rubbed his fingers over his forehead and temples. 'Other than a headache.'

Victoria smiled. 'No, I don't think we did. All we have is four more suspects who could have done it but say they didn't.'

The Commissioner leaned his elbows on the table and looked down at his notes. 'So what have we got? John Marsters and Lou Farmer both had a motive and the opportunity. They could have been in it together. They were certainly both keen to give as little away as possible. Which would suggest they are hiding something—possibly their intention to do away with Mrs Marsters, if Mr de Brouwer is to be believed. Which is not implausible, given the conversation you overheard between them.' He flipped over to the next page in his book. 'George Helstone could also have done it. He was incredibly riled up about the amount of money being spent on the wedding, while he was still waiting for his investment money to be returned. If he knew he wasn't going to get it, that would have given him a serious motive. He doesn't strike me as a wealthy man. A financial loss of that magnitude at this stage in his life, would be ruinous.' He frowned at his notes. 'I suppose his wife could have been in it with him. Although I can't help feeling if she was she would have let it slip by now, given how much she chatters. Or maybe she did and I missed it when I stopped listening to her!'

Victoria laughed. 'Yes, she could be a very clever master criminal. Bury the confession in a whole lot of other nonsense to throw us off the track.'

The Commissioner picked up his pen and began absentmindedly tapping the end on the table. 'Maybe we'll get something in the next batch of interviews. Who have we got left?' He flicked back to the front page of his notebook. 'Your friend, Miss Latchmore, and her grandparents, Bill and Eleanor Springfield. Perhaps we'll get something useful out of them.'

'It's possible, although at this stage, I'd say we've got more chance of getting something concrete out of forensics.'

The Commissioner leaned against the backrest of his chair and gazed up at the ceiling. 'What would I do now if I were Hercule Poirot?' He placed his fingertips together and closed his eyes. 'I would sit back and think. Then I would have an epiphany and call everyone together to show them how clever I am.' He opened his eyes and sat upright. 'Maybe that's what we should do; get everyone together.'

Victoria raised an eyebrow. 'We could; except, as we don't know who the murderer is, we're not going to look very clever.'

'Maybe someone will break down and confess while we've got them all in the room.'

Victoria laughed. 'That doesn't sound terribly plausible to me. I think you might need Eleanor's help to come up with an alternative dénouement.'

The Commissioner smiled. 'Maybe I just need lunch.' He glanced down at his watch. 'It is nearly two-thirty already.'

Sixty-One

Victoria pulled the front door of her suite closed and turned to the Commissioner. 'What about the Bar and Billiard Room for lunch? It should have quietened down by now.'

The Commissioner grinned with boyish delight. 'Sounds perfect to me.' He gave his stomach a small pat. 'I must say, I'm feeling a bit hungry again.'

Victoria smiled, glancing down at his small paunch as they set off towards the Grand Staircase. Given his unparalleled appetite for good food, she couldn't help thinking that his wife had her work cut out, preventing his paunch from growing any larger.

They walked on along the landing in silence, the Commissioner keeping time with Victoria's step. He fixed his gaze pensively on the floorboards. 'What did you think of Lou Farmer? Do you think she knows about the Ponzi scheme?'

Victoria thought about the question for a moment, casting her mind back to Lou's well-rehearsed answers when asked about it. 'I think she knows a lot more than she's telling us.'

'Yes, I agree. It's just hard to know which parts she's holding back information about. John Marsters is more or less the same. I'm not convinced he's quite as oblivious of the day-to-day running of their company as he likes to make out.'

Victoria smiled. 'Maybe the threat of facing justice in Singapore might be enough to loosen his lips. You're a bit tougher here, than we are in the UK. Mind you, I think he's partial to a good meal—the prison food here is probably marginally better.'

The Commissioner chuckled. 'Yes I think our food has a touch more flavour than your English cuisine.' He threw an arch smile across at Victoria. 'If we can call it that.'

Victoria laughed. 'Steady on, we do a very good fish and chips.'

'Yes that is true—*and* a very good Stilton cheese. That's one thing we don't do well in Asia; we don't make good cheese. You Europeans have got that covered.'

They passed the small lounge at the end of the atrium and rounded on to the landing above the staircase. As they made their way slowly down, Victoria fell silent. She couldn't get rid of the feeling that there was something obvious they were missing. She had felt it strongly during the interview with Nick; but for the life of her, she didn't know what it was or what Nick had said that had prompted the feeling.

Perhaps, she should just leave it for her subconscious to work on. The more she tried to force the memory, the further it slipped away.

As they descended the final flight of steps, she turned her attention instead to the throngs gathered for afternoon tea in the lobby. It was a busy day and it took her a moment to realize that Eleanor Springfield was standing amongst the mingling crowd.

She looked beautifully elegant in a classic Chanel suit. The cream jacket was edged in black and the skirt finished just below her knee in a hem of cream fringing. She wore three strings of pearls around her neck and impressively for a woman of eighty-nine, her cream shoes, trimmed with black toes, had small kitten heels. Even in the heat, she hadn't dispensed with her stockings.

She caught Victoria's eye and smiled. Making her way over to the staircase, she took an affectionate hold of Victoria's hand. 'I have been so wanting to come and see you to know how you're getting along. But I didn't want to interrupt the investigation.' She turned to the Commissioner. 'This must be your partner in crime, whom I have heard so much about. Or perhaps, I ought to say, your partner in solving our crimes.'

The Commissioner's face broke into a beaming smile. He bent his head down towards Eleanor. 'Mrs Springfield, I am delighted to meet you. I am a great fan of yours. I have read every one of your books.'

Eleanor looked uncharacteristically bashful. 'Commissioner, I hope you are in jest. You should not be wasting your precious time reading my books. They are just a little bit of fun. There is nothing serious in them.'

'Which is exactly why I read them. I deal with serious crime every day; I don't want to read about it. I want my leisure time to be pleasurable. I'm a huge fan of Agatha Christie and Sir Arthur Conan Doyle. Although I must say, I do think your books are superior.'

'Well, that is very kind of you to say, Commissioner.' The lively sparkle in Eleanor's eyes dimmed and her expression became more solemn. 'How is everything coming along? Are you making any progress?'

'We're making progress, but in very small steps. Unfortunately, the resolution isn't coming quite as quickly as it would in one of your novels.'

The twinkle returned to Eleanor's eye. 'The wonderful thing about being a crime novelist, Commissioner, is that we can go back and fill in missing clues at the end, to tidy everything up. Alas, real life is not quite so accommodating.'

The Commissioner laughed. 'No, it certainly is not. Criminals seem to like making our lives as difficult as they possibly can.'

'I am quite sure you will get to the bottom of it all, eventually. Time is a wonderful problem-solver.' Eleanor glanced down at her brass walking stick. 'Although not for old age, apparently.' She gave the pearl handle a gentle tap. 'Well, I had better not hold you two up any longer. You have got work to do and it's time I got back upstairs to Peyton.'

'How is she doing?' Victoria asked. 'Is she feeling any better today?'

Eleanor gave a small, sorrowful sigh. 'She is finding it very hard. She didn't get a wink of sleep last night. I gave her one of Isabelle's sleeping tablets earlier, so she could get some rest. Bill is upstairs with her, at the moment.' She gave Victoria's hand a tender squeeze. 'But she'll come right. She is a tough young woman with her whole life ahead of her. We'll get her home, just as soon as we can and take good care of her. Bill's looking forward to spending a bit of time with Peyton. There has been a lot of tension between the two of them, over the past few months, so it'll be a good chance to make amends and put everything behind them.'

'I wanted to ask you about that,' Victoria said. 'You mentioned it, the other night in the Writers Bar, but we got interrupted. What was causing the tension between them?'

Eleanor shook her head, her forehead creasing into a troubled frown. 'It seems so trivial now, with everything that has happened, but Bill has been terribly worried. Peyton wanted to give all of her money to James to invest for her. Bill tried telling her it wasn't a good idea to put all of her eggs into the one basket; he wanted her to spread her risk out over a number of different investments. But you know how stubborn Peyton can be. She didn't want to listen to a wise old head like Bill's. Apparently, James knew better. Bill had a lot of arguments with her about it. In the end, thank goodness, she did at least agree to a delay, so Bill could look over everything. I don't like to speak ill of the dead, but I am very pleased that problem has gone away. I was in agreement with Bill, but I'm not sure Peyton would have taken his advice in the long-run.'

Victoria nodded. 'I think you're right, Eleanor, I don't think she would have. I'm just so pleased Bill spoke up when he did. The delay has proved to be very timely. We've just found out that Winstanley & Marsters is being investigated for running a Ponzi scheme. There could be hundreds of millions of pounds involved.'

'Oh dear Lord.' Eleanor tightened her grip on the pearl handle of her walking stick. 'Peyton would have lost everything.' She turned her clear blue eyes on the Commissioner. 'I do not like to condone the taking of life, Commissioner, but whoever is behind these murders has saved my granddaughter a lot of heartache—and an enormous amount of money.'

Sixty-Two

As Victoria had anticipated, the Bar and Billiard Room was pleasantly quiet when they arrived. Only a few diners lingered, their hushed voices wafting across the room, mingled with the faint clanging of pots and cutlery in the kitchen. The waiting staff hovered unobtrusively in the background, quietly making preparations for the dinner service.

The maître d'hôtel glanced across at the new arrivals and hastened over to greet them. 'Miss West, it is lovely to see you again.' Her attentive gaze took in the Commissioner. 'A table for two?'

'Yes, thank you, Corrinne. Perhaps, something in the corner, out of the way.'

Corrinne smiled. 'Of course, follow me.'

She collected two menus and led them across to the far side of the restaurant, to a table tucked into the corner, beside one of the high-arched windows. Glancing outside, Victoria was delighted to see the heavy rain had eased to a drizzle. Perhaps in a few more hours, the grey mist would clear completely.

She settled into her seat, and was just opening the menu, when the familiar tones of Patricia Helstone's gratingly high-pitched voice, drifted across the restaurant. Victoria cringed.

'I can see them over there, George. I'm going over to see what's happening. It's ridiculous not knowing when we'll be able to leave!' With a cantankerous frown, Patricia hoisted her handbag up on to her shoulder and stalked across the room. She glowered at the Commissioner. 'Is there any more news? We've been sitting at lunch, waiting to hear something.'

The Commissioner closed his menu with a polite half-smile. 'I'm afraid we don't have anything further to report at this stage, Mrs Helstone, other than what we told you when we spoke, about an hour ago. But please, rest assured we are working as quickly as we can, to get to the bottom of everything. We do appreciate that this is a very difficult time.'

'Of course it is!' Patricia's voice went up a notch. 'And on top of everything, we're stuck here in a foreign country. Surely, you can't expect us to stay indefinitely. We're due to fly out! I don't know what we're going to do if we miss our flight.' She turned to her husband. 'That's something we need to look into, George. John is going to be in the same situation.' She glanced down at the small silver face on her watch. 'We really must get back up to him; we've been gone for over an hour!' She inclined her head towards Victoria. 'He's in a terrible state. This whole thing has been extremely upsetting for him. And I'm worried about Tim. He's never had to deal with anything like this before.'

Victoria laid her menu down on the table. It was clearly going to be a while, before she was going to be able to read it. 'I'm sure it must be extremely difficult for him. As it is for everyone.'

'Oh, you've no idea! He suffers from anxiety. I don't know how he's going to cope with all of this. Thank goodness, George and I are here. John wouldn't have been able to manage with Tim on his own. We really must get back up there, George.' Pulling the drooping strap of her handbag up, she cast a disapproving glance down at the Commissioner. 'It seems we're not going to get any more information for the time being.' She pointed to the bill folder in George's hand. 'We need to find somebody to give that to, before we leave.' She stretched her neck out like a meerkat, searching for a waiter. As soon as she spotted one, she snatched the bill folder from George and charged off in pursuit.

George gave Victoria and the Commissioner a weak smile. 'I had better go after her. She won't remember what room we're in.'

The Commissioner stared in disbelief, as George trotted dutifully after his wife.

The stunned look on his face made Victoria smile. 'A pleasant woman, don't you think?'

The Commissioner turned his wide-eyed gaze to Victoria. 'That isn't quite the phrase I would have used.' He glanced across at Patricia, commanding the waiting staff with a jabbing finger. A mischievous smile quivered on his lips. 'I don't suppose *she's* allergic to peanuts?'

Victoria laughed. 'Careful, you're starting to sound like Isabelle.'

'I'm beginning to come round to her way of thinking. Perhaps, we should leave the killer to it.'

Victoria pointed at the menu lying on the table in front of him. 'I think you need to get some sustenance into you. You're sounding a bit light-headed.'

The Commissioner opened up his menu, smiling. 'Yes, perhaps, that might help.'

He traced his finger down the list of starters on the first page and had just stopped on the onion and anchovy tart, when Victoria caught sight of Peyton hurrying across the restaurant towards them, her pale face looking drawn and strained.

Victoria pushed her chair back and made to stand up, but Peyton stopped her, placing a hand on her shoulder. 'I am so sorry for interrupting; I know you're both really busy.'

The Commissioner rose from the table. 'It is no problem at all, Miss Latchmore. Please—' He pulled a chair out for Peyton. 'Take a seat. We were just about to order some lunch, if you would care to join us.'

'Thank you, but—' Peyton placed both hands over her stomach. 'I can't face eating anything, at the moment. I just came down very briefly to ask you both for a favour.'

The Commissioner's arched eyebrows rose a little. 'Of course. We are here to help in any way we can. What is it that you would like us to do?'

Peyton gave a small, grateful sigh. 'I wondered if you might be able to give everybody an update as to the status of the inquiry? I know you're interviewing all of us individually, but everyone is coming and asking me what's going on. I don't know what to tell them; I don't have any more information than they do. I guess they are all just anxious about catching flights or changing them, if they have to. Although Nick and Kate are talking about getting a lawyer to represent them; they seem quite upset by everything.'

The Commissioner gave a faintly satisfied smile. 'I am quite sure they are. But with regards to your request, Miss Latchmore, I'd be more than happy for us to call everyone together, after we've had a bite of lunch. In fact—' He threw a sly glance across at Victoria. 'We were just talking about doing precisely that.'

Peyton's wan face warmed into an appreciative smile. 'I would be so grateful, thank you. I'm really sorry for putting you both to all this trouble; it's just that I don't have the energy for dealing with everyone, right now.'

Victoria smiled at her friend. 'You're not putting us to any extra trouble at all, Peyton, so stop worrying about it. We're more than happy to give everyone an update.' She raised an arch eyebrow at the Commissioner. 'Such as we are able to, at the moment. Unfortunately, there's not an awful lot to tell, at this stage.' She reached out for Peyton's hand. 'Then can we get together with you for a chat?'

'Of course, you can interview me, whenever you need to. I want you to catch whoever did this.'

Victoria squeezed her hand. 'We will, Peyton, I promise you. Are you sure you don't want to stay and have something to eat with us? You look like you could do with some food.'

Peyton shook her head. 'I honestly can't stomach anything right now. I tried eating a cookie, earlier, and it made me feel nauseous. I think I'll just head back upstairs and see you both after lunch, if that's okay?'

Victoria nodded. 'Of course, that's okay.'

The Commissioner watched Peyton for a moment, until she was out of earshot. Then he reassumed his seat.

Victoria picked up her menu and smiled at him. 'Well, Monsieur Poirot, if your suspects are being gathered together, you had better get those little grey cells working and figure out who the murderer is.'

The Commissioner laughed. 'I'm afraid they are not capable of working very quickly, these days.' He stared thoughtfully at the leather cover of his menu. 'Mind you, I don't mind the idea of getting everyone together. It'll give us a chance to put a bit of pressure on them all. You never know, something might come out of it.'

Victoria raised an eyebrow. 'You mean, put the cat amongst the pigeons. That was Eleanor's idea at dinner, last night, and we ended up with a dead body because of it.'

The Commissioner opened his menu, throwing a dry smile across at Victoria. 'At least we'll be prepared for it, this time.' He turned the page over and ran his eye down the list of main courses. 'I think I might go for the pizza with Italian sausage. What are you going to get?'

Victoria froze, staring at him. Every drop of blood in her body came to a stop.

The Commissioner gave her a slightly bashful smile. 'You look horrified. That's exactly the look my wife would give me. I know it's not terribly healthy. I suppose you're going to order a salad, are you?'

Victoria shook her head. 'No, I wasn't thinking about the pizza. I was thinking about the sausage.' She pushed her chair back. Her mind was racing. 'It could be the link to our murderer.'

Sixty-Three

Despite the Commissioner's long stride, he trailed behind Victoria as she marched along the landing, towards the Noel Coward Suite. His gaze fell to the four-inch heels on her black Saint Laurent pumps. 'How do you walk so fast in those things?'

Victoria stopped in front of the Noel Coward Suite door. She turned to him and smiled. 'Practice.'

The Commissioner raised a doubtful eyebrow. He then glanced at the door. 'Are you going to tell me what all of this is about?'

Victoria reached out for the bell, shaking her head. 'Not yet—I need to check a couple of things, first.'

'But you have an idea who the murderer is?'

Victoria nodded. 'Yes. But if I'm right, it's not the answer either of us want.'

Inspector Yew opened the door. She smiled at them both. 'Please come in.' Leading them across to the small dining table in the entrance foyer, she picked up a sealed plastic bag and handed it to Victoria. 'This is the pen you were asking about. We haven't had it checked for fingerprints as yet, but we will do so.'

Victoria took the bag, with the Montegrappa pen inside, and turned it over in her hand. She saw what she was looking for and smiled.

The Commissioner peered over her shoulder. 'Have you found something?'

'Yes.' Victoria pointed to the gold band at the bottom of the barrel. 'Do you see this bit of engraving, here?'

The Commissioner squinted. He pulled his head back to get a better focus. 'Yes, although I can't quite make it out. Does it say & Co?'

Victoria nodded. 'It does. And if I keep turning the pen around, you'll see that it says Winstanley & Co.'

The Commissioner stared at her. 'Is that significant? Has it got something to do with our murderer?'

'Yes, it most certainly has.' She turned to Inspector Yew. 'Did you look into the fingerprints on the dinner plate?'

The inspector nodded. 'Yes, I spoke with forensics and they agree with you. A napkin would have wiped more of Beverley Marsters' fingerprints off the plate.'

The Commissioner turned his confused gaze from Inspector Yew to Victoria. 'What on earth are you both talking about?'

Victoria smiled. 'Come with me. I'll fill you in on the way to my suite.'

Sixty-Four

Victoria stood at the far end of the dining room, leaning against the delicate white frame of the French doors, while the Commissioner ushered the last of the wedding guests into position around the table. He seemed to be enjoying his role as the great detective about to unveil the murderer. Victoria was happy to leave him to it. It wasn't a role she had any desire to undertake. It upset her to even think about it. The police had to do their job; she knew that. But she couldn't derive any pleasure from solving the crimes, she just felt sadness now. If only she had understood everything earlier, she might have prevented the murders.

She pushed the gloomy thought from her mind and turned her attention, instead, to the courtyard and the rain still falling beyond the balcony, in a soft, grey mist. A shaft of sunlight briefly muscled its way through the clouds, catching the small droplets and casting an eerie silver light over the hotel.

As the last of the guests settled into their seats, Victoria brought her attention back to the dining room. The Commissioner worked his way around to where she was standing and paused for a moment, running his gaze around the table. The murmuring conversations ceased and every set of eyes turned in his direction.

Kate de Brouwer shifted in her seat, her jaw set and her eyes fixed squarely on the Commissioner. 'I presume you are not expecting any of us to answer more questions without a lawyer present?'

The Commissioner responded to her hostile tone with a patient smile. 'Mrs de Brouwer, the purpose of calling everyone together was to give you an update on the investigation. There has understandably been some anxiety for information.'

Tim crossed his arms and slumped down in his chair. 'That's an understatement.'

John placed a restraining hand on his son's arm. 'Let us just listen to what the Commissioner has to say.'

Tim pulled his arm away. 'We know what he has got to say; he thinks one of us is the killer.'

'We don't know that, son. The police have to do a very thorough investigation, that is all. I'm sure the Commissioner now realizes nobody in this room had a reason to harm James or your mother.'

'I'm afraid, Mr Marsters, that is incorrect.' The Commissioner rocked forward on to his toes. 'Unfortunately, many of the people in this room had a motive for doing exactly that. That is one of the aspects of this investigation that has made it so challenging. Therefore, it is important for everybody here to understand that until a formal arrest is made, you all remain live suspects at this point in the investigation.'

'Live suspects!' Patricia pinched her vivid pink lips together. 'How ridiculous! Why would one of us have been involved? Surely, there is no evidence to support that.'

'On the contrary, Mrs Helstone.' The Commissioner took his notebook from the breast pocket of his jacket. 'We have a substantial amount of evidence to support that. And in fact, since we called you all together, further evidence has emerged.'

George folded his arms, leaning against the backrest of his chair. 'I think we would all be interested to know what that evidence is, Commissioner.'

The Commissioner inclined his head in George's direction. 'Let me take you back to the beginning of our investigation. As you are all aware, a message was delivered to Mr and Mrs Marsters, yesterday afternoon, at one o'clock, informing them that James Winstanley had been kidnapped, followed by a ransom demand for a payment of 60 million dollars for his release. Threats were made against his life, if the family contacted the police, and so, they chose not to do that. However,

Miss Latchmore—' he rested his gaze on Peyton. 'Had the good sense to talk to her friend, Miss West. Given the amount of knowledge the kidnapper appeared to have, about the wedding and the family's movements, it seemed clear to Miss West that the kidnapper was either one of the wedding guests or was receiving information from one of them. Given her background in security, she made some enquiries, and it quickly became obvious to her that the kidnapping was a hoax.'

Peyton sat forward in her chair, her face deadly pale. 'What?'

The Commissioner nodded. 'Yes, I am afraid to say there was no kidnapping. It was a hoax concocted by Mr Winstanley, with the help of his mother and stepfather.'

A flash of fiery indignation flared in Lou's eyes. 'That is an absurd allegation. Why would John be involved in staging his own stepson's kidnapping?'

'Because Winstanley & Marsters is in very serious financial trouble, Miss Farmer. Without an immediate, large injection of cash, the company will be forced into liquidation.' The Commissioner ran his gaze along the full length of the table. 'Some of you may remember being asked if the name Nigel Delamore meant anything to you. Mr Delamore works for the Serious Fraud Office in London. They are currently investigating allegations that Winstanley & Marsters is running a Ponzi scheme.'

George's mouth fell open. His yellow complexion turned ashen as he shifted his wide eyes from the Commissioner to his brother-in-law. 'A Ponzi scheme? Is this true, John?'

Lou reached out and took hold of John's hand. 'Of course it is not true; the whole thing is a lie. Besides, it doesn't make any sense. Why would they have sent a ransom note to themselves?'

The Commissioner settled his gaze on Lou. 'Because the Marsters and Mr Winstanley anticipated Miss Latchmore would pay it. All the signs were that she was infatuated enough with Mr Winstanley to do just that.' He thrust his hands into the pockets of his trousers and slowly paced around the dining table. 'We have conducted an investigation into the bank accounts listed in the ransom demand.' He paused behind John's chair. 'They were all established using shell companies in order to disguise the identity of the true owners. However, after a considerable amount of probing, it became clear that the beneficial owners of all the accounts are John Marsters, Beverley Marsters and James Winstanley. So there is no doubt about their complicity in the kidnapping hoax and their attempt to defraud Miss Latchmore. There was also only one way Mr Winstanley's phone could have got on to the room service trolley.' His gaze bore down on John. 'The butler did not leave the trolley unattended until he reached the door of the Marsters' suite. It was at this point that Mrs Marsters, by her own admission, went out on to the landing. Therefore, she is the only person who could have placed it there.'

All traces of expression had drained from Peyton's white face. She turned to look at John. 'Is what he says true?'

John looked helplessly at his son and then at Lou. He darted a flustered glance towards Peyton, but quickly shifted his uneasy gaze from her face to the tabletop.

George stared, wide-eyed, at his brother-in-law, his fingers gripping the edge of the table. 'Does this mean all of our money is lost?'

John quickly shook his head. 'No—no it doesn't. Your money is with Bankcorp; it is quite safe. In fact, everything is fine. We just need a little bit of time to sort things out, that's all.'

The Commissioner raised a sceptical eyebrow. 'I am afraid time is not on your side, Mr Marsters. Nor do I think is Bankcorp. Our initial investigations into the company suggest they are also running a fraudulent operation. However, I am primarily concerned with crimes committed on Singaporean soil. Fraudulent activity committed in the United Kingdom falls within the jurisdiction of our British counterparts. Naturally, we will work with them on any extradition requests they might make. In the meantime, we will continue our investigation into the kidnapping hoax—which I might remind you, Mr Marsters, is a serious criminal offence under Singaporean law.'

Keeping his eyes fixed on the assembled guests, the Commissioner strode back to join Victoria at the head of the table. 'When it was discovered that Mrs Marsters' death was not accidental, we struggled to find an immediate link between her murder and her son's alleged kidnapping. At this point in the investigation, Miss West had completely discounted her initial theory that the kidnapping was a hoax. It didn't seem to fit with Mrs Marsters' death. We, therefore, focused our attention on attempting to identify a motive for her murder. Of course, we had a finite list of suspects. We knew the murderer was in the Padang Suite during dinner, last night. And as no staff member went near the table where the peanut crumbs were found, whoever killed Mrs Marsters had to be one of the dinner guests.'

'This is ridiculous!' Patricia straightened the front of her teal cardigan. 'None of us had a reason for wanting to murder Beverley.'

'I am afraid that once again I must contradict you, Mrs Helstone. There is more than one person sitting in this room who had a reason for wanting Beverley Marsters dead. I believe, Miss Farmer—' the Commissioner turned his attention to Lou. 'You once commented that you and John would be better off without her.'

Lou's clasped hands tightened in her lap, her anxious gaze darting from John to Tim.

Tim sprang forward, the moment her eyes met his. 'It wasn't me; I didn't say anything.' He turned his desperate gaze on the Commissioner. 'Look, Lou didn't kill my mother, okay? You can't pin any of this on her. She didn't have any reason to do it.'

'Miss Farmer was overheard speaking with Mr Marsters, very soon after his wife's death, in a manner that suggested they enjoyed a close— one might even say, intimate—relationship.'

Lou's mouth fell open and for a moment she sat motionless, staring at the Commissioner. But she quickly regained her cool-headed demeanour and faced him stoically. 'John and I have absolutely nothing to be ashamed of, Commissioner. Our relationship is and has always been, purely platonic. My closeness to John is no different to how I have felt towards the whole family. Any implication otherwise is objectionable.'

The Commissioner bowed his head in acknowledgement. 'I perfectly understand your feelings, Miss Farmer. However, with an investigation of this nature, we need to consider all possibilities. And Mr Marsters was heard saying to you, "this will all be over in a couple of days and we'll be on a plane back to England". I'm sure you will agree those are not the words one would expect to hear from a grieving husband.'

The expression on Lou's face hardened. 'They are the words I would expect to hear from a man attempting to comfort a grieving friend and colleague,' she retorted. 'When your informant heard those words, Commissioner, we were all under the impression that James had been kidnapped. Our sole focus was getting him back and returning to England with Beverley's body, so we could all grieve in peace. None of us imagined we were going to be accused of murder. The whole idea is preposterous.'

A faint smile crept on to the Commissioner's lips. 'I'm afraid murder is a preposterous business, Miss Farmer. Unfortunately though, we are not able to dismiss it on that basis, and given your close involvement with the family, both on a personal and professional level, we had to consider that you and Mr Marsters had access to the offshore bank accounts listed in the ransom demand. Therefore, should you have wished to collect the full ransom payment for yourselves, you were in a position to do so, with both Mrs Marsters and Mr Winstanley out of the way.'

Lou started forward in her seat, but the Commissioner raised a hand to stop her. 'But of course, you and Mr Marsters were not alone in having access to that information.' He turned his gaze on Nick. 'Mr de Brouwer also had knowledge of the accounts, having helped to set them up. Additionally, his precarious financial situation suggested to us that he may have been prepared to risk going after the ransom payment as well, in order to prevent his own downfall. He would only have had to keep Mr Winstanley's body hidden for twenty-four hours, in order to pull it off.'

Kate threw a sharp, enquiring glance at her husband. But he kept his eyes fixed steadfastly on the Commissioner.

The Commissioner strolled around to the other side of the table. 'Yet, despite Mr de Brouwer's obvious motive, we could not consider the death of Mrs Marsters in isolation. It seemed improbable to us that there was no link between her death and that of her son's. Mr de Brouwer was playing golf at the time of Mr Winstanley's murder and therefore had a solid alibi. However, we do know that his wife was in the room where Mr Winstanley's body was found, at around the time of his murder.'

'Kate?' Peyton stared at her, dumbstruck.

Nick spun his head round so sharply to look at his wife, that Victoria heard the vertebrae in his neck crack. Kate turned away from her husband, crossing her legs and arms and keeping her attention firmly glued on the Commissioner.

The Commissioner met her gaze and held it. 'We already knew that Mrs de Brouwer had lied to us. She claimed that she did not leave the hotel, yesterday. And yet, camera footage taken on Bras Basah Road shows that she did leave the hotel, at around the time Mr Winstanley was murdered.'

Kate sat bolt upright in her chair. 'I didn't leave the hotel, I—' she stopped abruptly. 'Oh my goodness, I did. I completely forgot. I went across to the mall to buy some chocolate. But that was all. I must have only been gone for about twenty minutes.'

The Commissioner acknowledged her confession with a small nod. 'We also had to take into consideration, Mrs de Brouwer, that at dinner last night in the Marsters' suite, you were holding a plate with chilli crab on it. A strange choice, I would have thought, for a committed vegetarian.'

Kate's expression clouded over with confusion. 'I didn't have any chilli crab, last night. I don't eat seafood.'

'That was George's plate, Commissioner.' There was a hint of irritation in Nick's voice. 'I asked Kate to take it for him while he went to fill up his wine glass.'

'And yet, your wife was standing in the doorway holding it, so distracted that she didn't notice Miss West passing right in front of her.' The Commissioner frowned in thoughtful contemplation. 'Perhaps, preoccupied with how she was going to get the nuts into Beverley Marsters' food.'

Kate fixed a firm glare on the Commissioner. 'I was preoccupied with a phone call I had received from my office. It may surprise you, Commissioner, but as a business owner, I do have matters other than this investigation on my mind.'

The Commissioner smiled. 'Thank you, Mrs de Brouwer.' He turned his attention to the rest of the table. 'Which brings us to the murder weapon. As many of you are aware, the knife used to stab Mr Winstanley belonged to his brother. Given the recent nature of the purchase, Mr Tim Marsters naturally became a prime suspect in our inquiry. Our suspicions were further raised when camera footage emerged of him threatening his brother with the same knife, the evening before. In addition, we have found traces of blood in the suite he shares with Miss Avery-Smythe.'

Tim flung himself forward in his seat. 'I've already told you; I didn't kill him!' His frantic gaze darted around the table. 'He was my brother.' He fell back in his chair, tears brimming in his eyes. 'Jesus Christ, why won't anyone believe me?'

John reached out to his son, putting a comforting arm across his shoulders. 'The Commissioner is not accusing you, Tim. He is just pointing out the evidence he has.'

The Commissioner nodded. 'Exactly so. And in fact, Miss Avery-Smythe has informed us that she took the knife from your suite and gave it to Mr Winstanley on the morning that he was murdered.'

Every set of eyes around the table turned to look at Zara. A fiery blush spread over her face, seeping out into the roots of her red hair. Tim stared at her. 'You gave my knife to James?'

'Yes. I was worried. You had made so many stupid threats with it. I wanted to get it out of our room.'

The Commissioner left the dining table and walked slowly across to the French doors. He stood there silently, for a moment, watching a heavy, black cloud drift over the hotel. As the sky darkened, the rain began to fall with renewed vigour; the opaque sheets cascading into the courtyard below. He turned back to face his audience. 'Miss Avery-Smythe's admission regarding the knife suggested to us that, contrary to our initial thinking, Mr Winstanley's murder may not have been pre-planned. Anyone visiting him in the Noel Coward Suite could have seen the knife and made use of it. Therefore, we had to ask ourselves: *who* made use of it?' He turned his attention on Curtis. 'Mr Butland had withheld critical information from us. It was possible that he had done so in an attempt to hide his guilt.'

Curtis shifted uncomfortably in his seat. 'What reason did I have, for killing anyone?'

'I would have said that you had a number of reasons, Mr Butland.'

Curtis stared at the Commissioner. 'Like what?'

The Commissioner moved away from the dreary half-light filtering in through the French doors and stood beneath the bright halo of the chandelier. His boyish features took on a more sombre expression. 'When you sold your company, recently, I understand your portion of the sale was significantly less than Miss Latchmore's. Perhaps you were trying to re-balance the books by taking money from your former business partner that you felt was rightly yours. If that were the case, our initial thinking suggested that you might have been behind the ransom demands. Of course, when we realized the kidnapping was a hoax, perpetuated by Mr Winstanley and the Marsters, we had to adjust our thinking. At which point, it occurred to us that, given your excellent hacking skills, you could have discovered the fraud and seen an opportunity to redirect the ransom money.' The Commissioner paused for a moment, and then raising a pointed finger, took a purposeful stride towards Curtis. 'Or perhaps, you didn't like seeing the money that you had worked so hard to earn, being spent recklessly by Miss Latchmore's fiancé and you wanted to protect her. Miss Latchmore had spoken of giving all her money to Winstanley & Marsters to invest for her. Perhaps, it was your intention to prevent that from happening.'

Curtis spun round in his seat to face the Commissioner. 'I don't care what Peyton does with her money.'

'Yet, you cared enough about Miss Latchmore that you were prepared to lie to the police for her. Had you uncovered the kidnapping hoax, you might have felt the need to take more drastic action to safeguard her interests. A desire to protect our loved ones can drive us to extreme measures, Mr Butland.'

Isabelle stirred in her seat, throwing the Commissioner a sharp glance. 'If you are going to use that logic, you should accuse me also.' She pushed her chair back and rested a perfectly manicured hand on Curtis' shoulder, indignation burning in her eyes. 'Curtis was not alone in his desire to safeguard the interests of my goddaughter. He is a good man and his chivalry does not make him a murderer any more than it does the rest of us.'

The Commissioner tilted his head towards Isabelle with a small, respectful nod. 'Madame Sauveterre, you are, of course, quite correct. Indeed, I believe you yourself expressed on many occasions, a desire that your goddaughter should not marry Mr Winstanley. Perhaps, you also considered taking extreme measures to safeguard her.'

'Had the opportunity presented itself, Commissioner, I can assure you I would not have shrunk from the task.' Isabelle spoke quickly and fiercely; then turned abruptly from him and sat back down in her seat.

Curtis shook his head. 'This is total madness. Neither of us killed James and Beverley to protect Peyton. Peyton is quite capable of protecting herself; she doesn't need our help.'

'And yet you felt the need to protect her by not telling us that she had deleted messages from Mr Winstanley's Privatechat account.'

Peyton shot a startled glance across at Victoria. Victoria met her gaze and held it. The childhood they had spent together in Africa and the years of their friendship that followed, flashed through her mind, and an overwhelming feeling of sadness welled up inside her.

The Commissioner walked slowly around to the other side of the dining table. 'Of course, the messages Miss Latchmore deleted may have been of a highly personal nature and she wished to prevent them from being seen by a third party.' He stopped and fixed his gaze directly on Peyton. 'But they could also have been messages that incriminated her. Because it is true, is it not Miss Latchmore, that you, more than anyone else in this room, had a reason to murder James Winstanley and his mother?'

A horrified gasp escaped from Zara. 'Peyton?'

The entire room went deathly quiet as everyone turned to look at Peyton's pale face and impassive expression. Only the incessant patter of the rain outside, broke the silence.

The Commissioner moved a step closer to her. 'You were the victim of multiple betrayals, were you not? Your fiancé and his mother had attempted to defraud you by suggesting you invest the proceeds from the sale of your company with them, knowing full well they were running a Ponzi scheme and any money you gave to them, would be irretrievably lost. When those efforts failed to yield results quickly enough to prevent their financial ruin, they then attempted to defraud you through a kidnapping hoax.'

A momentary flush coloured Peyton's white cheeks. 'I didn't know anything about the Ponzi scheme or the kidnapping hoax. I have only just learned about all of this now.'

'We only have your word for that, Miss Latchmore. And you may also have discovered your fiancé's infidelities.' The Commissioner threw a glance towards Kate and Zara. 'Mr Winstanley was not a particularly careful man. Perhaps, that is why you were so eager to get into his Privatechat account. Perhaps, you wanted to hide evidence of his affairs, so that no suspicion would fall on you.' He moved slowly around behind Peyton. 'Of course, it is also possible that you discovered he was married and that the child you had asked him never to speak of, was the product of that marriage.' He fixed his gaze firmly on Peyton. 'The discovery of any one of these betrayals, Miss Latchmore, could have driven you to act in the heat of the moment without considering the consequences. Put them all together and we have the strongest motive for murder in this room.'

Peyton stared at the Commissioner. 'This is ridiculous. I have no idea what you are talking about. James doesn't have a child; he's never been married. And there haven't been any affairs.'

Eleanor's fingers tightened their grip around the pearl handle of her walking cane. She pushed herself up out of her chair. 'My granddaughter is quite right, Commissioner; this is ridiculous. You surely do not expect us to believe that Peyton had anything to do with these murders?'

The Commissioner directed a reverential bow in Eleanor's direction. 'I appreciate it is not a possibility that you would wish to consider, Mrs Springfield. However, as police officers, we must work with the facts as they present themselves—no matter how unpleasant that task might prove to be.' He stood for a moment in silence; then, very slowly, made his way around to the head of the table. 'It was at this point in the investigation that Miss West's involvement in the case proved invaluable.' All eyes shifted in one swift movement to Victoria, like spectators following a tennis match. Victoria took in the expectant faces, but she nodded for the Commissioner to continue. He ran his gaze silently along the table. 'When we discovered James Winstanley's body in the Noel Coward Suite, we found a Montegrappa pen on the floor. We assumed it belonged to Mr Winstanley. It had the Winstanley name engraved on it, but curiously, there were three "C"s engraved underneath the name. Miss West happened to notice them. They were perplexing, because they didn't seem to have anything to do with the Montegrappa brand or James Winstanley. It wasn't until this afternoon, during our interview with Mr de Brouwer, that their meaning became clear. The Roman numerals, XXV, on the sleeve of his polo shirt, prompted Miss West to think back to the three "C"s on the pen.' Thirteen sets of eyes shot across to look at Nick's shirt. "C" is the Roman numeral for 100, therefore three C's denote 300. Winstanley & Co, the bank owned by James Winstanley's father, Roger Winstanley, has been in business for three hundred years. This had been mentioned to Miss West by both Mrs Springfield and Madame Sauveterre. It, therefore, became clear that the pen didn't belong to James Winstanley, but to his father, Roger Winstanley. It was a commemorative pen for the 300th anniversary of Winstanley & Co. We didn't make the connection when we found it, because in order to preserve the evidence, we didn't turn the pen over. Had we done so, we would have seen "& Co" engraved on the back. Once the full inscription was revealed, it was clear that the pen couldn't have been dropped by James Winstanley, as he had never met his father. In which case, Roger Winstanley must have given the pen to someone else and that person dropped it in the Noel Coward Suite—very likely after they murdered James Winstanley.'

Eleanor sat forward on to the edge of her chair. 'Who did Roger give the pen to?'

The Commissioner interlaced his hands behind his back. 'I understand, Mrs Springfield, that your husband consulted for Winstanley & Co when they set up in New York. I believe you mentioned to Miss West that they had enjoyed each other's company immensely and Mr Springfield was sorry that he wouldn't be seeing Roger Winstanley again, here at the wedding. It is, therefore, possible—given the warmth of their relationship—that your husband was the recipient of the pen.'

Bill's bushy eyebrows shot up above the thick tortoiseshell rim of his glasses. 'I don't remember him giving me a pen.'

'It is perhaps not an event that would stick in your mind, Mr Springfield. Particularly if you had not been using the pen yourself. But given our tendency to leave these things lying around, it is possible that your wife may have picked it up.' The Commissioner paced slowly down the length of the dining table until he was standing behind Eleanor. 'We know you were both concerned about your granddaughter investing all her money with Winstanley & Marsters. Given your connections in the finance world, Mr Springfield, it is possible you uncovered the Ponzi scheme they were running. You may even have discovered the hoax kidnapping. Given you are both naturally very protective of Miss Latchmore, you may have decided to act. You said yourself, Mrs Springfield, that whoever was behind the murders had saved your granddaughter a lot of heartache and an enormous amount of money. The knife wound that killed Mr Winstanley did not require a great deal of strength; merely precision. As a crime novelist, Mrs Springfield, I have no doubt that is something you would have researched, at some point in your career.'

Eleanor turned slowly around to look at the Commissioner. 'I am extremely well-versed as to the best place to plunge a knife into the human body, Commissioner. But I can assure you, I do not extend my murderous endeavours beyond the written word.'

The Commissioner smiled. 'You will understand though, Mrs Springfield, that it was a possibility we had to consider.'

Bill heaved a sigh of relief. 'I am mighty pleased to hear that it was only a possibility. I know our days are numbered but we sure as heck didn't intend to end them with a noose around our necks.'

Eleanor settled back in her seat. 'I presume, Commissioner, that you do intend to tell us who Roger gave the pen to?'

Victoria glanced across at the Commissioner. Perhaps, it would be better if she took over. He seemed to be enjoying his role a little too much. She was about to step forward, when she felt a text message vibrate in her pocket. She pulled her iPhone out and cast a quick glance down at the screen. It was a message from Bee. She unlocked the phone and as she began to read the text, the tension drained from her body. At last, everything made sense.

Seeing Victoria staring at her phone, the Commissioner moved across to where she was standing. He bent his head close to hers and addressed her in a voice low enough not to be overheard, 'Is there a problem?'

Victoria turned her phone around, so the Commissioner could read the message.

He took a moment to digest the contents; then slowly raised his eyes to meet Victoria's. 'Terminal cancer.' He gave a very faint, but sad, smile. 'Do you know, in an odd sort of a way, I'm relieved.'

Victoria nodded. She felt a mixture of sadness and relief as well. 'Yes, me too.'

She placed her phone back into her pocket and lifted her gaze, taking in, one by one, all the faces turned in her direction. She took a deep breath and very slowly walked around to where Peyton was seated. She stood behind her, resting a hand on her shoulder. As Peyton reached up to take hold of it, Victoria felt a stab of sorrow in her chest. She gave Peyton's fingers a squeeze, and then sliding her hand free, turned her attention back to the table. 'Roger gave the pen to the same person who put the nuts into Beverley's food last night. We know from our investigations, that the killer prepared a plate from the buffet, identical to Beverley's. Having put the nuts into the food, they then swapped that plate for the one Beverley had prepared for herself. Which means Beverley handled two plates during dinner—her original plate and the one the killer swapped it with. But there was a curious issue with the fingerprints on the two plates. Only Beverley's prints were found on both plates and on the first plate Beverley handled, the prints were smudged in such a way that suggested whoever had handled that plate after her, had been wearing gloves. We had initially thought the plates had been handled by someone holding a napkin. But forensics confirmed our suspicions that a napkin would have wiped off more of Beverley's fingerprints.' Victoria turned to look at Kate. 'Kate had come to my attention, because she was holding a plate of crab, which as a vegetarian, she doesn't eat. Therefore, we had to consider the possibility that she had prepared that plate in order to swap it with Beverley's. But Kate wasn't wearing gloves. I remember noticing her nail polish. However, there was somebody at dinner last night who *was* wearing gloves. That same person isn't vegetarian, but they also don't eat crab; and yet I remember Nick putting crab on to their plate. I had forgotten all about it until we were sitting down at lunch today. The Commissioner ordered pizza with Italian sausage and that jogged my memory. At dinner in La Dame de Pic on Tuesday evening, Kate wasn't the only person who didn't have the standard menu. Someone else substituted the crab in the first course. They were served quail sausage instead. As soon as I remembered that, everything fell into place. That same person wore gloves during dinner last night; they had crab on their plate when they shouldn't have, and Roger Winstanley could have given them a pen. Forensics are currently checking the fingerprints on the pen to confirm my suspicions. But as much as it upsets me to accept it, I don't believe I am mistaken.' Victoria slowly turned, a lump rising in her throat as her gaze settled on the woman she had looked up to, ever since she was a child.

Isabelle rose from her seat, reaching an unsteady hand out for her box of Gauloises Blondes. She turned away from the table and walked across to the French doors, throwing them open. The muggy heat from the afternoon rain poured in, enfolding the dining room in its long tentacles. She took off her blue coat and tossed it over the back of a rattan armchair. Her skeletal arms seemed so fragile in the sleeveless sweater she wore, underneath.

Placing one of the cigarettes between her red lips, she flicked open the top of her lighter. The orange flame leapt out, caressing the end of the tobacco with its burning tongue.

Isabelle inhaled deeply; then, lifting her head, slowly breathed out a long ribbon of smoke, watching the writhing coil drift out towards the courtyard and vanish; the white vapour melting into the gloomy afternoon light. She placed the cigarette back between her lips and drew in another deep breath. Slowly, she let the smoke escape from her mouth.

Turning her back on the stunned faces around the dining table, Victoria walked slowly across to the doorway and stood watching Isabelle. For the first time, seeing a frail old woman and not the formidable fashion designer she had always known.

Isabelle took another long draw on her cigarette. Without shifting her gaze from the courtyard, she spoke in a hoarse voice, so low it was barely audible. 'No, you are not mistaken.'

Peyton pushed her chair back and rushed across to her godmother. 'Isabelle! Why? Why on earth did you do it?'

Isabelle spun round, obstinacy shining in her eyes as she stared straight at Peyton. 'I did it because James and his mother were insatiably greedy. They would stop at nothing to get what they wanted. I watched them attempting to destroy Roger. They would have brought down a noble family with hundreds of years of history, to satisfy their own selfishness. They did not care whose lives they ruined. Roger is a man of integrity, I have known him for a long time, and they wanted to crush him because of a mistake he made in his youth.' She placed the cigarette between her lips and turned away. 'They had to be stopped.'

Victoria stepped outside onto the balcony. 'You could have let the authorities deal with it, Isabelle. Roger had enough evidence against them on the Ponzi scheme to get a conviction.'

Isabelle turned slightly towards Victoria. 'By then, it would have been too late for Peyton. They needed money and they were determined to get it any way they could. I knew nothing about the kidnapping plot; I have only just learned of that. But I knew of their thirst for money, and how vicious they could be when someone like Roger got in their way. I knew they would have destroyed Peyton; I knew it in my heart.' She turned away, her voice choked with emotion. 'I could not let them do that. I love her too much.' Tears glistened in Isabelle's eyes. 'Maybe what I did was wrong. But perhaps, one day, Peyton, you will forgive me.'

Peyton shook her head. 'Why didn't you come and talk to me?'

'And say what? That I had killed your fiancé and his mother?'

'No, that you were *planning* to do it.'

A faint smile crept on to Isabelle's lips. 'I did not plan it. It happened because there was no other option.'

'No other option? There were a hundred other ways we could have dealt with this.'

Isabelle wheeled round. 'There was no other way. They had a hold on you and you wanted to believe in their love. That hope in you was too strong to fight. I tried to talk you out of this marriage, but you would not listen. I know without any doubt, that if James were alive, he would still have a hold over you. But his love was a lie. I saw him yesterday in the Noel Coward Suite—' She raised her chin, and turning her head, cast one venomous glance at Zara. 'With her.'

Peyton turned. Zara stared at her, her huge eyes wide and a crimson blush spreading from her pale cheeks down into the collar of her pink blouse.

An awful stillness gripped Tim's freckled face as he turned to look at Zara, his expression frozen in a mixture of horror and disbelief. 'James?'

Peyton's eyes darted back to look at her godmother. 'What are you saying, Isabelle?'

'I am saying that what the Commissioner has told you is correct; your fiancé was unfaithful. I confronted him. I told him I would not let the marriage go ahead. And I said I would never let him get his straying hands on your money. He laughed. He said you loved him and would listen to him, not me. And he was right. I have always felt that he did not love you and only wanted your money, but in that moment, I knew it for certain. And I knew without a doubt that if he were not stopped, he would destroy you. In the same manner that he was attempting to destroy his father. His mother would have done the same.

'Roger told me about the Ponzi scheme, but I knew if I told you, James would deny it and tell you that I was against him. And you would have believed him. But when he laughed at me, yesterday and said he would take as much of your money as he wanted, I realized they intended to use you to fund their fraudulent activity. And I was not prepared to let them do that. They were ruthless and had stolen the life savings of thousands of people; they would not have spared you. He was laughing in my face, Peyton. Laughing at me—pfff, that does not matter. But laughing at his betrayal of you, that I could not bear. The knife was lying beside me on the table and before I knew it, it was in my hand.' Isabelle stood stock-still for moment. 'Then at dinner, last night, I saw Beverley's false love for you, and I knew you were still not safe. Her son's death was not going to stop her; I knew how cruel Beverley could be. I had seen what she had done to Roger and I was not going to let her do the same to you. So, I saw the jar of nuts on the mini bar, and I picked them up. I had nothing to lose. We all knew about her allergy, and she had told us where she kept her EpiPens because she wanted us to help her if she had an attack. Yet never in her life, did Beverley help anyone. The only thing she knew how to do, was destroy people. And she would have destroyed you, if I had not stopped her.' Isabelle's hand trembled as she lifted the cigarette to her lips. 'I had a duty to protect you, Peyton. I made that promise to your parents.'

'They didn't mean for you to commit murder! For God's sake, Isabelle, the death penalty still exists here in Singapore.'

Victoria walked across to one of the rattan armchairs. She sat down facing Isabelle. 'I don't think that makes any difference now, does it?'

Isabelle sank down into the chair beside Victoria. A long, thin plume of smoke rose from the smouldering ash between her fingers, like a serpent coming up out of a basket. Slowly, she shook her head. 'No, it does not make any difference now. I have already received my death sentence.'

Peyton stood stock-still in the doorway. 'What are you talking about, Isabelle?'

Isabelle inclined her head. 'My body is riddled with cancer. The doctors give me a few more weeks; that is all.' She reached into the pocket of her coat, taking out a vial of pills. 'These help with the pain for now, but very soon, it will become unbearable and then I shall take all of them together. I do not wish to spend my last days in a hospital being fed drugs through a machine.' She turned her gaze to the courtyard and the coconut palms standing tall and erect, becalmed against the steady stream of the afternoon rain. 'I would rather die here.'

Victoria reached out, placing her hand on top of Isabelle's. 'Wouldn't you rather go back to France?'

Isabelle shrugged. 'I am not sentimental about these things. France will always live in my heart. And my legacy will live on through my work.'

Despite what she had done, Victoria couldn't help but admire Isabelle. She had the conviction to live life on her own terms, right up until the bitter end. The courage she had shown, knowing what the consequences of her actions would be, was extraordinary. Victoria had underestimated her. She had always thought Isabelle incapable of doing anything that didn't serve her own interests. And yet, here she was, sacrificing herself for Roger—and Peyton.

Isabelle stood up. She walked across to the edge of the balcony and leaned against the thick, concrete balustrade. With her back towards Victoria, she looked out over the courtyard, her thick, husky voice barely louder than a whisper. 'I would like you to do one thing for me, Victoria.'

'Of course, Isabelle. I'll do anything I can.'

The hand that held the cigarette shook a little. 'Ask the Commissioner to give me twenty-four hours.'

Victoria went to push herself up out of the chair to go to Isabelle. But Isabelle raised a hand to stop her. 'That is all I need.'

Slowly, Victoria lowered herself back down. With that one gesture, she understood everything. She nodded, feeling the sting of tears in her eyes. '*D'accord, je comprend.*'

Sixty-Five

The Commissioner stood silently in front of Isabelle's suite, his gaze taking in the majestic cream door, before coming to rest on the brass doorbell. The 'Do Not Disturb' light glowed, innocuously, in the centre. He drew in a deep breath. Then straightening his jacket and brushing the grey lapels, he glanced across at Victoria.

She gave him a small, reassuring nod and he reached out for the doorbell.

They waited. But no sound came from within. The Commissioner leaned towards the door, straining to listen. He gave a small knock. Still nothing. He frowned, turning to Victoria.

She reached into her pocket and took out a key. Passing it over the magnetic lock, she depressed the handle and slowly pushed the door open. Total silence greeted them. Victoria called out, 'Isabelle?'

Still, not a sound.

Quietly, she closed the door and they moved into the living room. A box of Gauloises Blondes lay open on the coffee table, alongside an empty bottle of Domaine de la Romanée-Conti, Montrachet, Grand Cru 1973. Victoria looked towards the bedroom. The dull, afternoon light filled the room, throwing faint shadows against the walls, but there was no sign of movement within. She went across and stood in the doorway.

Isabelle's lifeless body lay on the bed, perfectly arranged in a black velvet suit encrusted with row upon row of pink jewels. A fringe of pink feathers edged the jacket and created a frill on the bottom of the knee-length skirt. Around her neck, the feathers blended into her blonde hair, arranged in a perfect halo on the pillow. Her lipstick and nail varnish were a perfect match for the soft pink feathers.

Victoria went over and stood beside her. She looked so peaceful, as if she had taken her last breath without a trouble in the world. An empty wine glass and her vial of pills lay on the bedside table beside her.

The Commissioner came gingerly into the room and stood beside Victoria. His gaze rested on Isabelle's frail, lifeless body. 'You knew, didn't you?'

Victoria nodded. 'Yes. I thought she would want to end things on her own terms.' She settled her gaze on Isabelle's tranquil face. 'I can't say I blame her. Even without the murders, this is what she intended to do. She didn't want to die in a hospital; let alone a prison.'

The Commissioner's melancholy expression softened. He looked around the room: the lavish white furnishings, the beautiful blue and white floral carpet, the Ming style lamps and the four wooden posts framing the funeral bed. He slowly nodded his head. 'I can think of worse places to die.'

As he spoke, the sun briefly broke free from the clouds and cast long fingers of bright light over Isabelle's peaceful figure. Victoria smiled. 'Yes, so can I.'

She moved across to the bedside table and picked up a Raffles Hotel envelope with the Commissioner's name beautifully scripted on the front in Isabelle's large, rounded handwriting. She passed it to the Commissioner. 'It's for you.'

He tore the envelope open and pulled out a single sheet of Raffles Hotel notepaper. Frowning, he turned it over. 'It's in French.'

Victoria held out her hand. 'Would you like me to translate?'

The Commissioner nodded. 'Yes, please. My schoolboy French was never very good and that was a long time ago.'

Victoria took the sheet of paper from him and sat down on the bed, beside Isabelle.

Dear Monsieur,

Victoria will have, by now, told you everything you need to know. There is nothing for me to add, other than to confirm in writing that I am guilty of the murders of James Winstanley and Beverley Marsters. I think you understand my reasons for committing the crimes.

It is regretful you have wasted your time on such a sordid affair. I apologize to you for that. In a small way, I would like to make amends. Please take your wife to my store in Takashimaya. I have left instructions with my staff there to fit her for a new wardrobe. This season will be the last Isabelle Sauveterre range designed by me and I do not want her to miss out. By the time your children have left home, I do not know what designer will be putting their work to my name, or whether or not they will be worthy of it.

Regarding any of my other affairs, please revert to my goddaughter and sole heir, Peyton Latchmore. I have left instructions with my lawyers for her.

Please also accept my gratitude for the twenty-four hours you have given me. Had my guilt not been discovered here in Singapore, it was my intention to write a full confession upon my return to France with instructions for it to be forwarded to you after my death. In lieu of that, I trust this short note will suffice.

Yours,
Isabelle Sauveterre

Victoria slowly folded the letter and inserted it back into the envelope. Her gaze drifted outside to the magnolia trees; their white flowers shimmering beneath the grey skies with the last remnants of the morning rain. So Isabelle had lied—she *had* wanted to return to France.

Sixty-Six

Peyton and Victoria lay down, side by side, on the huge king-sized bed in Eleanor and Bill's suite. They watched Eleanor tapping, with great concentration, on her keyboard, while Bill stood at the foot of the bed, packing their clothes neatly into a large, black Samsonite suitcase.

Lazing in their bedroom brought back memories to Victoria, of when they were teenagers living in Ethiopia. Peyton's grandparents would come over from America on holiday and they would both lie on their bed, watching them unpack. Eleanor had always been shopping in New York and they couldn't wait to see what new outfits she had bought for them.

But the happy anticipation that had filled the air on those occasions was missing now; replaced by a veil of sadness—each of them feeling it in their own way.

Victoria reached out and took hold of Peyton's hand. She gave it a small squeeze. 'How are you feeling?'

Peyton laid her hand on her stomach. 'Sick.' She rolled over to face Victoria, drawing her knees up and squashing the soft feather pillow into a more comfortable shape under her head. 'I just can't believe how stupid I was.'

Victoria rolled her head over on the pillow to look at Peyton. 'You weren't stupid. You trusted James and his mother because you are a decent, trustworthy person. *They* are the ones who let *you* down.'

Eleanor glanced over the lid of her laptop. 'Victoria is absolutely right. You have nothing to be ashamed of. James wasn't worthy of your trust, but that doesn't mean your trust isn't worthy. You must not let that one bad experience make you bitter and change who you are.' She smiled lovingly at her husband. 'If Bill and I had done that, we might never have got together and had sixty wonderful years of marriage. We must always be willing to trust someone—because one day, you'll find somebody worthy of it.'

'I know and I keep telling myself that. But I just feel so bad about Isabelle.' Peyton's blue eyes filled with tears. 'I should never have allowed her to get tied up in all of this.'

Bill glanced up from the suitcase. 'Sweetheart, you are not responsible for what Isabelle did. The choices she made were hers and hers alone.'

Victoria smiled at Bill. 'Exactly. Besides, she'll be in her element up there.' She glanced towards the ceiling. 'She'll be getting everyone sorted out. The angels will be in new outfits by the end of the week.'

Peyton laughed—and as if to punctuate her lighter mood, the doorbell chimed at the same time. She sat up on the bed. 'That'll be Curtis.'

Bill laid the shirt he was folding down into the suitcase. 'I'll go let him in.'

Watching Curtis stroll into the bedroom with Bill, Victoria had to look twice at him to make sure she wasn't hallucinating. 'Curtis, I never thought I would see the day. You've had a haircut!'

Curtis laughed. 'Yeah, Peyton said it was getting a bit out of control. So I thought I'd better go and get it dealt with. I never get the time to do it, back home.'

'Well, you look very smart. But you'd better watch out; she'll have you in a new wardrobe, next.'

Peyton gave a faint smile. 'There is no point embarking on the impossible.'

Curtis looked down at his blue flip flops. 'What's wrong with the way I dress?'

Eleanor smiled at him. 'Absolutely nothing, Curtis. You ignore the two of them.'

Curtis' cheerful disposition had lightened the mood in the room and Victoria couldn't help thinking how nice it was, having him back as part of the family again. It felt just like old times—almost as if the whole interlude with James had been nothing more than a bad dream.

Bill popped his head around from behind the wardrobe door and smiled at Curtis, 'Got your safari suit all packed up?'

Curtis laughed. 'I knew there was something I needed to go shop for.'

Bill raised his bushy eyebrows, behind the thick rim of his glasses and nodded at Curtis' orange boardshorts. 'You're not going to find any surf beaches in Botswana; it's all landlocked.'

'Botswana?' Victoria propped herself up on her elbows and looked suspiciously from Curtis to Peyton.

Peyton gave her a coy smile. 'Curtis is going to come to Botswana with me, after the funeral. Granny and Grandpa talked us into it. Curtis has never been to Africa before and I love it over there. And as Granny says, I can't let James ruin everything.'

Victoria returned her smile. 'I think that is a fantastic idea. There's nowhere like Africa to get your chakras back in alignment and start afresh. And Eleanor is right; you must not let James ruin another minute of your life. He's done quite enough damage. The sooner we all forget about him, the better.'

'That's exactly what Granny said.'

Curtis glanced down at his watch. 'Hey, it's one thirty. Is there anything I can do to help? The cars are picking us up at two. I'm all done. My bags are down in the lobby, already.'

Eleanor glanced across at Peyton. 'How are you doing with your packing, sweetheart? Do you want Curtis to come and help you?'

'That would be fantastic, thanks Curtis. My brain isn't quite operating as well as it should be. I could do with someone keeping an eye on me.' Peyton swung her legs off the bed and stood up. But she stopped immediately, with her hand pressed against her forehead. 'Oh wow, I'm having a head rush.'

Curtis took hold of her arm. 'Have you had anything to eat today?'

Peyton shook her head. 'Not really. I had some fruit for breakfast, but that was all. I just can't stomach anything at the moment.'

Bill took the last of the clothes from the wardrobe and carried them into the bedroom. 'Why don't you get her a can of soda on the way out, Curtis? There's a fridge in the pantry. Try to have a little bit, sweetheart. You need something inside you until you get your appetite back, even if it's just sugar.'

Peyton nodded. 'I will. I feel okay now though; I just stood up a bit fast.'

Curtis linked his arm through Peyton's and gently guided her into the living room. As he did so, Victoria gave a small gasp of delight. The sun had suddenly broken out from behind the clouds, casting long shafts of cheerful, bright light into the bedroom. After three days of solid rain, surely, that had to be a good omen.

As soon as the front door closed, she turned to Eleanor and Bill with a playful grin. 'Maybe Isabelle will get her wish, after all.'

Behind her laptop, a glint of mischief sparkled in Eleanor's eyes. 'Bill and I are certainly hoping so.' She gazed wistfully towards the front door. 'James at least did her one favour. He taught her how to love. Before she met him, she was so closed off from everybody. We began to despair of her ever getting married. But James broke that pattern and I think now, her heart will be more open. And often, the harder we fall, the greater is our joy that follows.' She glanced at the time on her laptop. 'I don't want to hold you up, Victoria; I know we need to be downstairs, shortly. But I did want to ask you if you managed to talk to Peyton? Was it her that deleted the messages from James' Privatechat account?'

Victoria nodded. 'Yes, it was as I half suspected. She had sent him some photos that she didn't want anyone to see. She felt terrible not telling me about it. Although, I think she was impressed with Curtis's loyalty.'

Eleanor smiled. 'Curtis is a good man. I do hope things work out between them. He's not too upset, is he, that Peyton got more money from selling the company than he did?'

'No, not at all. I asked him about it, because he did sound quite resentful when I spoke to him. He was only upset about James spending everything *he* had worked so hard for; he doesn't mind Peyton having the money. In fact, she's already offered to split it with him, but he's turned her down. He said he doesn't need any more. Unlike James, I think he's more interested in Peyton, than her money.'

Eleanor's eyes sparkled with fondness. 'Yes, I think he is.' She closed the lid of her laptop. 'Do you know I feel rather sad about John getting caught up in all of this. I can't help but feel he was an unwilling participant.'

Bill's head popped up from behind the suitcase lid. 'You have got far too good a heart, my dear. That man knew exactly what he was doing.'

'Yes, he did.' Victoria sat up and shifted the pillows to one side so she could rest her shoulders against the cool leather headboard. 'He's not the complete bumbling fool he appears to be. Although, he did nearly give himself away, when he came charging into the Padang Suite, not realising Peyton and I were sitting there. If only I'd been a bit quicker, I might have worked out the kidnapping was a hoax then.'

Bill paused with Eleanor's blouse lying half-folded on the bed before him. 'Why, what was it that he said?'

Victoria drew her legs up into the lotus position, keen to stretch out before being stuck on a plane for fourteen hours. 'He said he'd been down to concierge and the front desk, but nobody had seen anything. I assumed he meant he'd been out looking for his stepson, but I think what he'd been doing was checking the staff hadn't seen James going into the Noel Coward Suite. Still, he managed to cover his blunder when he saw us and did an excellent job of looking astonished when the ransom demand came through. In fact, both he and Beverley made a superb job of that. They turned out to be much better actors than I would have given either of them credit for.'

'They certainly did,' Eleanor agreed. 'They had me fooled. I thought Beverley looked especially dreadful.'

'She did, but I think that was a lack of make-up, more than anything else. The only time I saw her without it, was straight after the kidnapping and I'm sure that was deliberate.'

Eleanor rested her clasped hands on top of her laptop. 'They thought of everything, didn't they?' A small frown creased her forehead. 'The only thing I don't understand is if James was already dead, who sent the ransom demand?'

'Beverley. John had Privatechat set up on his phone and it looks like everything was pre-programmed into it. When Peyton and I went to their suite, John wasn't there but Beverley was, and I remember her clearing a few things off the sofa and taking them into the bedroom. I assume that was when she set the messages in motion. I think the plan was for her to be with Peyton when they came through, so she could keep control of everything.' Victoria unthreaded her legs and recrossed them the other way. 'It was a brazen strategy, and it all hinged on Peyton not calling the police. They obviously backed themselves, because they made no effort to cover their tracks. John placed the order with room service from his mobile, and when we checked his phone, the call was still showing on the log. He hadn't attempted to clear it.'

Eleanor lifted her bag up on to the desk and slipped her laptop inside. 'That's a psychopathic personality for you. They have a grandiose sense of their own self-worth and absolutely no ability to feel empathy. They can also be very promiscuous.' She shook her head. 'To think James was being unfaithful to Peyton right under our noses and had a wife and child nobody thought to mention.'

Victoria stretched her knees down with the heels of her hands. 'I think everyone was as taken in by James as Peyton was. Kate certainly seemed to believe his stories. I think she genuinely thought their affair meant something and she was helping him through a difficult time in his life. But then as you said, that's a psychopath—they can be very charming.'

'Yes, they certainly can be that.' Eleanor zipped her bag closed. 'I still do wonder about John though. I can't help thinking he was taken in by James and Beverley, like everyone else. I know you'll say

I'm being too soft, Bill, but I did come to like John in a funny sort of a way. I can't imagine how that son of his will cope, if he goes to prison.'

Bill snapped the suitcase lid closed. 'I don't think having to stand on his own two feet will do him any harm. In fact, it will probably be the making of him. He's intelligent enough—he has just been a little over-indulged.'

'Yes, he certainly has been that.' Eleanor turned to Victoria. 'What about the blood in his room, did you get to the bottom of that?'

Victoria swung herself up off the bed and went over to help Eleanor with her bag. 'It was his own blood apparently, he cut himself with the knife when he was showing it to Zara.'

'And what is he going to do now; is he travelling back to London?'

Victoria nodded. 'Unfortunately, he doesn't have much say in the matter. With no money to stay here, he's catching his flight home.'

'But John is being kept here?'

'Yes, for the time being. He's facing charges for the kidnapping hoax. Then I presume the UK will want to talk to him about the Ponzi scheme. The SFO have already started proceedings against Nick for the six million pounds missing from his Client Money Account. I imagine John will be in their sights next.'

Eleanor rested her elbows on the writing desk and slowly, shook her head. 'What an extraordinary ending to what should have been a beautiful holiday. Life certainly can be a lot stranger than fiction.' She glanced across at Bill as he slipped the packed suitcase down on to the floor. 'Well, I suppose we had better start making our way downstairs.' She pushed herself up out of the chair. 'We don't want to miss our flight to Paris.'

Victoria smiled. 'No, we definitely don't want to do that. I'd better go back to my suite and sort out my bags. Isabelle would never forgive us if we arrived late for her funeral.'

* * *

Victoria stood on her balcony, looking out at the lush, tropical gardens in the courtyard, the bright afternoon sun illuminating the fan-shaped leaves of the traveller's palms, vibrant and green after all the rain. She did love Raffles Hotel and was sorry to be leaving it so soon—especially now that the sun had finally reappeared.

It was strange to think that only five days ago, she had been looking forward to spending her holiday lazing by the pool in the tropical heat. She should have been reading the diaries of Gertrude Bell on the roof terrace and Peyton should have been blissfully happy on her honeymoon in Botswana. But instead, they were all still in Singapore, dealing with the aftermath of James' duplicity. Shakespeare himself couldn't have come up with a more elaborate tale of greed and betrayal. But then, James and his mother paid the ultimate price for their treachery. And now, John was going to have to face the music on his own. It was unlikely he would ever be a free man again.

She had to agree with Eleanor; it was hard to see how Tim was going to cope, having lost his mother and brother with little possibility of seeing his father free again. And Zara was unlikely to stick around, even if he wanted her to. If their relationship wasn't already over, Victoria suspected it soon would be. Still, he did have Lou. There seemed to be a lot of affection between the two of them. She was still unsure if Lou had known about the Ponzi scheme; she suspected she didn't, but either way, it was difficult to see her abandoning the family she had been a part of, for so long. Tim could probably rely on her.

The Helstones would be struggling. She hadn't warmed to Patricia, but they had lost their nest egg and nobody deserved that—especially at such a late stage in life. She gave a heavy sigh. It was awful to think how many people would be affected. It looked as if the Ponzi scheme would run into the hundreds of millions of pounds. And there were Nick's clients as well. He would most likely be going to prison for the money he had stolen from them. There would be no more designer clothes and bottles of champagne for him, for a while. She couldn't see his and Kate's marriage surviving, either.

Victoria shook her head. To think so much misery had been caused by greed and a desire for more money than anyone needed, to be happy. She thought about her upcoming trip to the Middle East. It was going to be a tough assignment, but there was something to be said for good old-fashioned hard work. That had always been Isabelle's philosophy and one of the reasons Victoria admired her so much. It was hard to believe she was never going to see her again.

She gave a small shrug to drive away the thought and stepping back inside, cast one final glance about the room to make sure she hadn't forgotten anything. Then, slowly, she walked through her suite to the entrance foyer and out onto the landing. Closing the door gently behind her, she made her way downstairs to the lobby.

Mario and the Commissioner were waiting for her, standing to attention beside her luggage at the concierge desk. She smiled as Mario stepped forward. Taking hold of her outstretched hand, he made an elaborate, sweeping bow and raised it to his lips. 'Miss West, you must return to us again soon—but for a *real* holiday, next time.'

Victoria gave his hand an appreciative squeeze. 'I shall look forward to that, Mario, thank you.'

The Commissioner extended his hand towards her. 'We shall do our very best to keep the country trouble-free for your next visit.' A mischievous twinkle glistened in his eye. 'Although I will keep my police department on standby, just to be safe.'

Victoria laughed. 'That is probably a very good idea, if my last two visits are anything to go by.'

Mario joined in the laughter, and then with an almost imperceptible gesture, signalled for the doorman to approach. Narajan stepped forward and lifting Victoria's bags from the floor, carried them outside to the waiting Daimler, its engine purring in anticipation on the gravel driveway.

Victoria gave Mario and the Commissioner one final, parting smile; then stepped outside on to the red carpet and into the glorious warmth of the Singaporean sunshine.

She took her seat in the Daimler, bidding one last, fond farewell to Narajan, as he closed the door behind her. The chauffeur pulled out of the gravel driveway, gliding the car gently round onto Beach Road. Victoria turned and cast one last glance back at the grand, white façade of Raffles Hotel, as it slowly receded behind them—its magnificent colonial architecture silhouetted against the vibrant blue sky.

Acknowledgements

First and foremost, I would like to thank Kathy Gale for her inexhaustible patience, encouragement and meticulous editing. Without her guiding hand this book would never have seen the light of day. A huge thank you also to the wonderful team at Raffles Hotel Singapore. In particular, I would like to thank Leenu Tarani and Jesmine Hall for supporting my murderous endeavours and allowing me to take a very small part in writing this new chapter in Raffles' rich literary heritage.

Thank you also to Nora Nazerene Abu Bakar and the fabulous team at Penguin Random House for guiding this book into production.

To Chris Soh and Wenya, thank you for the fabulous cover design. Graham Howard and Kevin Fitzgerald CMG, thank you for your incredible support. Thank you also to Cendrine Piper for sharing your medical knowledge.

And a special word of thanks to Ravi Karawdra for the brilliant advertising ideas. To my dear friend Cynthia Vongai, thank you for your never-ending support.

And finally, to my beloved partner in crime, Roy Savage. Without your endless love and support the first words of this book would never have been written. Thank you for sharing this adventure with me.